D0459628

Titles by Jennifer Ashley

The Mackenzies

Shifters Unbound

The Scandalous Mackenzies

JENNIFER ASHLEY

BERKLEY SENSATION, NEW YORK

**BERKLEY
SENSATION**

**An imprint of Penguin Random House LLC
375 Hudson Street, New York, New York 10014**

THE SCANDALOUS MACKENZIES

A Berkley Sensation Book / published by arrangement with the author.

ISBN: 978-0-425-26627-4

PUBLISHING HISTORY
Berkley Sensation mass market edition / September 2015

PRINTED IN THE UNITED STATES OF AMERICA

10 9 8 7 6 5 4 3 2 1

Cover art by Gregg Gulbronson.
Handlettering by Ron Zinn.
Cover design by George Long.
Interior text design by Kelly Lipovich.

Penguin
Random
House

Contents

The Scandalous Mackenzies

The Untamed Mackenzie

Chapter 1

Lloyd Fellows's small fists beat into the dirty face of the older boy, bloodying the mouth that had taunted him. *Your mum's a whore, your dad was a scabby old man, and you're a bastard, a bastard.*

Now the older boy was howling, his teeth on the pavement and blood running down his face. Everyone knew not to taunt Lloyd of the hot temper, but sometimes it was hard to resist. Lloyd always taught them to respect his fists.

Besides, his dad wasn't a scabby old man. His dad was a duke. When Lloyd had been very little, he'd been sure his father would come along in a golden coach and take him away from the squalid streets of London to his palace in Scotland. There Lloyd would have all the toys he wanted, horses, and brothers to play with. His dad had other sons, his mum had told him, and she'd told him Lloyd deserved everything *they* had.

Years passed, and no golden coach came down the back lanes of working-class London. Wiser now, Lloyd knew the duke was never coming.

Until today. Today, he'd learned, because Lloyd made it his

business to know everything that happened in this part of town, his father's ducal coach would be passing along High Holborn to Lincoln's Inn Fields, where he would be visiting solicitors. Why the duke would visit the solicitors, Lloyd had no idea, nor did he care.

His plan was to stop the coach by any means possible, present himself to his father, and tell the man he needed to take care of Lloyd and his mum. Simple as that.

The duke had never sent money, letters, any word at all that acknowledged he'd fathered Lloyd Fellows. *Fellows* wasn't even his true name—his mother had taken it, pretending to be married to a Mr. Fellows who'd died long ago. Lloyd's mum had been a tavern maid, a duke had charmed her, gotten her with child, and then left her. The duke had never spoken to or looked at them again.

Today, Lloyd would change that. He'd put on the clothes he wore to church whenever his mum bothered to take him and headed up to High Holborn.

Except the little oik, Tommy Wortley, decided to waylay Lloyd and begin his taunts. Lloyd could have thrown them off, but Tommy had brought friends, and rocks. When the stones had started flying, Lloyd had grabbed Tommy and slammed him into the wall, and the fight had commenced.

Now Lloyd was bloody and filthy, his best shirt torn. His mum would tan his hide. But it didn't matter. Time was running out.

Lloyd delivered one final blow, leaving Tommy writhing in the mud, and he took off, running in his usual swift stride toward High Holborn.

He barely made it. He darted through the crowd, brick in hand, avoiding the grabs of the irritated men he pushed aside.

There was the coach, tall and polished, pulled by matched gray horses. As it came closer, Lloyd watched the burly coachman in his red coat and tall hat, knowing that the coachman could scatter all his plans if he wasn't careful.

The coach came into full view. Black, with its wheels and points picked out in gold, it bore the crest of the Duke of Kilmorgan on the door—a stag surrounded by curlicues and words Fellows didn't understand. Lloyd's father, Daniel Malcolm Mackenzie, was the thirteenth duke in the Scottish line and the first in the English line. Lloyd had spent his childhood teaching himself all about dukes and how they became dukes. This duke had been given a high honor by Queen Victoria to be recognized in England too.

Lloyd waited for the strategic moment, then he let fly the brick, right at the coachman. His aim was not to hurt or disable the man, but to make him stop the coach.

The brick hit the coachman in the hand. The coachman dropped the reins in surprise, and the coach veered. A cart coming the other way skittered to a stop in the thick traffic, and the cart's driver swore loudly and vehemently.

The coachman quickly caught the reins and tugged the horses right again, but a bottleneck had already happened. The coachman stood up on his box and told the cartman what he thought, finishing with *Get out of the way, you piece of dung, this is a duke's coach.*

Lloyd slipped through the morass to the stopped carriage. The coach was a tall box rising above him, shining and clean, except for what mud had splashed on it this morning.

One of the windows went down, and a man put his head out. He had a mass of dark red hair and thick red sideburns, a dark red beard just starting to gray, and a full moustache. From behind all this hair, which was carefully groomed, blazed eyes yellow like an eagle's.

"Get this pox-rotted coach moving!" the man shouted. "You! Boy!"

Lloyd blinked. The duke, his father, had fixed his gaze on him and was speaking to him. Lloyd opened his mouth, but no sound came out.

"Yes, you there. Gaping like a fish. Go see what's wrong."

Lloyd worked his jaw, trying to remember how to speak. "Sir," he managed. "I—"

"Go to it, boy, before I come out and beat you."

I'm your son.

The words wouldn't come. Lloyd stood, frozen, while the man who'd sired him, the lofty Duke of Kilmorgan, glared down at him.

"Are you an imbecile?" The duke ripped open the door, showing he wasn't concerned about preserving his finery or position by climbing down from the coach into the street. He grabbed Lloyd by the ear and shook him hard. "I tell you to do something, boy, you obey me. Get out there and tell that cart to move."

The man didn't even offer a coin, as other aristos did when they commanded boys on the street to do things for them. The duke's fingers pinched hard, and Lloyd felt a blow across his chin.

"Go." The duke shoved him away.

Lloyd stumbled back. The years of dreaming, hoping, pretending this man would come for him and take him to a golden castle shattered at his feet.

How could he have been so stupid? Lloyd was old enough now to understand that many men saw women as merely bodies on which they took their pleasure, nothing more. So had the duke done with Lloyd's mother. Lloyd's existence was nothing but an accident of nature.

Disappointment, heartbreak, and fury welled up in him and, as usual, came out through his fists. Lloyd launched himself at the duke, screaming in berserker rage.

"Bastard! Bloody, dung-eating, stupid, bloody *bastard*!" Lloyd pummeled the duke, blows landing on the man's chest, stomach, arms, and one lucky one across his face. The duke's nose spouted blood as easily as Tommy's had.

The duke seized Lloyd by both shoulders, his strength astonishing. Then he had Lloyd on the ground and started beating him with large fists, kicking him with heavy boots made from the finest leather.

Lloyd tucked himself into a ball, protecting himself with his arms, his rage keeping him from crying. After a long time and much pain, he was pulled to his feet by a dark-uniformed, tall-helmeted constable.

"This gob of filth attacked me," the duke snarled at the policeman. Blood ran down the duke's face, which he swiped at ineffectually with his handkerchief. "Take him off the streets."

Lloyd didn't struggle. He'd been nabbed by constables before. The best way to get away from them was to pretend compliance and then twist free later and lose himself in a crowd. The constables were usually too exasperated to bother giving chase to one little boy.

"Yes, sir," the constable said.

"*Your Grace*," the duke growled at him. "Learn some manners."

A footman had come off the back of the coach and now silently waited at the open door to help the duke back inside.

That was when Lloyd saw the other boy. A lad of about Lloyd's own age, his dark red hair and golden eyes marking him as the duke's son, was climbing down from the coach. The boy wore a kilt of blue and green plaid, a black coat, an ivory silk waistcoat, ivory-colored wool socks, and shoes that were as finely made as his father's boots.

No one was looking at the boy except Lloyd. All eyes were on the duke, the footman lending a beefy arm so the duke could climb back inside.

The other boy, as arrogant as his father, walked up to Lloyd, but Lloyd swore he saw a gleam of satisfaction in the boy's eyes. The boy brushed past Lloyd, pretending not to see him, but Lloyd felt the coldness of a coin against his palm.

The duke's son said nothing at all as he headed for the coach. The duke bellowed down at him. "Hart, get your arse back inside. Hurry it up."

The footman held out a hand to the boy called Hart, but Hart ignored it and leapt with agility back into the coach. The traffic cleared, and the coach pulled away. Hart Mackenzie looked out the window as the coach passed, his gaze meeting Lloyd's. The two boys stared at each other, one on either side of luxury, until another coach passed between them, and traffic swallowed the duke's carriage.

"Come on, lad," the constable said, his hand still firmly on Lloyd's shoulder.

Lloyd closed his hand around the coin until the ridges of it creased his palm. He walked away with the constable, so numb that he went all the way inside the police station before he remembered he should try to get away.

Chapter 2

"Louisa, dear, just see that the bishop isn't left alone, will you?"

Louisa looked down the sloping meadow from Mrs. Leigh-Waters's Richmond house to watch the Hon. Frederick Lane, Bishop of Hargate, enter one of the tea tents. Hargate was in his forties, young for a bishop, marginally handsome, and lately had made no secret he was hanging out for a wife.

Lady Louisa Scranton, unmarried, her father dying in scandalous circumstances which had left the family nearly penniless, must be, in Mrs. Leigh-Waters's eyes, in want of a husband.

Hargate fit the criteria for an aristocrat's daughter—wealthy, second son of an earl, successful in his own right. Hargate had reached his status young, but he had connections, many of whom were here at this garden party, attended by Mrs. Leigh-Waters's handpicked guests.

A bishop's wife would have money, respect, and standing. Louisa was highly aware she needed to marry well—in fact, she'd entered the Season this year with every intention of doing so. So why, when it came to the sticking point, did she feel a great reluctance to be alone with Hargate?

"Of course, Mrs. Leigh-Waters," Louisa made herself say. "I'll look after him."

"Thank you, my dear." Mrs. Leigh-Waters beamed at her. *I'll have Louisa married off in no time,* the lady was no doubt thinking. *Quite a feather in my cap when I do.*

Louisa gave her a kind smile and hurried after the bishop.

Mrs. Leigh-Waters's house commanded a view down a hill to the river. The April day was a fine one, the weather not too hot, clouds in the sky but not threatening rain. The land stretched away on the other side of the river to be swallowed in haze.

The expanse of lawn had been commandeered for the garden party, with seats and little tables scattered about, pathways lined with ribbon, a croquet set being brought out by the footmen. Ladies in blues, greens, yellows, golds, lavenders, and russets moved about, the spring breeze stirring feathers, ribbons, braids, and false fruits stuck into the ladies' hats. Gentlemen in casual suits of monochrome gray or tweed filtered through the ladies. Tea had been served in the tea tents at the bottom of the hill, and many guests still carried cups and little plates of treats. An idyllic English afternoon.

The guests chatted to each other as they waited to begin the croquet match, which would be cutthroat and rather expensive. Members of high society gambled fiercely at everything.

Louisa ducked away from them into the white canvas tea tent, which was empty except for the Bishop of Hargate and white-draped tables holding tea things. The elegant china cups and saucers were patterned with sprays of roses, as were the three-tiered trays with the remains of petit fours and profiteroles. As most of the party had already refreshed themselves, only a few clean plates and cups remained.

"Ah, Lady Louisa," Hargate said, sounding pleased. "Have you come to join me?"

"Mrs. Leigh-Waters did not want you left on your own."

"She's a kind lady, our hostess." Hargate looked at Louisa with every eagerness, which Louisa found odd in a man her father had done his best to ruin.

Louisa's father, Earl Scranton, had convinced other men to give him money for investments, which were either never made or failed utterly. Earl Scranton had been paying the first investors with what the others had given him, pretending the money came from his cleverness at buying the right stocks. Finally when his true investments failed, he had to confess he could pay none of the money back. In the space of a day, Earl Scranton had moved from respectable and wealthy to complete ruin. A good many other gentlemen's fortunes had gone with his. Hargate hadn't lost everything, but he'd lost much, though he'd managed to build it back in a relatively short time.

Louisa moved calmly to a table, trying to behave as though none of it had happened. A lady wasn't supposed to know about or understand such things, in any case. "Tea, Your Grace?"

"Of course. Thank you."

Louisa had been taught to be an expert at pouring tea. She trickled the soothing liquid into two china cups, dropped a lump of sugar and dollop of cream into the bishop's tea, and handed him the cup.

She left her own cup sitting on the table and lifted two dainty, cream-filled profiteroles, which hadn't wilted too much in the April warmth, onto one of the petite china plates. Louisa had a weakness for French pastries, even those that looked a bit limp.

"I've been meaning to speak to you, Lady Louisa," Hargate said, an odd note in his voice. "What a fine chance that we are here alone."

Chance, my foot. Hargate and Mrs. Leigh-Waters had contrived this meeting between them, they must have.

Hargate reached out his free hand and seized Louisa's. He closed his fingers so tightly she'd never be able to release herself from him without jerking away. Hargate looked into her eyes, his full of something like glee. "You will do me much honor to let me speak to you, Louisa."

Oh dear, he was about to propose.

Louisa could refuse him, of course, but she knew she risked great disapproval if she did—*Haughty creature, turning down such a fine match; did she truly think she'd have the opportunity at another? A girl from a scandalous family cannot afford to be so high and mighty.*

On the other hand, if Louisa accepted Hargate, she'd have to marry the man. He was everything a young lady should want in a husband, as Mrs. Leigh-Waters no doubt thought, but

Louisa had never much liked him. Hargate was pompous, talked at length—usually about himself—and was quite hopelessly, well . . . *dull*.

"Your father and I had business dealings," Hargate was saying. "And you of course know what happened with those."

Yes, Louisa was reminded of it every day. When everything had fallen apart, Lord Scranton had died of the shame. Louisa and her mother, on the other hand, had to continue to live with the shame.

"Water under the bridge," Hargate said. "I assure you. I'd never hold it against you, Louisa. That is, I won't, if you consent to be my wife."

And if Louisa refused him, he *would* hold it against her? Louisa stared at him, not certain she comprehended. Was he trying to *blackmail* her into marriage? From Hargate's smile and expression, Louisa thought he might be.

I can't marry him.

As Louisa gazed at Hargate, trying desperately to think of a way out of this troubling conversation, another face swam into her mind. This one was hard rather than handsome, a man with unruly dark hair and hazel eyes that held a glint of gold.

A working-class man, an illegitimate son, his mother a tavern maid, everything an earl's daughter was supposed to shun. And yet, Louisa remembered the power of his kiss, the strength of his hands. His rough whiskers had burned her lips, and she'd tasted his mouth.

That kiss had occurred at Christmas, and it had been Louisa's idea, her impulse. Likewise had been the kiss at the wedding before that at Castle Kilmorgan. Louisa's impulse had turned into a sort of madness, and now she could not forget Lloyd Fellows, no matter how hard she tried.

But she'd felt more alive pressed against the hard doorframe while he'd kissed her, the sounds of the Christmas party in the distance, than Louisa had any other day of her life, especially this one, in this tea tent at a perfect English garden party.

She wet her lips. "Your Grace, I—"

"You know it is for the best," Hargate said. "No one else will marry the daughter of the gentleman who ruined him. Save your respect and accept my offer."

Hargate's eyes took on a hard light, giving Louisa a glimpse of a meanness she'd not seen in him before. "Your Grace, you are kind, but—"

"You have no dowry; your cousin, the new earl, is a frugal man who keeps you and your mother on a small allowance—all this is common knowledge. Your Mackenzie in-laws have sordid reputations few decent families wish to be connected with. Your name has been discussed at my club, and only my admonition has stopped gentlemen saying disparaging things about you. You have few champions, Louisa, and I am one of them. When you are my wife, I will stop all gossip about you."

Gossip? Louisa blinked in shock. About what? A little panic fluttered in her heart—the kisses with Mr. Fellows rose in her memory again, not that they were ever far away. Had someone seen?

No, she'd been careful about that. Louisa had approached him only when she was certain they'd be alone, although once the kisses began, she couldn't swear to anything else happening around them, not even an earthquake. Someone might have seen her, and in Louisa's circle, with its rigid rules for unmarried misses, those kisses would ruin her.

Or perhaps Hargate simply meant the speculations about Louisa in light of her older sister's scandalous elopement. Not only had Lady Isabella run off with a *Mackenzie*, she'd then left him, walking out of his house and obtaining a legal separation. But instead of retreating to quiet solitude, Isabella had gone on hostessing soirees and balls as though she saw nothing amiss. Most of society expected Louisa to follow in Isabella's footsteps. Never mind that Isabella and Mac had been reconciled and now were blissfully happy—their outrageous behavior was what everyone remembered.

The bishop was offering to save Louisa from any sort of shame. All she had to do was marry him.

"And I will drop any pursuit of the money your father owed me," Hargate said. "You can tell your cousin the estate would be released from that debt."

"Your Grace . . ."

Hargate let go of Louisa's hand to touch his fingers to her lips. "Say nothing until your answer is *yes*, dear Louisa. I'll wait." He took one step away and raised his teacup to his lips, as though he would stand there and sip tea until she capitulated.

Louisa, anger rising, stared down at her profiterole, looking for inspiration in the rather runny cream. Bloody cheek he had, cornering her and demanding she give in to him.

Why on earth *did* Hargate want to marry her? He could have his pick of unmarried ladies, many of whom were at this very garden party, who would gladly marry him for his standing, wealth, and when a seat came empty, his place in the House of Lords. Plenty of young ladies with respectable families and good dowries would have already started planning the wedding as soon as they walked into the tea tent. What was Hargate up to?

Louisa drew a breath, hardening her resolve. "Your Grace, I . . ."

The bishop looked up at her over his teacup, and as he did, Louisa noted that his face had lost most of its color. His cheeks had taken on a greenish tinge, and Hargate's breath hitched.

"Are you all right, Your Grace? Perhaps we should adjourn to the open air."

If Hargate had eaten something that disagreed with him, that would put paid to this awkward proposal. Louisa caught the bishop's arm, ready to lead him out and give him over to the ministrations of their hostess.

"Loui—" Hargate had to stop to draw a breath. He coughed, staggered, and coughed again.

Louisa began to be truly alarmed. "Come outside with me, Your Grace. We'll take you to the house, where you can rest out of the heat."

Hargate tried to take another breath. His eyes widened as air eluded him, and he dropped his teacup, splashing tea across the grass. He sagged against Louisa, his eyes and mouth wide, his chest heaving, but no air moving inside.

"A few more steps is all," Louisa said, trying to support him. "You'll be all right once we get outside."

Hargate took one more step before his legs buckled and he fell heavily against Louisa's side. Down went Louisa's plate, which she realized she was still clutching, the plate breaking, creamy profiteroles smearing on the dead grass.

"Your Grace."

Louisa couldn't hold him. Hargate landed on his back, Louisa on her knees next to him, her blue and brown striped skirt spreading over the tea-dampened grass. Hargate's face had gone completely gray, and hoarse little gasps came from his mouth.

A doctor. She needed to fetch a doctor. One was here at Mrs. Leigh-Waters's garden party, a very famous one called Sir Richard Cavanaugh.

Louisa scrambled to her feet. "I'll find Sir Richard. Don't worry. Help is coming."

As she ran out, the heel of her high-heeled lace-up boot caught the teacup Hargate had dropped, smashing it to bits.

Louisa dashed into the open air, scanning the guests in desperate search of Sir Richard. There he was, speaking with Louisa's sister, Isabella, and another old friend of Louisa's, Gilbert Franklin. Both Isabella and Gil turned with welcoming smiles as Louisa panted up, but Isabella's smile faded in concern.

"Darling, what is it?"

"Hargate . . . in the tea tent. Taken ill. He's collapsed. Please, Sir Richard. He needs you."

Sir Richard, a short and lean man with dark hair going to gray and an arrogant manner, seemed uneager to set aside his tea and rush across the lawn at Louisa's request. "What seems to be the matter with him?" he asked.

Louisa resisted the urge to grab the man and shove him down the hill. "Please, you must hurry. I think he is having a fit. He can't breathe."

"Good Lord," Gil said, managing to sound pleasant even with his worry. "We'd better see to him, Cavanaugh."

Sir Richard frowned, then finally he sighed, passed his teacup to a footman, and gestured for Louisa to lead him to the tent.

He walked too slowly. Louisa had to wait for Sir Richard, she holding the tent flap open impatiently while he sauntered in. Isabella, Gil, and Mrs. Leigh-Waters followed, along with a smattering of curious guests.

Sir Richard at last showed concern when he saw Hargate, who hadn't moved. Sir Richard went down on one knee next to the bishop and looked him over, felt his pulse points and his heart, then leaned down and sniffed at Hargate's mouth.

The doctor gently closed the bishop's wide, staring eyes before he got to his feet. His arrogant look had grown more arrogant, but it was more focused now, more professional.

"He is dead," Sir Richard announced. "Nothing I can do for him. Send for the police, Mrs. Leigh-Waters. The bishop appears to have been poisoned." He looked at Louisa when he said it, his accusing gaze like a stab to the heart.

Chapter 3

London was Lloyd Fellows's home. He knew every street from Whitehall to the East End, from the Strand to Marylebone and all points in between. He'd known them as a boy living in St. Giles with only his mother to raise him. He'd learned more as a constable walking a beat, and even more as a detective sent to every corner of London and beyond.

Fellows knew every street like he knew his own name—who lived where, what businesses, legitimate or illegal, were where, and what people walked the streets and when. He knew every corner, every passage, every hidden staircase. Metropolitan London might be divided into districts by the government, and into cultural areas by the people who lived there, but to Fellows, London was one, and it belonged to him.

This fine April afternoon, he entered a dark passage off Crawford Street, aware of what awaited him at the end. His constables weren't with him, because the culprit they were pursuing had changed course, and they'd split up to surround him.

Fellows was after a murderer, a man called Thaddeus Waller, who'd been nicknamed the Marylebone Killer. Waller had brutally murdered his brother and brother's wife, then covered up the crime and pretended grief, even taking in his brother's children to raise.

Fellows, recently promoted to detective chief inspector, had investigated the deaths with a ruthlessness that had alarmed his superiors. But he'd uncovered fact after fact that pointed to Waller as the killer. Finally Fellows had obtained a warrant for Waller's arrest and had gone with his constables to Marylebone to bring him in.

Waller had seen them coming and used his own wife and his brother's children as hostages. Fellows's fury had wound higher as Waller had held a little boy out the upstairs window, threatening to drop him to the cobbles if the police didn't go away. The lad had cried weakly in terror as he'd hung helplessly, high above the street.

Fellows had left his constables to catch the boy if he was dropped, stormed upstairs and kicked his way into the flat, his rage making him not care what weapon Waller decided to draw on him.

Waller's terrified and weeping wife at least managed to drag the boy back in through the window. When Fellows burst in, Waller had jumped through the window himself to the street one floor below. The constables tried to grab him, but Waller had fought like mad, they'd lost hold of him, and he'd fled.

Fellows had swung himself out the window right after him. He'd chased Waller through crowded streets to the passage where the man now hid. Fellows knew this passage. It was narrow and dark, twisted sharply to the right at its end, and emerged via a shallow flight of stairs to another street.

He sent his constables around to the stairs to bottle in Waller, while he dashed into the passage alone. Waller was going to fight, and Fellows knew his constables stood no chance against him. Although they were good and robust lads, they didn't understand dirty fighting or what a man like Waller could do.

Fellows had grown up with dirty fighting. He knew about the destructive power of bits of brick in his hand, the various ways small knives could be used, and how to pit an opponent's own weight and reach against him.

Waller would know the constables waited for him above. He'd make a stand. He'd killed his own brother, for God's sake, had killed more men in the past, and wasn't above using a child as a shield.

Fellows was one man, alone. But he knew that if he waited for help, Waller stood a chance of getting away. Fellows wasn't going to let him.

The passage was dark, shielded from the April sunlight by high, close-set buildings. Fellows couldn't see much, but he could hear.

Waller tried to mask his breathing, but the heavy intake of it was too thick to hide. The scuttle of rat's claws on the cobbles also came to Fellows, as well as the clatter of carts on the streets outside, the wind pouring between buildings. Fellows pinpointed each sound, identifying and cataloging it as he moved to the source of the breathing.

The attack came swiftly. Fellows sensed the first swing of a massive fist and ducked. He rose, bringing up his elbow to slam the man in the diaphragm.

Fellows was rewarded with a blow to the head, one that darkened his world a moment. He dragged in a breath, trying to find his equilibrium, before another punch to his skull sent him to his knees. Waller didn't waste breath laughing or gloating. He slammed his arm around Fellows's neck and started to choke him.

Fellows shoved himself to his feet and threw his weight forward. Waller grunted and his hold loosened. Fellows dug his hands into the man's shoulders and continued the momentum of the throw, ending up slamming Waller against the wall of the narrow passage.

Waller grunted and stumbled but swiftly regained his feet. He came at Fellows, roaring, no longer trying to be surreptitious. The constables poured down the stairs from the other end, against orders, their clubs ready.

Fellows and Waller fought, close and desperate, in the confined space. Boulder-like fists slammed at Fellows's face. Fellows ducked under the man's reach, came up abruptly, and smashed his fist into Waller's jaw. The jaw broke, and Waller fell, screaming.

He grabbed Fellows on the way down, and Fellows felt the

prick of a knife under his arm. He jerked away and punched Waller full in the face.

And kept on punching. Fellows's rage was high, with a white-hot fury that blotted out all reason. He couldn't see or hear—he only knew that this man had caused terror and death, and hadn't held back from hurting harmless children.

"Sir," one of the constables said. "He's down."

Fellows kept on punching. Waller was mewling, broken hands curled around himself. Blood poured from his nose and mouth to stain the already-grimy cobbles.

"Sir?" One of the younger constables dared seize Fellows's arm. The touch dragged Fellows back from the dark place he'd gone, and his awareness slowly returned.

Waller lay still, hoarse sounds coming from his mouth. The young constable was eyeing Fellows nervously, hand still on his arm. The boy barely had whiskers to shave, and yet they'd sent him out to chase a madman. The constable at the moment looked as though he wasn't certain who was more dangerous— the killer or Fellows. Fellows felt a surge of feral delight.

He drew back his square-toed boot and kicked Waller squarely in the ribs. "That's for the little lad," he said. He straightened up, wiping his mouth. "Arrest this filth and get him away from me," he told the constables. "We're finished here."

Fellows turned away from a killer who'd slain at least five people and regularly beat his wife and children, found his hat, put it on, and walked back onto his streets.

Before Fellows returned to the Yard, he went back to Waller's flat to tell his wife Waller had been caught and arrested. He'd waited to see the man securely locked into the police van and trundled away to face a magistrate before he'd gone.

Mrs. Waller, Fellows knew, had nothing to do with the murders; she was a victim as much as any of the people her husband had killed. She'd been the one who'd saved the children, not Waller. Fellows went to tell her she was now safe from her husband.

The residents of the area did not like policemen. They hadn't much liked Waller, the Marylebone Killer, but even so, they'd been closemouthed when Fellows had questioned them.

Now the men and women on these streets stopped what they were doing to watch Fellows pass. Fellows knew his face was bruised and bloody, but his walk and his grim look would tell the others who'd won the fight.

Mrs. Waller was upset, confused, grieved, and relieved at the same time. She promised she'd look after the children and keep them well, and Fellows believed her.

The rooms she lived in weren't a hovel, but they weren't a palace either. Fellows handed her a few coins before he left. He also stopped and had a word with her landlord, saying he'd be back if the landlord turfed out Mrs. Waller because her husband had been a murdering bastard. She needed help, not blame.

Fellows left, hearing muttered words behind him. But he hadn't come here to make friends. He'd come to stop a killer and save a family, and that he'd done.

Now he needed a bath, a thick pint of beer, and a good night's sleep.

But it wasn't meant to be. First he'd have to report to his superiors, then spend the rest of the day and into the night writing up a concise documentation of the investigation and arrest. The reward for his valor would be paperwork.

Fellows walked into his office to cheers. Word had already gotten around how he'd landed the Marylebone Killer, embellished, no doubt, by the constables who'd been on the scene.

"Well done, sir!" Detective Sergeant Pierce sang out as Fellows entered his inner office. "Fought your way through three men, single-handed, did you, sir? And then dragged out our killer by the hair, him begging for mercy?"

"Exactly," Fellows said, and Pierce laughed.

Fellows collapsed to the chair behind his desk, drew out a clean handkerchief, and dabbed at the wounds on his face.

"Don't get too comfortable, sir," Sergeant Pierce said, annoyingly cheerful. "One's come over the wire from Richmond. Asking for you specifically, Chief."

Bloody hell, what now? "I'm on leave, Sergeant. Starting immediately. That is, after I spend all night writing a boring report."

"Sorry, sir." Pierce didn't look one bit sorry, the sod. "Detective Chief Super wants you to take this. Police in Richmond telegraphed. A bishop dropped dead at a fancy garden party in the middle of a load of toffs. They think it's foul play, and they want a detective from the Yard. They want it handled with kid gloves, and they specifically want you."

Fellows scrubbed his hand through his hair, finding it stiff with blood. "If they want kid gloves, why do they want *me*?"

"I suspect 'cause you're related to a toff—a duke, no less."

Since the day it had come out that Fellows was in fact the illegitimate son of the Duke of Kilmorgan, he'd gotten hell from his colleagues. They either looked at him with contempt or went so far as to bow to him mockingly in the halls. Laughter was always present.

Fellows decided he could either play superior officer and quell them, or he could look the other way. He'd gained back his respect by making a rude gesture when he bothered to notice the jibes, then completely ignoring them. Fellows also worked hard to show he was damn good at his job, better than most, and did not let his accidental aristocratic blood hamper him.

Sergeant Pierce went on, "I suspect that if we do have to arrest one of the nobs, the Richmond boys would rather it be one of us who does it. They have to go on living there while we can scuttle back to Town."

"They want us to do the dirty work, in other words."

Pierce grinned. "On the nose, sir."

A jaunt to Richmond to clear up a problem among the upper classes was not what Fellows wanted at the moment. He'd meant to finish his report, go home, bathe, sleep, pack, drop in at his mother's to say hello and good-bye, and then board a train. He had a week's leave coming. His half brother, Cameron Mackenzie, had suggested Fellows stop in at the races at Newmarket next week. Fellows, though still uncomfortable with his newfound family, didn't mind the horse races. Any man might enjoy himself at a racecourse. He'd planned to go to the seaside and stare at the water a while, then make his leisurely way to Newmarket for the racing meet next Monday.

But he was a policeman first, and if he had to postpone his trip, then he did. Policemen didn't get days off.

Fellows rubbed his hair again. His face was already dark with new beard, and then there was the blood all over him. He didn't feel in any way fit to face a house party of people convinced a man who'd died of overeating and apoplexy had been murdered.

But there was nothing for it. "We go," Fellows said in a hard voice. "It's our job."

Sergeant Pierce lost his grin. "We?"

"I'll need my dutiful sergeant for this one. Let me go wash my face, and we'll be off. Fetch your hat."

Fellows took some grim satisfaction from Sergeant Pierce's crestfallen look as he headed off to the washroom to make himself presentable.

~~~

"He's dead, all right," Sergeant Pierce said an hour or so later.

He and Fellows knelt next to the body while a doctor called Sir Richard Cavanaugh stood nearby and gave them his medical opinion in the most condescending way possible.

"Histotoxic hypoxia," Sir Richard said. "See his blue coloring? Prussic acid, most likely. In the tea, I would think, a fatal dose. Would have been quick. Only a few moments from ingestion to death."

Fellows disliked arrogant doctors who presumed ahead of the facts, but in this case, the man was probably right. Fellows had seen death by prussic-acid poisoning before. Still, he preferred to hear conclusions from the coroner after a thorough postmortem, not to mention a testing of food and drink the victim had taken, than speculations by a doctor to the elite.

Fellows ordered Pierce to gather up what was left of the broken teacup with the liquid inside, and also the full teacup that stood next to the pot on the table. He had Pierce pour off the tea still in the pot into a vial for more testing. Fellows scraped up cream from a pastry that had been smashed on the ground, and the remains of the plate that had held it, handing all to Pierce.

He left Pierce sealing up the vials with wax and had a look around the tea tent. Unfortunately too many people had trampled in here; the place was a mess. The grass was filled with footprints—ladies' high heels, gentlemen's boots, servants' sturdy shoes—all overlapping one another.

The local police sergeant stood well outside the tent as though washing his hands of the affair. Fellows approached him anyway. The fact that the local police had sent no one higher than a sergeant meant the chief constable wanted to keep well out of the way. He wondered why.

"Your thoughts, Sergeant?" Fellows asked the local man.

The sergeant shrugged, but the man had a keen eye and didn't look in the least bit stupid. "The doc says poison in the tea, and I don't disagree. The young lady they think did it is in the house—my constable's on the lookout up there. She's an aristo's daughter, though, so the lady of the house didn't want the likes of us questioning her. Says we had to wait for you." The sergeant gave Fellows a dark nod. "Better you than me, if you don't mind me saying so, guv."

He meant better *Fellows* lost his job for arresting a rich man's spoiled daughter, which was exactly what could happen. Fellows's Mackenzie connections might be able to save him from a lawsuit by the girl's father, but his career could be over.

Not that Fellows wanted to go begging, hat in hand, to his half brothers for their charity. An invitation to the races was one thing. Owing a monumental obligation to Hart Mackenzie was another.

"Go help Sergeant Pierce," Fellows growled at the man. "I'll need statements from everyone. Who was where and what they saw—in minute detail. Understand?"

The sergeant did not look happy, but he saluted and said, "Yes, sir."

Fellows left him behind and made for the house and the aristocrat's daughter. He reflected as he approached the large house that running down a killer six feet three and weighing eighteen stone was much more satisfying than having to face a silly girl who probably didn't understand what exactly she'd done. She likely felt herself perfectly justified in poisoning a man who'd annoyed her. She'd be highly strung and more than a little mad, or else too stupid to realize the consequences of her actions.

Fellows looked up at the giant brick house trimmed in white, strategically positioned for a view to the river at the bottom of a meadow. The very rich lived here, the sort who existed in their own world, with their own rules; no outsiders need enter.

He climbed the marble steps at the rear of the house and stepped into the dim coolness of its interior. Mrs. Leigh-Waters, the lady of the house, hurried toward him from the front hall. She was a large-bosomed woman with hair pressed into tight, unnatural curls, and was garbed in a gray bustle gown that made her look a bit like a pigeon.

"I'm so glad you've come, Chief Inspector," she gushed. "They've always spoken highly of you, which is why I told the chief constable to telegraph you. The local constables can be a bit . . . hasty . . . and she needs a bit of sympathy, doesn't she?"

"Of course," Fellows said, forcing his tone to be polite. "I will keep the interview brief."

"Thank you." Mrs. Leigh-Waters sounded relieved. "I'm certain she will thank you too."

She led Fellows through the cool, high-ceilinged hall whose draped window at the end cut out most of the light. Mrs. Leigh-Waters tapped on a door halfway along and opened it to a sitting room with back windows overlooking the garden and the view.

Two women rose from the sofa to face him. Fellows halted three steps inside the room, unable to move.

The features of the two red-haired women were heart-breakingly similar, the younger a little taller than the older. The older wore a gown of bottle green with black buttons up its bodice. The younger woman's gown had a blue and brown striped underskirt, the blue overskirt folded back to reveal a lining of blue and brown checks. Her bodice was buttoned to her chin with brown cloth-covered buttons. Fellows noted every detail even as his gaze fixed to her face.

The older sister, Lady Isabella, was married to Lord Mac Mackenzie, one of Fellows's half brothers. The younger sister, Lady Louisa Scranton, had petal-soft skin, lips that could kiss with heat, and a smile that had been haunting Fellows's dreams since the day he'd met her.

Louisa stared back at him, as frozen as he, her lips slightly parted.

Isabella unlinked herself from Louisa and came forward. "Thank heavens you're here," Isabella said to Fellows, both relief and worry in her voice. "They're claiming *Louisa* did this, can you imagine? You'll clear this up and tell them she didn't, won't you?"

Chapter 4

Isabella spoke, but Fellows could see only Louisa. Louisa looked back at him, fixed in place, her face as white as the plaster ornamentation on the cornice above her.

The other two ladies in the room faded, as did the sound of voices outside the windows, the sunshine, the fine afternoon. Fellows could be alone in a whirling fog, where nothing existed but himself and Louisa.

At Christmas this year, Fellows had found himself alone in a hallway with her in Hart's obscenely large house. Louisa had tried to talk to Fellows, bantering with him as she did the other young men at the celebration. Fellows had only heard her voice, sweet and clear, then he'd had her up against the doorframe, his mouth on hers, her body pliant beneath him. Fellows could still taste the kiss, hot and beautiful, and remember his need for her rising high.

She was the aristo's daughter the doctor and local sergeant were convinced had poisoned the bishop. Lady Louisa Scranton, earl's daughter, the woman Fellows dreamed about on nights he couldn't banish thoughts of her any longer.

He'd have to pull himself from the investigation. He'd never be able to get through it, because anything Fellows found against Louisa he'd toss aside or try to pin to someone else. He knew he'd do anything to keep from seeing this woman led away in manacles, put into a cell, charged and tried, convicted and hanged until dead.

The proper thing would be to excuse himself, summon Pierce to take her statement, and tell the Yard they needed to assign another detective to the case.

Another detective who might find evidence that Louisa had committed murder. Fellows's heart beat sickeningly fast. If he backed away, Louisa might be convicted for the crime by people too impatient to prove she could be nothing but innocent. That she *was* innocent, he had no doubt.

Now was the time to speak. To say good day to Mrs. Leigh-Waters and explain that Sergeant Pierce would take over the questioning of Isabella and Louisa.

Fellows opened his stiff lips. "It shouldn't be too much to clear up, ma'am. I'll need to speak to Lady Louisa alone."

"Are you certain?" Mrs. Leigh-Waters fluttered. "Perhaps she should wait for her family's solicitor . . ."

No solicitors. No witnesses. Fellows needed to hear what Louisa had to say without any other person present.

"A preliminary questioning is all, Mrs. Leigh-Waters," he said firmly.

"Then her sister at least should stay with her."

Mrs. Leigh-Waters was perfectly right to try to protect Louisa from an unscrupulous policeman, not to mention being alone in a room with a man at all. But Fellows couldn't question Louisa in front of anyone, not even Isabella, not even Sergeant Pierce. He had to be alone with her, to get her to tell him what had happened, so he could keep her safe.

"Please," Fellows said, gesturing to the door. "Lady Isabella, you too."

Isabella gave her sister a look of concern. Louisa shook her head, the movement wooden. "I'll be all right, Izzy."

Isabella studied Fellows a good long time before she agreed. "Please send for me if I'm needed. Never worry, Mrs. Leigh-Waters. Mr. Fellows is a perfect gentleman." Isabella's look told Fellows he'd better *be* a perfect gentleman or face her and explain why not.

Fellows returned the look neutrally. He'd fenced with Lady Isabella before.

Isabella took Mrs. Leigh-Waters's arm and led the reluctant woman from the room. He heard the door close, their footsteps in the hall.

When it seeped through Fellows that he and Louisa were alone, his awareness narrowed to her. How her body was a perfect upright, how the curve of her waist and bend of her arms softened her posture. Her striped gown made her look taller, her bosom a soft swell under all the buttons.

Lovely, lovely femininity. Fellows was no saint, but he hadn't been with a woman in a good long while, long enough not to be able to look upon Louisa Scranton without wanting her.

No, it wouldn't matter if Fellows came to her sated and exhausted from weeks of passion—he would still want her.

He gestured with a gloved hand to the sofa. "Please, sit."

Throughout the exchanges, Louisa had remained rigidly still, as though turned to the biblical pillar of salt. Now she moved to the sofa, her movements jerky. Her face was paper white, her red hair making it whiter still. From this stunned face, her eyes burned.

Fellows knew he should not sit on the sofa next to her. He should pull a hard chair from the other side of the room and angle it away from her so he wouldn't risk his legs touching her skirt.

But then he thought again about how they'd stood in the doorway of the empty room last Christmas, the revelry far away down the hall. How Louisa had flowed into him, her lips seeking his, her body soft against his. She'd instigated the kiss, and Fellows hadn't been able to stop himself turning it into a taste of passion.

He did not seek the other chair. He sat on the sofa with Louisa, putting at least two feet of space between them. Then he stripped off his gloves, took a small notebook and pencil from his pocket, flipped to a clean page, and wrote: *Interview with Lady Louisa Scranton, witness.*

"Take me through it, Lady Louisa," Fellows said, not letting himself look up from the notebook.

"Take you through what?" Her voice was brittle. "How I watched the Bishop of Hargate die?"

Fellows kept his eyes on the page. "I need to know exactly what happened. It's apparent he was poisoned, and I'd like to know how and by who. You went inside the tea tent . . ."

Louisa drew a sharp breath. "We had some tea. The bishop was talking to me about . . . about his recent travels to Paris. Then he looked ill, started struggling to breathe, and he fell. I thought he was choking, and I ran and fetched Sir Richard. By the time we returned, the bishop was dead." Louisa shivered, her hands moving restlessly.

Fellows resisted the urge to reach over and give her a comforting caress. "Did you drink any of the tea?"

"No. I never had the opportunity."

Fellows made his hand write the notes. "But you had a cup of tea. There were two cups—one broken on the ground, one on the table near a teapot. The cup on the table was presumably yours."

"Yes, I poured it. But I didn't want tea just then, so I set it down to drink later."

"Why did you do that?"

When Louisa didn't answer right away, Fellows made himself look up from his notebook.

Louisa was staring at him, no shyness in her. The light in her eyes was angry, very angry, but behind her defiance he saw great fear.

"Why didn't you drink?" Fellows asked again, this time watching her.

"Because I did not want tea at the moment." Louisa said every word slowly and deliberately. "I was speaking with the bishop. I didn't want to spill anything."

"You were eating tea cakes."

"Profiteroles," Louisa said. "Choux pastry filled with cream. I took two but I didn't eat because I was having a conversation. I could not be very dignified stuffing cream and pastry into my mouth, could I?"

Fellows had a sudden flash of her licking cream from the profiterole, then taking a dainty bite. Her red lips would part as her teeth bit down, cream would cling to her lips, then she'd lick it away. Slowly.

Fellows tightened his grip on the pencil. "Continue."

"That is all. The bishop coughed and fell. I told you, I

thought him choking or fainting. I had no idea he was dying . . ." She shivered again.

Fellows wanted to throw his notes to the floor, pull her to him, and enfold her in his arms. He'd stroke her hair, kiss her, shush her. *It's all right. I'm here. I'll keep you safe.*

He remained rigidly on his end of the sofa. "Then what did you do?"

"I rushed out of the tent looking for the doctor. Sir Richard said the bishop had been poisoned and looked at me as though I'd done it. Isabella brought me to the house." Louisa opened her hands. "And here I am."

Here they both were. The police had been summoned, and Mrs. Leigh-Waters, likely at the insistence of Isabella, had asked for Chief Inspector Fellows to come and take over.

Fellows closed the notebook and set it on the tea table next to the sofa. He folded his hands and leaned forward slightly, a posture he hoped didn't threaten.

He was a master at threatening, had had many more than one criminal fling themselves at his feet and beg for mercy. But mercy wasn't his job. Fellows's job was to track down and arrest murderers, as he had earlier today, and bring evidence to their trials. Mercy was left to judge and jury.

But he'd do everything in his power to keep Louisa Scranton from standing in the dock at the Old Bailey, facing a jury who'd find her guilty of murder. He'd do anything to avoid the judge looking at her and voicing the awful phrase, *Take her down.*

Fellows held her gaze. "I need you to tell me the truth, Louisa. Did you poison him?"

Louisa's eyes widened, then she was up and off the sofa. "No! Why on earth should I?"

Sincerity rang in her every word. She was innocent, Fellows knew it. But he was not who had to be convinced—the rest of the world must believe it too.

"Perhaps you didn't mean to," he suggested. "Perhaps you put something in the tea and didn't realize what it was."

"I gave him *tea*. I dropped in one lump of sugar and a dollop of cream. I'm very certain it was sugar and cream. I *have* served tea before."

Fellows did not reach for his notebook. He'd had Pierce take the sugar bowl and pour off the cream as well.

"Or you thought to make him sick," Fellows went on. "You didn't realize what you gave him would kill him."

Louisa stared in shock. "*No.* Inspector, you know me. I would never be so cruel. I am telling you, I did not poison the bishop's tea, deliberately or accidentally. I would never do such a thing. You have to believe me."

Her desperation sang of her innocence. But Fellows had heard the same tone from lying murderers—they were masters at it. If Sergeant Pierce were in the room, he'd say, "That's what they all tell me, love," and be on his way back to London to apply for an arrest warrant.

Facing a magistrate would be traumatic for Louisa. She needed to understand that. Fellows's next words were what he knew a stern magistrate's would be. "You were alone in the tent with him, no one else near. He died, and if we are right about what kind of poison it was, it acted swiftly. That fact will get out. Newspapers like a murder, especially in the upper classes. The bishop had given your father trouble over their financial dealings. No one else had time to put poison into his teacup. Only you. So you tell me what happened, exactly what you saw—*who* you saw. I will keep you out of jail and away from the courts at all costs, Louisa, but I'm going to have to work very hard to do it."

Louisa listened to the speech in the same shock, but color returned to her face in a furious flush. "What are you saying? That you don't believe me? I thought you knew me. Why are you . . . ? How *dare* you?"

Fellows was on his feet, his professional persona evaporating. "For God's sake, Louisa, *help* me. My sergeant is even now listening to fifty accounts of you going into the tea tent alone with Hargate. Why did you?"

She blinked, dragging in a deep breath as she tried to calm herself. "I don't remember . . . No, I do. Mrs. Leigh-Waters asked me to make sure the bishop was looked after."

"And you do everything Mrs. Leigh-Waters says? You let yourself be alone with unmarried gentlemen to please Mrs. Leigh-Waters?"

"You are making this sound sordid. It wasn't like that. You don't understand."

Fellows was over her, the scent of violets that clung to her floating to him. "Then tell me why."

"Mrs. Leigh-Waters didn't want him left by himself," Louisa said stiffly. "And apparently he wanted to speak to me."

"What about?"

Fellows stood too close to her, could feel the warmth of her body, see the smoothness of her skin as her pink flush deepened. "None of your business what about," she said. "It was a private conversation."

"Between friends?"

"*Yes.* Why are you talking to me like this? I'd thought *we* were friends. Why are you accusing me?"

Fellows curled his big hands. "Right now, I am the best friend you can have. But you have to tell me everything. What you were speaking about, why you decided to be alone with him. Why I should believe you didn't deliberately poison him."

Louisa's breath tangled his for an instant before she stepped back. She put her hands to her temples, red curls snaking around her fingers. "This has to be madness. I didn't kill him."

"You expect me to take you at your word?"

"Yes, I do." She glared up at him. "An English*woman's* word is as good as an English*man's*."

"Not in my world." Fellows made his voice hard. "In my world, everybody lies. They might think it for a good reason, but they lie. And those lies hurt. They can even kill."

"You come from a terrible world, then."

"Oh, it's bad, all right." Fellows gave her a wolfish smile. "And I don't want you to be part of it. So tell me, Louisa, *why did you go off alone with the bishop?*"

The tears that flooded Louisa's eyes made his heart pound. But they weren't tears of sorrow, they were tears of rage and embarrassment. "I don't want to tell you," she said. "It had nothing to do with his death."

"You can't know that. It might have everything to do with it."

Louisa had opened her mouth to argue, but she stopped. She turned away again, still massaging her temples, moving to the window. The light silhouetted her, her gown gently swaying as she walked.

The vulnerability in her stance nearly undid him. Fellows wanted to go to her, slide his arms around her from behind, kiss her hair when she leaned back to him. He wanted to caress her, as though she belonged to him, and say, *It's all right, love. I'll take care of everything. You don't worry about any of it. I'm here.*

If Fellows touched her, he wouldn't let go. He'd draw her into his arms again, crush her up to him, let their mouths meet. He'd taste her, drink her, and let the rest of the world go to hell. He'd take her away with him, anywhere, to be safe, alone with him. Never letting go.

When Louisa turned back to him, her face was blotchy red, the tears wiped away, but one still damp on her cheek.

"You're a policeman," Louisa said. "From what Mac and the others have told me, you're very good at it. A detective first, they've said. Like a bloodhound on the scent."

Fellows dragged in a breath, pulling his thoughts back from burying himself in Louisa and never coming out. "Flattering."

Ian Mackenzie had once lumped Fellows's dedication in with the Mackenzie family's madness, saying Fellows's focus on catching criminals was as intense as Cameron's brilliance with horses, Mac's with painting, or Ian's with numbers and total recall.

"If I tell you, the good policeman, everything, it will end up in a report on a desk, will it not? The foolishness of Lady Louisa Scranton in black and white, for all to see. Shall I then find it splashed across every newspaper and scandal sheet in London?" Louisa gave a half-hysterical laugh. "Why not? They played out my sister's marriage and near-divorce there. They'll quite enjoy themselves over me."

Fellows held up his empty hands. "My notebook is over there. Whatever you say to me, in this room, will go no further. I'll write it into no report. What you tell me will be between you and me, I promise you. You'll have to take me at *my* word."

"And why would you, the good policeman, not write down every syllable I say?"

Because I'd do anything for you, Louisa.

"Because I'm not always the good policeman," Fellows said. "Never mind what the Mackenzies tell you about me— sometimes I'm just a man."

Just a man who remembered every brush of her lips, every

touch, their impulsive kisses, the stolen moments. *I shouldn't have done that,* she'd whispered after the first time. *But I've been wanting to kiss you.* Fellows's world had changed that day and hadn't righted itself yet.

"I want to trust you," Louisa said.

"I want to trust *you*."

Louisa looked away, head turned, but not bowed. She was courageous, elegant, beautiful. Fellows wanted her with the intensity of a small sun. Somewhere not this overly large sitting room where she could walk so far away from him, somewhere he could close her in his arms, lay her head on his shoulder, and simply be with her.

"Very well, I'll tell you," Louisa said. She looked back at Fellows, her green eyes luminous with unshed tears. "Mrs. Leigh-Waters encouraged me to go alone to the tea tent with the Bishop of Hargate, because she knew he would propose to me there."

Chapter 5

Isabella's maid had laced Louisa's stays too tightly. She could not draw a proper breath, couldn't keep her voice from sounding scratched.

She hated the way Inspector Fellows was looking at her— *Chief* Inspector now; he'd won his long sought-after promotion. His hazel eyes were steady but behind them were questions, skepticism.

This man, this half Mackenzie, always unnerved her. He was as tall and strong as his brothers, and possessed their air of confidence so acute it was almost arrogance. His hair, a dark shade of auburn, had been cut short, now rumpled as though the wind had caught it. Unshaved whiskers were dark on his bruised and battered face, and his eyes were red-rimmed.

But the hazel eyes that looked out at her showed anything but exhaustion. Fellows watched her with the keenness of a hawk, one waiting for the right moment to strike its prey.

The abrasions on his face had stunned Louisa almost as much as seeing him again. She wanted to touch him, ask in concern what had happened to him, try to make his hurts better, as though she had a right to.

The wild streak in the rest of the Mackenzies had been

honed in Fellows into a ruthless need to pursue whatever criminals he believed needed to be pursued. He was just as single-minded as the rest of the family, but not as scandalous, because he kept a very tight rein on his emotions.

Fellows waited, not saying a word. The hawk would let his prey come to him.

Louisa drew another breath, or tried to, silently cursing her tight corset. "And yes, he did propose."

"And you said . . . ?"

"I never had the chance to answer. As I tried to think of a way to let him down politely, he took ill."

Fellows's expression didn't change. "You were going to refuse him?"

"Yes."

"Why?"

I thought of you, and I couldn't. "Why?" She wanted to laugh again. "Because I did not want to marry him. I knew we wouldn't suit."

Fellows's expression still didn't change. "Because your father defrauded him?"

Louisa flinched but had to nod. "I was surprised Hargate wanted to propose to me, in light of that."

"Curious."

"Yes, it was." Humiliating too. Something she did not want to discuss with Mr. Fellows.

Fellows looked her up and down, and when he spoke again, his voice was mild and even. "I've spent years listening to people lie to me, Louisa. I've learned what exactly it sounds like. Up until this moment, you've been telling me the truth. Now you are lying. Why?"

With any other man, Louisa might hold her head up and demand him to cease badgering her, but with Fellows, she couldn't. He knew too much about her. He knew she liked kissing him, liked the smoothness of his lips, the taste of his tongue.

Her face burned. "You are presumptuous."

"It isn't presumption," Fellows said, keeping the mildness. "Or assumption. Why did you refuse the Bishop of Hargate? He's rich, has plenty of titles in his family, and a lofty position. He should have been a good match for you."

His indifferent tone made Louisa's heart sting. "I should

have married him for his wealth and position?" She gave him a mirthless smile. "Is that what you're asking?"

"It is why people of your class marry, isn't it? A business arrangement. Marriage is for connections and money; love is sought with mistresses."

In spite of the uncaring words, the look in Fellows's eyes was bitter. Louisa knew his history—the now-deceased Duke of Kilmorgan had dallied with a tavern maid, got her with child, then deserted her. When Fellows's mother sought the duke to tell him about the baby and ask him for help, he'd denied Fellows was his.

Fellows's Mackenzie blood was obvious, however. At one time he'd worn a thick moustache to hide some of his features, but now that he went about clean-shaven, the resemblance to the old duke and to Hart Mackenzie was clear. Fellows had never spoken of his parentage to Louisa, but she knew the duke's denial of him had hurt him deeply and driven him most of his life.

"My reasons for refusing the bishop have nothing to do with this," Louisa said. "I promise you. I didn't poison him, and I'd like to go home now."

Fellows took a step toward her, his carelessness gone, menace returning. "*I* will determine what has to do with Hargate's death and what doesn't. You need to tell me everything, or else you'll be stammering it in front of a magistrate. He will also know when you are lying, and unlike me, he'll turn everything against you. Because you're an earl's daughter, instead of being hanged or sent to prison, you *might* be put into a home for genteel ladies who have gone insane, but then again, you might find yourself up before a judge who wants to make an example of you." Another step, the light in his hazel eyes sharp. "Or, you can tell me everything, and you won't have to face a magistrate at all."

He was unnervingly close. Louisa smelled the outdoors on him, the fresh April wind mixed with the scent of coal smoke that clung to the wool of his coat. His words terrified her, because she knew he was right. She knew how it looked—she alone with the bishop, she serving him tea, he dropping dead at her feet. Louisa was a young woman from a scandalous family, and who knew what she might do?

His deep voice rumbled around her, stern and harsh, but Louisa wanted to cling to it, to let the sound comfort her. While he meant to frighten her, he was asking her to trust him with the truth, and with her life. He was right that she had no one else to help her.

She clenched her hands and said the words in a rush. "The Bishop of Hargate told me he would release my family from any obligation to repay him if I married him. Repay him what he'd lost because of my father, I mean. He'd relieve us of that debt and the shame of it, but only if I consented to be his wife."

Fellows's eyes became even more focused, frighteningly so. "He told you this in no uncertain terms?"

Louisa nodded. "Oh, he made it very clear."

Fellows went silent for a few moments. Clouds slid across the sun, thick enough to erase the happy spring sunshine and plunge the sitting room into gloom.

When Fellows spoke again, his voice was quiet. "You know you have just outlined a perfect motive for killing him."

"Yes, I do realize that." Louisa swallowed on dryness. "It is one reason I was trying very hard *not* to tell you."

"One reason? What is another?"

"The other reason is because it is so very embarrassing."

Fellows studied her, his eyes still. His left cheekbone bore a deep cut, the blood dried. Black bruises surrounded the cut, the bruises moving up to his temple. The right side of his mouth had taken another cut, and scrapes decorated his cheek. Again, Louisa wanted to reach up and touch his face, to ask if he was all right. She curled her fingers into her palms.

"Did anyone else know the terms of this proposal?" Fellows asked abruptly.

"I have no idea. Mrs. Leigh-Waters knew, or guessed, the bishop would propose to me, but whether she had any hint he would try to blackmail me into accepting, I do not know."

"Even if she didn't know, the story will come out sooner or later," Fellows went on in his matter-of-fact voice. No false comfort for Louisa, just unvarnished truth. "Hargate might have confided in his valet that he planned to coerce you into marrying him, or his solicitor. Or he might have boasted of it loudly at his club or a meeting of his vestry, who knows?"

"Well, *I* didn't know until he sprang it on me in the tea tent,"

Louisa said. "That's a point in my favor, is it not? If I'd decided to poison him, I would have had to prepare beforehand. But I had no reason to prepare, because I had no idea what he meant to ask me. Surely that proves my innocence. I would have had to bring the poison with me to the garden party, and I assure you, Inspector, I have no vials of poison about my person."

"Proves nothing. You might have known about Hargate's proposal in advance. Servants gossip. Solicitors and vestrymen gossip too. You might have seen yourself pushed into accepting him and decided the only way out of marrying a man who demanded your body in exchange for forgiving your father's debt was killing him. You could have brought the vial in your pocket or a reticule. Afterward you could have dropped the bottle in the tea tent, or surreptitiously tossed it into the garden as you walked through it, or even hidden it in this room while you waited for me. Or you might have it in your pocket now."

Louisa's lips parted as she listened, something cold seeping through her body. His words . . . *demanded your body in exchange for forgiving your father's debt* . . . were inelegant, even harsh, but again, he was not sparing her. Truth was often ugly.

"Yes, I *might* have done any of those things. But I did not. It's ridiculous."

"Just show me," Fellows said.

She blinked. "I beg your pardon?"

"Show me what you have in your pockets, Louisa. Believe me, if you are arrested and searched, you'll be treated far less gently at a police station than you will here by me. So show me."

Louisa's frock had one pocket, in the skirt, its opening hidden by the peplum of her bodice. She jammed her hand inside and pulled out a handkerchief, a pencil on a ribbon, and a tiny notebook.

"There. That is all."

Fellows came to her swiftly. He gave her a measuring gaze and then pushed aside her hand and slid his own into her pocket.

Louisa's breath hitched. The corset cut into her again, and spots danced before her eyes.

Fellows didn't touch her. She felt the warmth of his hand between skirt and petticoat, the strength of his fingers as they moved in the pocket. She looked up at him and found his hazel eyes focused directly on her.

The look in their depths made her dizzy. This man should be nothing to her—a member of the family her sister had married into, that was all. He was not of her world. He'd been born on the wrong side of the blanket, raised in working-class London, and had taken up the common profession of policeman.

But he'd compelled her from the first time she'd laid eyes on him, at a family gathering at Kilmorgan Castle. Louisa had seen how uncomfortable Fellows had been in a home that might have been his, how silent he'd been, how haunted he'd looked. She'd wanted to cheer him up, to show him that the past didn't have to mean a thing to the present.

She'd learned Fellows had a biting, deprecating sense of humor, often directed at himself, but he was also happy to direct it at those around him. He had the powerful personality of the Mackenzie men, but one turned in a different direction from theirs. While the brothers had been raised with money and power, Fellows had faced the world in all its ugliness. He'd had no protection but himself.

Now Fellows stood very close to her, and Louisa wanted to kiss him again. The first time she'd done so, she'd told herself she felt sorry for him. But she knew it had been more than that.

It was more than that now. The need to kiss him rose like an uncontrolled fire. It sent Louisa up on her tiptoes in her high-heeled boots, making her lean into him, wanting to feel his strength and his warmth.

Fellows's eyes started to close, his body coming down to meet hers. The hunger she saw, before his lids hid his eyes, sparked an answering hunger deep inside her.

Louisa drifted into him, welcoming his heat. She felt the touch of his breath, which would be followed by his lips . . .

Then wasn't. Fellows jerked back, eyes opening, a hard light entering them.

He lifted his hand out of her pocket. Between his broad fingers was a small bottle of cut glass with a little stopper, a tiny amount of liquid inside it.

Chapter 6

Louisa, still ensnared by the kiss that hadn't happened, stared at the bottle uncomprehendingly. "What is that?"

"That is what I am asking you." Fellows's voice was harsh.

"I don't know." Louisa held up her hands. "It isn't mine."

"It was in your pocket." His gaze grew even colder.

"You must have put it there then. I certainly didn't."

"Louisa." Fellows lifted the small bottle in front of her face. "I need you to explain this to me."

"I didn't put it there," Louisa repeated in desperation. "I cannot help it if you don't believe me. I don't even know what it is."

"It's a perfume bottle," Fellows said. "But this is not perfume."

"I can see that it's a perfume bottle. How do you know it's not perfume inside it?"

"Wrong consistency."

Hysterical laughter tried to bubble up again. "And you're an expert at what ladies carry in their perfume bottles?"

"I am an expert in the many ways people kill other people and try to cover it up."

Louisa's eyes widened. "I've *told* you. I didn't kill him."

"Someone is going to a lot of trouble to make it look as though you did. Why?"

"Well, I don't know," Louisa nearly shouted. "Perhaps someone did not want Hargate to marry me. Perhaps the poison was meant for me, or it was in the teapot, for us both. Only I didn't drink it."

Fellows's eyes flickered, but he went on remorselessly. "Bit of a gamble, wasn't it, to pour the poison into the correct cup of tea then put the bottle into your pocket? Who did you see when you went into the tea tent?"

"*No one.* It was empty. Hargate was already inside by the time I arrived, but no one else. I noticed no one leave—the rest of the guests were outside waiting for the croquet match."

Fellows shoved the perfume bottle into his pocket. He gazed down at Louisa a moment longer, his brows coming together, then he turned abruptly and walked away from her. He made his way to the window and looked out, every line of his body tight.

His broad back, covered in black, showed his strength. If life had been different, if Fellows's father had married his mother and the birth had been legitimate, this man would now be a duke.

Fellows turned back. When he spoke, his voice was stern and solid, worthy of any duke's. "You entered the tea tent and saw someone crawling out the other side."

Louisa shook her head. "No. I told you. The tent was empty, except for the bishop."

Fellows walked to her again. "You saw someone—maybe only a glimpse of them—ducking out under the back of the tent. They must have pulled up a stake to loosen the canvas."

"I . . . ," Louisa trailed off, her mouth drying.

Fellows wanted her to say this, was handing her the script. All she had to do was repeat the words, and he'd write them down.

"I can't lie," Louisa said weakly.

"Better to say it to me now than to a judge and jury, after you take the oath. Tell me what you saw, Louisa."

Louisa bit back a cough. "I thought . . . Yes, I thought I saw someone scrambling out under the other side of the tent."

"Man or woman?"

"It was too quick. I couldn't see."

"Color of their clothing?"

"Dark, I think. But as I say, I couldn't see."

Louisa closed her mouth, not wanting to embellish. *Keep a lie very simple,* her brother-in-law Mac had once told her. *The more you invent, the more you have to remember. It's tricky, lying. That's why I never do it, myself.*

"I couldn't see," Louisa finished.

Fellows's hazel eyes glinted in the room's dim light. Then he nodded, picked up his notebook from the table, moved back to her, and wrote down the words while she stood a foot away from him.

His fingers were inches from her, his eyes quietly fixed on the paper. His sleeve moved to show the cuff of his shirt, enclosing a strong wrist and forearm. His hands were tanned from the sunshine, the liquid color going back under the linen of the shirt, as though he had the habit of rolling up his sleeves outdoors. His knuckles were scratched, from whatever fight had given his face its cuts and bruises.

Louisa felt his stare. She looked up from her study of his hand to find his gaze on her. Never taking his eyes from Louisa, Fellows closed the notebook and slid it and his pencil into his pocket.

She expected him to say something, anything, to break the tension between them. Or to touch her. They'd shared two kisses, both of them intimate. Louisa could still feel the doorframe at her back from the kiss at Christmas, Fellows's body the length of hers, his hand on her neck as he scooped her to him.

The silence stretched. Louisa was dismayed by how much she wanted to kiss him again, even after he'd interrogated her. He was the only man she'd ever kissed, the only man she'd ever wanted to.

If she touched his cheek, she'd feel the bristles of his whiskers, the heat of his skin. She could lean to him and indulge herself in another taste of him. The Mackenzie who was not a Mackenzie so fascinated Louisa that she could barely keep her thoughts together when he was in a room with her.

"Louisa."

Louisa realized she *had* started to rise to him, and thumped back on her heels. "That's all I remember."

"It's enough. Are you staying in London with Isabella?"

Louisa nodded, feeling giddy. "Yes, for the Season. My mother is in Berkshire with Cameron and Ainsley." Why she felt she needed to report that, she didn't know.

"Good. Stay in tonight. And for the next few nights. Cancel your engagements and pretend you're sorry Hargate is dead."

"But I *am* sorry . . ."

"No, you're stunned and shocked, but you're not grieved. This man wanted to marry you, for whatever his reasons, and everyone at this party saw you go into the tent alone with him. You need to behave as though you had interest in him, a friendliness toward him, and no contempt. If anyone knows Hargate planned to coerce you into marrying him, and they say so to you, you must have no idea what they mean. Hargate never mentioned your father, or your father's debt to him. You thought Hargate loved you, and you were at the very least flattered by his interest in you. Understand?"

Louisa nodded numbly. "I must lie and say I liked him, because otherwise no one will believe the truth that I didn't kill him."

"You had the best opportunity. Easy for you to slip poison into his teacup while you poured out for him, then slide the bottle into your pocket so deeply a cursory examination wouldn't reveal it. Most policemen would balk at putting their hands very far into an earl's daughter's pocket."

"But not you."

Louisa saw him draw one quick breath, but his reply was as hard as ever. "This is life-and-death, Louisa. Behave as though you liked him, and spare yourself the noose."

Louisa looked at him for a long time, Fellows staring back at her. Finally, she nodded.

"Good," he said. She saw the smallest flicker of relief in his eyes, but nothing more. "Stay here. I'll tell Isabella to come to you."

Louisa nodded again, tears burning. Through the blur she saw Fellows's face soften, then he lifted his hand and brushed her cheek.

Louisa thought he'd say something to her, maybe go so far as to apologize for upsetting her, giving her a gentle word to make her feel better. But no. Fellows caressed her cheek with callused fingers, the sensation sending heat through her body.

Then he withdrew his touch and walked stiffly past her and out the door. The sound of it closing behind him was as hollow as the pain in Louisa's heart.

~~~~~

Fellows made Sergeant Pierce clear everyone out of the tea tent. Too many people had trampled in here after he'd gone, the grass and dirt even more of a mess than it had been before. Someone had knocked over a small table, spilling yet another set of tea-cups to the ground.

Once he and Pierce had convinced them all to go, including Mrs. Leigh-Waters, who wanted to linger, Fellows went over every bit of the tent on his own.

He ended up on his hands and knees on the far side of the tent, looking for signs that someone actually had crawled in the other side. But the stakes that held the tent were driven firmly into the ground, and the dirt here hadn't been disturbed.

Fellows disturbed it. He tugged up one stake and gouged the area with his boot.

He was aware of the magnitude of his actions. Misleading the police or covering up a crime could have him arrested, possibly convicted and sent to Dartmoor to break rocks along-side the men he'd helped put there.

He didn't care. Louisa was innocent, and he wouldn't let her go down for this crime. Fellows had been a detective long enough to know when a person was guilty and when he or she was not. His instincts were never wrong. The only time he'd been wrong had been in a case involving Ian and Hart, and in that instance he'd let his hatred for the Mackenzie family over-ride his instincts.

Wasn't he letting his emotions do the same now? some nig-gling part of him asked.

No.

He'd made an error of judgment when he'd thought Hart and Ian Mackenzie had committed a few murders, but at the same time, Fellows had known those men to be capable of it, Hart especially. Fellows himself was capable of murder as well.

Not Louisa.

Few truly good people existed in this world, and Louisa Scranton was one of them. She had a fiery temper—he'd seen that a time or two—but she also possessed a vast kindness and generosity that made her beautiful. She was like a firefly, bright and energetic, lighting up those around her.

Fellows would do everything in his power to keep her safe.

He finished arranging the scene of the crime as he wanted it, took a few more samples from the smashed tea things, and departed the tent.

～～

The Bishop of Hargate's funeral two days later was well attended. Louisa went with Isabella and Mac, the three of them standing a few feet behind Hargate's family and friends.

Rain trickled down, spotting the black umbrellas, which had opened like dark flowers as soon as sprinkles began. The tiny drumming on the canvas made Louisa's already tight nerves stretch tighter.

Mac held an umbrella over Isabella, his arm around his wife's waist. He was never embarrassed at displaying that he'd married for love, which Louisa had always found rather sweet. The Mackenzies were volatile, emotional men. She didn't think they knew *how* to hide their feelings.

The other Mackenzie who stood at the very edge of the crowd was volatile and emotional too, but he kept a tight rein on himself. Lloyd Fellows wore severe black today, his hat in his hand as he bowed his head for the prayers. Rain darkened his hair—no umbrella for Chief Inspector Fellows.

Three days had passed since the bishop's death. Louisa had followed Fellows's dictate that she remain inside and away from the Season's social whirl. She understood why, but the confinement chafed. Though Isabella's house was cheerful and full of children, Louisa had been happy even for the excuse of the funeral to come out into open air, as chilly and dank as it was.

The churchyard contained many prominent people—both above and below ground—Hargate being no less prominent. Hargate's father was an earl, and marriages had made him cousin to a marquis, another bishop, and a few baronets. The crowd at the burial ground today must encompass several pages of *Debrett's*.

The two Scotland Yard detectives stayed well back, being

respectful of the family's grief. But Louisa knew Fellows was watching, looking for signs of feigned sorrow among the guests, a betrayal of glee that Hargate was gone.

The bishop who conducted the service finished with the usual prayers about man being dust and his life on earth nothing. The casket was lowered, and Hargate's family sadly bade him farewell.

As the crowd dispersed, Louisa moved next to Hargate's mother and offered her condolences. She was rewarded with a cold stare. Hargate's father gave Louisa a look of open viciousness before he and his wife turned their backs and walked away from her.

Louisa moved back to Isabella as though nothing untoward had happened, but her heart was hammering, and she felt ill. Hargate's parents had just cut her dead, and the entire gathering had witnessed it.

Isabella closed her fingers around Louisa's arm. "Never mind, darling. They're upset. Only natural."

"They think I killed him," Louisa said numbly. "Don't they?"

"Please don't think about it, dearest. We'll go home and have lots of hot tea and stuff ourselves with cakes. You know this will blow over when Inspector Fellows clears it all up."

Inspector Fellows had resumed his hat, but he remained on the edge of the crowd, watching every person walk by. He wasn't part of them, and his stance said that he didn't want to be.

He saw Louisa. Their gazes met, held for a heartbeat, two. Louisa grew hot in spite of the chill rain.

Finally Fellows gave her a nod and lifted his hat. Louisa nodded back as politeness dictated, but her head and heart ached.

~~~~~

Louisa usually found it soothing to sit in Mac's studio and watch him paint. But the day after the bishop's funeral, she paced restlessly in the wide upper room while her brother-in-law slapped paint onto canvas.

His children were there—Aimee, Eileen, and Robert—Aimee and Eileen playing together, baby Robert fast asleep. Mac Mackenzie, clad in his kilt, old boots, and loose shirt, his hair protected by a gypsy scarf, painted in a kind of frenzy, never looking away from his canvas or palette.

When Louisa paced past him for about the twentieth time, however, Mac dropped his palette with a clatter and thrust his brush into oil of turpentine.

"Louisa, lass, for God's sake, sit down. I can't concentrate with you rushing past a dozen times a minute."

Louisa bit back snappish words and sat down with a thump on the threadbare sofa. The sofa was old and thoroughly worn from children playing and napping on it. Louisa knew Isabella modeled for Mac on it, and not for modest pictures. Little Robert had been conceived on it, Louisa believed. A very family-situated sofa.

"I beg your pardon, Mac. I am tired of being confined to the house." Hearing nothing, knowing nothing. Fellows had sent no word and had not called himself. "It's a bit frustrating." An understatement, but Louisa had been bred to be so very polite on every occasion.

Mac softened. "Aye, I know. I'm sorry. Forgive my temper."

"You're an artist," Louisa said lightly. "You can't help yourself."

Mac burst out laughing, a big, booming Mackenzie laugh. "A good excuse. Ashamed of myself for employing it. Why don't you tell Isabella to take you out? No reason you should sit here day after day. If anything had happened . . . was wrong . . . the good Fellows would tell us, yes?"

Mac's stammering around the subject did not give Louisa heart. He meant that if policemen were about to swoop down and arrest Louisa, Fellows would warn them.

"Be kind to her, Papa," Aimee said. "She's afraid people will accuse her of poisoning the bishop."

Aimee was five years old, nearly six. Mac and Isabella's adopted daughter had red hair a similar shade to Isabella's, steady brown eyes, and a burgeoning intelligence. Unkind people made out that Mac was Aimee's father in truth, her mother one of Mac's models, and Isabella a fool to take Aimee into her home.

The truth was harsher—her father had been a man who'd tried to kill Mac, her mother a Parisian woman who'd died of illness and neglect. Mac's and Isabella's compassion had saved this little girl. Aimee was turning into a sweet, amiable, and clever child. She knew she was adopted, but the only parents she remembered were Mac and Isabella.

Mac stared at Aimee now in surprise. "Where did you hear talk like that, wee girl?"

Aimee returned his look without blinking. "You and Mama. And a few ladies who came to visit Mama yesterday. I hid in the second drawing room and listened to them talk. I like to look at the ladies in their dresses. Some of them are beautiful, though Mama's dresses are the prettiest."

Mac had his mouth open. On a big man wearing a kerchief, the expression was comical. "Aimee . . ."

"Perfectly all right, Mac," Louisa broke in. "We shouldn't hide things from her. Aimee, sweetie." Louisa took Aimee's hands. "It is true that some people will say I killed the Bishop of Hargate, but that is untrue."

Aimee still looked troubled. "The ladies said you hated him for what happened with your father. And one said you'd been his lover. What does that mean, exactly?"

Mac's Highland Scots became pronounced. "Lass, never listen to the likes of women such as they. I'll tell Morton not to allow them into the house again. And don't repeat such things to your mother."

"I wouldn't," Aimee said. "That's why I'm asking you and Louisa."

"God save me," Mac muttered, and went to find his palette again.

Louisa squeezed Aimee's hands. "What they said is untrue as well. The bishop and I were acquaintances only, and I was not angry with him. I did nothing to hurt him."

Aimee nodded, her eyes round. "I know you didn't."

Relief touched her. Louisa knew Aimee didn't entirely understand the implications of the situation, but the girl trusted her, and Louisa wanted to do nothing to violate that trust.

"And Aimee, lass, you're not to talk of it anymore, with anyone," Mac said sternly. "Not even within the family."

Eileen, who was nearly three, watched them, her fingers in her mouth. Her little brother Robert slept on a pile of clean drop cloths, on his tummy, his fists curled beside him. His hair stuck up in little spikes, his Scots fair skin a stark contrast to the brilliant red of his hair. The boy could sleep anywhere, at any time, no matter what fireworks were going off around him. Louisa found that adorable; Mac only growled that he was another stubborn Mackenzie.

"Don't scold her, Mac," Louisa said. "She wasn't to know. You may talk of it with *me* all you like, Aimee." She smoothed the girl's wiry red hair. "No secrets inside the family. Those outside might not understand, which is why we're not speaking of it to them."

Aimee nodded. "All right, Aunt Louisa. Why do people think you poisoned him?"

"Because I was nearest him at the time. But I give you my word, I did not."

"I believe you." Aimee climbed up onto Louisa's lap and gave her a warm kiss and a hug. "Don't be afraid, Aunt Louisa. You're safe here."

Louisa felt anything but safe, but her eyes grew moist at the sentiment. Now, if only Lloyd Fellows would believe her. Not to mention put his arms around her and reassure her that she was all right.

Mac turned back to his canvas. He was working on a picture of a group of horses. He'd done the preliminary drawings in Berkshire at Cameron Mackenzie's training stables, and was now painting it. The horses galloped across a pasture, manes and tails flying, muscles gleaming. Because Mac painted in the new style, the lines weren't solid, but the wildness of the beasts came through—even more than if he'd made every line exact. Louisa could almost hear the hooves pounding, the snorts and whinnies, and smell the grass, dust, and sweat.

"Tell Isabella to take you out," Mac repeated. He yanked his brush from the jar and rubbed it clean on a rag. "A good ride in the park or something. Our grooms don't need to be hanging about like loose ends. Give them something to do."

In other words, *go away and let me work.*

"Isabella is busy," Louisa said. "She's frantically finishing preparations for the supper ball, as you know. I ought to be helping her." She fixed Mac a look. "So should you."

"I *am* helping her. I'm minding the children. A good husband knows when to stay out of the way of the whirling household."

"A fine excuse," Louisa said, feeling the first amusement she'd had in days.

"Papa likes to hide up here," Aimee said. "Morton and Mama bully him if he goes downstairs."

Mac grinned. "She's not wrong. Driven away by my wife and my butler. What is a man to do?"

Enjoy himself with his art and his children. Louisa envied him, and Isabella. They were so happy together, exactly matching each other in spirit, love, and vigor. Louisa knew Isabella would prefer to be up here with him, watching her handsome husband paint, playing with the children she loved so well.

But Isabella was a hostess at heart as well, leading the ladies of the Season. She was also keeping up her social schedule, Louisa knew, to dare anyone to say that anything was wrong. Louisa would be at the supper ball tonight, by Isabella's side, helping to greet guests, engage shy young ladies in conversation, or smooth ruffled feathers of older ladies. This gathering would be utterly respectable, for debutantes up to the most redoubtable matrons, and Louisa would be in the middle of it.

She'd go mad. Louisa gently set Aimee on her feet and sprang up. "You're right, Mac. Staying in will only make me more irritable." She went to him, lightly kissed his paint-streaked cheek, and left the room, not missing Mac's grin or his look of relief.

It also did not help her that Mac looked much like the man she could not banish from her thoughts. The near-kiss she'd shared with Fellows in Mrs. Leigh-Waters's drawing room burned her almost as much as the true kisses had. She kept feeling the heat of his body against her, his hard fingers on her cheek.

Out.

A young lady couldn't simply walk outside in London and charge alone down the street. It wasn't done. Louisa had to play by every rule she possibly could until the true culprit was found. All eyes were on her, she knew.

She asked Morton to fetch Isabella's carriage, convinced the housekeeper to release a maid to accompany her, and made her way to visit Eleanor, the Duchess of Kilmorgan.

Fellows's investigations didn't take him often to Mayfair. Murders in London were most likely to happen at the docks or in slums where gin and desperation overrode sense, and knives came out. Mayfair was for the polite crimes of embezzlement and fraud and, long ago now, dueling.

The death of the Bishop of Hargate was a crime of Mayfair. Though the event itself had taken place in Richmond, every single person at that garden party had a London residence for the Season, all of them in Mayfair.

Fellows knew Mayfair as well as he did the rest of London, because he was thorough. The people who walked these streets, though, were not the ladies and gentlemen who lived there, but the tradesmen and domestics who worked it. Those who reposed in the houses wouldn't consider strolling more than three doors down without a carriage.

For the past three and a half years, Fellows had made use of a new base of operation in Mayfair, the Duke of Kilmorgan's mansion on Grosvenor Square. Once Hart, the duke in question, had officially acknowledged Fellows as part of the family, he'd made it known that Fellows could walk into and out of the Grosvenor Square house anytime he chose.

Fellows mostly didn't choose, but he'd relaxed enough in the last few years to realize that taking Hart up on his hospitality could be convenient. Since Hart's marriage to Lady Eleanor Ramsay last April, it had become even more convenient.

Eleanor knew everyone. She not only knew them but knew everything about them. If anyone could tell Fellows about the people at the Richmond party, it was Eleanor.

Fellows took an omnibus to Hyde Park, then walked through the park to Park Lane and north. This took time, but Fellows liked to think as he walked, and he enjoyed the open green spaces of the park. For Fellows the boy, London's city parks had been his idea of pristine countryside. He'd sneak away from home and play in Hyde Park, St. James's Park, Green Park, or Holland Park, until someone reported an urchin in their garden spaces, and a constable chased him away.

On Park Lane, whose giant houses grew more ostentatious by the year, he noted a moving van outside the mansion formerly belonging to Sir Lyndon Mather. It must have been sold yet again—that made three times in the last three years. Unlucky, that house must be. Fellows had never liked Mather, though Mather had inadvertently guided Fellows to the right path to solving the High Holborn murders. Nothing about that case had ended up as Fellows had ever dreamed it would. It had led, indirectly, to him meeting Lady Louisa Scranton.

Fellows turned onto Upper Brook Street and walked to Grosvenor Square and Hart's house. Hart's first footman had the door open for Fellows before he reached it.

"Good afternoon, sir," the footman said, reaching to relieve Fellows of his coat and hat as Fellows stepped into the wide front hall. A staircase wound up through the middle of the house, spring sunshine lighting it from windows at each landing. The balustrade was elegance itself, the airy space quiet, beautiful, and at peace.

Fellows's father had lived here. The old duke had walked up and down these stairs, no doubt growling at his footmen and butler to jump to do whatever he commanded. Hart had traversed the stairs as well, as the boy Fellows remembered from that day on the street when Fellows had pummeled the duke, the duke had beaten him, and Hart had given Fellows a coin. Hart didn't remember the encounter—at least he'd never mentioned it. Fellows had never mentioned it either.

Fellows wondered briefly if the stern-faced Hart had ever slid down the banisters as a boy. Hart had been wild in his youth, so perhaps he had. Then again, he'd always maintained strict control over himself, so maybe he'd forgone the pleasure.

"Her Grace is in the morning room upstairs," the stately butler who stood at the bottom of the stairs said.

Fellows shook himself out of his woolgathering and returned to the task at hand. He thanked the butler, mounted two flights of stairs, and made for the sunny sitting room at the rear of the house.

He knew the way, because whenever Fellows visited, Eleanor insisted they have tea in her sitting room. Eleanor had redecorated this room after she'd married Hart, filling it with peach and cream colors, comfortable furniture, soft carpets, and Mac's paintings. A cozy retreat, filled with feminine grace. One of the Mackenzie dogs, Old Ben, was generally in residence. The hound liked to curl up near the fire in the winter, or lie on his back in a sunbeam in the warmer months.

Old Ben was there now, his soft doggy snore sounding between the words of the women sitting together, April sunshine touching them both. One lady was the duchess—Eleanor. The other was Louisa.

Chapter 7

Louisa got to her feet. Fellows couldn't force his gaze from her, even though Eleanor was also rising, coming toward him, a smile on her face. Louisa wore cream and peach like the colors in the room, a fall of soft lace at the neckline of her bodice. Red ringlets of hair straggled against her throat, making him want to lift them and lick the soft skin beneath.

"So kind of you to call, dearest Lloyd," Eleanor said. She walked past Louisa, who stood unmoving, and reached out for him.

Eleanor took Fellows's hands, rose on her tiptoes, and kissed his cheek. The Mackenzie women were impulsively affectionate, and Fellows had learned to tolerate them. Cameron advised him to take it like a man, though Hart seemed to understand Fellows's discomfiture.

Louisa was in no way inclined to come forward and join the welcoming kisses. She barely gave Fellows a civil nod.

"Sit down and have coffee," Eleanor said, still holding his hands. "I know you loathe tea."

She half dragged Fellows toward the sofa where Louisa had sunk down again. Fellows broke away from Eleanor and moved to a balloon-backed chair at the writing table. The fact

that it had been turned around to face the ladies meant someone else had been using it and recently departed.

Eleanor saw his assessment. "You've missed Hart. He's off
to tell the House of Lords what to do. He so enjoys it."

Hart Mackenzie at one time had departed the House of
Lords in a quest to become prime minister. He'd backed away
from that for Eleanor, for his family, for his life. But he still
enjoyed politics, and according to the newspapers, was a force
to be reckoned with.

Fellows waited for both ladies to sit down again before he
took his seat. His mother had taught Fellows that much—no,
had shouted manners into him. No one was going to say her
son had the manners of gutter trash, she'd declare. He was
going to rise above himself, he was. Didn't he have a duke's
blood in his veins?

"Now, then," Eleanor said. She poured coffee from a pot,
handed the cup to Louisa, who had been sitting in stiff silence,
and indicated she should take it to Fellows.

Louisa had to rise to do it, and Fellows sprang to his feet.
They met halfway across the carpet, Louisa holding out the
cup and saucer, Fellows reaching for it politely.

The look Louisa gave him was anything but polite. She was
enraged, her eyes smoldering with it. She was angry at Eleanor, and she was angry at Fellows.

Fellows closed his hands around the cup. Louisa quickly let
it go, making certain their fingers didn't touch. She turned
from him and sought the sofa before Fellows had the chance
to say a word.

"You've come to tell us about the investigation," Eleanor
said once Louisa had resumed her seat.

Fellows sank to the chair again, balancing the coffee. He
hadn't come here for that, but he didn't argue. "My sergeant
and I have interviewed everyone who was at the garden party,
some of them twice. I looked over Hargate's flat in Piccadilly,
but found nothing to suggest he'd angered someone enough for
them to poison him. I will speak again to those who were closest to the tea tent. Unfortunately, no one saw anything. They
were too busy talking, drinking, and wagering on the upcom-
ing croquet match."

"That sounds typical," Eleanor said. "High society takes its croquet seriously."

Fellows thought he heard Louisa make a small noise in her throat, but he couldn't be certain. "No one claims to have seen anything, at least not what they'd say to the police. But the person Louisa glimpsed made certain to escape on the side of the tent facing the empty meadow, so we're not surprised no one saw him."

He said the lie without a flinch. Louisa didn't flinch either but focused rigidly on her teacup.

"What about the poison?" Eleanor went on. "How was it administered? In the tea?" She waved her own teacup fearlessly.

"Traces of prussic acid were found on the broken pieces of teacup the bishop held. None in Louisa's." That had been a great relief. Even if she'd drunk from her cup, Louisa would have been safe.

On the other hand, the fact that she'd by chance chosen the innocent cup woke Fellows up at night cold with fear. What was to say the poison hadn't been meant for Louisa in truth? Perhaps Hargate had poisoned the cup himself then drunk the wrong one by accident. Or had there been no target—only a madman waiting to see which guest dropped dead?

Either way, Louisa had survived a close call. Fellows, who hadn't prayed since he'd been a boy and forced to church on occasion, had sent up true thanks to God for that.

"No poison in the teapot, then?" Eleanor asked.

"None. In the bishop's teacup only." Fellows took a sip of coffee, which was rich and full, the best in the world. Of course it was. "Lady Louisa, since you are here, I'd like you to tell me—think carefully—why you picked up that particular cup to hand to the bishop."

Louisa lifted her shoulders in a faint shrug. "It was the easiest to reach." Her voice was tight, as though she hadn't used it for some time and hoped she wouldn't have to. "A clean one, placed on a tray. I had to reach all the way across the table for one for me. I poured Hargate's first, to be polite."

"So, if Hargate had gone into the tea tent alone, or someone else had, and wanted tea, they'd have reached first for that cup?"

"Yes. It would have been natural." Louisa paled a little. "How horrible."

"Deliberately killing another person so cold-bloodedly and letting an innocent receive the blame, that is horrible, yes." And too close to home. Fellows wanted the man—or woman—who'd done this. He'd explain to them, slowly and thoroughly, how they'd enraged him, and what that would mean for them.

He turned to Eleanor, who'd listened to all this with interest in her blue eyes. "I've come to ask you, Eleanor, to tell me about Hargate. I want to know who were his friends, his enemies, and why someone would want to poison him."

"So you are taking the assumption that he was indeed the target?" Eleanor asked.

"In a murder like this, even if it seems arbitrary, malice is usually directed at one person in particular," Fellows said. "If the killer wanted to cause chaos and much harm, he'd have poisoned the entire pot, or all the cups. Not just one, for one person alone."

Louisa shivered. "Gruesome."

"The world is a gruesome place," Fellows said to her. He wanted to shove aside his coffee, go to Louisa, sit next to her, put his arms around her, and hold her until her shaking stopped. "It never will be safe, as much as we tell ourselves we can control danger or even hide from it."

Louisa looked back at him, her green eyes holding an equal mixture of fear and anger. He liked seeing the anger, which meant she hadn't yet been broken by this ordeal. But there would be much more to come. Fellows longed to comfort her, to shield her from the horrors, to kiss her hair and tell her he'd make everything all right for her. But at the moment, he was trapped into being the good policeman, with no business wanting to touch her, hold her, kiss her.

He made himself drag his gaze from Louisa and continue. "Now, Eleanor, tell me about Hargate."

Eleanor's eyes widened. "What information can *I* give you? Louisa knew him much better than I did. She'll have to answer."

Louisa shot her a look that would have burned a lesser woman. Eleanor sipped tea and paid no attention.

"I didn't know him all that well," Louisa said, when it was

clear Eleanor would say nothing more. "He was ambitious and became a bishop rather young, and he had family connections that helped him. But everyone knows this."

"He was charming too," Eleanor said. "At least, some people thought so. I never found him to be, but I'm told he had a persuasive way about him. He charmed his way into every living he held, apparently. The only person who ever blocked him was Louisa's father, Earl Scranton, and he and Hargate had words over it."

So had every single person Fellows interviewed told him; they'd told him as well that Earl Scranton had later taken much of Hargate's money in fraudulent schemes.

"Why did your father cause problems for him over the living?" Fellows asked Louisa.

Louisa shrugged, looking past him and out the window. "Father didn't approve of young men getting above themselves. The living at Scranton is quite prosperous, and Hargate wanted it. He was the Honorable Frederick Lane then. My father didn't like him and didn't want him to be the local vicar. He found Hargate foppish, and said he preferred an older clergyman."

"Simple as that?" Fellows asked.

"As simple as that." Louisa looked at him again, her eyes green like polished jade. "Hargate was angry, of course, but once he began his rise to power, he forgave my father. Well, he said, rather deprecatingly, that taking my father's church would have held him back, so it was all for the best."

"Forgave him enough to let your father invest money for him?" Fellows asked.

Louisa's smile was thin and forced. "Investing with my father became the fashionable thing to do. Everyone wanted to say they'd of course entrusted their money to Earl Scranton."

All the worse when the scheme came tumbling down. "And Hargate was angry when everything fell apart?"

Eleanor broke in. "Of course he was. So many were, unfortunately. But when I spoke to Hargate earlier this Season, he seemed unconcerned about it. No grudges there. But Hargate's family have always given him piles of money, even though he was the second son, and he never had to worry much about the ready. Seems to me Hargate led a charmed life. He would have found a seat in the House of Lords soon and lived happily ever after. Well, happy except for being a bit bullied by Hart. But then his luck ran out, poor man."

"And I need to find out who killed him, and quickly. That's why I've come to you for help," Fellows said, looking at Eleanor.

Eleanor contrived to look surprised again. "I don't know what I can do."

She did know, but she was making Fellows spell it out. "You know everyone. When *I* talk to them, they see a policeman prying into their affairs. No, don't bother telling me I'm one of the family and they should treat me as though I'm a true Mackenzie. I'm the illegitimate son and always will be. When *you* talk to them, they see their friend Lady Eleanor Ramsay. They'll tell you things they'd never dream of telling me."

"And then I report it all to you." Eleanor gave him a severe look. "You are asking me to spy on my friends."

"I am, yes."

Eleanor's severe look vanished, and she beamed a smile. "Sounds delightful. When do I begin?"

"As soon as you can."

"Hmm, Isabella's supper ball would be a good place to start. Absolutely everyone will be there. She's hired assembly rooms for it, because her house is far too small for such a grand event—even this house isn't large enough to hold the entire upper echelon of English society. Besides, Hart has become quite tedious about having any large affairs here now that there's a baby in the house, although I—"

Eleanor broke off when a small cry—more of a grunt—invaded the silence, even over Old Ben's snores. Fellows saw now what he'd missed by focusing all his attention on Louisa—a bassinet hidden behind the sofa, its interior shielded from the sunshine by a light cloth.

Eleanor rose immediately, went to the bassinet, and lifted out a small body in a long nightgown. "Here's my little man," she cooed, her voice filling with vast fondness. "Forgive my abruptness, dear friends, but I wanted to pick up my son before he started howling. He can shatter the windows, can little Alec."

Fellows had risen automatically as soon as Eleanor left her seat. Eleanor lifted the boy high, gazing at him in pure rapture. "Did you have a good nap, Alec? Look, Uncle Lloyd has come to see you." Eleanor turned the baby and held him out to Fellows.

Fellows looked at a sleep-flushed face, tousled red gold hair, and the eyes of Hart Mackenzie. At the age of four months, Alec—Lord Hart Alec Mackenzie, Eleanor and Hart's firstborn—already had the hazel golden Mackenzie eyes and the look of arrogant command of every Mackenzie male.

As Fellows stood still, unwilling to reach for this little bundle he might drop, Alec's face scrunched into a fierce scowl. Then he opened his mouth, and roared.

Fellows had heard plenty of children cry in hunger, in fear, or in want of simple attention. Alec's bellowing possessed the strength of his Highland ancestors, calling out for blood.

Old Ben woke up with a snort, looking around in concern. Eleanor laughed, turned Alec, and cuddled him close. "There, now, Alec. The inspector can't help looking at you like that. He scrutinizes everyone so." Alec's cries quieted as he snuggled into his mother's shoulder. Ben huffed again then laid his large head back down.

"If you'll excuse me," Eleanor said. "I must return this lad to the nursery for his afternoon feeding. Tell Louisa what you wish me to do, and thank you for keeping us up on the matter."

So saying, she gathered Alec tighter and breezed out of the room before Fellows could say a word.

The closing door left him alone with Louisa. She looked up from her place on the sofa to where Fellows stood, awkwardly holding his coffee cup.

"You may leave if you wish," Louisa said. She wanted him to, that was plain.

Fellows remained standing but set down the coffee. "I'm glad to report I was able to make the investigation turn its focus from you," he said, trying to sound brisk and businesslike. "You're not to be arrested unless there's evidence solid enough to bring you before the magistrate. The coroner and my chief super don't want to risk putting an earl's daughter in jail unless the chance of making the charges stick is very high. I've convinced my sergeant and my guv that the story of the man escaping from under the tent wall is true."

"It's very good of you."

Such a stiff and formal response from the woman he wanted

to gaze at him in soft delight. His heart burned. "No, it's very bad of me to lie to my own men, but I am trying to keep you out of Newgate."

"And I am grateful to you, make no mistake."

"But angry you have to be grateful to me," Fellows said, his words brittle.

"No, not angry. It's just . . ." Louisa heaved a sigh, pushed herself to her feet, and paced the sunny room. Ben watched her without raising his head. "I'm confused. I don't know what to do, or how to think or feel. How I *should* think or feel. Or how to behave."

"It's a bad business," Fellows said tightly.

"And now you're trying to help me, and I'm being horribly rude. I . . ." Louisa swung around, her peach and cream skirts swishing. "Nothing in my life has prepared me for this. Even Papa defrauding all his friends was not as difficult to understand—you'd be appalled how many wealthy gentlemen are bad at simple business matters. But watching a man die and then being accused of killing him—*that* I have no idea how to parry."

"Being accused?" Fellows asked sharply. "Has someone said that to you?"

"No, but they are all thinking it. I can *feel* them thinking it. Out there." She waved her hand at the windows. "Even you think it."

"I don't. That's why I'm trying to find the culprit."

"If you didn't have a doubt, you wouldn't go to such pains to keep me from being arrested."

Fellows stepped in front of her, forcing her to stop. "Let me make this clear to you, Louisa. You're right that everything at this moment points to you. But if you believe our system of justice will prove your innocence, only because you're innocent, you are wrong. If a judge gets it into his head that you're a giddy young woman who goes around poisoning potential suitors, nothing will change his mind, not the best barrister, not the jury. Most of the judges at the Old Bailey are about a hundred years old and regard young women as either temptresses or fools. Would you like to face one of them? Or a gallery of eager people off the streets, coming to mock you? Journalists writing about what you look like standing in the dock? Every expression, every gesture you make?"

Louisa's face lost color. "No, of course not."

"Then let me do my job and keep you out of court. I wish you didn't hate me for it, but if the price of keeping you free is your hatred, so be it." And a hard price to pay it was.

Louisa's eyes glittered with tears. "No, I don't hate you. You must know that. I never could."

She was too beautiful. Her hair was coming down in soft little ringlets, the red shining in the April sunshine. Many English aristocratic families had Anglo-Saxon ancestry, and it was evident in Louisa—pale skin, bright hair, eyes of brilliant green. Fellows could drown himself in her beauty and never want to come up for air.

He caught her hands. The touch of her warm flesh sent his heart pounding and swept away the last fragment of his self-discipline.

He pulled her by her fisted hands against him, her soft body becoming the focus of his world. Fellows heard nothing, saw nothing but her beautiful face and eyes, her lips parting as he came down to her.

The first taste was intoxicating. Sweetness clung to Louisa's lips from the tea she'd drunk, laced with sugar and cream.

He needed more. Fellows opened her mouth with his, sweeping his tongue inside. Louisa made a noise in her throat, and clutched the lapels on his coat. She kissed him clumsily, unpracticed, but eager.

She smelled of lilacs and dusty silk, and a warmth that was all Louisa. They were alone in silence and sunshine. Fellows slid his arms around her, finding the curve of her waist. Her bodice's smooth fabric was thin, the bones of her corset the only barrier between him and her soft skin.

If he could strip away the layers of her—satin, lawn, lace—and touch her, he knew he'd fill the gaping hole in his life.

She was against him now, her breasts to his chest, her fingers tightening on his coat. Fellows tasted more of her. Her lips were soft, hot, but seeking, learning . . . wanting. He was hard for her, growing harder by the second.

I need her. I would do anything . . .

A sound outside the door made Fellows break the kiss. Louisa backed away, her eyes wide, breath coming fast. Fellows let her go, finding his fists clenched, his heart pounding, raw emotion tearing at his control.

But he needed control. They were in the Duke of Kilmorgan's London house, with servants moving to and fro outside the door, the lady of the house likely to enter at any moment. Eleanor had slyly left them alone, but if she opened the door and found virginal Louisa in Fellows's arms, he ravishing her mouth, even Eleanor wouldn't be able to look the other way.

Louisa's fingers went to her lips. The first time she'd kissed him, she'd smiled warmly at him. The second time, Fellows had left her abruptly and hadn't seen her reaction. Now Louisa looked stunned, even ashamed.

Fellows made himself move around her to the door. He knew he should say something, a polite good-bye, but he couldn't. Politeness had gone to hell and didn't matter.

He found his hand shaking as he reached for the door handle, then he was in the hall, and going down the stairs, the encounter over.

No, not over. Fellows might have left Louisa behind, but he felt her hot kiss linger on his lips for the rest of the day and on into the night.

~~~~~

"Why aren't you coming, exactly?" Louisa asked Eleanor six hours later.

"Because I am quite unwell." Eleanor lounged on a sofa in her bedchamber, looking perfectly healthy as she bounced Alec on her knees. She wore a dressing gown instead of a ball gown, and was nowhere near ready to leave for Isabella's supper ball.

Louisa in her finery had arrived at Eleanor and Hart's, having agreed that Hart and Eleanor would escort her tonight. A young, unmarried lady did not go to a ball alone. When Louisa had argued that she could simply ride over to the assembly rooms with Isabella, Eleanor had negated the idea. If Louisa went with Isabella, she would be the sister working behind the scenes, not the young, eligible earl's daughter announced to the crowd arriving with the Duke and Duchess of Kilmorgan.

Louisa had also questioned the need for them all to leave from the Grosvenor Square house—Hart and Eleanor could collect her from Isabella's on their way. But no, Eleanor wanted them all to be seen leaving from the ducal mansion. She seemed adamant.

Usually it was easier to simply agree with Eleanor when she was determined, because she could talk any argument to death—Eleanor would go off onto many and varied tangents until everyone forgot what the original disagreement had been. What Eleanor wanted wasn't unreasonable, so Louisa had given in before Eleanor had time to launch into one of her impossible speeches.

But now it seemed that Louisa was to go to the ball escorted by Hart, Beth, and Ian, while Eleanor remained at home to nurse a cold.

Cold, my foot.

Louisa said, "You do remember that Mr. Fellows asked you to converse tonight with the guests from the garden party?"

"Oh, you can do that, dear. And Beth can help you. She's very good at making others open up."

That, at least, was true. Beth, married to the elusive Ian Mackenzie, was good at winning people over. But the thought of approaching the garden party guests unnerved Louisa a bit.

"Hart will be annoyed," Louisa tried.

"Hart prefers I stay indoors and make my apologies if I don't feel well. He never dances at balls anyway, and if he does not have to worry about me there, he's free to spend the time coercing gentlemen into doing things for him. He so enjoys that. And he does not mind in the slightest escorting you. He calls you the only sensible woman in the family."

Flattering from Hart, who tolerated so very few. "Hardly kind to you or the other Mackenzie ladies," Louisa said.

"Hart also enjoys being rude. But in this case, I agree with him. Run along, dear." Eleanor blew her a kiss. "You look absolutely beautiful in that gown. Isabella has wonderful taste, does she not? And it strikes just the right note."

The gown was indeed beautiful. Isabella had taken Louisa to her modiste at the beginning of the Season to have Louisa fitted with an entire wardrobe, and had insisted on paying for the lot. Louisa had kept her protests to a minimum. She didn't want to be ungrateful for her sister's kindness, she did need the clothes, and also, it was true, Isabella had exquisite taste.

The ball gown for tonight was a cream and light sage green confection, the décolletage baring Louisa's shoulders, the satin of the bodice hugging her waist. The underskirt was draped with cream lace, with a shimmering sage moiré overskirt pulled back and puffed over a bustle. The gown spoke of spring and light breezes, and set off Louisa's red hair and green eyes to perfection.

Louisa crossed the room, leaned down, and kissed Eleanor's cheek. She had no worry about catching Eleanor's cold—she had as much chance of flying out the window.

"I don't know what you're up to, but I'll go," Louisa said. She pressed a kiss to Alec's forehead. The lad clutched at her hair, but Louisa gently untangled his tiny fingers, kissed him again, and left them.

Hart waited outside the front door at the carriage, stepping back so Louisa could be handed in first. He did not look pleased, but he greeted Louisa civilly enough and handed her into the landau himself.

Louisa understood now why Eleanor had asked her to come to the house tonight—with Louisa here, Hart would not steadfastly refuse to go without Eleanor. Eleanor apparently counted on his sympathy and liking for Louisa to override his annoyance, an event that would be more certain if he had Louisa standing before him.

Beth and Ian were already in the coach, sitting opposite each other. Beth gave Louisa a warm hello and squeezed her hand as Louisa sat down beside her. Beth was with child again, already about four months gone, though her gown had been made to not show it yet. Louisa was surprised she'd wanted to come tonight, but Beth was a strong and resilient woman who loved soaking up enjoyment from Isabella's parties.

Ian had his head turned, gazing out the window at passing traffic, and said nothing at all. Louisa knew him well enough not to be offended—Ian might be thinking deeply about some mathematical conundrum and not even realize she'd entered the carriage.

Hart swung in next to his youngest brother, a footman shut the door, and the carriage lurched into traffic.

The two gentlemen rode in the rear-facing seat, leaving the front-facing one for the ladies. Louisa put aside her mixed feelings about the ball and studied the two Mackenzie men. Both wore formal frock coats and waistcoats, wool kilts of Mackenzie blue and green plaid, thick socks, and finely crafted leather shoes. The landau was generously sized, plenty of room for all, but was still crowded by the two large Scotsmen.

The brothers were much alike and yet entirely different. Hart was the most reminiscent of their Highland ancestors, with his hard face and arrogance—an arrogance Louisa had seen soften a long way since he'd married Eleanor. Now behind the imperious glint in Hart's eyes was the look of a man who'd found happiness. Rest. Peace. Love.

Ian too had found peace. He still possessed a restless energy, one that could focus with amazing precision on whatever task he wanted to undertake. Ian could dive into a complex, impossible mathematical problem, close his eyes, and find the solution in his head. He'd become so famous for this that mathematicians, physicists, and astronomers throughout Europe wrote to him for advice.

Ian had come to love with great difficulty, but once he'd found Beth, his life had blossomed. He was still shy, preferring to spend time home alone with Beth and his children, or at most, with his extended family. He didn't like crowds, and he had the unnerving tendency to spring into a conversation with a non sequitur—though his declarations made perfect sense once Louisa worked out how he'd arrived at that particular statement.

Louisa liked Ian, finding him a unique man in the midst of a society that strove for perfect sameness. She thought him refreshing.

Perhaps the same sort of interest in the unique was what drew her to Inspector Fellows. She didn't want to think of him at the moment, but she hadn't been able to think about much *except* him after the searing kiss in Eleanor's sitting room this afternoon. This kiss *he* had instigated, though Louisa had instantly and readily succumbed. She could still feel the press of his lips, his hard muscles under his coat, the strength of his hands as he held her.

Fellows had broken the kiss and abruptly walked away, and

Louisa couldn't blame him for that. He was trying to investigate a murder, and she should let him get on with his job. Their mouths falling together every time they were alone had to cease. They needed to be comfortable with each other, friends.

Friends. The word sounded so empty.

The landau halted in the street, a little way from the assembly rooms, inching forward with the line of carriages depositing guests at the door. So many carriages, so many people.

As they at last reached the entrance, and a footman snapped open the door, realization struck Louisa with an ice-cold slap. Eleanor had sent Louisa to go among those from the garden party and ask questions because she wanted Louisa to report directly to Fellows herself. It would stand to reason, El would explain in all innocence. Louisa had asked the questions; she would best know how to relate the answers.

The glint in Eleanor's eye, her secret smile, her decision to leave Louisa and Fellows alone in the sitting room this afternoon . . . Louisa wanted to groan with dismay. Eleanor was a romantic—the only explanation for how she'd remained in love with Hart all these years. Now she was inventing a romance for Louisa.

Louisa hid her disquiet under a sunny smile for Hart, who held out his arm to her. Hart shot her a look of grave suspicion then schooled his expression to a neutral one and led her inside.

Chapter 8

"Lord and Lady Ian Mackenzie," the majordomo announced. "The Duke of Kilmorgan, Lady Louisa Scranton."

The assembly rooms, giant spaces with tall, arched ceilings and wide chandeliers that dripped with crystal facets, already teemed with people. The ladies glittered under the light—diamonds, emeralds, rubies, and sapphires flashing rainbow colors on gowns of equally rainbow shades. Gentlemen and lords in white ties and flowing black coats moved among their ladies.

Everyone within hearing range of the majordomo's booming voice turned to watch the duke and his party arrive. Any other night, Lord Ian and his nobody wife, Beth, might have been the object of scrutiny. Tonight, all eyes focused on Louisa.

The weight of their stares fell on her. The looks ranged from pure curiosity to sordid interest to outright disgust and disapproval. Here was a young woman who probably had poisoned the Bishop of Hargate, and she arrived bold as you please on the arm of the lofty Duke of Kilmorgan. Yes, he was her sister's brother-in-law, but she was using him to shield her, wasn't she? A proper young woman, who was an unmarried miss no less, should stay home and show the shame she ought.

The stares followed Louisa, in a pause that would have been

awkward had not an orchestra already been playing to enter-
tain the arrivals. Louisa's pretty heeled slippers now seemed
too tight, her dress too garish. Hart's solid arm was the only
thing that kept her upright as they moved to the receiving line.

Hart, not oblivious to the scrutiny, leaned to her and spoke
in a low voice. "Face them down and to hell with them."

Hart straightened up again, saying nothing more, but Louisa felt a little better. She drew a breath, rearranged her expression, and smiled warmly at a knot of young ladies who stared
openly at her.

Hart was right, as usual. Louisa could do this. After all, she
hadn't killed Hargate, and she had nothing to be ashamed of.

"Good girl," Hart said. He gave her arm a pat with his strong
hand.

They reached their host and hostess, Mac and Isabella, who
stood at the top of the long line of guests. Isabella's dark blue
satin ball gown was elegance itself, but she was careful not to
outshine the other women present. Her role as hostess was to
make the ladies of the *ton* feel welcome and special, not belit-
tled, and Isabella took that role very seriously.

She gathered Louisa into a hug and kissed her cheek before
she grasped Hart's hands and kissed him as well. Isabella
didn't seem surprised in the least that Eleanor had not come
with them. Louisa frowned at her, but Isabella turned away to
greet Beth and Ian before Louisa could say a word.

"I'm glad you braved it." Mac squeezed Louisa's hands in
his large ones before he kissed her cheek. "Remember, Louisa, we are always here to catch you."

They were, especially Mac. Mac had been the one who'd
pulled Isabella and Louisa's family out of the fire when Earl
Scranton's fraud had been found out. If not for Mac and his
machinations, Louisa's family would never have survived.

"Thank you, Mac," Louisa said, heartfelt.

Hart turned Louisa loose once they'd finished the greet-
ings, he and Ian making straight for the gaming rooms. Beth
took Louisa's arm, and the two ladies headed for the withdrawing rooms to straighten gowns and repin hair.

This night should be the same as any other since Louisa's
come out. Louisa knew as many people as Isabella did, and
even her father's behavior hadn't lost Louisa her friends.

Money ebbed and flowed, Louisa hadn't been to blame, it was vulgar to worry about finances anyway, and a good marriage could put everything right for her again. Louisa knew half the girls in London and was close friends with half of those—had been their bridesmaids, held their first children, gossiped with them, shared their memories of growing up in privileged Mayfair and country estates.

Louisa was not as well acquainted with the ladies who happened to be in the withdrawing rooms, but though they stared, they softened under Beth's friendly smile—most people did. Louisa began to relax. As long as everyone was polite, the ball would be fine.

Louisa left for the main assembly rooms with Beth and quickly spied a knot of her friends. They were watching her, none of them making any pretense about staring at her and murmuring to one another. Louisa felt suddenly chilled.

Hart's words came back to her: *Face them down and to hell with them.*

Nothing for it. Louisa could not cling to Beth all night. She slid away from Beth as Beth turned to other guests, and approached the ladies and gentlemen clustered together, watching her come.

"Adele, how are you?" Louisa held out her hands to a young woman she'd known since they'd been toddlers. "What a lovely gown. You are all the rage tonight."

Lady Adele returned Louisa's kiss on the cheek, but stiffly. "We hardly thought to see you here tonight, Louisa."

"I did mean to stay home—I've been rather upset, as you might have guessed—but my sister coaxed me out. I couldn't refuse her, when she had her heart set." Louisa smiled, as though to say, *What can you do with older sisters?*

"Of course, but Louisa . . ." Adele smiled, but the smile was cool and condescending. "In spite of everything, you have never been anything but tasteful."

Implying Louisa was not being tasteful now. Louisa saw that the rest of the group agreed with Adele. She'd known these people from childhood, had played in nurseries with them, ridden ponies with them, had made her debut with them. She'd flirted with the gentlemen, giggled with the ladies. And now they gazed upon her as though she were a stranger from a remote land.

"As I say, Isabella wished me to see friends," Louisa said, pretending not to notice. "She thought I'd feel better in company."

"It *is* a lovely gown," another lady said, looking Louisa up and down. "Very . . . bright."

"Jane," Louisa said, all but stopping herself from snarling at her. "You've known me long enough to know I dislike hints and insinuations. If you believe I should put on mourning and bury myself at home, say so clearly and have done. I did not know the Bishop of Hargate and his family very well. It's a terrible thing that happened to him. My sympathies lie with his family, of course, where they should. It would be unfair to them for me to claim the entirety of the grief, as though what happened to the bishop was about me and my feelings alone."

Jane flushed, but she remained resolute. "Very well, Louisa, I'll be plain. Putting on a pretty new dress and sailing in all cheerful as though nothing had happened isn't quite the thing, is it?"

"I am anything *but* cheerful," Louisa said, striving to keep her tone even. "My sister thought the gown would put me in better spirits. She and my sisters-in-law convinced me to come, because they thought I should go out and see people. I'm certain they believed I'd find sympathy among my oldest and dearest friends."

Instead of being admonished, the ladies and gentlemen looked annoyed, and Adele laughed. "Louisa, my dear, it's becoming a dangerous thing to be your friend."

One of the gentlemen laughed as well. The four young men behind the ladies were those she'd played tag with in the meadows of Kent and danced with after her come out. One gentleman looked at Louisa as though he'd never seen her before, and another was glancing about for a way to escape without appearing rude.

"I do beg your pardon for my sister Jane," the gentleman who'd laughed said. "You see, Mama has told her—and me—to stay away from you. I'm afraid your dance card won't be very full tonight. Word is circulating that you're *poison*." He laughed again, proud he'd made a joke.

"You aren't funny, Samuel," Jane said. "But it's true, Louisa. We have been advised to keep our distance."

"I see." Louisa's chest tightened as she looked at them, finding no sympathy in their faces. "I see now what years of friendship can count for." She'd cared for Adele and Jane, but their expressions were stony tonight, all caring gone.

"Not their fault," Samuel said. "It's just that murder is so sordid. Not the done thing, you know." He mimed stabbing with a knife, still grinning.

"I did nothing to him." Louisa gave Samuel a hard look. "I had hoped my closest friends would believe me."

"It doesn't matter, does it?" Samuel asked. "No chap is going to risk being at your side tonight, Louisa darling. He'll always worry about taking a sip of his tea, or his claret, or his port, or his brandy, or his—"

"What the devil is this?" a new voice said.

Louisa started, and looked around to see the Honorable Gilbert Franklin, who'd stopped in time to hear the last comments. Gilbert was one of Louisa's oldest friends—they'd lived next door to each other as children, and Louisa had been maid of honor to Gil's sister last summer. She hadn't seen much of either of them since, until Gil had turned up at Mrs. Leigh-Waters's now-infamous garden party.

Gilbert cast a disparaging gaze over the little group. "Are you telling me, Sam, that after all these years, you still have no idea how to behave to a lady? I believe that in this glorious England, we think a person innocent of a crime until proven otherwise, do we not? Doesn't Louisa deserve that same faith? Or at the very least, your respect?" Gil spoke in pleasant tones, as he always did, but his look was sharp, his words direct.

Samuel had the grace to be abashed. Gilbert was well liked, and now the others looked embarrassed, no longer laughing.

"How are you, Louisa?" Gil stuck out his hand and squeezed Louisa's when she put hers into his. "I'm happy to see you tonight. I know you have been painfully upset, and I'll wager none of these louts have decided to rally 'round and make you feel better."

Adele bridled. "*Really*, Gil."

"Yes, *really*, Del," Gil said. "I never thought you so heartless. Louisa, I believe the first set is forming in the ballroom. Will you do me the honor? And if your dance card has remained empty tonight, I will happily fill it."

The others had gone deathly silent. Gil's strong fingers remained around Louisa's hand.

Louisa's heart pounded. Every part of her had been wanting to flee back across Mayfair to the sanctuary of Isabella's house, where she could go up to the nursery and make herself feel better sitting with the children. Being around Isabella's children always comforted her, and *they* did not believe her a murderess.

Now Gil's wash of sympathy nearly undid her. He was handing Louisa a lifeline, coming to her rescue. Refusing him and running would be as churlish as Adele and her friends were being to Louisa. The Hon. Gil was well liked, well-bred, well-dressed, attractive, wealthy, and intelligent. His stamp of approval could save her life.

Louisa smiled at him in true gratitude. "Of course. I would indeed love to dance. Excuse me, my friends. I hope you enjoy Isabella's entertainments."

She wouldn't cut them dead, much as she longed to. She would not be as petty as they were being. She bowed graciously to the collective group, who had to return the bow or be forever branded as uncouth.

Gil led Louisa away, keeping such a quick pace she didn't have time to say anything to him until they stood in line for the opening dance, an old-fashioned country dance. Waltzing would take up the rest of the night—with pauses for Scottish reels, since this was a Mackenzie party after all—but Isabella always opened her balls with country dances.

Gil knew these dances as well as he knew everything else. Gil had always been there, in the background of Louisa's life, she now realized. He'd been brother to her dear friend, playing with the two girls as children, teaching them cricket in their adolescence, escorting them to parties after their come outs, quietly shrugging off their praise about his academic honors at university. Gil was the perfect gentleman, so perfect one didn't always notice him, because he did his best to efface himself and not push in front of others.

On the other hand, everyone in Louisa's set considered Gil's opinion highly important. If Gil had taken Adele's and Samuel's part this evening, her social ruin would have been assured. The fact that Gil had admonished *them* would be all over Mayfair by the end of the set.

"Thank you for taking pity on me," Louisa said as they came together in the dance.

"Nonsense, Louisa, I meant every word of it."

"Nevertheless, it was kind."

Gil gave her a warm smile. "You deserve much more than to be snubbed by Samuel and Jane, believe me."

The dance took them apart, but Gil's smile remained, like an anchor in the swirling madness. Louisa knew he'd done her a great favor, simply from the goodness of his heart. She'd have to find a way to thank the man who'd just saved her from being an outcast at her own sister's ball.

How the devil Hart had talked him into stuffing himself into this suit and walking into Isabella Mackenzie's supper ball, Fellows had no idea.

His mother had been all for it, though. Fellows hadn't mentioned the invitation to his mother, because he knew exactly what she'd say. But Isabella must have written to her, because she brought it up immediately when Fellows had visited her earlier this evening.

The Mackenzie wives had taken to writing to Mrs. Fellows, who loved receiving the letters from the women she termed the "la-de-da ladies." She read every single missive out to Fellows, and she wrote back to them. She'd been invited to the ball as well, and she laughed about it.

"Imagine me in a ballroom with a bunch of toffs," she'd said. "A right git I'd look. I was a tavern maid like me mum before me, and my sister was too, and that's all there is to that." She'd softened. "It's a kindness, I know. They don't really expect me to come. But *you*, my boy—you go and show them there ain't nothing wrong with you. You're the son of a duke, and you should have *been* the duke. Now you go and show Lord Hart you're the better brother."

"Huh," Fellows said, falling into the cadence of his youth. "A right git *I'll* look in a fancy suit, Mum, and you know it."

"Don't throw my words back at me, boy. You're not so big I can't still smack you about."

Catherine Fellows was five feet high, a bit rotund from the ale she liked to drink, and had wrinkles lining her face from the laughter she loved so much. Lloyd towered over her with the tallness of the Mackenzies, coupled with their strength.

"You're half my height, woman," Fellows said, ruffling her hair fondly. "*And* you've got the tongue of a viper."

"Yeah? Then I have half a mind to buy a posh dress and go to this do, just to show you. I'll drag you along by your ear, see if I don't."

"Leave off, I'm going. And not because of you. If you think *you* can scold, you've not had the four Mackenzie ladies stand in front of you and ask you why you didn't do what they asked. Frighten a man out of ten years' growth, they can."

"I think they're sweet girls," Catherine said, abruptly ceasing her bantering. "Good manners. So kind to me. No, indeed, you can't disappoint them." Her look turned shrewd. "What about Lady Louisa? Does she frighten you out of ten years' growth?"

Fellows often discussed his cases with his mother, who for all her talk about being only a tavern maid had good perception about her fellow man. A lifetime of carrying about ale in a public house, she said, had honed her understanding. In Fellows's opinion, she'd have made an excellent detective if she'd been born male. Her insights had helped him see a case clearly more than once.

Those insights, unfortunately, made Catherine realize that Fellows viewed Louisa as more than a suspect, and more than simply his sister-in-law's younger sister. He'd been careful to bury the fact that he thought about Louisa day and night, waking and sleeping. Every time he drew breath, in fact. But Fellows had learned long ago that he could never hide things from his mother.

"Let it lie, Mum." Fellows leaned down and kissed her forehead.

"You're every bit as good as her, you know," Catherine said. "Your dad was a duke. *Her* dad was only an earl. And now her distant cousin is earl, and stingy from what I hear."

"I'm a police detective," Fellows said. "I'm let into the great houses by the tradesman's entrance. That's the end of it."

"Doesn't have to be," Catherine said.

Fellows pretended not to hear, gave his mother another kiss, and departed. Back at his flat—four large rooms in a building off the Strand that had recently been refurbished—he dressed in the coat and waistcoat Eleanor had bullied him into being fitted for by Hart's tailor. Under that was a new lawn shirt, high collar, and cravat.

On bottom . . . Fellows studied the blue and green Mackenzie plaid kilt laid out across his bed. He'd worn it before, at Christmas at Kilmorgan, feeling strange with wool wrapping his hips, air circulating his thighs. Scotsmen had to be mad.

But Fellows was a Scotsman, or at least half a Scotsman, one of the family Mackenzie. He'd spent his boyhood trying and failing to be acknowledged by them. And then he'd hated them. The hatred had wound so long and so deep it was difficult to put aside.

He was tired of anger. Anger was a poison, leeching into a man and stealing everything he was. While anger had allowed Fellows to reach great heights in his profession, he'd also jeopardized his career and even his life because of it. Now he might jeopardize Louisa.

He put on the kilt and combed his hair, or tried to. His hair never stayed put, the short strands going wherever they wished. At least he'd had time to shave.

Nothing he could do about the healing bruises and nicks on his face, though. Evidence of his fight with the Marylebone Killer was still present. The bruises were now turning yellow and green, the cuts scabbed over, but dark red.

If Isabella didn't like them, he couldn't help it. She'd already seen them anyway.

And Louisa? She likely wouldn't be there. Fellows had told her not to go out until this was over, and Louisa had seemed inclined to agree. Louisa had spirit, but she was no fool.

So it was with great shock that Fellows walked into the assembly rooms to see Louisa waltzing with a handsome young man, laughing up at him, her eyes bright, joy on her face.

Chapter 9

Fellows had entered the assembly rooms through a side door, not wanting to endure the nonsense of the stiff-necked major-domo shouting his name to all present. How bloody stupid would that sound? *The Duke and Duchess of Almond Paste, the Princess of Peach Pie, and . . . er . . . Detective Chief Inspector Lloyd Fellows of Scotland Yard.* The company would suppose he'd come to arrest someone.

If Fellows could clap cuffs around the wrists of the young man dancing with Louisa, he'd do it in a trice. Fellows's eyes narrowed as he assessed him. Expensively dressed—well, he would be if he'd been invited here. Golden hair gleaming under the chandeliers, every strand of that hair in place. Handsome face, just hard enough not to be feminine, skin unmarred by bruises or cuts.

The young man danced with ease, gliding Louisa around the ballroom without missing a step. The perfect gentleman.

Louisa looked up at her partner with laughter in her eyes, talking easily with him, smiling at him. She looked relaxed and happy, not stiff and frightened as she had this afternoon when Fellows had entered Eleanor's sitting room. And then Fellows had given up on discipline and kissed Louisa. Hard.

She'd gazed at him in anger and fear . . . no wide smile, no sparkle in her eyes. Those were reserved for the young man currently with his hand on Louisa's waist. A fist tightened around Fellows's heart until he could barely breathe.

Something in the back of Fellows's mind told him to find his host and hostess, to speak to them, to pretend to be civilized. But Fellows couldn't pull his gaze from Louisa. The rest of the ballroom didn't matter, nor did the people in it. The only thing that existed was Louisa dancing on light feet, tiny diamonds glittering in her hair, her froth of cream and green skirts spinning around and around. She wore a black ribbon with a white cameo around her throat, which emphasized her lush femininity as well as her erotic beauty.

The splendor of her—the whole of her—was like a physical blow. As Fellows stood, alone among a sea of people, watching her, he realized what she meant to him.

Everything.

"What's the matter, Uncle Fellows?" a voice said beside him. "You look like someone has just punched you in the gut."

Daniel Mackenzie, Fellows's tall nephew, had stopped next to him, a glass of whiskey in his hand. Daniel already had the hard look of his father, Cameron, though his lanky body still showed his nineteen-year-old youth.

"Or maybe punched you in the face," Daniel continued, casting a critical eye over Fellows's bruises. "I take it the other bloke looks worse?"

Fellows's gaze went back to Louisa. "The other bloke is in Newgate awaiting trial. And, yes, he looks worse."

Daniel chuckled. "Good for you. A villain, is he?"

"One of the worst. Don't waste sympathy on him."

"I'll take your word for it." Daniel turned to look where Fellows's attention had been dragged. "Ah. That explains the gut blow."

Fellows wrenched his gaze away from Louisa again. "What the devil are you talking about?"

"I'm not a fool, Uncle. Our Louisa is beautiful. Why wouldn't you fall for her?"

In all his life, Fellows had never considered marrying, no matter how many dalliances or flirtations he'd had. He'd assumed himself too buried in his work, too ruthless and suspicious, or simply not interested in marriage. He'd never seen a good example of it, had he? He'd spent his childhood wishing he belonged to a family who'd made it clear he wasn't wanted. He'd grown up with a mother angry at a rich man who'd charmed her, used her, and cast her aside.

None of that had relevance now. As Fellows looked at Louisa, he knew why he'd never married. He'd been waiting for her. And now she danced and laughed with a young man of her class who held her admiration.

"She's not exactly *our* Louisa," Fellows said. "Yours, maybe."

He felt Daniel studying him. His irritation rose. Daniel gave him a knowing, and also sympathetic, grin. "Ask her to dance," Daniel said.

"I don't dance." He gave a self-deprecating laugh. "Never had a dancing master."

"I advise you to learn. Ladies love a gentleman who can spin them about the floor. Once they know you can dance, they'll follow you anywhere."

"You speak from experience?"

"Aye, that I do."

None of the Mackenzie men had ever had trouble attracting women, and Daniel, despite his youth, was no different. The ladies here, of his age and a few years older, were eyeing him with interest. Daniel was young, virile, handsome, and rich. He would come into the money left to him in trust by his mother when he was twenty-one, and would inherit everything Cameron had at Cameron's death. Then he'd be a wealthy man indeed, and powerful. The fact that he stood a few steps removed from a dukedom only added to his desirability.

"Watch yourself," Fellows advised. "One of these hopeful mamas will have you in the noose before you know it, if you're not careful."

"I'm always careful," Daniel said, speaking with confidence above his years. "But the matrons have started flinging the debutantes at me, haven't they? Some of these girls are barely out of the schoolroom. They should still be in short skirts and pigtails."

"That's aristos for you. Marry young, repent for many years to come."

"And put seventeen heirs in the nursery while you're at it,"

Daniel finished. "Cynical, Uncle. Whatever happened to true love?"

"Love is for the middle class," Fellows said. "The poor can't afford it, and neither can the rich."

"A sad thing to say, but probably true. These mamas who are eyeing me like sharks would be devastated to know I don't plan to marry for many years. First, I'm going to travel the wide earth, and then learn how to build all the machines I have in my mind. The world's on the brink of great change. Many people fear the change, but I want to be at its forefront, looking down its throat."

"The enthusiasm of the young," Fellows said.

"Not only the young. I know plenty of older chaps ready to face it with me. Now if I can ever find a *lady* like that—*she's* who I'd marry."

Fellows had already returned to watching Louisa. "Perhaps you and Louisa should make a match of it."

Daniel's attention came back from his future, and he bent his shrewd stare on his uncle. "Louisa and I have become great friends," he said, as though choosing his words with care. "But no. I don't believe we would suit."

"Maybe not now. In a few years, though . . ."

"No. I'm thinking that in a few years, she won't still be waiting."

Daniel was right. Louisa shone with brilliance. She was kind, warmhearted, and stronger than she understood. As soon as Fellows proved her innocence and all this blew over, Louisa would be snapped up by any of a string of eligible bachelors. The newspapers would make much of the marriage between the earl's daughter and some sprig of aristocracy. She'd marry in glory, and then be gone. She might greet Fellows at family parties, but Louisa would have her own life, no longer connected with his.

Louisa and her partner whirled closer to the corner in which Fellows and Daniel stood. Daniel lifted his whiskey glass in salute. Louisa smiled back at him, then her gaze landed on Fellows.

Her smile vanished, and the light drained from her face as though someone had extinguished a lamp. She stumbled. The gentleman with her caught her, so smoothly no one but Fellows and Daniel saw the near fall.

The gentleman said something to her, and Louisa laughed. The light returned, she spun away from Fellows, and resumed the dance.

Fellows felt as though someone had crushed all the air out of him. He might as well be lying at the bottom of a pile of bricks, with no hope of clawing his way out.

When he could manage to speak again, Fellows asked sharply, "Who is *he*?"

"Gilbert Franklin. The Honorable. His dad's an earl. England's bloody thick with earls, don't you think? Can't turn around without tripping over one. He was at the notorious garden party, you know. If he's sweet on Louisa, he might have a reason to do in Hargate. You could always arrest him and ask him."

Daniel wasn't smiling, but amusement definitely hovered near. Fellows turned a cold look on him.

"I don't arrest people and get them convicted for my convenience," Fellows said. "My job is to find true villains and keep them from hurting others."

Was Daniel cowed at the admonishment? No, his grin broke free. "Ah ha—so you admit it would be to your convenience."

Fellows scowled. "You probably should go off on your world travels soon, Danny. Might take the cockiness out of you."

"I doubt that." Daniel gave him a tip of his glass. "I doubt it very much."

Daniel turned and sauntered away. Fellows watched him go, reflecting that however arrogant Daniel was, he was smart and too perceptive for his own good.

He looked back at the dance floor, but Louisa had gone. Fellows craned to see her, but her shining red hair glittering with diamonds had vanished.

Fellows circled around the crowd to search for her again, even while he growled at himself for doing it.

~~~~~

"I'm fine, really," Louisa said. Gilbert had her seated on a divan at the end of the ballroom. He'd brought lemonade and an ice, and then sat down and held them for her while she partook. "You don't need to stay with me."

"I need to look after you," Gil said reasonably. "You might have a sprain, and it would be my fault. It is either this or I carry you out of the ballroom in my arms, and what would people think?"

"Don't be so silly." But Louisa smiled. Gil had the knack of making people feel better.

She'd stumbled in her too-high heels because she'd seen Lloyd Fellows standing at the edge of the ballroom. He'd been wearing a kilt—one of the Mackenzie plaids that Hart had thrust upon him. It fit him well, hugging his hips, smooth against his thighs, showing his strong legs below its hem. He wore a coat as finely tailored as any man's here, though it looked better on him because he had the body to fill it out.

The bruises from whatever brawl he'd been in were obvious on his face, though he was clean-shaven tonight. He looked like a warrior who'd taken time off fighting to look in on civilization.

No, Fellows didn't fit among these soft-faced people. There was still too much of the brute Highlander about him for civilized company. He fought battles out in the world so the ladies and gentlemen in this ballroom could walk about in peace.

"Louisa?" Gil was looking at her. She'd missed what he'd just said.

"I do beg your pardon. I believe my ankle hurts more than I thought it did." She lied, but Louisa needed a reason to cover for her distracted state.

Gil looked concerned. "Shall I fetch Isabella? Call for your coach?"

"No, no. I only wrenched it a bit. I'll sit here quietly and watch the dancing."

"Then I will sit with you."

Gil handed the empty ice bowl to a passing waiter, fetched another lemonade for Louisa and champagne for himself, and sat down with her again. Not too close—no one in the ballroom seeing them seated on the far sides of a divan would think anything inappropriate was afoot. Then again, the two of them even occupying the same piece of furniture might start people talking. Anything for gossip.

"Really, there is no need for you to miss enjoying yourself," Louisa said. "I will be well."

Gil leaned closer. "Louisa, you weren't well when I first spied you here. That idiot Samuel talks more than his brains should let him, and his sister and Adele were being vicious. I'd rather not leave you alone to their knives again. Besides, I can enjoy myself quite well sitting with you."

Louisa's face heated at the same time something inside her warmed. "You're very flattering tonight."

"Not at all. I was unbelievably distressed about what happened at the garden party. I wanted to comfort you there, but I was shunted away home. I came here tonight hoping to see you again. And I have."

Louisa smiled at the same time she let her gaze rove the ballroom. She couldn't see Fellows anywhere. Had he made for the card rooms? Or left the ball altogether? "You've always been a friend, Gil," she said, more to keep up her end of the conversation than anything else. "So kind to the hanger-on of your sister."

"Oh, I think you know I've always viewed you as far more than a hanger-on, Louisa. Or a friend."

Louisa, with difficulty, pulled her attention back to Gil. His expression was serious, no teasing. She tried to laugh. "I'm not sure I'm in the proper mood for flirting, Gil, dear."

"And you know it is not flirting."

Gil's affable blue eyes held something quiet and heartfelt. Oh, dear.

But, then again, why not? the sensible side of Louisa asked. Gil was the obvious answer to Louisa's current troubles as well as her quest for matrimony. Louisa still wanted to marry—she wanted a home of her own, respect, children.

An unmarried miss had little say in the world. She lived with her married sister or brother or childhood friend, and was a helper, a companion, an appendage. A married woman, on the other hand, was viewed with respect and even admiration if her marriage was a good one. She could become a great hostess, a leader of her set, a powerful force in her world.

The Honorable Gil was one of the most respected gentlemen in England. He would one day be an earl. Louisa had known him all her life, and they rubbed along well together. His friends were her friends. Gil and Louisa would, in fact, make the perfect couple.

So why did her heart beat too quickly as she caught a glimpse of Inspector Fellows again, her hands grow moist, and her feet long to thump to the floor and carry her away from both of them?

Louisa drew a sharp breath. "Gil—my dearest friend—I'm not sure I am strong enough to hear declarations tonight."

Instantly Gil went solicitous. "Then I won't make any. Not tonight. Don't worry. I'm not the pestering sort. But I will sit here and make sure no one *else* pesters you."

"Thank you. It's good of you."

"If you'd like to think so."

Gil sat for a moment with her in silence, giving her time to master herself, then he started up with a conversation that had nothing to do with the two of them, Louisa's predicament, or the poisoning.

He was nice, really. Kind. Generous. Warmhearted. Completely different from the man who came around the dancers in his kilt, a tailored coat stretched over his strong shoulders. He held a champagne glass in one hand, looking as though he didn't know what to do with it, and walked beside Mac Mackenzie, paying half attention to whatever Mac was jabbering about.

Fellows saw Louisa and sent her a sharp look, then one to Gil. The look stabbed Louisa all the way through, and then the blow doubled as Fellows started to turn away again.

Mac, with seeming nonchalance, blocked Fellows's escape. Fellows would either have to turn back to the divan or push Mac bodily aside to get around him. The look on Fellows's face told Louisa he preferred to shove his way out, but at the last minute he let Mac chivvy him toward the divan and the two sitting there.

Gil rose to meet them. "Mac, how are you? Well met, Chief Inspector. Can you tell us how the case is going? If you've found the man responsible yet? Or are you allowed to say?"

Gil asked with sincere curiosity, and also with obvious concern for Louisa's part in it. Mac's expression said he showed the same concern. Only Fellows looked furious. He did *not* want to discuss the case at all, and Mac and Gil pushing him into it made him angry.

"It is all right, Chief Inspector," Louisa said quickly. "You do not have to tell us. I understand that more gossip about it would not be good."

If anything, Fellows looked even more angry. "There is very little to say. The investigation is ongoing. We are pursuing several leads."

"Have you had any luck tracing the chap Louisa saw rolling out from under the tent?" Gil asked in all innocence.

"Not yet."

"He's the guilty one, must be." Gil emphasized his words with little jerks of the hand that held his champagne glass.

"No doubt," Fellows said, his tone dry.

"It might have been a woman," Louisa broke in. "I couldn't be certain, as I said." She directed the words at Fellows, but he was watching Gil, assessing him. Possibly wondering how he'd look in handcuffs.

"No, a man," Mac said, shaking his head. "I'll wager it was a man in the tent. Stands to reason. A woman would be hampered by skirts and bustles and all the paraphernalia women seem to wear."

Gil smiled. "I find the paraphernalia charming."

"Entrancing," Mac said, winking at Louisa. "I call it utterly entrancing."

"An even better word," Gil agreed.

Fellows looked annoyed. Louisa could see that at this moment, he didn't find women or their paraphernalia charming or entrancing, or even remotely interesting. He was again stuck in a society party where he didn't feel comfortable, coerced by his brothers and sisters-in-law to do what he didn't want to do. *A fish out of water,* was the saying.

"It is good of you to help, Mr. Fellows," Louisa said, to try to fill the break in conversation. "I am grateful."

Fellows scowled at her. "It's a murder, and it's my job." He clicked the champagne glass onto the tray of a passing waiter and made a little bow. "If you'll excuse me, Lady Louisa."

He walked away without further word, and this time, Mac didn't try to stop him.

Chapter 10

The pain in Louisa's ankle became nothing to the pain in her heart as she watched Inspector Fellows fade back into the crowd, finished with her. Ladies and gentlemen parted for his broad frame, looking after him with curiosity. Louisa felt suddenly hollow, as though something important had just been lost to her.

"I beg your pardon, Louisa," she heard Gil saying, as though from a long way off. "And Mac. I think I've gone and put my foot in it."

Louisa turned back to him. "No, no. He's—"

"Bloody rude sometimes," Mac finished. "He's a Mackenzie. No need to apologize, Franklin, or for you to make excuses for him, Louisa. El and Isabella coaxed Fellows into coming tonight, and he didn't want to. He's busy. I don't blame him for being out of sorts."

"I shouldn't have needled him about the case," Gil said. "I admit I'm dashed curious, though, having been at the party myself. As well as being anxious for Louisa."

For heaven's sake. Men could excuse each other over the worst offenses when they wanted to—*oh, he didn't mean to overturn the entire dining table and swing out of the room on*

the chandelier; he was out of sorts because he lost ten guineas
at cards, poor fellow.

"If you will excuse *me*, gentlemen." Louisa got to her feet, pretending not to wince at the twinge in her ankle. "I should be assisting Isabella instead of lounging about. Thank you for all the dances, Gil. It was kind of you. Stay and converse with him, Mac. I won't need an escort across a room full of family and friends."

Gil and Mac both stared at her, then Gil remembered his manners and bowed, his expression polite. Mac only frowned at her. Louisa knew she'd be in for it when she got home—Mac and Izzy would sit her down and quiz her about her jumpiness, but for now, Louisa just wanted air.

At least Gil was courteous enough to let her go. Mac clearly wondered what she was up to, but he too let her go, his duties as host keeping him too busy to pursue her.

She was *not* following Mr. Fellows to ask him why he was so angry with her. Not at all. Louisa held her skirts as she slid past the crowd at the perimeter of the dance floor. She would not admit that her gaze roved them, looking for a broad-shouldered man in black with close-shorn, mussed hair.

Before the murder at the garden party, Louisa could never have moved through a ballroom without being stopped every few feet and pulled into delighted conversation. Tonight, too many people turned away when she flowed by, too many people pretended not to see her.

Louisa ground her teeth, her temper rising. They had no business snubbing her. She'd done nothing wrong. Her only crime had been foolishly letting Mrs. Leigh-Waters talk her into entering the tea tent with Hargate. If Louisa had refused and gone to wait for the croquet match with Isabella, she would even now be talking and laughing with her friends and acquaintances as usual, having a fine time at Isabella's splendid supper ball.

Strange how life could alter so greatly with one decision, one spin of a coin. Into the tea tent or not, speak to the bishop or stand with her sister.

Fellows's declaration that the world was not a safe place haunted her too. Of course it wasn't safe. But Louisa had lived a sheltered existence, growing up believing that bad things would always be kept far from her. She'd learned, too late, that this wasn't always the case.

Fellows, on the other hand, had lived life in its raw state, seeing all the horrors of it. He'd been raised on the backstreets of St. Giles, learning about crime and criminals firsthand. If the old Duke of Kilmorgan had been a kind man and had taken Fellows in to raise, his life would have been entirely different, perhaps as pampered and sheltered as Louisa's. Fellows could never inherit the dukedom, regardless, having been born out of wedlock, but the duke could have given him a good education, settled unentailed money on him, and allowed him to pursue a gentlemanly profession.

Another choice, in another time, that had changed a man's entire life.

Louisa reached the other side of the ballroom rather quickly, her ankle not hurting near as much anymore, but her temper was getting the better of her. By the time she ducked into a cool back hall, she wanted to scream or do something unladylike such as beat on a wall. To add to her frustration, she had not seen Fellows anywhere.

She knew she'd never be able to go back into the assembly rooms and speak civilly with anyone. *If* anyone condescended to even talk to her. But Louisa rushing out and home without a word to Isabella would look churlish and cowardly. As much as it hurt her, Louisa had to stay here and face them all, as Hart had advised her to. Make them know *she* was not in the wrong and had nothing to be ashamed of.

Having been to these assembly rooms on many occasions, Louisa knew there was a quiet room at the end of this hall—an office or some such. Though the office was not in use during the balls and other gatherings, guests sometimes slipped inside it to seek calm moments or for assignations.

Louisa hoped no dallying couple occupied its sanctuary tonight. She breathed a sigh of relief when she found the dim room empty, then jumped when a man stood up from the high-backed chair in front of the fireplace.

Her heart went to her throat when she saw the broad shoulders and glint of red hair of a Mackenzie. Then her breath went out again when she realized which Mackenzie it was.

"Ian." Louisa's legs shook as she made her way across the

small room and gave up altogether as she collapsed to the chair. "I'm glad it's you."

Ian pulled out the desk's chair and sat down on it, not responding to her statement. He might not know what she meant—or he might have understood, thought of five different answers, and decided to say none of them. That was Ian's way.

Silence settled over the room, which was lit only by firelight. Restful. Ian never expected a person to say something simply to say something. He had no use for banalities or meaningless conversation, for talking to pass the time. Louisa didn't ask whether she disturbed him. If she had, he'd have walked out of the room without a word and sought another refuge.

"I always wondered at your aversion to crowds," Louisa said. "Until tonight. Now I understand perfectly."

Ian's eccentricities were well-known and well talked about. Whenever he walked into a gathering, people stopped, stared, whispered. Even if they didn't whisper, Ian had difficulty with the focus of too much attention at once. He was better with one person at a time.

Ian said nothing about Louisa's sudden compassion, didn't nod, and silence descended again.

Presently, Louisa let out an exasperated breath. "I say botheration to the lot of them. They've damned me for having the misfortune of standing beside a man while he died. I was the object of pity before the garden party; now I am an object of disgust. Well, I am tired of it already, I must say."

Ian didn't answer. He was studying the room, the worn books in the shelves, the desk empty of papers, locked for the night. The office's one window was heavily curtained, shutting out the night, the only light the coal fire which would soon die.

"They expect Mr. Fellows to haul me away to jail," Louisa said, the words tumbling out. "They are wondering why he hasn't already done so. I think they were hoping he'd come tonight to arrest me. Wouldn't that have been titillating?" She gave a short laugh. "Well, they will just have to live without it. I didn't poison Hargate, and I refuse to be condemned for it. There must be *something* I can do to prove my innocence."

Ian had tilted his head back to study the ceiling. Louisa couldn't stop herself looking up at it too. It was quite pretty, laid out in squares of molding, with filigree in the corners of the squares. Instead of being whitewashed, the wood was in its natural state, rich walnut, which made the room both dark and elegant.

Ian probably hadn't heard a word Louisa had said. He did that sometimes, let a person babble on, not answering. In his head, he'd be working out a mathematical problem, or thinking of every word his little girl and boy had said today, or thinking about Beth and the baby she would have by autumn. This room, Louisa, the supper ball—this part of London, even— might not exist for him.

"I wish *he* understood," Louisa went on, not minding that Ian didn't answer. "If not for him, I would probably be in New-gate right now, or under house arrest. Something dreadful any-way, while men gathered evidence for my trial. But Mr. Fellows won't stand still and talk to me. What is wrong with me, Ian, that makes him turn away or not want to be in the same room with me at all?"

Ian still didn't answer, and Louisa had stopped expecting him to. "We are in completely different worlds, he and I, and I don't know if we can ever cross the chasm between them. I see him at places like this, and he is so unhappy. He doesn't want to be here." Louisa gave another laugh. "A bit like you, Ian. Mr. Fellows doesn't like this world; he prefers the one he made for himself. I wish he could see that his world is a good one. He *does* something. People like Gil are wonderful—Gil is good at making people feel happy. But he's never had to worry about anything in his life, has he? If everything were stripped from Gil, would he be the same? I know Lloyd would be. Even if all Inspector Fellows had worked for was taken from him, he'd still walk straight through it all, come what may."

Louisa stopped, finally running out of breath. The room had cooled with the night and dying fire. Ian sat comfortably in the darkness, the low firelight touching his face.

Louisa closed her eyes, deciding to be silent with him. She had nothing more to say, and her heart was burning.

"Mrs. Leigh-Waters," Ian said.

Louisa popped her eyes open. Ian had turned to her, watch-ing her. In the past Ian had had trouble looking into a person's eyes, but tonight he was relaxed, thoughtful, and easily meet-ing her gaze.

Louisa blinked at him. "I beg your pardon?"

"Mrs. Leigh-Waters," Ian repeated, as though waiting for Louisa to catch up.

"What about her?"

"You should speak to her."

Louisa tried to remember all she'd said since she'd come in and which part Ian was responding to. "You mean I should talk to her about the garden party again?"

Ian made a slow nod. "She invited the guests."

Louisa sat still a moment, turning his words over in her mind. What Ian said always had deeper meaning than his listener first supposed.

She invited the guests. Mrs. Leigh-Waters hadn't asked her entire social circle to her garden party—the guest list had been fairly exclusive. Why had she invited certain people and not others?

"Hmm," Louisa said. "I think I see what you mean."

Ian turned his head and looked away, finished with the discussion.

"Thank you, Ian."

A small clock on a shelf struck midnight. Outside the windows, church clocks in Mayfair and beyond took up the chime.

Ian rose, pulled out his pocket watch, checked it against the clocks, and made a minute adjustment. "I'll go to Beth now. She will be tired."

So that was why Ian had come in here—he was counting the minutes until he could take Beth home. Beth would have insisted on staying a polite amount of time; Ian would have insisted on an exact hour to take their leave. They always worked out their differences so beautifully.

"Tell Beth good night for me," Louisa said.

The clocks were still chiming, and Ian didn't wait on ceremony. He walked swiftly out of the room without a good-bye, as though he had to reach Beth before the last stroke of midnight. Ian pursuing his Cinderella.

They'd endured so much, Ian and Beth, had found each other through fire and fog. They deserved every moment of the happiness they had now.

Louisa supposed she ought to go home with them. Fellows had likely departed, and Louisa had no desire to return to the ballroom and paste a false smile on her face for a few more hours. Beth would not mind dropping Louisa at Isabella's on the way home.

Ian had already disappeared, however, by the time Louisa had made up her mind and left the office. She found no sign of Ian in the back hall or in the corridor that led around to the front door.

The foyer was still full of people, though not the crush that had filled it when she'd entered the assembly rooms earlier tonight. Louisa didn't see Ian or Beth there, going out, nor did she see Mr. Fellows. She did spy Daniel, who was talking with his usual animation to a knot of guests, no doubt charming them to pieces. Daniel was just nineteen now and already friends with half of England, not to mention all of Scotland and probably most of Wales.

A look into the games room showed her Hart Mackenzie lounging at a card table like a king among his subjects, in no hurry to depart. Cheroot smoke layered the air like fog.

Ian had likely decided to scoot Beth out a back door to avoid the crowd. Louisa made her way again to the little hall that led to the office, turning a corner beyond it to seek a rear door.

Inspector Fellows was there, his broad back to her as he opened the door, letting in a draft of cool spring air.

Louisa sped her steps, her anger returning. She raced forward and grabbed the sleeve of his coat, just as Fellows stepped out into the night.

Fellows swung around, eyes blazing, his hand going automatically to Louisa's throat, and the other balled into a hard fist, pulled back to punch.

In the next instant, he blinked. "Louisa. Bloody hell." He moved his hand so swiftly from her that she felt a warm breeze on her skin. "Don't do that."

Louisa stared at him. "Did you think I was a robber? In Mayfair assembly rooms?"

Fellows had taken a step back, but his hands were still clenched, his face flushed. "You'd be surprised where thieves lurk. Why aren't you in the ballroom, dancing with all your beaux?"

"I don't have any beaux, and I was looking for you."

"Why?"

The door was still half open, the two of them on the doorstep. Neither in nor out, neither forward nor back. Like their friendship, Louisa thought.

"You walked away," she said. "I was defending you. You snapped at me as though I'd insulted you, and then you turned your back and walked away."

Fellows gave her an impatient look. "I know I'm rude. I wasn't raised to this life."

"A poor excuse. You can be perfectly civil—I've seen you be. What did I do to earn your wrath this evening?"

Fellows reached behind her and pulled the door closed. They were alone in the night, in a dim passage steps away from the busy street. "Understand, Louisa, I can't discuss what I investigate with everyone in the ballroom. You and Mac are one thing, but Mr. Franklin himself was at the garden party. He is a suspect."

"Gil?" Louisa's eyes widened. "Surely not. Gil wouldn't hurt a fly."

"Hargate wasn't a fly. He was a pompous git from what I hear, and he proposed to you. From the way Mr. Franklin looked at you, he's happy the bishop is no longer around to be his rival."

"That is ridiculous . . ." But Gil had made it clear tonight he wanted to speak to Louisa about more than friendship. Perhaps not so ridiculous, but *Gil*? "I still don't think Gil capable of murdering anyone," she said, certain. "And in any case, we weren't asking for a summation of the case in minute detail. We only wanted to know if you'd discovered anything important."

Fellows looked down at her in angry silence, resembling a Highland warrior even more out here in the dark. Louisa's imagination made the tailored coat and ivory waistcoat become a linen shirt and great kilt wrapped around his shoulders; the glint of his watch chain blurred into the hilt of a dirk. He was powerful, strong, nothing tame about him. At any moment, he'd snatch her up and carry her off, a Highlander stealing himself a bride.

Louisa jumped when he reached out and seized her wrist. Reality and fantasy melded, and her heart pounded.

"Come with me," he said, voice hard. "If you want to understand why I can't give you the simple answers you want, come with me, and I'll show you."

He didn't wait for her to debate. Fellows pulled Louisa out of the passage and to the street, April wind rushing at them as they emerged into the wider avenue. Louisa could have protested, jerked away, run back to the safety of the assembly rooms. But she didn't. She let Fellows hold her, Louisa following her Highlander into the dark.

Fellows gave a sharp whistle through his teeth. A hansom cab a little way away jerked forward, the horse's hooves clopping as the carriage came toward them. Fellows had obviously already planned his escape.

He opened the door and all but shoved Louisa into the cab. She didn't have her wrap, but she had no desire to rush back inside to fetch it. The night was warm enough, Fellows might change his mind if he had to wait, and Louisa wanted very much to run off with him, wherever he was taking her.

Fellows gave the driver a direction she didn't hear then climbed in beside her.

Louisa knew she had to be mad, leaving with him without a word, but with Lloyd warm beside her, his animation exciting her, she wanted to go. Whatever damage Louisa did by her flight, she'd repair it in the morning. No looking back.

Fellows took hold of her wrist again, as though he feared she might climb out the other side of the hansom and run if he didn't. As the horse started, Fellows slid his clasp down to her hand, and their fingers twined. The pulse of it raced from hands to Louisa's heart.

The cab listed abruptly. Louisa let out a squeak in alarm as another man wrenched open the carriage door and heaved himself in, landing next to Louisa in the one-seated cab. He was another Highland warrior, this one exuberant and young. He settled himself in the small space, forcing Louisa closer to Fellows, and told the startled driver to keep going.

"Saw you leave," Daniel said, flashing his grin at both of them. "Couldn't let you rush off without a chaperone, now could I?"

Chapter 11

The offices of Scotland Yard were quiet and echoing at night, though not deserted. Constables went in and out from the ground floor on their duties. Detectives used the calm of night to work on cases or for writing up the paperwork that went with them. Talk had been ongoing about moving the cramped police offices to a larger building to be erected near the Victoria Embankment, where a new opera house had been started then abandoned years ago. Fellows had been hearing about this theoretical move for a long time—he wondered if he'd still be alive when it happened.

The few men on the ground floor glanced at Fellows in curiosity when he walked inside in his formal kilt and suit, escorting a young lady in a fancy ball gown and a younger man in kilt and coat. That is, the constables stared until Fellows gave them a look that made them scramble back to their duties.

Fellows had shown Daniel Scotland Yard before. Being a curious lad, he'd turned up not long after Fellows's identity had been revealed to the Mackenzies and demanded a tour. He'd wanted to know everything about the workings of the Metropolitan Police, thinking to perhaps become a detective himself.

After the tour, Daniel told Fellows he'd changed his mind—
he'd rather be an inventor. But maybe Scotland Yard would be
purchasing some of his inventions in time, he'd said.

Daniel gazed about him in as much curiosity tonight, and
Louisa looked interested as well. She was completely out of
place here in her cream and green bustle gown, diamonds in
her red hair, but she looked about without fear.

They had to walk up the two flights of stairs to Fellows's
office. Louisa shivered—it was always either too cold or too
hot in this blasted building. Before Fellows could turn back
and offer her his coat, Daniel had slid his from his shoulders
and wrapped it around Louisa. Daniel threw Fellows an apologetic look, but Fellows didn't comment.

He led them into his office. The small room held two desks,
one for himself and one for Sergeant Pierce, with a cubbyhole
for Constable Dobbs. The constable dealt with the bulk of the
menial work, such as sending telegrams and messages, typing
up handwritten notes, pigeonholing papers or fetching files, and
keeping his chief inspector and sergeant supplied with coffee
and tea, and in the case of Sergeant Pierce, thin cigarettes. The
smell of stale smoke clung to the rooms, though the charwoman
had cleared out the bowls of ash and spent butts hours ago.

The top of Fellows's desk was bare. Every night before he
left, Fellows shoved all the papers he was currently working
with into the deep drawers. The drawers looked like a jumbled
mess, but Fellows knew precisely where each item was.

He fished up the bulkiest stack, gestured for Louisa to sit at
his desk, and dropped the papers onto the desk's flat surface.

Louisa took the seat and looked at the tall pile in front of
her. "My."

Fellows started fanning out the stacks of papers. "My notes
on the suspect interviews," he said, touching a pile covered
with his painstaking handwriting. "These are Pierce's notes.
This is the pathology report on Hargate, and the reports on the
tea, the cups, the pot, the plates, the pastries. Photographs of
the tent, inside and out. This is the second set of witness interviews; this, notes of my search of Hargate's flat and my interview with his parents. Every single detail typed up here."
Fellows put a blunt finger on sheets of paper crowded with
typewritten characters.

Louisa stared at it all uncomprehendingly. Dobbs's typing left something to be desired—there were overstrikes, bad erasure marks, and penciled-in words everywhere. Hardly surprising that Louisa gazed at the report in perplexity.

"You can see why I couldn't make a detailed account of my progress," Fellows said. "Mostly because I don't know what my progress is. The truth is somewhere in that mess. If I go over it another fifty times or so, I might find some clear thread to pull."

Fellows had expected Daniel to give him suggestions, if he didn't just start reading the entire report right there, but when Fellows turned to look for Daniel, he found that the young man had gone. Where, Fellows couldn't imagine. He might have smelled the smoke and longed for a cheroot, he might have spied someone he knew—Daniel seemed to know everyone in London, upper-, middle-, or working-class—or he might have decided that Fellows needed a discreet chat with Louisa. No matter what his motive, Fellows and Louisa were now alone.

Louisa touched one of the pages. "You'll find it. That's what you do, isn't it? Look at a jumble no one else understands and discover a clear pattern?"

That was exactly what he did, but this time, Fellows was finding the way murky. "You have much faith in me."

"I've heard about your cases from Hart. He's very interested in what you do. You find people, you solve crimes that no one else is able to." Louisa looked up at him, her eyes full of confidence. "You'll solve this one. That was what I was trying to tell you before you dragged me away so precipitously from my sister's supper ball." Her smile returned, the warm one she'd bestowed on Fellows a few times in the past. He remembered every single instance. "If anyone saw us go, my reputation will be in tatters—even more than it already is."

"You'll not be ruined," Fellows said. "I'll make sure of it."

"Because Daniel is with us? True, I wager he'll spin a tale that he and I begged you to show us the inner workings of Scotland Yard until you capitulated." She shrugged, pretending nonchalance, though her shoulders were stiff. "It is all in the family, after all."

"We're not family," Fellows said abruptly.

Louisa shook her head, which made the diamonds glitter in the room's stark gaslight. "Indeed, we are, which is Isabella's fault. I never thought I'd find myself with five somewhat overbearing brothers and one energetic grown-up nephew, but when Isabella married Mac, that is what I got. I do like it, most of the time."

"You and I are not brother and sister." Fellows's words came out harsh and flat.

"Well, no, not by blood." Louisa smiled again, that heartbreaking, beautiful smile. "We have shared a kiss or two, after all."

He was going to die. Louisa sat in his office chair, decorating the room as nothing ever had, smiling her sweet little smile. She didn't belong here, and yet she brightened the space like a beacon.

"A kiss or two," Fellows said. "Is that how you think of them?" While he dreamed of them in the nighttime and woke up hot, sweaty, and hard. He had to stifle his groans so he wouldn't disturb the neighbors.

Louisa's smile wavered. "I imagined that was how you thought of them. The silly kisses of a silly girl."

Fellows came around the desk and stood over her, his breath hurting him. "I'm not like Daniel," he said, voice still grating. "Or your Mr. Franklin. Or those stuffed asses at the ball with lust in their eyes as they watched you dance. I wanted to pound the faces of every one of those bastards for looking at you like that."

Louisa blinked in surprise. "What are you talking about? They looked at me in disgust. Everyone believes I poisoned Hargate."

"And the idea that you might be a murderess excited them. Every male there wanted you, Louisa; I watched them want you. That's another reason I took you away from there tonight, another reason I urged you to stay home until this is over."

They stared at each other. Louisa's eyes were a beautiful green, slightly moist with tears she refused to let form. The men tonight had wanted her, Fellows had seen. Not only was she lovely in her froth of a ball gown, that black ribbon around her throat, but the taint of the murder made her even more seductive.

The same taint also took away some of the stigma for touching her—she was not the sweet innocent her set had thought her, or so they now believed. If they debauched her, it would be Louisa's fault, not theirs.

Fellows had to protect her from that. At the same time, he knew he was a hypocrite, because he wanted her as much as had any man there. Fellows didn't only dream of Louisa in the night, he dreamed of her every waking minute.

He couldn't stop thinking about her soft red lips in the kisses they'd shared. He couldn't cease imagining how her mouth would feel on other parts of him, especially the one that was hard under his kilt even now. He wanted to kiss every inch of her body, taste her skin, inhale her scent.

When he lay awake in his bed of nights, his imagination put Louisa in the room with him, she casually undressing with her back to him. She'd slowly strip off her gown, then what was under the gown, letting each piece of clothing loosen and fall. When she was clad only in her corset, her red hair rippling down her back, she'd look over her shoulder and give him her lovely smile.

Fellows made a noise in his throat. He could reach for her right now. She was alone with him, vulnerable. He could do anything to her, and nothing that came to his mind at the moment was honorable.

"Do you believe the same as they do?" Louisa was asking. "That I'm fast?" She let out a small sigh and another shiver. "I'm very afraid they might be right."

She waited for his answer worriedly, as though what Fellows thought mattered to her very much. The cameo at her throat beckoned him to lean down to lick her there. "Louisa, you're an innocent." He had to remember that. "Of that there is no doubt."

Louisa rose, her breath lifting her too-low décolletage in a dangerous way. "Then why do I think about kissing you every time I see you? I should be at my sister's ball, hoping one of the gentlemen I dance with will propose to me and solve my troubles. Instead, I ran off with you the moment you beckoned. Whenever I see you, I know I don't want duty and properness— I want the wicked things my brothers-in-law whisper to my sisters-in-law when they think I don't hear them. I want to do those things with *you*, not with the young men I was raised to expect to marry. Please, explain to me how I can be so innocent with those desires in my head."

Oh God. Fellows's body tightened. He wasn't good with words, was much better at chasing down criminals and then beating them until they stayed down. Words weren't his gift—persistence and his fists were. And now the woman he craved was asking him to explain away the basic animal instinct that burned inside him.

He cleared his throat. "Have you acted on these thoughts, either with me or other gentlemen?"

"No, of course not . . ."

"Then you are an innocent. You have no idea of the full of it."

"But I want to know." Louisa put her hand on his where it rested on the desk. "I want to know all these things. With you."

The world stopped. The flash of Louisa undressing, smiling at him over her shoulder, came to Fellows again, with force. He couldn't say anything, not even her name. *Louisa.* The beautiful, sweet word. She wanted him. What he desired, what he craved—she wanted it too.

Louisa nodded, her diamonds flashing again. "You see? I am a wanton. At least, I am where you are concerned. And I have no idea what to do about it."

Fellows had plenty of ideas. And he couldn't act on any of them, not without being as insidious as the most vicious criminals he'd chased to ground.

Louisa was alone with him, in his power, innocent, no matter what she claimed. She knew nothing of life, not in all the ugliness he'd lived through. And she was telling him she wanted to give that innocence to him.

So much heat washed through his veins that Fellows thought he'd fall. But cold followed hard upon the heat. Louisa trusted him. She had no idea what a man like Fellows was capable of. He could take her right here, to hell with virtue and respectability, and she wouldn't be able to stop him. She trusted him because he was now one of the Mackenzies, acknowledged as the half brother of her sister's husband. *All in the family,* she'd said.

But Fellows wasn't like the Mackenzies—he was worse

than any of them. For all the brothers' hardness and ruthlessness, Hart, Cam, Mac, and even Ian had a modicum of polish. Fancy schools and university, money, influential friends, and the right circles had given them a bit of a gloss.

Fellows had lived in squalor, his mother working harder than any woman should have to keep him fed. Catherine had stayed late into the night at the taverns, working her feet off for impatient tavern keepers, putting up with men trying to corner her. Fellows knew she'd let some of them corner her, for money, when she needed it. And he'd never blamed her for it.

The tamer Mackenzies had never had to watch their mother try not to cry as she counted out her coin for the night and realized it wouldn't be enough. Hart hadn't fed off tavern scraps grudgingly given, hadn't had to watch his mother work harder and harder for less and less as her prettiness faded. Fellows had determined, the day he'd been accepted as a police constable, that his mother would never have to work again. And he'd fulfilled that vow.

Louisa knew nothing of these hardships, and Fellows would do everything in his power to make sure she never did.

He could frighten her away from him. Make her go running back to the safety of Mac and Isabella's home, lock the door, stay there. He abruptly slid his hand to the back of her head, twisted her face up to his, and crushed his lips over her mouth.

Louisa gasped, lips parting. Fellows tasted the sweet and tart of the lemonade she'd drunk, brought to her by the insipid Mr. Franklin. The thought of Franklin made Fellows angry. He dragged Louisa closer, fingers tangling in her satin-smooth curls, the kiss turning hard.

She made a little sound, and he knew he was bruising her, but he didn't care. He meant to frighten her, meant her to jerk away and flee him.

She didn't flee. Louisa was warmer than the room, the heat of her mouth searing. Daniel's coat, still around her shoulders, smelled of cheroots, but her fragrance was all Fellows heeded.

He scooped his arm under her legs, easing her up onto the wooden desk. Perfect. Louisa sat on its edge, looking up at him, lips red with his kisses. Fellows cradled her head in his hands and kissed her again, deeper and fuller, locking her in place.

He jumped when her slipper brushed his leg. The point of her heel touched his wool socks then the bare of his thigh beneath the kilt. The little scratch of the heel jolted his need into a rampant fire.

Louisa was supposed to be frightened. She was supposed to fight away from him, shout at him that he should never dare take such a liberty. She should instruct him to never touch her, never to *speak* to her again. But Louisa's answering kiss was as frenzied as his. Her slipper went up and up, her leg wrapping his and holding on.

One swift thrust on the desk, and she'd be his forever. But this was wrong. Fellows should savor her, in a bed, perhaps in an elegant hotel on soft sheets. Louisa deserved that. But the desk was here, the room dark and empty, his yearning for her climbing.

Fellows forced his mouth from hers. Louisa looked up at him in need, her eyes half closed, her lips red, parted, swollen. Her body was soft, hands curled around the lapels of his coat.

"Louisa." He could barely get out her name. "No."

It was the hardest thing he'd ever said. Louisa released her hold on his coat, but only to slide her hands around his neck. "Lloyd."

The whisper was the first time he'd ever heard her speak his name.

He felt something break apart inside him, a breath of air that cleansed everything soiled within him. Fellows's arms went around her, and their bodies moved together down to the flat surface of the desk. Daniel's coat fell from Louisa's shoulders, pooling on the hard wood and all the papers beneath her.

Louisa made another little gasp as he kissed her again, and Fellows took advantage. He kissed her parted lips, licking them, suckling them.

She didn't stop him, didn't fight him. Louisa kissed him back, trying to imitate what he did, which was sweet and erotic at the same time.

Fellows moved from her lips to her throat and the black ribbon and cameo. Fellows bit the innocent cameo then brushed his tongue down the curve of her neck to her breasts. Soft skin rose above the neckline of her bodice, the slight salt taste of her making him want more.

She'd be damp and warm under the gown, the space between her legs moist and welcoming. Fellows wanted to taste her, to sink his tongue into her and take her goodness into his mouth.

He could have her. Raise her skirts, kiss her thighs, enjoy her delights and bring her to heights of pleasure. Louisa's restless hands in his hair, her leg still twined around his, told him she wanted him, wanted this.

Fellows licked across the top of her breasts, his tongue catching the fabric of the bodice. The satin's dry contrast to Louisa's skin only spiraled his need to near madness.

"Lloyd," Louisa said again.

Her beautiful, throaty voice caressed his name. Everything painful in him washed away on its sound . . .

Someone coughed.

Reality came crashing back into Fellows so hard he lost his next breath. He took his mouth from Louisa's breast and carefully raised his head.

He expected Daniel. Embarrassing, but Daniel might be trusted to keep silent. The lad already suspected Fellows's intense interest in Louisa. Fellows would apologize for taking the liberty and explain the situation, then ask that Daniel keep it to himself. *If* Fellows could explain.

The young man standing inside the doorway wasn't Daniel. It was Constable Dobbs.

Dobbs was about nineteen, eager to learn, eager to please. He had close-cropped blond hair, blue eyes, and a tall, Viking-like body.

Right now, his fair face was scarlet. "Sir."

"Out," Fellows said.

"Sir." Dobbs nodded nervously. "Sorry, sir."

Even as Dobbs turned for the open door, he peered surreptitiously at Louisa, trying to make out who she was. Catching Fellows's glare, he turned quickly away and sidled out, leaving the door open.

Louisa's eyes were wide with alarm, her breathing rapid as she struggled to sit up. Fellows helped her from the desk and steadied her on her feet. Louisa's hair was mussed, red ringlets straggling down her neck, her face as flushed as Dobbs's had been.

No apology came from Fellows's lips. He wouldn't apologize for doing something he'd longed to do with everything inside him.

"Dobbs won't say a word," Fellows said.

Louisa reached for the coat, not looking at him, her cheeks still red. "We should find Daniel."

She slid the coat around her shoulders. Fellows helped her settle it, but still Louisa wouldn't look at him.

The moment was fragile. One wrong word, and she'd be lost to him forever.

But there were no right words. Fellows wasn't elegantly articulate, like Mr. Franklin, or glib like Daniel. He'd learned plain speaking from his mother, as well as the value of keeping his mouth shut when the situation called for it.

He said nothing.

Louisa wouldn't look at him, but she didn't bow her head. She was a proud lady, from a long line of proud people. She was elegant and regal and wouldn't crumble to dust because a police detective kissed her on his desk.

Fellows led her out the door. Louisa didn't blindly rush away; she walked calmly with him through the empty corridors and down the stairs. Neither of them spoke or even looked at each other.

Daniel leaned on a desk inside the front door, talking and laughing with the sergeant there. When Daniel saw Fellows and Louisa, he straightened up in surprise. The sergeant quickly found something else to do, but Daniel's eyes narrowed as he looked them over.

Fellows led Louisa past Daniel without a word and out into the street. The hansom cab still waited outside. Daniel, who'd insisted on paying the fare, must have tipped the driver well.

Fellows handed Louisa into the cab. She gripped his hand without hesitation as she stepped inside, but still she didn't look at him.

"Take her home," Fellows said to Daniel.

Louisa leaned forward, finally meeting his eyes. "Aren't you coming?"

Fellows shook his head. "Have things to do, and my flat isn't far from here. Daniel will escort you home."

"That he will," Daniel said. "Good night." He didn't look pleased that Fellows was deserting Louisa, but at least he didn't argue. He climbed in after Louisa and settled onto the seat with a swing of kilt and a boisterous thump.

"Good night." Fellows closed the door to the hansom with a snap.

Louisa continued to watch him. Curls of her loosened hair fell forward, haloing her in red. Then the carriage jerked forward, and Fellows's view of her was lost.

Lost. A good word. Fellows remained on the street, watching the receding carriage for too long, until it disappeared into the April mists.

Chapter 12

"Do you want to talk about it?" Daniel asked.

Louisa jerked from her reverie, in which she saw, heard, and felt nothing but Lloyd's warmth around her, his mouth on her, his strong hands . . .

"Talk about what?"

"What happened upstairs," Daniel said. "I step away for five minutes, you come down flushed and mussed, not to mention distracted and upset. Did ye not like his attentions? Do I have to pummel him for you?"

Daniel, so young and eager—and so wide awake; did he never get tired?—watched her with a shrewdness that belied his youth.

Louisa couldn't answer. She sank into the hard back of the hansom's seat, stifling a sigh. Isabella's house on Mount Street wasn't impossibly far from Whitehall, but the hansom went slowly, and she knew the ride would be long.

"Ah," Daniel said when the silence had stretched a while. "So you *did* like his attentions. That's the trouble, is it?"

Louisa let out an exasperated breath. "I don't know what he wants. *That* is the trouble. I don't *know*."

"Well, ye have to understand that when a gent looks at a beautiful woman, such as yourself . . ."

Daniel left it hanging. Louisa sat up. "Yes, I know very well what you are implying. And you are very flattering. But I have no idea if he wants anything more than that. Or if I do. Blast it all, it's a terrible thing when I can't trust my own thoughts. *I* don't even know what I want."

"I think you do."

"Yes, of course I do," Louisa snapped. "I want to not have gone into the tea tent with the Bishop of Hargate. I want Mr. Fellows not to be so standoffish with me. I want to be his friend. More than his friend. I want . . . Oh, Danny, it's so confusing."

"Not really. You're falling in love with him. Or are already in love with him."

"But am I? Or just . . . overwhelmed?"

"Love is overwhelming. Look what your sister did when she met my uncle Mac. She lost her head and ran away with him the very night she met him. She was just eighteen, younger than I am now. Whatever Mac thinks, Isabella would never have done anything so reckless if she hadn't fallen crazily in love with him."

"She might have," Louisa said darkly. "Isabella was always headstrong."

"She *is* headstrong." Daniel gave Louisa another assessing look. "Let me guess—Isabella was the bold one, while you were always the good girl. The one who stayed home, behaved herself, never did anything to upset people. Am I right?"

"Yes." Louisa thumped her hands to the seat. "You are absolutely right. I never did *anything*. I stayed quiet and obedient and did what was expected of me. And what was my reward? People pitying me, whispering about my scandalous family. So I decided to look for a respectable husband to make them *stop* pitying me. Now I'm accused of murder, and I'm letting the detective in charge of the investigation kiss me senseless."

"Ah ha, is *that* what went on upstairs when my back was turned?"

"Yes." Louisa's face heated. "If you must know, yes."

Daniel grinned. "You didn't really have to tell me, you know.

The stars in your eyes, your hair coming down, the pretty flush on your cheek, all betrayed you."

"And you mustn't tell anyone." Louisa pinned him with a severe look. "Promise me, Daniel."

Daniel raised his hands. "Never worry. I always keep the confidences of my great friends. Now, what you have to decide is what you're going to do about this falling-in-love business. Ignore it and pursue your respectable marriage? With Gil Franklin, I'm thinking? You won't have to push hard for a proposal there, I'd wager. Or wait and see if Fellows tries to kiss you again? Or asks more of you?"

"He won't," Louisa said glumly.

"Which he? Won't do what?"

"Mr. Fellows won't ask anything of me. He barely speaks to me. I have no idea why he kisses me, except for the fact that I've thrown myself at him several times now. He must think me depraved. I'm not certain he's wrong."

Daniel watched her. "This is all fascinating. I had no idea it had gone this far."

"Nothing has gone *far* at all," Louisa said in exasperation. "I'm behaving like a flighty, ridiculous woman who's been sitting on the shelf so long she's starting to go mad. It's the only explanation for my insanity. You're right—I should tell Gil I welcome his attentions, marry him, and have done."

Louisa turned abruptly to the window so Daniel wouldn't see the tears in her eyes. If she married Gil, she could never let herself be alone with Fellows again. She couldn't trust her own body not to react to him or trust herself to remain sensible and not succumb to desire. Even now she couldn't banish the sensation of Fellows's burning kisses, the feeling of his mouth on her skin, and the knowledge of how much she wanted him.

"Yes, live in misery the rest of your life," Daniel said. "That will show everyone."

Louisa turned back. Let him see the tears. What did she care? "It won't be in misery. Gil is a gentleman. He's courteous and kind, never rude, generous, good-hearted . . ."

"And dull. I hear it in your voice. You're trying to be fair to him because he is a good chap. But dull. You'd do the same thing every day, he'd never do anything unexpected, never make you wonder what was going on in his head. Gil is transparent. Makes him a fine bloke to play cards with, because I win every hand, but probably very tedious to live with."

Louisa wanted to hotly defend Gil, who'd been a friend to her tonight when no one else had, but the words died on her lips.

Daniel wasn't wrong. Louisa liked Gil immensely, she always had, but she didn't love him. She'd never be interested in him in the way she wanted to understand what was inside Lloyd Fellows. When she saw Lloyd, she wanted to follow him, be with him, listen to him, touch him, make him understand that he wasn't alone. Louisa was fascinated by Fellows's job, wanted him to talk to her about it and confide in her, and she wanted to confide in him.

She leaned her head back on the seat. "It's hopeless. Inspector Fellows is very conscious of his position in life, and mine."

"That is true. He's a snob. I've found that working-class chaps generally are. Any hint of getting above yourself is ruthlessly quashed. The posh should stay posh; the honest workers should stay honest workers. And Fellows has always seen himself as an honest worker. More so once he realized his dad was never going to acknowledge him. The working classes, now, they tolerate *me* because I'm such an honest bloke, and I don't try to change them."

Louisa had to laugh. "And you're not conceited at all."

"I'm all sorts of conceited, I know that. I'm very clever and see no reason to hide it. On the other hand, being clever is no assurance of being great or finding success. Success takes bloody hard work too. I know that. But we're not talking about me, Auntie Louisa. We're talking about you and Uncle Fellows. And what we're going to do about it."

"We will do nothing about it. I will marry Gil or remain a spinster, and Inspector Fellows will go on being a policeman. Perhaps he'll find a cheerful working-class woman to marry him, and his life will become simple and pleasant."

"Listen to yourself. Poor martyred Louisa. I predict that Fellows will solve this murder and then sweep you off your feet." Daniel shrugged. "Well, the sweeping-you-off-your-feet part might take a little nudge. But he wants to do it. It's a beautiful thing to watch the way he looks at you. Fellows glared at Gil tonight as though he wanted to find a claymore, learn how to use it, and finish him off. Or just pull out a pistol and shoot him."

Louisa gave up. She leaned across the seat in the rattling coach and kissed Daniel's cheek. "You are sweet, Danny. A complete madman, but a very sweet one."

"Aw, Auntie. You know I love you. I'm devastated ye won't pick me as your husband, but if not, I'm happy to help you land one of your own."

"Pish. You haven't fallen in love yet, so you don't understand how very awful it can be. I used to be a rational girl, and now I'm doing foolish things like running about London in the middle of the night and letting police inspectors kiss me senseless. I shall be all right. It will pass. And when you do fall in love, Daniel Mackenzie, I shall laugh at you."

"No fear of that. I enjoy ladies, as both friends and lovers, but I will let nothing stand in the way of my inventions."

"So say you. Well, here I am," she said as the carriage pulled to a halt in front of Isabella's house. "Thank you, Danny."

Daniel gallantly leapt down and handed her out. He surprised Louisa by pulling her into a crushing hug before he let her go. "Never worry, Auntie," he said softly. "I'll make sure all is well."

He gave her a kiss on the cheek, another hug, and then backed away and waved good night. Louisa hurried into the house, Morton the butler pulling the door open for her before she reached the doorstep. Daniel called good night again, leapt into the hansom, and rattled off.

Louisa wasn't sure whether to take hope from Daniel's words or worry about what mad thing he'd take it into his head to do. Either way, most of her thoughts were still focused on Fellows's kisses, the strength of his body on hers, the look of dark desperation in his eyes when he'd backed away from her.

She had to be right. It was hopeless.

Louisa went up the stairs, not stopping on the landing that led to her bedchamber. She kept climbing, up to the nursery to quietly slip inside and kiss the three sleeping children good night. She sat there after that, in the dark, watching them sleep, soaking in the calming silence.

"The guv's asking for you," Sergeant Pierce said to Fellows, looking apologetic. "Says now, sir."

Damnation. Fellows looked up from the fifty statements he was going over again, meticulously, trying to decide who was telling the truth. They were all lying—people did that to the police—but usually for reasons that had nothing to do with the case. Fellows had to sift through and pick out the important lies from the unimportant ones.

He'd been here since the early hours, after going home last night and trying to sleep. Not possible. Fellows had lain awake, staring at the whitewashed ceiling above his bed, which reflected every passing light, the moon, streetlights.

In the reflections he saw Louisa, her red hair coming down, the sultry look in her eyes when he'd lain her back on the desk. He heard her voice, low and vibrant, saying his name. *Lloyd.*

He'd do anything to have her say it to him like that again.

Sleeping being out of the question, Fellows had come in to see if he could make sense of all this mess.

"Now?" Fellows repeated irritably.

"Yes, sir. Says it's urgent."

Fellows heaved an aggrieved sigh, slammed papers aside, got to his feet, and headed out of the room. Constable Dobbs was just coming in with cups of tea, and the two met in the doorway. Fellows turned sideways to move past him. Dobbs turned red. The constable's hands shook so hard that tea sloshed from the full cups and splashed to Fellows's shoes.

"Watch yourself, Constable," Fellows snapped, then he was past and striding down the hall.

Detective Chief Superintendent Giles Kenton had been Fellows's superior for nearly five years. It had been Kenton who'd lifted his former superior's restrictions on Fellows's promotions, put in place when Fellows had been fanatically pursuing the Mackenzies for murder.

Kenton had made clear that Fellows needed to have a care in who he offended with his obsessive investigations. Kenton was a good man to work for, though, because he recognized that Fellows had a unique way of solving his cases and that his clear-up rate was better than most.

Kenton waved Fellows to the only other chair in his office, keeping his attention on the papers that littered his desk. That was a good sign. No sitting upright, hands on the desk, gaze trained on Fellows. Just Kenton doing what he usually did.

Kenton signed a piece of paper, blotted the paper, and clattered the pen to a tray, spraying a few ink droplets to his desk. Finally he pushed aside everything and looked up at Fellows.

Not so good. Kenton had a sharp light in his eyes that came from anger. "I'm pulling you and your team off the Hargate case," he said.

Fellows's answer was abrupt and instant. "No. You can't. I mean . . . No, sir. Please don't."

"I can and I will. Hargate was powerful, and his family is powerful, both his father's and his mother's. His friends are powerful. They are all busily screaming for our blood, wondering why we haven't closed this case yet."

Fellows couldn't stay seated. He was on his feet, fists clenched. "It's been less than a week. Cases like this can take months. Years. You know that."

"Yes, *I* know that. Civilians don't, especially posh ones. They either want the police to work miracles or else they complain we're a bloody nuisance."

"Then they should let me get on with my job. Having my chief super pull me in to twit me is wasting time."

Kenton gave him a severe look. "Are you finished?"

Fellows leaned his fists on the desk. "You can't take me off this case, sir."

"Listen." Kenton's voice lost its edge. "Fellows, you are the best detective on the force. I don't even qualify that by saying you are *one* of the best. You truly are *the* best. You'll make detective superintendent in no time, probably chief super beyond it, and likely higher than that. You're the best because you not only have good instincts, you're also careful and thorough. You follow up on everything. Unfortunately, Hargate's family wants a quick arrest. And they're wondering why the devil you haven't made one."

"Because I haven't found a culprit yet," Fellows said, trying not to shout. "As soon as I get a lead on the man seen crawling out from under the tent, I'll bring him in."

"Hmm, yes. Very convenient this bloke is, isn't he? He

gives you a good excuse not to pull together the evidence to arrest Lady Louisa Scranton."

"Because she didn't do it." The shout came then.

"Maybe not. But consider—once she's arrested and examined by a magistrate, and the magistrate determines her innocence, she'll be let go. End of the matter."

Fellows shook his head. "For God's sake, you know she can't afford to appear before a magistrate. He'll be compelled by Hargate's family to push her through to a trial, and they'll make sure the very best prosecutor in the country gets her convicted. The Scrantons haven't been well liked since Louisa's father ruined half the aristos in Mayfair. No one would fuss much if a Scranton was buried for this."

"Then Lady Louisa's family will come up with a barrage of solicitors to help her. You know that. Her ties to the Mackenzies will help too. And those ties are the exact reason I'm taking you off this case."

Fellows stood up, his fists tightening. "What the devil does that mean?"

"It *means* that you are the finest detective on the force—until you have something to do with the Mackenzie family. Then your common sense takes a dive out the window. You break rules, you don't sleep, you focus your energy on them and everything about them. Five years, wasn't it, that you tried to pin a murder on them? The duke had to threaten gents in the Home Office to get you to stop. And then you went behind everyone's back, chased Lord Ian Mackenzie to Paris, and tried a number of ways to get around the rules to land him."

"But I got to the bottom of the problem," Fellows said, voice stiff. "Murders solved. Case closed."

"You're quibbling, Fellows. You solved them, all right, but a woman died, and another nearly died in the process. I'm taking you off the case, because I can't explain to Hargate's father—an earl—and his mother—the daughter of a marquis—why you haven't arrested Lady Louisa Scranton by now. I imagine you don't wish me to tell them it's because she's your mistress."

Fellows's face burned. "Good Lord, sir. She is *not* my mistress."

"Then why did Dobbs charge in here bright and early this morning and tell me she was? Yes, he gave me the whole story of finding you ravishing the lead suspect in the Hargate case on top of your desk." Kenton's mouth tightened. "You need to speak to that lad about going over your head to spread tittle-tattle. A constable should be loyal to his own guvnor, whether that guvnor is ravishing suspects or not."

"I wasn't ravishing her," Fellows said. "Dobbs got it wrong." And he'd wring the boy's neck.

"Dobbs's exact words were: *He had her spread across the desk, knees up, and he were kissing her tits.*" Kenton mimicked Dobbs's youthful voice exactly. "Not something I wanted to hear, trust me."

"It doesn't matter what Dobbs saw or what he said." Fellows's voice hardened. "It doesn't matter what my feelings for her are either. Louisa Scranton is innocent. I know it. Whatever the world thinks of her, she did *not* kill the Bishop of Hargate."

"Climb down off your high horse. *I* don't care if you had her naked on her hands and knees and were giving her one up the backside. I care that Hargate's dad and mum and all the titles they're connected to want a result. My neck's being breathed on, and so I'm breathing on yours. You're too slow. I'm giving the case to Harrison."

"No." Cold fear spread through Fellows's body. "Harrison arrests everyone in sight then sorts out who did what. Sometimes he doesn't find out the truth until several people have been hanged."

"But he's fast and he gets his man. Or woman."

"No." Fellows leaned over the desk again, barely stopping himself from grabbing Kenton and shaking him. "Please. I promise I'll stay the hell away from Lady Louisa. Miles away if need be. But don't take me off the case. I'll find the culprit— I promise you. Don't leave her to Harrison's mercy."

Kenton gave him a severe look. "I've gone to the wall for you, Fellows. Several times. Worth it to keep you. But by God, you push it."

"If you give this to Harrison, sir, I'm off the force."

Kenton scowled. "Don't threaten me. I've been threatened by more frightening men than you in my time, believe me, including my own guvnor."

"I'm not threatening. If I'm off the case, I'm gone. I'll not stay where men arrest innocent young women only to prove they're getting things done. I'll go, and then I'll protect her from you any way I can." He paused. "Sir."

Kenton sat back in his chair. The look on his face said he knew damn well Fellows wanted to throttle him, but he put up no defenses. "You said you were going off to the races on Monday. To Newmarket."

"Yes, but I won't go. Keep me on, and I'll stay here and work—"

"Let me finish. You'll go. You need the day out. If, before you leave, you make an arrest—one that will stick—then I won't pull you from the case. If you haven't solved it before you go, then you're off."

Fellows stared at him in dismay. "That's only two days."

"Yes, it is. It's the best I can do for you."

"I mean it," Fellows said. "If I can't solve this case in two blasted days, and you pull me off, I'm gone."

Kenton raked papers back toward him. "Then you'd better solve it quick then, hadn't you?"

Fellows moved his fists from the desk again and straightened up. Kenton was finished, the interview over.

As Fellows walked to the door, Kenton cleared his throat behind him. "And stay away from the Scranton woman. I'll hold you to that. Unless you're escorting her to Bow Street and the magistrate, I don't want you anywhere near her."

"Yes, sir," Fellows said stiffly, and made his way through the building back to his office.

He walked in on Dobbs sitting on a wooden chair holding a hand to his bruised and bloody face. Pierce was wringing out his own hand, looking furious.

"Pierce," Fellows snapped.

Pierce betrayed no shame. "I was just explaining to Dobbs that he don't go around his chief inspector to tell tales, no matter what. You respect your team."

Fellows gazed quietly down at Dobbs, who gazed back, half fearful, half defiant. "Dobbs," Fellows said, his voice as chill as his stance. "It's not you peaching to my guv that I mind. If I'm wrong, I'm wrong. But if you ever speak about Lady Louisa again, especially in those words, to *anyone*, I will pound you until you can't walk. Understand?"

Dobbs swallowed. "Yes, sir."

"Now get me coffee and don't spill anything this time. Pierce, we're going to clear up this case before Monday. I want you to—"

"Monday?" Pierce said, springing up. "What the devil did the chief super say to you?"

"Monday," Fellows repeated. "We're dividing up the suspects between us, and we'll poke and prod until we get answers. I don't care who we annoy, provoke, or just plain make hate us. We're not out to make friends; we're out to catch a criminal. The first thing I want, though, is for you to find out everything—I mean absolutely everything—about the Honorable Gilbert Franklin. I want to know where he's been, what he does when he's there, what he has for breakfast, and when he shits it out again. All right?"

"Shits it out again," Pierce wrote down in his notebook. "Got it, sir. I'll start right now."

Chapter 13

That afternoon, Louisa sat once more in Mrs. Leigh-Waters's back sitting room. This time, though, Daniel was with her, and Louisa had come for a purpose.

The fact that Mrs. Leigh-Waters received Louisa at all encouraged her. Mrs. Leigh-Waters had always been a close friend to Louisa's mother and to Isabella, one of the few to stand by Isabella when Isabella had left Mac.

Today, the lady was full of sympathy for Louisa and also for Hargate. "I wake up with palpitations thinking about that poor man," Mrs. Leigh-Waters said, pressing a hand to her bosom. "What he must have suffered. It must have been quite distressing for you, Louisa, to watch him die. I am so sorry, my dear."

She sounded sorry, but also a bit morbidly curious. "Indeed," Louisa said. "Thank you."

"And you, Mr. Mackenzie," Mrs. Leigh-Waters said to Daniel. "So kind of you to stand by our dear Louisa."

"Not at all," Daniel said. He gave Mrs. Leigh-Waters his best I'm-young-but-very-intelligent-and-understanding smile. "Louisa is a favorite of mine."

"Of mine as well." Mrs. Leigh-Waters returned the smile, but with a glint in her eye. She looked back and forth between

Louisa and Daniel with obvious interest. Daniel was nineteen, it
was true, and Louisa years older than he, but such matches had
been made. Once Daniel had finished university and come into
his majority, he would be a very wealthy young man indeed.

Mrs. Leigh-Waters's eyes were truly gleaming now. Louisa
broke in hastily, "What I wondered, if you'll forgive me asking, is how you decided who to invite to the garden party? I
saw people here I hadn't in ages."

Mrs. Leigh-Waters blinked. "My guest list was quite large,
dear. My garden party is always an important Season gathering. I invite a wide circle, though I keep my list to those I like
best."

In other words, the gathering was large enough to be interesting, but exclusive enough for those invited to feel superior
over those who had not been.

"What Louisa means," Daniel said, "is that she's surprised
the Bishop of Hargate made your list. Louisa hadn't thought
you were particular friends. In fact, Hargate could be a prig-
gish and condescending oik, God rest him."

Mrs. Leigh-Waters flushed. "You are certainly forthright,
Mr. Mackenzie."

"But truthful. Hargate rose high in his profession very fast.
My uncle Hart figured he called in favor after favor and bought
his way to the top."

Hart would know. He'd used similar methods himself on
occasion, and he likely knew whose nest Hargate had feath-
ered to become bishop.

"Well, your uncle Hart might not be wrong," Mrs. Leigh-
Waters said. "Hargate did ask my husband for a word in the
right ear in exchange for him helping Mr. Leigh-Waters in
certain matters. It's often done, but with Hargate . . ."

"It was obvious and obsequious," Daniel finished. "Is that
why you invited him to the party? To repay what he'd done for
your husband?"

"No, no." Mrs. Leigh-Waters's flush went deeper. "If you
must know, I owed the bishop a bit of money, and he was nee-
dling me for it. I invited him at his request, intending to settle
the debt here."

"And did you settle it?" Daniel asked. He softened the
abrupt question with a smile, took a sip of tea, and then

gestured with his cup. "I mean, did you have the chance before . . . you know."

"I did, as a matter of fact. I gave him his hundred guineas. Well, most of it." Mrs. Leigh-Waters leaned toward them, lowering her voice. "Please don't tell my husband."

Louisa shook her head. "Never fear about that. Was it a gambling debt?"

"Pardon?" Mrs. Leigh-Waters looked surprised, then her face grew as red as the velvet curtains behind her. "Oh. Yes. Indeed. I had some very bad luck at cards and had to give Hargate a vowel for what I'd lost. I planned to pay him as soon as I could, but he was a bit impatient. For a man of the cloth, I must say, Hargate did not practice much forgiveness."

In fact, Hargate seemed to excel at all the deadly sins, Louisa thought, pride and avarice being the top contenders. But some gentlemen went into the clergy not because they had a calling or deep faith, but because, if they went the right way about it, they could make a good living and gain power. Hargate had been a power-seeker and hadn't much tried to hide it.

"I am sorry," Louisa said. "I know this is difficult for you."

Daniel gave Mrs. Leigh-Waters a cheerful smile. "At least your slate is clean. You were able to pay your debt, and all was finished."

"Not exactly." Mrs. Leigh-Waters put her hand over Louisa's, her eyes welling with tears. "Dearest Louisa, I must beg your forgiveness. I couldn't pay Hargate the entire amount. My pin money for the month was gone, and I could not ask my husband for more without telling him why. I didn't want Mr. Leigh-Waters to know. He doesn't approve of gambling."

This was the first Louisa had heard of it. Mr. Leigh-Waters was often seen around card tables at Isabella's parties, his wife the same. But Louisa smiled encouragingly and let Mrs. Leigh-Waters go on.

"Hargate threatened to go to my husband directly. I begged him not to. I asked what else I could give him, something to keep him happy until I could raise the rest of the money. He said—oh, my dear Louisa, I am so ashamed of myself now."

Louisa thought she understood. "Did Hargate ask you to arrange for him to speak to me alone?"

"Yes. Oh, my poor darling, I'm so sorry. I knew he meant

to propose to you. He often spoke of you as being the perfect bride for him. He wasn't wrong—you'd have made a very good bishop's wife." Tears trickled from the corners of her eyes. "I agreed, I'm afraid. Anything to keep him from going to my husband."

Mrs. Leigh-Waters's distress was true but seemed a bit much for a woman who'd owed a debt from a card game. Most people in Mayfair owed each other for losses at whist, faro, hazard, the American game of poker, any sporting matches, or even which side of the street a cat would walk down. Gambling mania was alive and well in the *haut ton*. Louisa knew men who'd lost pieces of untailed land, favorite horses, servants, and even houses to their friends. The bets were squared eventually, often good-naturedly. Wives whose husbands frowned on their gambling did try to be covert, but sympathetic friends often helped them pay. Mrs. Leigh-Waters had lied when she'd said her husband disapproved of gambling, though, but Louisa couldn't fathom why.

Daniel broke in, his voice quieter. "What did Hargate expect you to do, with respect to Louisa? Was letting him speak to her alone the end of it?"

Mrs. Leigh-Waters shook her head. "He wanted me to encourage her in the match if she proved shy. Talk her into it. Or bribe her, threaten her, whatever it took."

Louisa's eyes widened. "You promised him that?"

"I couldn't help it." More tears came, Mrs. Leigh-Waters's large bosom rising. "I was desperate, my dear. And I didn't see the harm. You told me yourself you'd decided this Season to look for a respectable husband. Hargate *would* have been a good match for you—would have helped you and your family."

"At the expense of her happiness," Daniel said. "If Louisa had accepted Hargate, I would have done anything to persuade her out of it." He shuddered. "I couldn't stick having Hargate for an uncle-in-law. Imagine having to be pleasant to him over pudding at Christmas. No, thank you."

"I would have refused him," Louisa said. "Hargate did try very hard to persuade me, telling me he'd forgive my family's debts to him if I married him. My family has paid back most of what my father owed him, but he intended to squeeze me for the rest of it. Horrid man."

Mrs. Leigh-Waters looked even more distressed. "Oh, Louisa, you mustn't . . ."

"Speak ill of the dead?" Daniel asked, before Louisa could answer. "It's not the done thing, no, but death doesn't change what a person was in life. Hargate wasn't above a bit of blackmail to get what he wanted. Key to most of his successes, I'd wager. He even tried to blackmail me once."

Mrs. Leigh-Waters wiped her eyes. "He did? What about? I mean . . . Oh, I beg your pardon, Mr. Mackenzie. I don't mean to pry."

Daniel shrugged. "Youthful indiscretions. I've had so many of those I had to tax Hargate a bit before I pinned down exactly which youthful indiscretion he was threatening to tell my father about. I told Hargate to tell him and be damned. Which he did. My dad came down on me hard, but I confessed my sins, Dad and I argued, he forgave me, we had a whiskey, and all was well." Daniel's relationship with his father in a nutshell.

"Rather mean of Hargate," Louisa said indignantly. "Did he ask you for money to keep quiet?"

"That and a word with Uncle Hart to hurry Hargate's chances of getting into the House of Lords. Only room for so many bishops' bums on the seats there. Someone has to die before another can come in the front door. Hargate wanted to be moved to the top of the list. I told him he was optimistic about Hart opening a way for him. Hart's harder to blackmail than anyone I know. Trust me. I've tried. My ears still hurt from the drubbing he gave me." Daniel rubbed the side of his head. "Of course, I was only ten at the time and not practiced."

Daniel's casual tone, dismissing blackmail as merely a nuisance, was having good effect on Mrs. Leigh-Waters. Her crying quieted, and she started to relax.

"Was he blackmailing you too?" Daniel asked her. "I'm sorry if he was."

Mrs. Leigh-Waters nodded. "Please, *please* don't tell my husband."

"No." Louisa squeezed her hand. "We understand."

Mrs. Leigh-Waters looked at them watching her, then she jumped. "But if you are thinking I poisoned Hargate to keep him quiet, I did not. I paid him, as I said, and set up the appointment for him to meet you. I knew he might try for more money in future, but I'd cross that bridge when I came to it."

Louisa wondered very much what knowledge Hargate had possessed that so shamed Mrs. Leigh-Waters, but she wouldn't ask. The poor lady had suffered enough without having to worry that someone else knew her secret. Hargate was gone now, and Mrs. Leigh-Waters was safe from him.

"Never fear," Louisa said. "I don't see how you could have killed him, anyway, if the poison was in the teacup. How could you know which cup he'd choose? Or which I'd choose to give him? It was me who handed him the cup. I am, unfortunately, the most likely suspect."

Louisa deflated. She'd come here hoping to learn much more. She'd discovered from their conversation that Mrs. Leigh-Waters did indeed have a motive for killing Hargate, but she had difficulty picturing Mrs. Leigh-Waters thinking of so intricate a way to administer the poison. Besides, would the lady risk killing the man in her own garden? In front of a large party of people?

Someone had. And that someone had shifted the blame squarely on Louisa.

"Thank you." Louisa squeezed Mrs. Leigh-Waters's hand again. "I'm sorry you've had to go through all this."

"And I you," Mrs. Leigh-Waters said. "Will you forgive me?"

"Of course."

Mrs. Leigh-Waters let out her breath, her relief plain. Louisa and Daniel exchanged a glance, silently agreeing to end the conversation, and they took the rest of their tea in peace.

⁓

When Louisa and Daniel left Mrs. Leigh-Waters's house, Louisa gave Mac's coachman directions to take them straight to London and Scotland Yard. She would try to keep Mrs. Leigh-Waters's confidences as best she could, but she wanted to tell Fellows what they'd discovered about Hargate. Immediately. As awkward as it would be to face Fellows again after last night, she wanted him to know.

Daniel agreed, and the coach headed east at a good clip.

When they reached Scotland Yard, however, the sergeant

downstairs told Daniel that Fellows was out. So was Sergeant
Pierce and Constable Dobbs. But they could always leave a
message.

Daniel returned to the coach, where Louisa waited, with this
information.

"I suppose I can leave him a message," Louisa said, unhappy.

"No." Daniel knocked on the roof of the coach and directed
the coachman to the Strand. "We'll wait for him in his own
lair. Might be a while, though. I say we fetch food and drink
on the way."

~~~

Sergeant Pierce had suggested to Fellows that they go back to
Richmond to reexamine the scene of the crime, but Fellows
negated the idea. As he'd contemplated before, this was a
crime of Mayfair. The players, and the answer, lay in that section of London.

Fellows began by visiting the Bishop of Hargate's father,
the Earl of Norwell, in Norwell's Berkeley Square house. Norwell didn't want to see Fellows, the butler informed them
when he answered the front door. He also said that Fellows
and Pierce should have gone down the stairs to enter the house
via the kitchen.

Fellows did tell Pierce to go down—it never hurt to culti-
vate those below stairs and learn the household gossip—but
Fellows remained squarely in the doorway.

"Tell his lordship that if he wishes me to find and arrest his
son's killer, and quickly, he'll speak to me," Fellows said to the
butler.

The man looked aggrieved, but at last he obeyed. Pierce
sketched a cheerful salute and departed for the kitchen.

The Earl of Norwell kept Fellows waiting in a reception
room for at least half an hour before the butler returned and led
Fellows up a flight of stairs to a study lined with books. The
room's high walls held a second floor of bookcases, reached by
an iron spiral staircase.

Norwell looked much like his dead son, handsome and lean,
though twenty years older. His hair was gray, his belly gone to
fat from too much rich food and too much port, his black
mourning suit making his pale face more sallow.

Norwell ran his gaze up and down Fellows, obviously not liking what he saw. "So you're old Kilmorgan's by-blow."

Fellows made a shallow bow, hiding the sting. "I have that honor."

Norwell grunted. "You look like him. Kilmorgan was a mean son of a bitch, and the current duke is no better."

Fellows took this stoically. He'd come to like Hart more and more as he got to know him, but he knew he'd waste his breath defending him to Norwell. Norwell was the sort of man who made his judgments and stuck to them, come hell or high water.

"How can speaking to me help you catch a murderer?" Norwell asked. "It was the Scranton bitch who did it, and we all know it. That entire family is mad."

Fellows clenched his jaw to keep his temper. "New evidence has come to light that tells me it was not Lady Louisa."

"What evidence? You're lying. The only reason you haven't arrested her is that she's connected with the Mackenzies, and you have an absurd loyalty to them."

"No, Lord Norwell," Fellows said in a hard voice. "I'm after the truth, no matter what. One reason I came here today is that I'd like to look over your son's bedchamber. His valet told me he often stayed in this house when he'd be in Town only briefly and didn't want to bother opening up his own flat. Is that correct?"

Norwell looked Fellows over again, neither agreeing nor disagreeing. "You're a bit above yourself, aren't you, Chief Inspector? You might be a duke's son, but you're still a bastard."

"Which has nothing to do with me looking at your son's rooms."

Norwell heaved a sigh. "What are you searching for?"

"I'll know that when I find it."

"This is ridiculous."

"I'm leaving no stone unturned," Fellows said firmly. "I want this killer found as quickly as you do and so am looking into every possibility. Don't worry, I will do no damage to your son's things, and leave everything as I found it."

Norwell again looked Fellows up and down, in the most condescending way possible. He heaved another sigh, this one sounding as though it came from his toes, turned away, and pushed a bell on the desk. The butler entered almost immediately—Fellows suspected the man had been listening outside the door.

"Take the inspector up to Frederick's old rooms," Norwell said. "Stay there with him, and don't let him steal anything."

Fellows didn't react at all to the statement. Norwell was grieving—Fellows allowed that. Otherwise, he'd be tempted to punch the man in the mouth. Fellows made himself turn his back and follow the butler out of the library without a word.

The butler led him up another flight of stairs. As they entered a large, dim bedchamber, Fellows bade him go down and tell Sergeant Pierce to come up. No one searched a room better than Pierce. He could find nooks and crannies that most missed, and he could do it rapidly and thoroughly. Fellows had always suspected that Pierce, in his youth, might have been a thief, but he'd never asked directly.

The butler looked put out, but he went. Slowly. The stairs creaked, one at a time, as he descended.

Fellows pulled open the heavy curtains, letting cleansing sunlight into the too-dark room. The room was musty— Norwell must have shut it up at his son's death and not allowed anyone in. Grieving people often wanted to hide away their loved ones' belongings.

The chamber was elegantly furnished, as befitting this Berkeley Square mansion. A tester bed with brocade draperies held prominence, a sofa stood near the fireplace, a writing table was positioned near the window, and a bookshelf full of leather-bound volumes took up part of one wall. Thick carpets covered the floor, and a dressing room with a wardrobe and a tall mirror opened off the main room.

Fellows took advantage of the butler's absence to start going through the writing table. He pulled out drawers, sorted through the few letters he found, and turned the drawers upside down to look for anything hidden beneath. He finished soon, the contents disappointingly sparse. Hargate's recent correspondence had been in his flat in Piccadilly, which Fellows had read when he'd searched there, but he'd found nothing of interest. Fellows wasn't certain what he hoped to find here, in Hargate's boyhood bedroom, but it was the one place Fellows hadn't searched yet.

By the time Fellows heard Pierce's step on the stairs, he

was under the large bed, looking beneath the slats for hidden treasures. Nothing.

Fellows crawled out and brushed himself off, and was on his feet pulling out books from the bookcase by the time Pierce and the butler arrived. Pierce, who prided himself on his forthrightness, shut the door in the butler's face. "Fetch us some tea, there's a good chap," he called through the door. "And coffee for the Chief Inspector. He don't like tea." He turned away and surveyed the room. "Anything, guv?"

"Nothing yet. See what you can make of it."

Pierce went to work. Fellows trusted his sergeant's skill, and for good reason. Pierce could feel every corner of a pillow without cutting it open, tell if a mattress or featherbed held any secrets. He checked every inch of wainscoting and the paneling around the windows, tested bricks of the fireplace, turned over chairs, and patted the curtains to see if anything resided between drapery and liner or inside the hems. Pierce flipped carpets up and tested floorboards, then went through the books and examined their bindings.

Undaunted by finding nothing, Pierce entered the dressing room. Fellows continued to look through the letters he'd taken from the drawer. Presently the banging and rustling in the dressing room stopped, and Pierce said, "Eureka, sir."

Fellows didn't get his hopes up. This had been Hargate's room when he'd been a young man living at home. Pierce might have found nothing more than a university lad's old stash of cigarettes or malt whiskey.

Pierce was crouching on the floor in the dressing room, having folded back the carpet. He'd lifted a loose board from the floor and now pulled out a square box that had been resting on the joists beneath.

The box was locked, but the lock was small and decorative, more to keep out those who would have respected his privacy anyway. Fellows put the box on the dressing table, took out a blunt tin nail he kept for such occasions, and quickly forced open the lock.

Would he find cheroots and love poems to long-ago schoolgirls? Fellows's heart beat faster as he lifted the lid.

He found a notebook. He took it out, noting that it was clean and crisp. Almost new.

"Ah," Pierce said. "Wonderful things, notebooks. Can tell you so much about a chap. His personal thoughts. Locked in a box under the floorboards."

Fellows sat down on the chair at the dressing table and opened the notebook. As he'd suspected, it wasn't a straightforward, written journal of everything the bishop had been up to, whom he'd angered, and who wanted to kill him. It was a series of cryptic notes, but Hargate had been kind enough to date them. He'd made the last entry the morning of the garden party.

"Bring the box," Fellows said grimly. "We're taking this."

Chapter 14

Lloyd Fellows's flat was in a lane off the Strand in a respectable house that retained some of the elegance of the past. The landlady was gracious enough to let Louisa and Daniel upstairs to Fellows's rooms once Daniel explained who they were—and charmed her with his smiles and youthful innocence. He portrayed innocence very well.

The flat had four rooms—a sitting room which doubled as a dining room, a small office with a cluttered desk, and a bedroom with a bath chamber beyond. Daniel solved Louisa's problem of wondering if she would ever dare enter Fellows's bedroom by opening the door and barging in himself. Of course, Louisa had to follow to make sure he stayed out of mischief.

"He won't mind," Daniel said. "I come here all the time for a bit of a chat. Ah, there it is." He picked up a book from Fellows's bedside table. "I lent him this a while ago. Thought it might be in here."

Louisa gave him a sharp look. It would be just like Daniel to pretend he'd given Fellows the book in order to have an excuse for snooping in the man's bedroom.

She ought to tell him they should leave the room and close

the door. But Louisa stood in the middle of it, absorbing everything about Lloyd Fellows.

His bed was large, with low posts and no hangings. Neatly made, the pillows plump, a quilt folded across the bottom. Louisa wondered if his mother had sewn the quilt.

The room was small, most of it taken up with the bed. Fellows didn't have many decorative touches, except a few photographs in frames on top of the high dresser. Louisa moved to look at them.

One photo was of his mother, taken when she was younger. Louisa had met Mrs. Fellows at informal Mackenzie gatherings—the photograph showed she'd been vivacious and pretty when younger, and her eyes held shrewd intelligence, much like her son's.

Another photo was a full-length portrait of a very young Lloyd, in his policeman's uniform, probably taken when he'd first joined the force. He stood stiffly, proud, his helmet tucked under his arm.

The third photograph was of Louisa.

Louisa looked quickly behind her, but Daniel was busy flipping through the book he'd found. Louisa turned back to the photo, her heart hammering.

The photograph was a casual one, taken by Eleanor during one of Louisa's visits to Kilmorgan—Eleanor enjoyed taking photographs and developing them herself. Louisa stood in the garden at Kilmorgan Castle, sunlight on her face, climbing roses around her. The sepia photo showed the roses as white, but in reality they were very light pink. Louisa's hair looked a shade of brown instead of bright red, her dress darker than the pretty green it had been, but overall, the photograph was a good one. Because Eleanor was skilled at photography, Louisa wasn't standing ramrod-stiff, her face and eyes washed out from the light, but was smiling, her pose natural.

How the photograph had gotten onto the dresser in Lloyd Fellows's London bedchamber, Louisa had no idea. Eleanor might have given him a copy. Or perhaps Daniel, who'd just ingenuously said that he'd been here many times before, had.

Louisa bit her lip as she turned around. The open door beyond the bed led into his bathroom, where she told herself she wouldn't go. But the window gave full light into the little room, showing her a mug and shaving brush on his washstand, towels neatly hung, a large bathtub with a tap. Fellows was a very tidy man, or else the landlady provided a competent maid. Nothing was out of place.

Louisa wanted to enter the bathroom and touch the shaving brush, an object of masculinity. She wanted to connect to Lloyd through it, feel again his strength, heat, the weight of him on her.

She'd never erase the imprint of his mouth on hers, the taste of him on her tongue. And she wanted more than kisses. Last night, if the constable hadn't arrived, Louisa would have let Fellows carry their passion on the desk to its conclusion. She'd have slid off her drawers and raked up her skirts, welcoming him into her arms and inside her body.

Louisa, who should go to her marriage bed a virgin, would have thrown virtue aside for the joy of being with Lloyd at least once. By the social rules she lived by, Louisa would then have had to withdraw herself from the marriage mart after that, because no man wanted to discover on the wedding night that his bride was soiled goods.

But Louisa would not have cared. Even now she felt nothing but deep regret that they'd been interrupted.

"We should wait for him in the sitting room," Louisa said abruptly.

Daniel looked up. "Eh?" He closed the book and shrugged. "Just as you like."

Daniel led the way back to the sitting room, and Louisa made herself shut the door of the enticing chamber behind them.

Fellows walked home in the dark, his thoughts piling one on top of the other. Hargate's notebook had revealed much. Fellows had left the book in its box firmly under lock and key at the Yard, but Fellows's notes on it burned in his pocket, waiting for him to have the time to sit and go over them.

He might be lost in thought, but Fellows knew the placement of every single person on the street with him as well as those lurking in dark passages, what they were doing, and, if he'd seen them before, who they were. Those he hadn't seen before, he made a note of in the back of his mind to look for again.

Denizens of the night always left Fellows alone, however. Though he wore a suit no different from that of any other businessman returning home late from work, somehow even those who knew nothing about him stayed far from him. Fellows was trouble, they sensed, and they didn't want to deal with that much trouble.

Fellows let himself into the house with his key, walked up the quiet stairs, and used his flat key to open the door to his sitting room.

Daniel looked up from the sofa where he'd been reading a book. He didn't spring to his feet, because Louisa was dozing next to him, her head on Daniel's shoulder.

Fellows stopped in the act of dropping his hat to a chair. Louisa was so serenely beautiful, her face flushed, her body limp against Daniel's, her red curls across her cheek.

Fellows drew a sharp breath as he imagined her head on *his* shoulder, better still, on his pillow with him lying next to her. The vision was so sharp, so desirable, that he couldn't move. He needed it to be true.

Daniel touched her shoulder. "Louisa."

Louisa frowned in her sleep, moved against his arm, then she opened her eyes. She stared in puzzlement at Fellows a moment, then she came fully awake, and sat up, pushing her hair from her face.

Fellows closed the door behind him. "You can't be here."

Daniel put his book aside and got to his feet. "A fine way to greet your family."

Fellows finally set his hat on the chair, stripped off his gloves, and dropped them on top of the hat. "I meant Louisa. She can't be seen anywhere near me until this investigation is closed."

Louisa rose, still trying to press her hair back into place. Fellows wanted to tell her it looked much better mussed—he wanted to go to her and muss it some more.

"I am in the room with you, Chief Inspector," she said. "You may tell me directly that you want me to go."

Fellows fixed his gaze on her and her alone, and wished he hadn't. "I want you to go."

"Not yet," Daniel said. "We didn't come for a social call. We came to tell you something."

Fellows still looked at Louisa. Her gown today was a brown broadcloth she'd covered with a jacket of burnt orange, autumn colors that went with her pale skin and red hair. She was a confection he wanted to eat.

It took a moment before Fellows realized Louisa was speaking to him, her eyes full of anger. "The Bishop of Hargate was blackmailing Mrs. Leigh-Waters. I told you he tried to blackmail me into marrying him, but I've learned that he also tried to blackmail Daniel."

"I know," Fellows said.

Louisa stopped, surprise pushing aside her anger. "You know? How?"

"Not about Daniel." Fellows shot his nephew a look, which Daniel returned with a guileless one. "But I know about Mrs. Leigh-Waters."

"This is interesting," Daniel said. "Was Hargate blackmailing any others?"

"I'm not discussing the case with you, Daniel."

"No?"

"No." But Daniel was perceptive. Hargate's book, once Fellows had deciphered his somewhat simplistic letter and number substitution code, showed he'd carried on an active round of blackmailing. A few of his victims, besides Mrs. Leigh-Waters, had been at the garden party. "The murderer doesn't need to know in advance what line of inquiry I'm taking," he said to Daniel.

"Of course not," Louisa said, sounding reasonable. "We should let the chief inspector do his job, Danny."

"Yes," Fellows said dryly. "Please do." He stepped aside and signaled with a wave of his hand that they should go.

Daniel didn't move. "If you're thinking of Mrs. Leigh-Waters as the murderer, I don't think she did it, if my opinion is worth anything," he said. "I don't think she'd have the courage."

"Nor do I," Louisa added. Her belief in the woman was clear in her eyes. "And there's the question of the poison—how it got into the tea, or at least the teacup, without Mrs. Leigh-Waters being there to make sure the right person drank it."

"Yes," Fellows said slowly. Louisa's words made the part

of his thoughts still tangled in the case begin to work. "And I think that's it."

Daniel and Louisa looked blank. "What?" Louisa asked.

"The answer to the entire problem."

"Ah," Daniel said. "You know how it was done?"

"Not yet. But I have possibilities to check. I planned to think about it tonight, alone, and then ponder while I sleep. I need sleep." Fellows hadn't gotten any the night before, that was certain.

Daniel looked resigned but nodded at him. "We'll leave ye to it, then. Except you have to tell us what you discover. We're pining to know."

"I'll send you a telegram," Fellows said in his dry voice. He opened the door. "Thank you for the information. Good night."

"Right you are." Daniel held out his arm to Louisa. "Auntie?"

Louisa didn't look at him. "I'd like to remain a moment, Daniel."

"No," Fellows said immediately. If Louisa stayed in his rooms, with his bedchamber steps away, he'd never be able to let her out again.

"Daniel," Louisa said.

"I shouldn't let you," Daniel said. "I'm the chaperone, you know."

"He is right," Fellows said to Louisa. "You can't stay up here with me."

"For heaven's sake, he can wait outside the door, which you may keep unlocked. If Daniel hears me scream, he will rush in to my rescue. I need to speak with you."

Fellows's hand stilled on the doorknob. He could not let her stay, blast the woman. But she stood stubbornly, as though rooting herself to the floor.

Daniel decided for them. Because neither Fellows nor Louisa moved, Daniel picked up his hat and gloves and walked out past Fellows, the hem of his kilt swinging.

"I'll be kicking my heels at the end of the hall," he said. "Shout when you're ready, Louisa."

Fellows remained at the door, holding it open. "Daniel, she can't stay."

"Best humor her," Daniel said. "Else she gets terse, and I'll have to ride all the way to Isabella's with her like that. Do me a favor and let her speak her piece."

Fellows had no sympathy. But he knew Louisa wouldn't budge unless he lifted her over his shoulder and carried her out. And if he touched her, he'd carry her straight to the bedroom.

Daniel grinned and turned away as Fellows finally swung the door shut. Fellows heard him whistling in the hall.

"Begin," Fellows said to Louisa. "Then leave."

He kept himself beside the door. Safer there—the entire sitting room lay between him and her.

Louisa wore brown leather gloves that hugged her fingers. Fellows couldn't stop his imagination putting those gloved hands on his bare chest, feeling the cool leather on his hot skin. She'd move her hands down across his abdomen, roving to the hardness that strained for her.

"Why do you have my photo in your bedchamber?" Louisa asked.

Fellows started, pushing his fantasies aside. Louisa looked at him expressionlessly, without anger, or disgust, scorn, or any other emotion he'd expect her to have. He kept a picture of her without her knowledge, and she only asked him about it in a calm voice. *How* she'd discovered he had it, Fellows hadn't the slightest doubt.

"I will throttle Daniel Mackenzie," he said.

"You have three photographs on your dresser," Louisa said slowly. "One of your mother, one of yourself in your police uniform. Natural enough. And you have me."

Any lie would sound ridiculous. There was no reason in the world Fellows should have her photograph, except one.

"I don't often see you," he said. "I have the photo so I can look at you in the stretches of time between."

She regarded him in silence a moment, as though considering his answer. "Did Eleanor give it to you?"

"She did."

"Did you ask her for it?"

"No," Fellows said. "But when she offered it, I didn't refuse."

Louisa swallowed, the movement faint in her slender throat. "I, on the other hand, have no photograph of you."

"I don't often have one taken. Haven't in years."

"Eleanor would do it," Louisa said.

"No doubt."

Another pause. Shakespeare would have had trouble writing this play. His characters talked and talked, spilling out streams of poesy. So many words, when silence spoke volumes.

"That photograph of me was taken a year ago," Louisa said. "Just after Eleanor and Hart's wedding."

"I believe so, yes."

"You've had it all this time." Louisa lost her frozen stance and stepped forward. "You've had it all this time, and you've not said a word. You haven't said *anything*."

"Would it have done any good?"

"I think it would have done the world of good." Louisa's voice increased in volume. "But how could I know? How can I know anything of what you're thinking? You hide so much."

Fellows came out of his rigidity. "I don't have much of a chance to speak to you, do I? Every time I see you, you're at a party of some kind, surrounded by friends, laughing with them. You're where you belong. You're part of their world, with people you understand, and I am not."

"What are you talking about?" She glared at him. "You are in that world now. You're part of the Mackenzie family. They've welcomed you with open arms."

"They have, yes." His tone went ironic. "They've been adamant to erase the part of my life when I lived in penury. Their remorse is touching. The only one not wallowing in guilt is Ian, because I don't think he understands the meaning of the word."

Louisa flushed. "Do you think *I'm* wallowing in guilt?"

"You feel sorry for me, Louisa. You've told me."

Her face reddened further. "You think I've kissed you out of *pity*?"

"You might believe otherwise, but yes."

"Is that what you truly think? That I'd be so . . . *patronizing*?"

"Aren't you?" Fellows knew he made her angry, but maybe if she grew furious enough she'd go, and stay away from him. "You told me once that I looked as though I needed cheering up. Poor Inspector Fellows—like a beggar standing outside the window, gazing at a feast he's not allowed to have." He'd felt that way often enough as a lad, especially the day he'd watched the boy Hart climb back into the sumptuous Mackenzie carriage and ride away with their father. Fellows had been left behind, outraged and bereft, and dragged off to a police station. That was the day he'd decided to become a policeman.

Louisa's eyes were starry with anger. "How can you say that? How can you know *anything* about my feelings for you? You've never bothered to ask me!"

"I don't remember you bothering to ask *me* before you coaxed me onto a ladder with you, or dragged me under the mistletoe."

Louisa moved to him, halting close enough to him that he could breathe in her scent. Dangerous. "I don't recall *you* pushing *me* away," she said.

Was she mad? "Dear God, what sane man would? There you were, beautiful and wanting to kiss me. Last night you wrapped your arms around me and pulled me down to my desk with you. Only a saint would push you away, and I assure you, I am no saint."

Louisa took a breath, pulling her voice down from a shout. "Why are you trying to make me angry? You are being deliberately cruel. Why?"

"Because you can't be here. I said that when I came in. We can't be together, Louisa. No declarations, nothing." Fellows tried to speak steadily. "If anyone discovers me even talking to you, the investigation will be compromised. I'll be pulled from the case and a detective assigned to it who cares nothing for truth, only for arrests and convictions."

She looked puzzled. "But I'm not the only suspect now. Hargate was a blackmailer, with many other victims. You said you had ideas."

"And by your own admission, Hargate was blackmailing *you*. You still had a motive, still are a very good suspect. So until this investigation is over, we don't see each other, we don't speak. If I have anything more to ask you regarding Hargate, I'll send Sergeant Pierce to you. Do you understand?"

"Well enough." Another of the small silences fell. "What about when the investigation is over?"

"I don't know." Fellows drew a breath. "There is still . . . I don't know."

"And yet, you have my photograph."

They looked at each other a long moment. Everything spoken and unspoken hovered between them, waiting to be shattered.

Then Fellows moved around and past her, making himself give her a wide berth. He strode to the bedchamber, slammed inside it, grabbed the small photo from the dresser, and slammed out again.

He thrust the photograph at her. "Take it."

Louisa didn't reach for it. "Why? It's yours."

"Take it." Fellows grabbed her wrist, pulled her gloved hand to him, and slapped the framed photo into it. "Give it back to Eleanor, keep it for yourself, give it to Mr. Franklin. I don't give a damn."

"You're horrible."

"Yes, I am. Best you know that. Now get out."

Louisa stared at him, her mouth open, red lips moist. It was all Fellows could do not to sweep her up, deposit her on the sofa, strip off her clothes, and have her. Now. Hang the investigation.

And then Louisa might truly hang. No, Fellows would never let that happen. Even if he had to stay away from her from this point forward, let her marry another man, and never see her again, he'd do it to keep her from harm. Louisa's life was worth far more to him than his own happiness.

Louisa didn't hurry to obey. She looked up at Fellows for a long time, then clutched the photograph to her chest.

"I'll go," she said in her quiet voice. "I understand how it will look for the investigation if it's thought we are having a liaison. But I won't stay away forever."

"When that time comes, no doubt we'll argue again," Fellows said.

"Do plan on it." Louisa turned from him, snatching up the hat she'd left on a side table. "When I hear someone else has been found to be the culprit, I'll seek you out again. I doubt you'll send *me* word, so I won't wait for it." She dropped the photograph into her pocket, thrust the hat onto her head, and turned to the mirror to stab two hatpins through the hat's crown.

Fellows watched her, mesmerized, as Louisa turned back to him, the hat perfectly in place. She gave him a last glare then marched past him and out the door without a good-bye. Despite her words, the slam of the door behind her spoke of finality.

~~~~~

Fellows spent the next two days frantically going over his notes, questioning those he felt should be reexamined, including Mrs. Leigh-Waters and the interesting reason Hargate had blackmailed her. She'd had an affair a dozen years ago, the notebook said. The affair had ended, Mrs. Leigh-Waters told Fellows tearfully. The gentleman in question had married and gone to live in Boston with his American wife, and they never corresponded. But her husband had never learned of it.

Hargate had somehow found out and decided to torment her about it. Hargate had found out many things about many people. He'd used the leverage over them to obtain money, favors, positions, and his bishopric.

Any number of people might have wanted to kill Hargate, yes, Fellows thought in frustration. But only one of them had figured out how to put the poison into the right teacup.

By Monday morning, Fellows had not uncovered who. At least, not with enough evidence to convince Chief Superintendent Kenton.

Fellows was ordered to take the train to Newmarket. A police van drove him to King's Cross station, a constable making sure he boarded. Kenton, understanding Fellows's desperation, said he wouldn't officially assign Inspector Harrison to the case until Fellows returned. Fellows would have until after the races to come up with an answer. But he had to go to Newmarket.

When Fellows arrived in Newmarket, the entire Mackenzie brood already there, the horse-mad aristos of England were abuzz with the latest gossip. The Honorable Gilbert Franklin had proposed to Lady Louisa Scranton, and wedding bells were sure to ring before midsummer.

Chapter 15

Louisa loved the racing season, loved traveling with Cameron Mackenzie and his growing family to Epsom Downs, Newmarket, Goodwood, Doncaster. The Mackenzies had a private box in the stands at each course, usually full of the family cheering on Cameron's horses.

All the Mackenzies had gathered for this Newmarket race, including the duke and duchess. The children had come to Newmarket as well, though they were currently at the hired house under the watchful eyes of their nannies. Cameron, Daniel's father, tall and harsh-voiced, stayed in the box only a short time, impatient to get back to his horses. Cameron bore a deep scar on his cheek, evidence of his former unhappiness. Louisa watched Cam's second wife, Ainsley, rise on her tiptoes to kiss that scar before he left. Softness flashed into Cameron's eyes, and the look he gave Ainsley was full of heat and fierce joy.

Cameron left the box, pausing to say something to Daniel on his way out. Daniel laughed out loud, looking exactly like his father in that moment.

"Excellent weather for it," Gilbert Franklin said next to Louisa.

Eleanor had enthusiastically invited Gil to attend the races with them. Isabella, when informed, had been less than pleased. Izzy had been cool to Gil since he'd called at the Mount Street house the morning after Louisa's encounter in Fellows's flat. Gil had asked to speak to Louisa alone and then proposed to her, even going down on his knees to do it.

Weeks ago, Isabella had been happy to help Louisa with her idea of using the Season to try to find a husband. Now that Gil, the perfect match, had made it clear he wanted Louisa to be his wife, Izzy barely stopped shy of snubbing him. That she didn't approve was obvious.

Gil put his warm hand on Louisa's arm, and her shaking started again. Every time Gil touched her, Louisa trembled. Any other woman might believe herself madly in love, half swooning at the touch of her beloved, but Louisa knew better. She shook because she felt as though she'd boarded a wrong train, and that train was rocketing off into the wilderness, no way to stop it.

When Louisa saw the unmistakable form of Lloyd Fellows approach Cameron near the track below, she became suddenly sick to her stomach.

"Are you all right, my dear?" Gil asked her in concern.

She really should be more grateful to him, she knew. Gil was like clear water, soothing, never troubling. Louisa ought to be glad, after all the upsets in her life, to lie still and let the water trickle over her.

Fellows, on the other hand, was fire. Fire burned. Even the spark of him was enough to sear her to the bone. Louisa always hurt when she was with Fellows, and merely looking at him talking to Cameron made her ache.

Fire and water. Water should put out the fire and ease the pain. Then again, fire that was hot enough jumped over water and continued its destruction.

The next race began, and Louisa tried to pull her attention to it. One of Cameron's horses was running in it, as well as horses he trained that belonged to other gentlemen. Cameron never bet on his own animals, but the other Mackenzies usually had a flutter. Cameron's horses were always short odds to win, but it was fun to wager a little. Today, Gil had gone down to the bookmakers and put money on all the races for him and for Louisa.

Gil didn't sit so close to Louisa that he would cause a scandal, but he did keep his arm near hers, so that their shoulders were nearly touching. When he turned to her and smiled, it was like the sun coming out. Louisa ought to be deliriously happy.

The horses started. The crowd surged to its feet, including everyone in the Mackenzie box, and the noise began. Ian was the only one who didn't cheer on the horses, but he held his hands ready to clap when his wife did. He still didn't entirely understand the concept of cheering and clapping, but he'd learned to mimic, so others would not point out his eccentricities. Beth cued him these days, her gentle guidance helping him over many a rough moment.

Cameron's horse, Night-Blooming Jasmine, running in the mare's race, easily pulled ahead of the others. Jasmine ran as though she could do this all day, then perhaps have a romp in the pasture afterward before going home to enjoy a good grooming. The other horses sprinted to catch up to her, but Jasmine leisurely galloped around the track, pulling even farther ahead in the last furlong. She finished first by a long measure.

The Mackenzie box exploded with noise, Daniel and Mac standing on the railings and shouting the loudest. Ian abandoned clapping to put his arm around Beth and give her a hard squeeze. Beth was more important to him than a horse winning a race.

"I had no doubt," Ainsley said, smiling. "Jaz is a wonderful horse." She credited Jasmine with helping her and Cameron through their rough courtship.

"An excellent win." Gil abandoned propriety to slide his arm around Louisa's waist. "A little something to feather our nest, eh?"

Isabella, standing on Louisa's other side, gave Gil a formidable frown. Gil assumed she was unhappy about the arm around Louisa's waist, and withdrew, sending Isabella an apologetic grin.

"I'm very thirsty," Isabella announced. "Louisa, will you accompany me to the tea tent?"

Mac turned around to her. "No need to bestir yourself, my love. Danny and I will rush down and procure for you anything you wish. You too, Louisa; ladies."

Isabella's cold look dissolved into a smile. She touched

Mac's face, the love in her eyes beautiful to see. "No thank you, Mac. I am making an excuse to take a stroll and speak to my sister. We're going to gab like mindless females."

Mac raised his hands. "Far be it from me to stand in the way of that."

"Beth, come with us," Louisa said quickly. Isabella was going to scold, she knew it, but Louisa might avoid the worst of it if Beth came along to mitigate.

"If it's all the same, I'd rather not." Beth fanned herself. She didn't look tired, but she also didn't like to rush about too much these days.

"I'll come," Ainsley said. She gave Gil a smile when he bowed and helped her across the box to where Louisa and Isabella waited. "Eleanor will make certain you aren't abandoned, Mr. Franklin."

"Indeed." Eleanor moved from her seat and to the one next to Gil. "We will have ever so much to talk about, now that you want to become part of the family."

Hart sent his wife a suspicious glance, and Louisa seconded it. Whenever Eleanor got that mischievous look in her eyes, there was no telling what she'd say or do. Fortunately Hart would be near to quell her if necessary—or to try to quell her, at least. The only person who didn't tremble and obey the mighty Hart the instant he growled was Eleanor.

Isabella pulled Louisa and Ainsley away, and the three of them left the box to pick their way down the stairs to the tea tents below. Louisa reflected that she never wanted to see another tea tent in her life, but Isabella had her arm firmly through Louisa's, and there was nothing for it but to follow and find out what she wanted.

The tea tent they reached was full, ladies in their finest gowns and beautiful hats greeting each other as though it hadn't been only a day or two since they'd been together in London. They chatted while filling their plates with pastries, finger sandwiches, petit fours, scones and clotted cream.

As Louisa walked in with Isabella on one side, Ainsley on the other, ladies paused, ceased talking, watched. They didn't quite cut Louisa, but they didn't greet her openly either.

Louisa heard the whispers begin as Isabella escorted her to the food tables. "Gilbert Franklin actually proposed to her.

Would he marry her if he thought her a poisoner, do you think?" "All I say is, he'd better be careful when he drinks his morning tea." Titters. Laughter.

Izzy said nothing to anyone, and kept Louisa close. Ainsley, on the other hand, greeted ladies and waved to friends, behaving as though no one openly and rudely discussed Louisa.

Isabella stayed with Louisa as they loaded their plates. Louisa lifted a profiterole onto a dainty flowered plate and flashed back to holding a similar plate with a cream puff at Mrs. Leigh-Waters's party. She'd been looking at the profiterole when Hargate had started to choke and gasp. She shivered.

Ladies who seemed to decide they didn't want to risk offending Ainsley and Isabella, the wives of the influential Mackenzies, ventured to engage them in conversation, and Louisa was left relatively alone.

Louisa wondered anew why Isabella had brought her down here. To help her overcome her fear of tea tents? Or to make her face the ladies who stared at her?

She took a determined sip of tea. Then Louisa set down her cup, snatched her pastry from her plate, and took a large bite.

Cream slithered out of the soft crust and smeared across her mouth. Of course it did. Louisa reached for a handkerchief and found Isabella no longer by her side. Ainsley either. They had become swallowed by friends and acquaintances, absorbed into the chattering mass.

Louisa did see Lloyd Fellows look into the tea tent, lock his gaze to her, give her the barest nod, and then turn away.

Drat it. He had to choose that moment to spy her, didn't he? When she had cream smeared across her lips, her eyes wide as she looked frantically about for Isabella.

Other ladies were staring at her, and their gazes were not friendly. She heard someone say behind her, "Shame on Mr. Franklin for leaving better girls in the starting gate."

Louisa slammed the plate to the table and walked out of the tea tent, scrubbing her mouth with her handkerchief. Ladies parted to let her pass, their hostile looks barely veiled.

She emerged to see Inspector Fellows heading for the stables. Louisa kept a good distance and part of the crowd between her and him as she followed, pretending she was doing nothing more than wandering about looking at horses.

Had Louisa understood his minute signal that she was to follow him? Or had it been her wishful thinking? She'd welcome the chance to explain to him about Gil. The situation was not what Fellows thought—what anyone thought. Fellows would understand, perhaps, but only if she had a chance to speak to him.

Fellows walked into the far end of one of the long rows of stables. Few people lingered there—a couple of grooms were leading horses out, but that was all. The bulk of the spectators, owners, trainers, and jockeys were in the stands or on the track.

No one bothered about one stray lady in pale yellow as she crossed behind horse vans and stable blocks and ducked into the last stable yard. This stable block wasn't much in use—a few horses poked their heads over the stall doors as Louisa entered, curious as to who was coming to see them.

The peace and coolness of the stables started to soothe her. Louisa loved horses. As a child, she'd sought refuge in the barns whenever her lessons in deportment drove her mad, or when the household was too busy making a fuss over Isabella to pay attention to Louisa. No one had much noticed where Louisa had gone.

She spied Fellows. He stood at the end of the line of loose boxes, his hand on a horse's nose. He was talking to the animal, the horse basking in his attention.

Louisa walked toward him, heels clicking on the cobbles. Fellows heard her, turned, and scowled formidably. He didn't call out; he waited until she neared him, then he walked away from her into an open, empty stall.

He knew Louisa would follow. She ducked inside the stall to find him standing on freshly strewn hay, his arms folded, eyes glinting in the dim light. *Fire.*

The shade of the stall was soothing. So were the scent of horses, the pungent smell of feed, and the mellower smells of leather and soap.

"Did anyone see you?" Fellows asked.

"No. I was careful."

"Good."

"Then I was right," she said. "You wanted me to follow you?"

"Yes. I need to talk to you. About Franklin. You can't marry him."

His gruff tone made her heart beat faster. At the same time, her anger rose. "I see. Do the police approve all marriages now?"

"Only yours. You are engaged to him?"

His voice was calm, but full of rage. Louisa looked into his hazel eyes to find the fire high.

"No," Louisa said. She wanted him to know. "The truth is, Gil did propose. I admit I didn't discourage him from asking. He'd spoken to my mother and my cousin before he called on me. Such an old-fashioned gentleman, don't you think? They were delighted."

"And were *you* delighted?" Fellows watched her closely.

Louisa rubbed her arms, suddenly chilled. "It was very kind of him. Considering my current notoriety, it was brave of him to declare his intentions. But in all honesty—and no one but the family knows this—I haven't given him my answer yet. So no, I am not officially engaged to him."

Fellows lost his stiffness in an instant. "Thank God." The words flowed with relief.

Louisa regarded him in surprise. "I thought you'd be pleased to hear I was engaged. That would keep tongues from wagging about me and you, wouldn't it? And prevent you being taken off the investigation. I am letting people believe as they wish until I give Gil my final answer."

"Why the devil should I be pleased?" His rage was back. "Use the betrothal as a blind if you want, but tell him no. You can't marry Gilbert Franklin."

"Why not? I believe you made it clear that you and I are not suited. Never will be. That you have no intention of trying to make us suit." Louisa unlaced her arms to pick at her tight gloves. "You made it painfully clear."

"This has nothing to do with what is between you and me. You can't marry Franklin for the very simple reason that he is already married."

Louisa had drawn a breath, ready to argue, then the breath lodged in her throat. *"What?"*

Fellows gave her a grim nod. "The Not-So-Honorable Mr. Franklin about six years ago married a woman in a village outside Rome. He has four children by her."

Louisa staggered. She reached her hand out to the board

wall to steady herself. Not enough support. She turned to put her back against it.

"Four children . . . No, that can't be. You must be mistaken. You must have the wrong Mr. Franklin."

"It's not a mistake." The words were flat, final.

"But . . ." Louisa wet her lips, finding a bit of cream she hadn't managed to wipe away. "Good heavens, why didn't you tell me before this? I've been considering accepting Gil's offer. *Seriously* considering it, because *you* gave me no hope."

"I didn't know until yesterday evening. I ordered Sergeant Pierce to find out everything he could about Franklin, especially after his name turned up in Hargate's notebook of sinners. I only had the telegrams from Rome last night. A copy of a parish register will follow in the post. Franklin married her all right. Legally. She's the daughter of a farmer. But I suppose an earl's son knew he needed a more acceptable bride to please his family and friends."

Louisa remained against the wall, unable to make herself stand. Part of her continued to argue. The Roman police had to be wrong. Fellows was wrong. It must be a mistake.

But Louisa knew Lloyd Fellows. He was thorough. He would not make a statement like this until he was absolutely certain of its truth.

Disbelief fled, and along came anger. Louisa balled her fists. "That absolute *rat!*" She pushed herself off the wall and started to pace. "How *dare* he? To think, I felt *sorry* for him!"

Her agitated walking brought her up against Fellows, or maybe he'd stepped in front of her. He stood quietly, a rock she could cling to, a calm in the storm.

"And you say Hargate was *blackmailing* him?" Louisa asked. "Bloody hell." The expletive came out—from Louisa, who'd been raised to never dream of swearing. "I can scarce believe it. Devil take all men." She looked up at Fellows, who watched her from his solid height. "And you!" Her fists came up, and she thumped them once to his chest. "You made me fall in love with you. You made me start to believe you cared for me in return, and then you pushed me away. And I don't mean because you were worried about risking the investigation. You implied that, even after the investigation was over, there'd be no hope. How dare you?"

She pummeled him a few times, but he didn't move, didn't flinch. When Louisa wound down, Fellows said, "In love."

The words were flat, calm, as though he was too stunned to put more emotion behind them.

"Yes, in love. Good heavens, why else would I chase you about and throw myself at you like a ninny? I convinced myself I wanted a respectable marriage—to save my family's reputation and to keep from being pitied, I thought. But I lied to myself. Pursuing a marriage was only an excuse to forget about *you*. But then you started to let me hope. And *then* you took that hope away."

Louisa's fists moved again, and Fellows grabbed her flailing hands.

"Louisa. Stop." He frowned down at her, his hazel eyes holding something she didn't understand.

"Why?" Louisa tried and failed to jerk away. "Why shouldn't I shout at you? You deserve to be shouted at!"

"Louisa." Fellows shook her once, hard. "You have to . . . stop."

Louisa looked up at him, startled out of her frenzy. Fellows studied her a few heartbeats more, then he dragged her against him.

"You have to stop, sweetheart," Fellows said. "Because I love you so much, it's killing me."

Chapter 16

Fellows couldn't believe he'd said the words, but he didn't want to take them back. Not with Louisa gaping up at him, a fleck of cream still on the corner of her mouth.

When he'd peeked into the tea tent and seen her closing her mouth around the profiterole, the cream smearing across her lips, he'd had to turn away before he rushed in and hauled her out. Not only out of the tea tent, but out of Newmarket and back to London and his flat where he could have her all night. He'd smothered a groan, hoping no one noticed his sudden hard-on, and walked away with difficulty.

Fellows had wanted to catch her attention, because he needed to warn her off Mr. Franklin before it was too late. Betrothals could be as binding as marriage, especially if the marriage settlements had already been put in motion. Even if Louisa hated Fellows for the information, he refused to stand by and let Mr. Franklin lie to her and ruin her.

He'd gotten Louisa to follow him here so they wouldn't be seen together. But now, alone with her, in the dim coolness of the stall, Fellows knew his mistake.

Louisa was tight against him, her eyes full of fire, her lips brushed with cream. He could no longer resist her—he only had so much strength. He leaned down and licked the side of her mouth.

The sparks he'd seen inside her ignited. Louisa twined her arms around Fellows and pulled him down to her for a full, hard, and desperate kiss.

They were not leaving. Fellows scraped her to him, his hand in her hair. Her hat came away and fell to the hay, and he was pulling her up into him, his arm solidly around her.

Louisa kissed him with urgency. Her hands scrabbled on his back, his neck, his shoulders. She wasn't an experienced kisser, not seductive and sultry like a courtesan, and Fellows didn't care.

She was his. A few steps had her against the wall. Fellows lifted her, hooking his arm around her hips. Her skirts came up as her leg twined around his. Fellows pushed the petticoats out of the way to find her warm thigh, bare under the lawn of her loose drawers.

He broke the kiss to touch his lips to her face, her hair. "Louisa," he said, the whisper hoarse. "Marry me."

Her intake of breath was sharp. "What?"

"Marry me. I can promise you damn all, but I need you in my life. I'll take care of you better than that bastard Franklin ever could."

"I know." Louisa touched his face. "I know."

"Then say yes. You are so high above me it makes my head spin to look at you, but I can't let you go. Those bloody aristos will use you and make you miserable. I promise I will never do that." He touched his forehead to hers, brushed a hard thumb across her cheek. "*Please*, Louisa."

"Yes." Louisa let out a breathless laugh. "Yes, I will. I'll marry you. Dearest Lloyd."

"Thank God." Fellows's prayer was heartfelt. "Thank God."

He sank to his knees and pulled her down with him, cradling her in his arms as he laid her down on the soft hay. His fervent hands unlaced her drawers and pulled them off, moving her skirts to cushion her. This was not what Fellows wanted for her, no elegance here, but he couldn't stop. His was a crude and fierce need, animal-like—fitting that they were in a stable.

Louisa didn't stop him or push him away. She slid her hand through his hair, the desire in her eyes reflecting his.

Fellows got his buttons open, his trousers loosened. He moved his hand to her bare thigh again, then higher, his fingers sinking into her breathtaking heat. Louisa started, and he softened his touch, knowing she'd not felt this before.

He gently stroked her opening, feeling the wetness increase. She was excited for him, needy. His cock pulsing with the rapid beating of his heart was just as needy.

"I won't hurt you," he said, or thought he said. "I promise."

She nodded, her eyes growing heavy with pleasure. Fellows's fingers continued their dance, and Louisa's body became more and more pliant. She murmured something in bliss, her smile widening and warming.

Fellows laced his arm behind her hips and lifted her to him; at the same time he fitted himself to her and slowly, slowly pushed inside.

His world changed. A mix of wild excitement and incredible tenderness spiraled through him, in addition to the wonder of being tightly inside her. Her head went back, eyes closing.

Her small gasp as he broke through her barrier made him stop. Fellows caressed her, soothed her, his hands shaking. He knew he'd hurt her; he hadn't wanted it to.

"Are you all right?" he asked her softly.

"Yes, I'm . . ." Louisa rose to him, her body knowing what to do. "I'm all right. I love you."

Whatever Fellows tried to say in reply was incoherent. He slid on inside her, a crazed feeling flooding him as they connected.

He lost all sense of time, of place. He was with Louisa, bodies together. Her fingers, still hugged by leather gloves, brushed his face. The cool of them lent a sharp contrast to the heat of her. Erotic, joyful.

Fellows kissed her, their lips seeking each other's, bruising. He thrust inside her, growing stronger as she opened more for him. This beautiful woman with her soft scent, her sweet body, was *his*.

"Louisa," he said. "Louisa. Bloody *hell*."

Too soon, too soon . . . His climax hit him. He kept thrusting into her, Louisa crying out with it and her own pleasure, her gloved fingers gripping his shoulders.

Fellows went on, hips rocking. He needed her, needed all of her. He couldn't form the words, but the thoughts were there.

You are the beauty I've been seeking all my life. My existence was dark, grim, full of struggle, until you. You are the light that pushes the darkness away. When I'm with you, I can see my way, and I can breathe again.

All that came out was, "I love you."

Louisa smiled, her eyes soft with the passion of what they did. "I love you too. My dearest Lloyd."

And that was enough.

They were sitting up together against the wall, she on his lap. Louisa felt stretched and different. The world looked different to her too, as though colors she'd never seen before had suddenly become clear to her.

She leaned against Lloyd's shoulder, he with his arm around her. They'd kissed quietly for a long time on the hay, then he'd withdrawn, lifted Louisa to his lap, and held her close.

Louisa didn't want to leave for the harsh light of the afternoon, not yet. They sat on the giving hay, not speaking. Basking.

Lloyd took her left hand in his, slid off her glove, and pressed a kiss to her third finger. "I will give you a ring. It won't have nearly the diamond Franklin would have given you, but it will be something."

Louisa wanted to laugh. "I'd rather have a band of tin from you than the Kohinoor diamond from Gil. What you give me will be true."

He continued to caress her finger. "If I hadn't told you what I told you about Franklin, would you have accepted him?"

"No." Louisa could say it honestly and decidedly. "I would have turned him down. I thought at one time he'd be the perfect husband for me. But perfection . . . It's cloying, dull sameness."

Fellows laughed his dry laugh. "Well, I am nothing like perfection."

"You're better. You're *you*." Louisa squeezed his arm. She belonged to him now, and she liked that feeling. "Gil is apparently a liar, a cheat, and a manipulator. Hargate was even worse." She lifted her head. "You don't think Gil killed Hargate for knowing his secret, do you? I'll not forgive Gil for deceiving me so dreadfully, but I'm not sure he'd go so far as murder."

"You would be surprised who would go so far as murder."
Fellows gave her a soft kiss. "Would you consider beginning
your life as a policeman's wife by helping me catch a killer? I
don't have the evidence to apply for an arrest warrant yet, and
I have to be careful about it. I won't push you to help me,
because there is some danger involved. I won't lie about that."

"Of course I'll help," Louisa said. "I'll gladly assist you
proving I didn't do it. I'd gladly assist you even if I hadn't been
suspected. I didn't much like Hargate, but I watched him
die—I wouldn't wish such a terrifying death on anyone."

"Before you agree, wait until I tell you what I have in mind,"
Fellows said. "I had planned to ask Eleanor to help, because
she's resilient, though Hart would throttle me when he found
out what I asked her to do."

"*I'm* resilient." Louisa sat up and took his hands. "Please, I
want to help you. You've done so much for me."

"Thank you." A grim light entered Fellows's eyes then. as
the police detective returned, and he outlined his plan to her.

~~~

Louisa entered the family's box a different woman than when
she'd left it. She'd spent a while in the horse stall putting herself to rights, Lloyd having to pick bits of hay out of every
piece of Louisa's clothing and her hair. He'd laughed as he'd
done it—she loved his laugh, the deep, warm one that held
none of his self-deprecation or bitterness.

Louisa had left the stable yard alone, pretending she'd done
nothing but linger to pet the horses. She made her way back to
the Mackenzie box, nodding and smiling at ladies who still
watched her with contempt.

Ainsley and Isabella had already returned to the box, both
of them giving Louisa sharp looks when she entered.

Gil greeted her warmly. "Louisa, my sweet, I was worried
about you. Where did you disappear to?"

Louisa shrugged, hoping her warm face and the new softness in her body didn't betray her. "Chatting to people is all.
And looking at horses. I love horses, you know."

"Well, it's good to have you back to myself," Gil said.
He smiled his warm smile, full of friendliness, no less

sincere than when she'd left him an hour ago. Louisa had felt slightly guilty to receive his kind attentions then; now he only irritated her. What a difference an hour made!

Gil sat next to her and again moved close without being too obvious. But now the movement seemed possessive and arrogant, as though Gil implied he knew exactly how to behave and Louisa did not.

"I long to travel," Louisa said to him. "To lands far away. Don't you?"

Gil raised his brows at the non sequitur. "Yes, I enjoy travel. But there's something to be said for good old England, isn't there?"

"That's true, but I very much enjoy my journeys to Scotland. Such wild land there, some of it quite rough. But beautiful, I think. Land untouched by any but God."

"Yes, Scotland can be lovely," Gil agreed, obviously wondering why on earth she'd brought it up.

"But I've never been abroad. I wasn't able to have a Grand Tour. Perhaps we could go together, Gil. I'd especially love to see the Italian cities: Florence, Venice, Rome. Shall we go to Rome?"

Gil stared at her as though she'd lost her senses. "I suppose. Rome is a bit crowded. Hot in the summer. Loud."

"Is it? But there is so much history there, and art. And I thought you partial to the city."

"Well, yes, it can be beautiful," Gil said, still bewildered. "But really, I think we ought to stay in northern climes. For instance, Paris in the summer is heavenly."

"I think I'd prefer Rome. I hear some of the outlying towns are very pretty. Perhaps you can introduce me to your acquaintance there."

Gil looked at her in confusion for a few moments longer, then Louisa saw him realize that she knew. His brows came down, lower, lower, in puzzlement, worry, anger.

"Louisa."

Louisa patted his arm. "Do not worry, Gil. I wouldn't make any sort of trouble for you. But it is a bit unfair to her, isn't it? Oh, and to me. Marrying me under false pretenses, I mean."

The last statement brought the other conversations in the box to a halt. Heads turned. Gilbert suddenly found himself under the scrutiny of four pairs of Mackenzie eyes, and the equally stony stares of the Mackenzie wives.

Gil's face lost color. "It isn't . . . the marriage wasn't legal."

"I have been told that it *was* legal without doubt," Louisa said. "From a very good source. I am certain she insisted on it, wise lady. I think you'd better confess your sins, Gil. To your parents, to your friends, to me. Is bringing your true wife to England such a difficulty?"

"Louisa." Gil tried frantically to lower his voice, but too late. "It was nothing. A youthful indiscretion is all. Long ago."

Daniel broke in. "Ah, those youthful indiscretions. Always come back to haunt one, don't they?"

Mac laughed. "You're too young to have youthful indiscretions haunting you, Danny."

"Don't be so certain," Ainsley said. "You'd be amazed what comes to light about our Daniel. But you were speaking of *your* indiscretions, Gil. Do not let us interrupt."

Gilbert kept his gaze on Louisa. "You must believe me, Louisa. I was very young. It was mad and brief, and over."

Louisa's anger had climbed down a long way since she'd first learned Gilbert's guilty secret. Wild happiness had erased most of her outrage. Now she could pity him, but the anger was still there. Gil had cold-bloodedly decided he'd lie to Louisa, and to his true wife, to deceive everyone. It was base and mean.

"I would believe you, Gil," Louisa said. "But *four* children? Four little ones hardly indicates that you've left the affair far in the past."

Gil dropped the innocent look. "Bloody hell."

"A wife and four children, Mr. Franklin?" Hart's eagle gaze skewered him.

"Indeed," Louisa said. "They live in a village near Rome. Gil married her . . . about six years ago, was it, Gil? I imagine you realized your father would kick up a fuss if he discovered you'd married an Italian farmer's daughter, so you decided to take an English wife of noble birth to keep him happy."

Gil seized her hands. "No, Louisa. I asked you to marry me because I want to marry *you*. I will divorce her. I am having difficulty, I will admit—she's Catholic and won't hear of it. But I promise, I'll get out of it. I have my best solicitors on it."

Louisa tried to withdraw her hands, but Gilbert held them hard. She shook her head, realizing as she did so, that a piece of hay still rested on her shoulder. Daniel had noticed it, according to the sudden shrewd look he gave her.

"It makes no difference to me whether you extract yourself from the marriage or not," Louisa said to Gil. "You must see that. I rather think you weren't going to tell me about it at all, were you?"

"I will obtain the divorce," Gil said stubbornly. "I won't hold you to anything, Louisa. We won't announce an engagement, even, if you don't want to, until it's done. But please, don't say no. I love you."

Hart had left his place in the corner of the box to take a seat next to Gil. "You're in a bad place, Franklin," he said. "Louisa is trying to tell you to take yourself away from her. I'll go further and tell you to leave England altogether. Go back to Italy and acknowledge your wife and children. If you don't think they'll be happy in England, then stay with them and settle down there."

Gil drew himself up. "Do not presume to tell me what to do, Kilmorgan. Your copybook is blotted far worse than mine."

"It's the nature of the blots that are important," Hart said. "Secret wives cause all sorts of legal complications. And then there are your children. Four, Louisa said? All yours?"

"Yes," Gil snapped.

"Then acknowledge them as yours. Raise them. Be a father to them. The cruelest thing you can do in this world, Franklin, is to not acknowledge your sons and daughters. Don't let them grow up believing their father doesn't want them."

Like Lloyd. He grew up knowing his father had rejected him. Hart understood that. Louisa read remorse in Hart's eyes for what his father had done.

"They've done nothing to deserve that," Louisa said in avid agreement.

"Louisa, please."

Louisa got to her feet. Gil, trained in politeness from the cradle, rose to his at the same time. But Louisa had reached the end of her patience with him. "I won't marry you, Gil. Not now, not if you obtain a divorce. You may as well go to Italy and stay there. I think you should leave at once. I'm sure you can find a train that will carry you to Dover this very evening."

"Louisa . . ."

"No, Gil. I'd like you to go now."

Louisa took a step away from him, intending to join the ladies. Gil reached for her, desperation on his face. Louisa sidestepped his outstretched hands, tripped, and came down on the same foot she'd wrenched dancing.

She cried out and started to fall. Gil snatched at her in true alarm and missed.

Another hand caught Louisa under her arm, lifting her up again. Ian. He frowned down at her, the look in his eyes telling Louisa he knew everything that was going on and everything that would come.

How he knew, Louisa didn't bother trying to understand. What Ian did and didn't know was always astonishing to her.

"Wretched foot." Louisa took a step and cried out again. Ian's grip tightened, and Daniel sprang to her other side, supporting her between himself and Ian.

"Sit down, Aunt Louisa," Daniel said. "I'll fetch Angelo. He's excellent at binding up fetlocks."

Louisa grimaced. "Thank you, Danny, but I believe I've done more to my fetlock than I previously thought."

"She's right," Isabella said worriedly. "We'll take you to a doctor, dear. I'm sure there are competent surgeons in New-market."

Ian looked at Daniel. "We will take her."

"We will?" Daniel blinked. "Yes, of course we will. Come along, Auntie. Ian and I will take care of you."

Isabella tried to follow, but Ian had Louisa hauled out of the box so quickly that Isabella got left behind. When Ian reached the stairs, he abandoned trying to help Louisa walk and simply lifted her into his arms.

Ian didn't much like touching people, or people touching him. He welcomed hugs from Beth and his children, tolerated them from his brothers and Daniel, but he slid away from everyone else. Now Ian cradled Louisa close, never minding that she clasped her hands around his neck to hold on.

Ian walked rapidly and grimly down the stairs with her, as

though he carried a Mackenzie dog that had hurt itself. And possibly, Louisa mused, Ian thought of Louisa as little different from them.

Daniel ran ahead and found the doctor Ian sought. The man's eyes widened when he saw Louisa, pale and hurt, and changed from the social gentleman to the professional.

"Bring her in here," he said, gesturing to one of the tents.

This one was empty, whatever use it had been put to finished, tables strewn about waiting to be carried away. Daniel made certain a table was clear, and Ian laid Louisa on it. Louisa bit her lip, trying to look brave.

One of Sir Richard Cavanaugh's lackeys hurried in with his bag and departed just as quickly. Sir Richard ran his hand competently over Louisa's ankle, and she made a noise of pain when he squeezed the right place.

"I'll need to examine it more closely—it might be broken. Gentlemen, if you'll go?"

He meant that he might have to expose Louisa's bare ankle. Daniel and Ian weren't closely enough related to her that it would be proper for them to see that. Silly, but Sir Richard had likely learned long ago to adhere strictly to the rules. Hence his knighthood.

"Wait for Isabella first," Daniel suggested.

Louisa waved him off. "No, please go. The quicker he finishes, the quicker I'll be out of pain. I'll be fine."

Ian, without a word, put his hand on Daniel's shoulder, turned the puzzled young man around, and marched him out of the tent. Daniel went, but with reluctance.

"Now then, Lady Louisa." Sir Richard worked the stopper from a small green bottle and held it out to her. "Take the smallest sniff of this. It will relax you and make you feel better."

Louisa regarded the bottle with suspicion. "What is it?"

"Just a sedative. See?" Sir Richard waved the bottle under his own nose. "Nothing noxious."

He held it out to her again. Louisa took a small sniff, smelling something sharp and sweet. She lay down on the table again, the pain almost evaporating, or at least receding to someplace far away. Louisa's limbs relaxed, and she drew a long breath.

"That's nice," she said.

"Just a touch of ether," Sir Richard said. "I don't want my examination to hurt you."

He picked up her foot, unlaced and drew off her boot, and slid his hand up her leg to take down her stocking. All quick, competent, professional. He rotated her foot this way and that, pressed her ankle, and then ran warm hands all over her foot.

"I don't think you've broken anything, fortunately, Lady Louisa. A mild sprain is all, though they can hurt very much. I'll bind the foot and give you something for the pain."

"Thank you." He was kind, really. "You're nice," Louisa said. Then she drew a breath. Why on earth had she said that?

"Lovely of you to say so, my dear." Sir Richard smiled at her, then something else entered his eyes. "You have beautiful legs, Louisa. A pity no one sees them."

Louisa's dry lips parted. "I beg your—"

She broke off with a little squeak as Sir Richard put his hand on her ankle again. It didn't hurt, but she watched, wide-eyed, as he caressed her leg all the way to the knee, the touch no longer that of a compassionate doctor. "Very nice," he said, his voice thick with pleasure.

Louisa wanted to shriek and kick, but the sedative he'd given her made her giggle instead. How very awful. Lloyd had been right after all.

"He generally is," Louisa said before she could stop herself.

"Pardon?" Sir Richard went on caressing behind her knee, his fingers sliding under the hem of her drawers. "Who generally is what?"

"Lloyd. He's always right about people. He's very clever."

"I'm certain." It was apparent Sir Richard had no idea who "Lloyd" was. He didn't connect the name with the police inspector who'd interviewed him—how very rude of him. "Louisa, my dear, you are quite a beautiful woman." Sir Richard withdrew his hand from her skirt only to slide it up her bodice and her bosom. He squeezed her breast, then started to undo the buttons that closed the bodice to her chin. "Let me loosen your gown, so you can breathe easier."

"Yes." The open buttons did let her draw a long breath. "Help," she tried to shout, but the word came out quietly.

"Hush now," Sir Richard said. "We don't have much time.

Someone will come soon. That makes it a bit more exciting, doesn't it?" He drew her placket apart and put his large, rather soft hand on her breast . . .

A very large fist connected with the side of Sir Richard's face. Louisa's eyes widened as Sir Richard staggered, blood appearing on his temple. He tried to keep to his feet, then he fell over like a tree in a storm and lay stunned on the wilted grass.

Louisa looked at the fist that had done the punching and recognized the black leather gloves Lloyd liked to wear. The punch had been very competent. Louisa tried to leverage herself up on her elbows, then she gave up and laughed.

Sir Richard struggled to rise. A large boot, this one belonging to Sergeant Pierce, landed on the man's chest.

"Now then, sir," Pierce said. "Just you rest there a bit."

The tent seemed to be full of people all the sudden. Ian Mackenzie, thunder in his eyes, put his booted foot on Sir Richard's chest as well. Sir Richard wasn't going anywhere.

The rest of the Mackenzies, including Isabella, took up the rest of the small tent. Gilbert, fortunately, was nowhere in sight.

Fellows had shrugged off his coat and now he draped it over Louisa. She smiled up at him and touched his strong hand. "Did I do all right?" she asked. "I'm sorry. I didn't know he'd give me such a strong sedative. I couldn't scream for help."

"You did fine. Thank you." Lloyd leaned down and kissed the top of her head. No one looked surprised, least of all Ian, the crafty devil.

Isabella was giving Fellows a hard look. "Do you mean to say, Chief Inspector, that you used my sister as *bait*?"

Daniel laughed. "It was well performed. I never suspected, until Ian told me."

"Ian knew?" This from Mac, who came to stand protectively near Louisa with Isabella. "Why did no one tell *me*? I'm still not clear on everything, come to think of it."

"I needed an ally who could keep his mouth shut," Fellows said. "And one who would look after Louisa. Ian was the obvious choice. Thank you, Ian."

Ian only nodded. At one time, Louisa had heard from Isabella, Ian had possessed fury to the point of violence against Lloyd, especially when Lloyd had tried to use Beth to get to Ian and Hart. Now Ian gave Fellows a satisfied look, an acknowledgment of camaraderie. He pushed a little harder on Sir Richard's chest with his boot, making Sir Richard cry out.

Fellows moved back to Sir Richard, took the iron cuffs Sergeant Pierce held out to him, and snapped them around Sir Richard's wrists. "Sir Richard Cavanaugh, I am arresting you for the murder of Frederick Lane, the Bishop of Hargate. I will take you to a magistrate, who will examine you and determine if there is cause to bind you over for trial."

"On what evidence?" Sir Richard scoffed. "You have none."

"Oh, I have plenty." Fellows tapped Sir Richard's doctor's bag. "All in here. And in your surgery, and at your house, and in the Bishop of Hargate's notes. I will try to make sure all the lady patients you've molested over the years, the poor women too afraid and ashamed to say anything against you, will be present in the gallery at your trial. Not enough justice for them, I think, but it will have to do. A man of your standing might wriggle out of a charge of indecent behavior, even sexual assault, but I intend to see you go down for murder."

Lloyd's voice was quiet but held the weight of authority. Sir Richard was furious, but he was down now. He couldn't fight.

Louisa, still drunk with sedative, raised her head and curled her lip. "You are disgusting," she said clearly. Then she found herself rushing back down to the table. "Oh, my." She reached for Lloyd and held his hand when he gave it to her. "I think I'll sleep now."

Lloyd kissed her forehead, his rough whiskers brushing her skin. "I'll be with you when you wake."

And he was.

Chapter 17

"You must explain all to us, dear Lloyd," Eleanor said from her place at the foot of the table.

A Mackenzie family dinner was taking place at the Duke of Kilmorgan's mansion on Grosvenor Square several days after their return from Newmarket. A family dinner meant all the Mackenzies, including Fellows and Daniel, Louisa, and Fellows's mother.

They dined informally, no place settings to conform to. The guests could sit where they chose, with whom they chose. The only structure to the table was that Hart sat at the head, Eleanor at its foot.

Ian claimed the chair next to Beth, Daniel was with his father and stepmother, and Mrs. Fellows sat next to Louisa, delighting in every moment of the gathering. She was highly pleased with Fellows's choice of bride and kept smiling broadly at Louisa.

"I knew he had good taste," she said. "You are the sweetest little thing, Louisa. You do know that?"

When Eleanor demanded the story, the rest of the table quieted. Fellows, on Louisa's other side, calmly laid down his fork.

"Louisa's hatpin," he said.

They waited for him to go on. When he didn't, Daniel said, "What are we supposed to understand from that? Play fair, Uncle Fellows. You have to tell the less clever of us what that means."

Fellows didn't smile, but Louisa could see he was enjoying teasing them all. He took a sip of wine, gave Daniel an acknowledging nod, and went on.

"When I saw Louisa sticking hatpins into her hat, it gave me the idea. If someone coated a pin or needle with a poison and stuck it into someone, perhaps that person might not die instantly, especially if it was a low enough dose. Or if the pin had been coated with a sedative instead of a poison, the victim might simply grow sick or perhaps fall unconscious. If Sir Richard Cavanaugh spoke to Hargate before he went into the tea tent, perhaps clapped him on the shoulder or shook his hand, he'd have the opportunity to stick something into him surreptitiously. Cavanaugh, as a doctor, would have needles at his disposal. Hargate begins to grow ill in the tea tent. Louisa runs out for the doctor. Cavanaugh comes to investigate, finds Hargate on the ground. A final prick of prussic acid finishes the job, or perhaps Cavanaugh poured it into Hargate's mouth while he examined him. He had the prussic acid in his doctor's bag, in a little bottle, along with his medicines and sedatives. He could also pretend to try to revive the man and wave the poison under his nose. Inhaling prussic acid can be just as deadly as imbibing it."

"But it was in the teacup, wasn't it?" Ainsley asked, puzzled. "The one Louisa handed to the bishop."

Fellows shook his head. "Cavanaugh saw it lying broken on the ground. Easy for him to drop a little poison onto the pieces after the fact. He made certain to lecture us, the plodding policemen, on how prussic acid killed a man, and pointed out an obvious way Hargate could have taken the poison. He also had a suspect at hand—Lady Louisa, whose father had swindled Hargate. Hargate was still demanding repayment from her family, and perhaps told Cavanaugh of his plan to ask her to marry him in exchange for forgiving the debt. Or Hargate told someone else, and Cavanaugh heard the gossip. In any case, Hargate was blackmailing Cavanaugh over Cavanaugh's practice of sedating women and taking advantage of them. The poison found in the teacup would point to Louisa, as would the bottle Cavanaugh managed to slip into Louisa's pocket. If Hargate had been standing with someone else when he died, no doubt Cavanaugh would have found a way to point to *them*. That was an advantage of killing a man at a large gathering—so many handy suspects."

"It is all so cruel," Isabella said angrily. "Especially to Louisa. If I hadn't been able to convince Mrs. Leigh-Waters to telegraph for you, the Richmond police would have arrested her."

"I hope someone would have sent for me even if Isabella hadn't telegraphed," Lloyd said, giving the table a stern look.

"Of course we would have," Daniel said. "You're the best detective in the Yard."

"Louisa is important to me." Fellows slid his hand over Louisa's. "Very important."

"Which is why you moved heaven and earth to help her," Daniel said. He grinned. "We tumbled to that."

"A June wedding," Isabella said. "Not much time to prepare, but Louisa will have the most beautiful gown and a lovely ceremony. All the trimmings. St. George's, Hanover Square?"

"No," Louisa said. "We've discussed it. A quiet family wedding is what we want. Not all of London gawping at us at a fashionable church. We'd like to marry either in Berkshire or at Kilmorgan. *Just the family,* Isabella." Louisa gave her a severe look, then added one for the duchess. "Eleanor."

Both ladies looked innocent. "You may trust us," Isabella said. "We'll give you exactly what you need. The world will be green with envy that they couldn't attend."

Louisa let out a sigh. "A *quiet* wedding, Izzy."

"Yes, yes, I heard you the first time."

Mac winked at Louisa across the table. "Don't worry. I'll rein her in if she gets too flighty."

"I am not flighty, Mac Mackenzie," Isabella said indignantly.

"Yes, you are, my sweet Sassenach."

Isabella's cheeks went prettily pink. She subsided, but Louisa knew she'd have to keep an eye on her sister. Isabella loved to come up with grand occasions.

"I won't have a mansion to take you to," Fellows said to

Louisa as other conversations began again. "I have enough salary for a modest house, but not in the fashionable district. And no hordes of servants. One or two at most. Are you certain you don't want to reconsider?"

Louisa leaned her head against his strong shoulder. "Those are practical things. We'll work them out. I am so very good at being practical."

Mrs. Fellows winked at Louisa. "Don't worry, dear. I have plenty of dusters put aside you can borrow. And I'll show you how to black a stove."

"Mum," Fellows said, half weary, half affectionate.

"I'm only teasing," Mrs. Fellows said. "But the dusters will be handy."

Lloyd didn't look convinced, but Louisa would show him she'd be fine. She'd grown up with every luxury handed to her, but she'd learned how empty that luxurious life could be. Her father had used his money and position dishonorably, had betrayed his friends' trust.

Louisa had discovered how to live simply once the money was gone, she and her mother staying alone in the dower house. It wasn't money and a title that made one honorable, Louisa had learned, but one's character and actions. And Lloyd had plenty of honor.

Ian alone hadn't spoken throughout the meal. He'd listened to Lloyd's explanation of Cavanaugh's actions then gone back to eating without a word. Now he put his arm around Beth and kissed her hair.

"What do you think, Ian?" Louisa asked him across the table. "Lloyd and I will do well together, won't we?"

Ian didn't answer right away. The table quieted, waiting for Ian's words of wisdom, but when it became clear he wasn't ready to respond, they took up conversing again. The family had learned not to push him.

Finally Ian looked at Louisa. He met her eyes full on, warmth and intelligence in his gaze. "I believe he loves you."

"I believe Ian's right," Fellows said quietly.

Louisa didn't answer in words. She tugged Lloyd down to her and kissed him, her heart in the kiss. She didn't care who saw, and neither did Lloyd. He put his arm around her and let the kiss turn passionate.

Daniel whooped, and the ladies applauded. Louisa broke from Lloyd, laughing.

Mrs. Fellows dabbed her cheek with her napkin. "Aw, look at that," she said. "You made your old mum cry."

Lloyd didn't smile. The look in his eyes when he leaned down and kissed Louisa again was full of love, and full of heat. Fire burned, but it also warmed.

Epilogue

The woods north of Kilmorgan were deep, isolated, quiet. The two men in kilts had walked a long way, Hart leading, his half brother following.

Fellows acknowledged that a kilt was good for walking in the woods. Thick boots and socks kept the underbrush from scratching his legs, and the wool of the kilt kept him warm as he and Hart made their way through the cool, dim forest.

Fellows's wedding to Louisa had been more or less a blur, and thoughts of it came to him in a series of images. He standing in the Kilmorgan chapel, a minister before him, Hart at his side as his groomsman. Aimee Mackenzie scattering flower petals down the aisle, Isabella Mackenzie following her. Then Louisa walking in on Ian's arm, and everything else fading.

Fellows knew he'd said the vows, put the gold ring on Louisa's finger, done everything right. But all he could remember was Louisa in ivory satin, her smile behind her gauze veil, the sweet-smelling yellow roses in her flame-red hair. Once Fellows was married to her, he'd lifted the barrier of the veil, taken her into his arms, and kissed her.

And kissed her. One taste of her had not been enough.

Only Louisa had existed for him as they'd stood in the sunlight coming through the chapel's plain windows. Her warmth, her touch, her love.

As the kiss went on, the rest of the family had started to clap, then to laugh, until finally, Hart had tapped Fellows on the shoulder and told him to take it to the house.

Fellows wasn't certain how he'd gotten through the wedding festivities afterward. It had still been light, the June sunshine lasting far into the night, when he'd at last taken Louisa to the bedroom prepared for them—one well away from the rest of the family.

That night was imprinted on his memory forever. Louisa and he under the sheets, Lloyd inside her, her light touch, her kisses, the little feminine sounds she made as she reached her deepest pleasure. Lloyd had touched her and loved her far into the night, until they'd slept, exhausted. As soon as morning light brushed them—very early—Louisa had wakened him with a kiss. She'd smiled sleepily at him, and Lloyd had rolled onto her and loved her again.

That had been three days ago. They'd spent most of that time in their bedroom. Daniel remarked, when they'd finally emerged, that he was surprised either of them could walk.

Today, Hart had wanted to take Fellows on a ramble through the woods. He wouldn't say why, but Fellows, being the great detective he was, realized the outing was important to Hart.

After about half an hour of tramping, Hart stopped. They were in a small clearing, woods thick around them, the evergreen branches shutting out the sky.

"This is where it happened," Hart said. "Where our father died."

Hart had told Fellows the true story of their father's death, after Hart's marriage to Eleanor. Not the widely circulated public version of the duke falling from his horse and breaking his neck, nor the story Hart had told the family, that the old duke had accidentally shot himself. Hart had told Fellows the truth. All of it. Only Hart had known, and he'd told only Eleanor.

"Father lived his life in hatred," Hart said now. "And he

tried to pass that hatred on to us. He hated me because I was his heir, and he knew I'd push him out one day. He hated my brothers because our mother loved them, and because I took care of them better than he ever could. He hated you because you reminded him he had no control over himself, or over the world, as much as he pretended to."

"I'm glad we finished with the hatred," Fellows said.

Hart looked around the clearing, the tension in him easing a bit. "Maybe the hatred made us stronger."

"I don't think so," Fellows said. "It kept us apart, and weak. Love is better."

Hart grinned. When he did that, he looked as he had as a very young man—handsome, devilishly arrogant, certain he'd rule the world. "Did Louisa teach you that?"

"Yes," Fellows said without shame. "As Eleanor taught you." He studied Hart for a time. "I kept it, you know. I still have it."

Hart stared at his abrupt change of subject. "Kept what?"

"The shilling you gave me when I was ten years old. You must have been about that age too."

Hart frowned. "I'm not recalling . . ."

"The duke's coach pulled up in High Holborn—he was on his way to Lincoln's Inn. A traffic snarl, of my making, stopped the carriage. The duke got down to see what was the matter. I'd planned to tell him I was his son that day. He was supposed to look astonished then welcome me into the coach and take me home with him. Instead, he beat me. You looked happy that I took my fists to him, and you gave me a shilling."

Hart's expression cleared. "I remember now. That boy was you?"

"You wouldn't have noticed a resemblance with my face so filthy. Not to mention bruised and bloody."

"Good Lord. I wish I'd known." He gave Fellows a grim smile. "Yes, I was happy you pummeled him. The man beat me every night of my life, so I was glad to see him get a taste of it. He beat me to make a man of me, he said. Well, he succeeded."

"Yes."

Both of them looked around the clearing again, where a man who'd made so many miserable had come to his end.

"They'll be wondering where we are," Fellows said after a time.

Eleanor and Louisa, their wives and lovers. "They will," Hart agreed.

"If they have to come after us, they'll scold when they get here," Fellows said.

"True. Then want to do something daft, like have a picnic."

"The ladies do enjoy a picnic. After a five-mile hike."

"I think we've been domesticated," Hart said. "The Highland warriors have gone soft."

Fellows shrugged. "I can do with a little softness now and again."

"Eleanor knew I could too," Hart said. "That's why she came back for me."

"They saved us from ourselves," Fellows offered.

"Someone had to."

The clearing had been a place of violence. Fellows imagined it, the gunshot, birds fleeing in a sudden rush of wings, the heat and smell of blood. The old duke, mean and thoughtless, falling dead. Hart breathing hard, the shotgun in his hands.

So much viciousness and cruelty. All gone now. The ground of the clearing was soft green, tiny yellow flowers blooming where the sun reached.

Without another word, the two men turned and started back for Kilmorgan.

They emerged from the trees near the river where Ian had taken the rest of the family fishing. They were all there—Beth and her children on a spread blanket; Mac's family nearby with Louisa and Fellows's mother; Ainsley and Cameron together; Daniel playing with his little sister; Eleanor and Alec on another blanket.

And Louisa. She smiled at Lloyd from where she reposed next to Isabella, and she rose to greet him.

Fellows met her halfway across the grass. He took her hands, and they shared a kiss, full of warmth, delight, and the sweet taste of sugared tea.

Louisa eased back down from her tiptoes and brushed her fingers across Lloyd's mouth. The simple wedding band glistened on her finger next to her engagement ring with its small diamond.

"Welcome home," she said.

"Thank you," Fellows answered. He meant the thanks for all, for all she was and all she'd done for him.

He drew her into his arms, and Louisa softly kissed him again. Laughter surrounded them, and the summer sunshine.

Scandal and the Duchess

Chapter 1

When he was *this* drunk, there was only one thing to do. Steven McBride laid the rest of his money on the table and got unsteadily to his feet.

"Divide it," he said to the assembled men, his Scots accent slurring. "I cannae see my cards anymore, and you'll have it off me anyway. Good night."

His friends and acquaintances, some as drunk as himself, either laughed or grunted and went back to their cards. *Bloody Scottish upstart,* he knew many of them thought.

Some thought much worse than that—those who knew the story—by their dark looks. *Army should have slung him out.*

Steven knew exactly why he was imbibing to his eyeballs on his leave, and why he'd come home earlier this year. Knowing why did not make it any easier to leave the card room, navigate his way down the stairs—who the devil had put the card room upstairs?—and stagger into the street.

He looked up and down for his carriage, then remembered he'd hired a carriage to bring him to the soiree tonight. Steven vaguely remembered dismissing it, blast it all, telling the coachman he'd make his own way home.

The November cold was bitter, a wind sweeping down the street to cut straight through Steven's uniform coat. Steven's regiment was currently in West Africa, a land of warmth. Bloody great heat, actually, but Africa was an amazing world full of amazing people. Nothing there like this frozen London passage, wind howling down it, stinging him even in his drunken state.

Which way were his lodgings? Steven didn't have a permanent house in London, so he usually hired rooms whenever he came to town—flats that catered to single gentlemen. He stayed in the same area each time, but rarely in the same house or even the same street. Sometimes he didn't bother with rooms at all and stayed in a hotel like the Langham.

The Langham—had a familiar ring to it. Was Steven living there now? Or had that been last year?

Steven realized he was standing befuddled in the street, buffeted by the wind. Passersby, what there were of them on this bone-cold night, were looking at him askance.

The pungent, grassy smell of horse dung caught his attention. A carriage clopped slowly by, the horses doing what horses did even when walking about. Wildcats in Africa were cagey about where they relieved themselves, hiding it from all but the most canny hunters. London horses simply let it fall to the street, and humans came along behind and swept it up for them. Which animal was the more clever?

Steven half jogged, half stumbled toward the carriage. A hansom, that's what he needed. He could tell the cabby to take him to the Langham, where they'd find him a room, whether he'd booked in already or not.

The shape was wrong for a hansom, but Steven was past caring. He had to get somewhere, or he'd fall down in the street and spend the rest of the night unconscious on the cobbles. Even in this part of London, even in this weather, he doubted he'd have much left on him when he woke up.

The carriage stopped. Wind cut Steven, making his eyes water. He folded his arms against the cold, and ran toward the carriage, head down.

A woman bundled in a thick cloak and hood came out of

the lighted house the carriage had halted before. As soon as she crossed the threshold, four or five other persons appeared out of nowhere to block her way.

"There she is!"

"Duchess . . . Your Grace . . ."

"Your Grace, my readers would love a description of your gown tonight . . . Are you still in mourning?"

"Your Grace, how did it feel to have ensnared a duke, only to have him perish in the wedding bed?"

"Your Grace, there are rumors of you carrying on a flirtation with the Earl of Posenby. Or his son. Some speculate both. Would you tell us which it is?"

Bloody journalists, Steven thought in disgust. They were after some aristo, more dirt for the scandal sheets. Steven had no idea who the cloaked woman was and had no interest. He only wanted to climb into the carriage—private or not, he'd pay the coachman handsomely to take him anywhere.

Of course, he'd just thunked a large wad of money to the game table. Steven wondered vaguely if he had any left as he made a lunge for the coach.

The cloaked woman broke from the vultures—"Your Grace, is it true you're wintering in Nice with a comte?"

She put on a burst of speed. Steven stumbled on his drunken feet, and he and the woman met in a crash of flesh and breathlessness.

Steven found himself landing face-first on a bosom of exceptional quality. The woman's cloak had pulled away, revealing a gown fairly modestly cut but giving Steven enough bosom to enjoy. His cheek rested on warm flesh, his lips pressed onyx beads, and he inhaled a heady, womanly perfume.

He heard a heart beating rapidly under his ear, and a voice vibrating through a body of fine plumpness.

"Oh dear."

Steven tried to raise his head—not that he wanted to—but he couldn't. He could only lever himself up by grasping the woman by the hips and pulling himself upright.

The hips were a warm handful, the thighs beneath her skirts and stiff bustle even better. Steven climbed the poor woman, unbending himself as he went.

Unfortunately, his legs had stopped working. They gave

way again, throwing his weight onto her. She retreated to compensate, but her back met the carriage door. Steven kept falling, his body landing full-length against hers, plastering her to the coach.

The woman's hood slipped down. Steven saw eyes of clearest green, a round face haloed by golden hair, flushed cheeks, and a wide mouth that begged for kisses. It would be rude to kiss her without asking first, but Steven didn't have the words to inquire.

His face and hers were very close together, the kissable lips an inch away.

"My dear fellow," the woman said breathlessly. "Are you all right?"

"No," Steven tried to say. "Damn, woman, but you're beautiful." The words came out a jumbled mess, in broad Highland Scots, but the journalists heard them.

"Your Grace, who is *he*?" "A regimental affair, is it? Or a Highland fling?" "What about the comte? And the earl?"

"Good Lord," came the impatient voice of Steven's angel. "Leave the poor man alone. Can't you see he's ill?"

"Falling down drunk is more like it," one of the journalists said, and laughed. "Who is he? Give us a name."

"You lot, clear off!"

The coachman had come down off the box, and flapped his hands at the journalists like a woman shooing chickens out of her garden. Steven wanted to burst out laughing. At the same time, a footman exited the house from which the woman had emerged and laid hands on Steven. Steven heard the cry of a constable coming up the street, along with the man's heavy footsteps.

"Off with you," the footman growled at Steven. The constable came faster, his tall helmet bobbing out of the gloom and making Steven laugh harder.

Laughter and the footman's heavy hands made Steven slide down the woman's body. He found the hard street beneath his knees, his face buried in her abdomen, the black bombazine of her gown smooth against his nose.

She smelled wonderful. The perfume didn't come from a bottle. It was *her*—soap and the scent of fabric, warmth and woman. Steven pressed his face to her belly, wanting to take his ease with her.

"Sir." Her hands were on his hair. Steven snuggled in

closer. If they'd been alone and without so many clothes, this would be the perfect way to finish the night.

She leaned to him, his angel, and whispered, "What on earth are you doing?"

"Loving you," Steven said. "You deserve every bit of loving a man can give you."

"Oh," she said. "You are very drunk, I believe. Perhaps the nice constable will see you home."

"No home." His home was a tent in Africa, under huge sky, in blessed warmth. "I have no home."

"Dear me, that's sad. Do you need money? Perhaps a meal?"

Steven's laughter returned. She thought him a homeless, helpless sot, and maybe he was.

The journalists surged forward. More people seemed to be on the street, and someone threw a stone. "Tart!" a woman yelled. "Be off with ye."

The coachman growled. He flung open the door of the coach and more or less hoisted the woman inside. Steven grabbed the door as it swung shut, hanging on to it to keep him upright. The coachman started to wrench him away, but the journalists pushed in, as did the sudden crowd. London loved a riot—best way to keep warm in the winter, Steven mused—any excuse to begin one.

"Miles, let him in. He'll get trampled."

Steven heard her voice, felt himself be hauled up under the arms by a man of amazing strength, and then he met the floor of the carriage. The door slammed, bumping Steven's booted foot. After a moment, the carriage jerked forward, and things splattered against it—the denizens making good use of the handy horse apples in the street.

The angel seemed to be speaking to him. Steven heard her clear voice but no words. He laid his head on her skirt, blissfully warm, and drifted off to sleep.

When Steven cracked open his eyes, it was daylight; at least as much daylight that could filter through the narrow, dirty window on a London winter day.

The narrow window went with the narrow room, wide enough only for a single bed and a corner washstand. That was all. No curtain or blind, no bureau, no cheerful fire, only a brick chimney that went up through the room and gave off a modicum of heat.

Where the hell was he? The last thing Steven remembered was a card game . . .

No, a cold London street, someone throwing things . . .

Green eyes, red lips curving into a little smile, and a scent like roses. Deep red roses, heady and intense.

Had Steven dreamed her? If so, he wanted to go back to sleep.

But the cold, Steven's pounding head, and details of the night were knocking for attention. He should climb out of bed, dress, and face his problems like a Scotsman and a soldier.

The bed was warm, and raising his head hurt like hell. Steven laid it back down.

He must have slept again, because when he next opened his eyes, the room was brighter. The door swung open, and in came his angel with a wooden tray heaped with crockery.

"Good morning," she said brightly. "Would you like some tea?"

Chapter 2

The unknown man stared at her over the bedcovers with bloodshot, sunken eyes in a face covered with stubble. Rose reminded herself he was a pathetic creature, a war veteran, likely in need of charity.

The former soldiers she'd seen eking out a living on the streets weren't nearly as handsome as this one, though. Winter sunlight burnished his short hair golden, his whiskers too. His hard face was the bronze color of someone who'd spent time in a climate hotter than England's. Rose had thought him older on the street, but she could see now that he was a fairly young man, battered and suntanned from his profession.

The man's eyes, other than being bloodshot, were a profound gray. He pinned her with that gray gaze as though she were an enemy soldier, not a kind young woman come to bring him breakfast.

"They called you duchess," he said in a voice strong despite his obvious hangover.

"Briefly," Rose said, carrying the tray toward him. The tray had small legs and was designed to go over the breakfaster's lap, much like one her mother had owned. The lady of the house always took breakfast in bed, her mother had told the child Rose, the privilege of a wife. What had become of that tray Rose sadly didn't know. "I was Duchess of Southdown," Rose said. "Still am, really—the dowager duchess now. What do they call you?"

The man ignored her question, his gaze becoming more focused. "What I mean is, if you're a duchess, why are you carrying trays to hungover officers in your garret? If this *is* a garret. Where the devil am I?"

He had a pleasant Scots accent and a nice rumbling baritone to go with it. A lady could listen to his voice all day and not tire of it.

"This is Miles's house," Rose said. "He didn't know where else to bring you. Or me. Miles is my coachman. Well, he *was* my coachman. I'm staying with him at the moment."

"Your coachman."

"That's right." Rose gave him an encouraging smile. "Now I have tea here, and plenty of toast with jam and butter, and a bit of sausage. Mrs. Miles makes a wonderful breakfast. Perhaps Miles can find a few odd jobs for you to do for a bit of coin before you go. Would you like that?"

The man's look turned to a glare—perhaps Rose shouldn't have mentioned the work; his pride was obviously intact. He didn't soften his gaze, but he struggled to sit up, his nostrils widening at the scent of the hot food. He was hungry, poor lamb.

The man's bare torso emerged from the blankets, and Rose swallowed and tightened her hold on the tray. His shoulders and chest were broad and sunbaked, his chest dusted with golden curls. The hard planes of his torso made her remember him falling against her, how she'd felt the steel of muscle beneath his soiled uniform coat.

This man had honed his body, had fought with it, if the scarred fingers, healed from breaks, told her anything. She could imagine women running their fingers down his chest, finding the hollows and planes of it, touching the dark areola that slid above the sheet.

The man saw her gaze and tucked the sheet under his arms, hiding most of his chest. But he didn't stammer or apologize for his nakedness in front of a lady, nor did he try to burrow back under the bedclothes. He simply reached for the tray that she'd frozen to, pried it out of her hands, and settled it across his lap.

"Where are my clothes?" he demanded.

"Pardon?" Rose blinked, tearing her gaze from the play of his thick-muscled arms as he uncovered the toast and poured tea.

"Clothes," he repeated. "I'm not wearing any. Where are they?"

The bareness of him went all the way down, Rose realized. She clenched her hands, since she didn't have anything else to hold. "Miles took your uniform away to be cleaned. It was dirty from the streets."

"London streets will do that." The man took a long drink of tea, and another, and another. The liquid had to be scalding, but he gulped it down and poured another cup. "You still haven't told me why a duchess is living with her coachman," the man said, lifting the first piece of toast. "And her coachman's wife." He put away the half slice in two bites and reached for another.

"I'm a duchess, because I married a duke," Rose said. "I was plain Miss Barclay before that, but my family is all gone now." The sorrow of that tore at her, and it always would. "I'm stopping with my coachman, because I'm skint. I had been staying with a friend, but she asked me to leave last night—or, rather, hinted strongly that I should go. Can't blame her, really. Journalists follow me about, waiting for me to do something scandalous, which happens all the time, unfortunately. I'm telling you this to warn you, because I'm certain the story of you coming home with me is all over London this morning. If you keep your head down, I think you'll be all right."

"Probably too bloody late for that," the man said. He downed two more half slices of toast. "Why is a duchess skint? Some aristos are impoverished these days, but dukes seem to do pretty well, overall. What about your widow's portion? Your dower house? Your jewels?"

All very good questions. "Ah, well, you see, much of my fortune is dependent upon the current duke, my late husband's son by his first marriage," Rose said. "My stepson is one of these modern men—he'd been rushing about being something in the City before he came into the title last year, and he learned all about profits and losses, turning land to the best use, investments and capital, and so forth. The wife of a former duke isn't much of an investment, is she?" Rose shrugged, pretending that the soldier's blatant masculinity didn't unnerve her.

At the same time, Rose found it easy to talk to him. The man kept eating—she hadn't seen such a healthy appetite in years—and he watched her, listening to every word. Rose wasn't used to someone who truly listened, not anymore.

"You must have settlements," he said between bites. "A widow's portion. Use of a house for your lifetime."

Rose nodded. "If all were well, I would. But my stepson is trying his best to prove that the settlements aren't valid. I have a solicitor to fight him, but he hasn't made much progress. I can't pay him much, you see, and my husband's solicitor now works for the new duke."

The man finished the toast and ate the sausages in about four bites. "You said your family was gone."

She gave him a sad smile. "Papa never had much but his connections, and he left me penniless. I'd been contemplating advertising for a post as a companion or governess when I met Charles . . . the duke. Soon after that, I became the second Duchess of Southdown." Rose let her thoughts go back to the fairy-tale glory of the wedding at St. George's, Hanover Square, the lavish entertainments afterward. Rose had been so happy that day. She was glad she hadn't known what was to come.

The man finished the last bite of sausage. "What happened?"

He sounded so interested that Rose peered at him. "You're not another journalist are you? Worming your way into my confidence with false pretenses?"

"Good God, no." The man laughed. When he did, he changed from hard-bitten soldier to a man of startling handsomeness, despite his unshaved face, sun-browned body, and shorn hair. "I'm only a grateful sinner, lass, glad of a warm bed and bit of breakfast."

His accent sent pleasant tingles down Rose's spine. "Not that it would matter. There is nothing about my life that hasn't been splashed across the newspapers. A young second wife is always food for gossip. I knew things would be difficult when I accepted Charles's proposal, but I never knew how vicious it could become."

"Gossips are all malicious," he said around the last swallow of tea. "Especially about beautiful women."

The flattery was delivered so even-handedly that Rose's face heated. She cleared her throat. "Now, I've told you my life story—what is yours? May I have a guess? Served your regiment faithfully for years, then they discharged you with nothing to live on? A common tale, I'm afraid. One of the charities my husband supported helps soldiers shunted unceremoniously back to England. They might be able to do something for you."

The man leaned back, breakfast over, and ran one hand through his shorn hair. "My story is that, in the regiment, I'm an honorable man. Outside it, I drink too much, gamble too much, and too much like . . ." He made a vague gesture, his cheekbones going red.

Rose broke into a grin. "Ah, the ladies. The downfall of many a man, as Charles used to say."

The man's gaze roved her, as though he tried to decide what to make of her. His look was thorough, that was certain. He would see a young woman in black, buttoned up to her chin, her only jewelry a mourning brooch and a string of onyx beads. Rose should really be in half mourning now or even out entirely, because Charles had been gone a year, but she couldn't afford to change her wardrobe. She'd likely be in black the rest of her life.

"You've been kind," the man said. "If you'll bring me my clothes, I'll leave you in peace."

Disappointment bit Rose, surprisingly so. She'd been enjoying speaking to him, pouring out things to him she'd been bottling up for nearly a year. Her girlhood friends, though they tried to be kind, didn't really want to *talk*. Not about things that mattered.

"You don't have to," she said quickly. "It's no bother, and as I said, Miles can find you things to do, so you can have some coin to take with you."

He rubbed a hand along his jaw. "What I'd truly like is a razor."

"That can be supplied. I'll ask Mrs. Miles."

Rose reached for the tray. In the confinement of the room, leaning down put her close to him, and she found his face a few inches away. His eyes were stormy gray, a beautiful color.

He did smell a little of whiskey, but the overall scent of him was warm, with a bite of spice. A man a woman would want to curl up with. No wonder ladies got him into trouble—he must attract them by the score.

"What is your name?" she asked, her voice barely working. "If you don't mind telling me."

"Steven," he said. The rumble flowed over her. "McBride. Captain, Twenty-Second Fusiliers."

Rose couldn't move. "Pleased to make your acquaintance."

His gaze moved to her lips, lingered there for a moment, almost as though he wanted to kiss her. Rose imagined it—his mouth would be strong, Captain McBride kissing her because he wanted to, not asking nicely for it. No politeness. Just desire, a man and a woman, and winter sunshine.

Rose dragged in a breath. She tried to make herself straighten up, but she couldn't. Captain McBride had a virile handsomeness behind the rough whiskers, not to mention a dangerous and compelling way about him.

Run away with me, Rose wanted to say. She longed to flee the constraints her life, the narrow confinement of mourning and shame, the rabid hunger of the journalists. She imagined herself roving the world with this man, both of them free and laughing, sleeping rough, snuggled together.

Poor and starving, shunned by gentlefolk, and prodded by constables. Ah yes, such a golden land she pictured.

Steven's expression changed, softening suddenly, and Rose realized she'd smiled at him. The hardness left his face, making him look so tender that Rose nearly dropped the tray.

He lifted one finger and brushed it across her cheek.

Compared to the way he'd clutched her last night, burying his face in first Rose's bosom then her stomach, the touch was nothing. But fire arced from his fingertips and shot swiftly down her body, lighting every feminine place.

Captain McBride slid his fingertip to her lips. Then his breath, warm and smelling of tea, touched her mouth.

"You'd better find me that razor," he said, his Scottish voice soft.

"What?" Rose blinked. "Oh. Yes. Of course. At once."

She made herself straighten up, the tray pressed hard to her stomach. Captain McBride kept his gaze on her, as palpable as his touch, as she backed away from the bed.

Rose forgot the room was so tiny, and she stumbled into the wall. She righted herself with a laugh, her onyx beads bumping her chest, and she swung away.

Now her skirt got caught on the bedpost. Rose tugged at it, but she couldn't grab it and hold the tray at the same time.

Captain McBride came halfway out of the bed, the covers sliding down to bare his chest, his side, the curve of his hip. Rose stilled, her eyes widening as he reached for the trapped skirt. She'd only seen a body like his in classic statues she was not supposed to look at. But cold marble had nothing on the living flesh of Steven McBride.

Steven tugged her skirt loose and sat back down, unselfconscious. Rose was free now, but she couldn't make herself cease staring at him. He noticed of course, but he said nothing, only met her gaze with a challenging one of his own.

Rose at last forced herself to turn away and open the door, but again, she had to juggle the tray to navigate the door handle.

A brown hand came around her and pressed the old-fashioned door handle down for her, Steven's strong arm pulling the door open. Rose had no breath. She knew she shouldn't dare peek behind her and look at him, but she couldn't help herself.

He'd managed to bring the quilt with him, wrapped around his waist. Even so, most of his upper body was bare, the heat of it pouring at Rose through her clothes.

"Thank you," she whispered.

Steven smiled, a devastating, knock-a-lady-down smile that had nothing feeble about it. Captain McBride knew Rose liked looking at him, and he didn't mind one bit.

She drew a stifling breath, yanked herself away from him, and scuttled out the door. Rose was halfway down the stairs when she heard his deep and satisfying laughter.

The duchess was scintillating. Not an adjective Steven used much in his life, but Rose Southdown was a lovely, lively woman. Her sad story, delivered with an oh-well-things-could-be-worse briskness tugged at his heart.

The coachman's wife, a plump and pink-cheeked woman, brought up the hot water and razor, and also the pile of Steven's clothes, brushed out and mostly clean. Steven was disappointed Rose hadn't delivered them herself, but he'd probably scared her away, coming out of the bed like that.

She'd been married, yes, but to a middle-aged man. Steven remembered meeting the Duke of Southdown once at a soiree at Hart Mackenzie's mansion. Southdown had been a pleasant enough chap in the English country gentleman sort of way. Hounds, horses, and farming had been his world. Though Southdown was a duke, the highest of the aristocracy, Steven couldn't help feeling the man would have been more at home talking in the pigsty with his steward about animal husbandry than making pleasantries in a Mayfair drawing room.

Rose's marriage meant she'd shared a bed with a man, but her shyness with Steven had been deep. Likely Southdown hadn't removed all his clothes when he came to his wife, only enough of them to do the business.

Or, perhaps Steven wronged the man. Who wouldn't look at that angel and not fling off his nightshirt and bear her down to the bed?

Mrs. Miles filled the basin, deposited Steven's cleaned and brushed uniform, gave him a cheery smile, and left him to carry on. Steven filmed his face with soap and carefully shaved his face. Felt good to wash away the stains of travel, too much whiskey, and whatever he'd fallen into out in the street.

He knew he was putting off the inevitable lingering here, but the inevitable was going to be difficult. He couldn't accomplish the task today anyway, he already knew that. So why shouldn't Steven take his comfort with the pretty and intriguing widow, cushioning himself against what was to come?

He was closing up the clasps on his uniform jacket when someone knocked on the door. To his "Come," the plain paneled door swung open to reveal Rose once more.

This time she had a newspaper in her hand, and her face over it was agitated. "I beg your pardon," she said, then she stopped and stared at him.

Steven said not a word as he finished doing up the buttons, straightening his jacket. Rose flushed as red as his army coat as she realized her mistake at thinking him a pathetic resident of the streets.

"I beg your pardon," she repeated. "But they've done it. Miles tried to break it to me gently, but I'm afraid they've included you too."

"Who has done what?" Steven asked.

For answer, Rose thrust a handful of newspapers at him. Steven turned the first one to where she pointed and read.

The Scandalous Duchess caught again, in the arms of Captain Mc—, a Fusilier in Her Majesty's Army. Will wedding bells ring, or will they play a different tune?

The second said, *Our favorite Duchess comforts a Scottish officer in the street. A Moral Tale.*

The third newspaper showed a cruel cartoon of Rose, her bosom exaggerated, and Steven, all arms and legs and chin, pinning her to the coach. The two weren't exactly copulating in the picture, but the cartoon strongly suggested it. *"Ken ye assist me, lassie?" Captain McB—, brother-in-law to those notorious Scots, the Mack—z—s, asks a favor from a Duchess, late of S—d—n. Nothing too sacred for Queen and Country.*

Nonsense, but when Steven looked up at Rose, tears stood in her pretty green eyes. "I'm so sorry," she said. "I seemed to have landed you in it."

The scandal sheets printed filth, and *she* was apologizing. Steven tossed the papers to the bed. "No, love, I'm sorry I've landed *you* in it. Don't worry, I've weathered worse. I'll take myself away, and the scandalmongers will forget in a few days, when something more juicy comes their way."

A shame, but there it was. Perhaps when Steven finished his duty and had leave again, he could find her and speculate on what might have been. That is, if another aristo hadn't snatched Rose up in the meantime. A woman as headily desirable as this one wouldn't stay alone for long, unless every man in London was blind and stupid.

Rose chewed her lower lip, a fine sight, and her brows drew into an agitated frown. "I'm afraid the scandalmongers will not let you get away so easily. They followed me home, it seems, or were bright enough to come here—I'm sure a few coins in the right hands let them know I spent the night in the coach house behind the duke's mansion. With you."

Looking into her eyes, Steven wished like hell he'd spent

the night in the way the journalists speculated. He and Rose in the narrow bed, cuddled under the blanket against the November cold, bare flesh to flesh.

Steven started to get hard at the thought, the buttons of his trousers suddenly too snug.

Rose watched him, worry for him in her expression. For *him*, Steven realized. For the drunkard who'd fallen on her and made her life even more wretched.

"We can slip you out the back," she was saying. "Or Miles can take you in the coach, perhaps quickly enough so they can't follow. To a train out of London?"

Yes, Steven could board a train for Scotland, bury himself at his brother Elliot's estate, fishing and playing with his niece and new nephew. Forget that he'd ever seen Rose Southdown and had the pleasure of being naked in her bed—unfortunately not in the way he'd have wished.

But no, he had errands to run, even if the result would be hell. He'd get away, but not lightly.

Or . . .

Steven shot her a sudden smile, his natural wickedness pushing aside all thoughts of running. "Send for your coach," he said. "Have it meet us in the front of the main house, or wherever the journalists are prowling. Put on your best frock, and come out with me."

Rose's eyes widened, but she looked curious rather than afraid. "What on earth for?"

"Because we're going to face them. If they want scandal, we'll give them scandal. We'll ram it down their throats. And then we'll turn the tables." He held out his hand. "Do you trust me?"

Rose's green eyes danced. "I have no idea. I've only just met you."

"Good. I'll tell you all about my ideas on the way."

"On the way where?"

"The Langham. I have a room there, but I'll have them put us in a couple of suites."

Rose's smile began, a wickedness matching his own. "Us?"

"This will take courage, but I'm certain you're up to it. Any woman who dragged a drunken, dirty lout home with her and carried breakfast to him in the morning has courage, in my opinion. Are we agreed?" Steven stuck out his hand again, and this time, Rose took it.

"Agreed."

Steven shook her soft, warm hand, but that was much too businesslike. He raised the backs of her fingers to his lips. "Agreed."

He wanted to haul her all the way against him and kiss her very kissable mouth, but Steven took pity on her and let her go.

"I will meet you downstairs," Rose said. Her eyes were alight, her face beautiful. *"Au revoir."*

She laughed and breezed out, leaving the room much emptier.

Rose knew she had to be mad as she hurried down to her own room, but she pushed the objections aside as she donned her Sunday best. The gown was black bombazine and quite plain, but looked well enough. Rose settled its small bustle and put the matching hat on her head.

Downstairs she walked out of the coach house and through the passage to the main house. The house's interior was dark and musty-smelling—Albert, the new duke, wasn't in residence, and rarely opened the place even when he was in Town. Charles would be so unhappy; he'd loved this house.

Rose swung open the front door, which had already been unbolted, and walked out, head high, to face the mob.

Most were journalists in black suits and hats, with three or four female scribblers in their midst. The women who followed Rose tended to be even harder on her than the men—the men at least could sometimes remember to be gentlemen. The women always let Rose have the worst of their opinions.

The crowd surged forward, intent upon her, but Rose remained firmly on the doorstep, glancing about for her carriage as though she didn't notice the scandalmongers. The coach was coming, driven by Miles, and when it stopped at the door, Steven got out of it.

Seeing him resplendent in his clean and brushed red uniform, the gold braid gleaming in the winter sunshine, Rose wondered how she'd ever thought him a pathetic castaway of the streets. Darkness, grime, and the rife smell of drink had convinced her, but there was no trace of dirt and alcohol now.

Steven stood tall and strong, his hatless head the color of sunshine. His hair was cropped close, as some military men's were, and he was clean-shaven, young gentlemen nowadays eschewing the heavy moustaches, beards, and mutton-chops of the older generation.

The journalists watched, agog, as Steven walked through them, took Rose by the arm, and led her to the carriage. At the carriage door, he lifted her hand to his lips, pressed a warm kiss to her glove, then helped her inside.

He jumped onto the carriage step, turning to beam a smile at the collected journalists. "Congratulate us," he said, then he sprang inside, snapped the door closed, and rapped on the roof to signal Miles to go on.

The coach jerked forward, the horses moving into a trot on this relatively empty street. A few intrepid scribblers jogged after them but gave up as the carriage turned a corner and was swallowed by thicker traffic.

"Congratulate us on what?" Rose asked as Steven settled into the seat opposite her.

Steven's grin beamed out, his eyes sparkling with merriment. "Our betrothal," he said.

Chapter 3

"Our . . ." Rose's words died as she clutched the velvet-cushioned seat. "I beg your pardon—our *what*?"

Steven's grin had faded, but he sat forward, animated, light glinting on the bright buttons of his uniform coat.

"Hear me out, love. If we tell the journalists we've been engaged all this time, they'll have to eat what they've been printing about you. Always entertaining, watching scandal-sheet scribblers backpedal."

"But . . ." Rose struggled for breath. Was he insane? She couldn't pretend to be engaged to him. She'd only just met him.

And yet . . . The camaraderie she'd sensed with Captain McBride was still between them. He was smiling, encouraging her, wanting her to dare to do this.

And why not? The journalists liked to print stories about Rose—from how much her wedding gown had cost to the shocking fact that the first duchess's jewels had been around her neck when she'd walked down the aisle. They hadn't, in fact, been jewels Charles had purchased for his first wife, but ones that had belonged to his mother. The first duchess had never worn those, preferring more modern pieces.

If the journalists were going to print stories, why not make certain they wrote about what Rose wanted them to? As Steven said, turn the tables on them?

She'd not had the courage to face them before. But with Steven beside her, Rose was again finding the playfulness she'd had when Charles had courted her—her willingness to ignore convention was one of the things that had attracted Charles to her. *Lively,* Charles had called her. And cheeky.

Rose sat forward to meet him, sunlight playing between them. "An enticing thought," she said, wanting to laugh. "But what happens when the charade is at an end? If they believe I jilted you, they will lambaste me."

"Not necessarily." Steven's gray eyes were alight, he looking less hungover by the minute. "I intend to make sure that by the time we are finished, you'll have plenty of money and can go anywhere you like, do as you please, to hell with what anyone thinks. I have access to some of the best solicitors in London— in all of Britain, in fact—both through my barrister brother and my Mackenzie connections through my sister. Those solicitors could make your stepson cough up what is legally owed you as well as bring suit against the newspapers."

Rose listened, excitement rising, while Steven rattled this off. "You thought of all this standing in your bedroom this morning, did you?"

Steven shrugged. "It came to me when you told me the vultures were lying in wait at the front door. I didn't want to leave you to face them alone. With one stroke, you can foil all your enemies." He slashed his hand down, brushing her knee in the process. Warmth blossomed there, and Rose wanted to both laugh and shiver.

It sounded like such fun—Steven was handing her a tendril of hope, one she wanted to grab and not let go.

She tried to make herself calm. "There is one catch in your plan, you know. If I am betrothed to you, my skinflint stepson will say he has no need to part with any brass at all. A husband takes care of a wife. I won't get the settlements if he believes I'm ready to marry again."

Steven gave her an admonishing look. "You leave that to me and the solicitors. Hart Mackenzie employs the best and most ruthless in the realm, and my brother Sinclair knows them all personally. The solicitors will work behind the scenes to bring you what you're owed, while in front of them, you and I will work to restore your good name." He lifted the window blind to look briefly out at the cold morning, then dropped it. "I've already sown the seeds, so you need to go along with it, don't you?"

The smile he turned on her as he said the last words crumbled any kind of objections. Steven McBride could make anyone do anything he wanted with such a smile, she decided, which did strange things to her heart.

Rose sank back to the seat, fanning herself with her black-gloved hand. "Why on earth would you do all this for me? You don't even know me."

"I'll say I'm repaying your kindness in taking me home when you thought I was a drunken vagrant. Most ladies would sweep their skirts aside or shout for the police. You felt sorry for me instead."

"I showed you a kindness, so you wish to pretend to be engaged to me?"

He shrugged. "The ruse also gives me a beautiful lady to escort about. You must keep up your end of it and accompany me everywhere. There are certain . . . attentions I wish to avoid on this trip. A respectable young woman at my side will be just the thing."

Rose shot him an amused look though she felt a twinge of envy. "The ladies again?" Women likely fell at his feet, and the fact that Steven had to stave them off meant they were many and determined. "Are you certain you wish to be hampered by a fiancée?"

Steven's look softened, as it had earlier in his bedroom, the hard man becoming a gentle one. "No man could be hampered by you, Rose."

Even the way he said her name, with a slight roll to the *R*, curled heat through her.

Rose cleared her throat. "We'll be closely watched. If you do encounter a lady you wish to spend time with, you'll have difficulty slipping away with all the journalists pressing against us." She meant to tease, but Steven gave her a serious look.

"Trust me, I'll not want to. I'm on leave for two months, one of which I'll spend in Scotland with my family. I'm not looking for frivolity." Steven's gaze moved down her tightly buttoned dress to the hips he'd clasped last night. "Though I can understand a gentleman wanting to be frivolous with *you*."

Rose blushed until she thought her face would scorch. "A business arrangement then," she made herself say. "You help me win back my money and reputation, and I guard you from unwanted attention."

"Exactly." Steven held out his hand, his grin returning. "Shall we shake on it?"

"You enjoy shaking hands." Rose held out her own. "We did this upstairs."

Steven closed his fingers around hers, the warmth of him coming through his gloves. He exuded so much strength, so much competence, that it filled her, bolstering her.

Rose could do this. If he was adamant about doing her a good turn, she could do him one when this was over. If Captain McBride managed to help Rose get the money Charles wanted her to have, she'd reward him well. Then she'd leave England and travel as she'd always wanted to. Hire a companion instead of being one, and go off to see the world.

The heat of his touch, however, made Rose's pulse flutter as it never had before. A voice whispered inside her that every moment spent in the company of Steven McBride was a danger to her, and Rose believed it.

<hr />

Memories of the previous day came to Steven as they rolled up to the Langham, a grand hotel situated where Regent Street transitioned to Portland Place. He *had* taken rooms here, but in his befuddled state of drink last night, Steven hadn't recalled that.

He'd sought drink not in his usual pursuit of entertainment, but to bolster his courage. His reason for returning to England early for Christmas was a sad one, which he'd have to face soon. Helping Rose would be a way to help him assuage the sadness and perhaps make up for the man he hadn't been able to save.

The hotel's manager, a well-dressed gentleman with a voice more posh than any duke's, came forward at Steven's beckoning as the doorman helped Rose out of the carriage. "A suite for the lady?" the manager repeated Steven's request. "Of course, sir. It is no trouble."

The man had always been accommodating to Steven, liking Steven's habit of tipping well, as well as liking his Mackenzie connections. The Mackenzies had been staying at the Langham for years, Cameron Mackenzie, Steven's brother-in-law, practically living there for long stretches at a time. The Mackenzie family had plenty of money, the McBrides, plenty of respectability—a fine combination.

Rose had already attracted a crowd who pointed and whispered as she swept in—the scandalous Duchess of Southdown was in their midst—highly entertaining. Rose pretended not to notice as she spoke cheerfully to the doorman. She slipped a small coin to the very young footman trying to carry all her bags at once, winning an adoring look from him. Rose had nothing, and yet she spared others what little she could.

The manager, obviously having decided that if Rose was now engaged to Steven, Steven might be able to keep her under some sort of control, turned away to bark orders at his underlings.

Steven moved back to Rose, ready to begin his role. Wouldn't be difficult, he thought as he neared her. She was a graceful and lovely woman, plump rather than painfully slender as fashion dictated. Ringlets of golden hair haloed Rose's face under her mannish hat—a creation with the brim curled up on one side and a black veil drifting down her back.

When Rose turned to greet Steven, her face flushing with her smile, something twisted in Steven's heart. She was speaking but he couldn't hear, and he couldn't move his gaze from her. Couldn't move his feet either, for that matter.

But Steven was practiced at verisimilitude, and he pasted a smile on his frozen mouth. "All right, darling?"

Rose's eyes widened at the endearment, but she checked her surprise. Her voice when she answered was breathless, just as it would be when they were in bed, when they'd finished . . .

Stop. Hard-ons in the lobby of the Langham were frowned upon. Must be.

"Yes, of course," Rose said. "Where shall I direct them to send my luggage?"

Steven forced the lump to leave his throat so he could

answer smoothly. "The manager has it well in hand." The obsequious man, indeed, had glided across the floor to give more orders to the footmen. "Shall we go up?"

Rose nodded and took Steven's offered arm, her body warm at his side. Steven led her through the staring crowd toward the staircase. They could have taken the lift, which rested between the sweeping flight of stairs, but Steven wanted everyone to see, to notice, to report.

On the first landing, as though oblivious of the men and women around them, Steven twined his arm around Rose's waist. He looked at her, only her, ignoring the rest of the world.

Easy to do, gazing into those beautiful green eyes, her face pink with excitement and a bit of guilt. Steven pulled Rose a little closer and brushed his lips across hers.

The tiniest kiss, that of a man unable to stop himself touching his beloved, but Steven's body nearly exploded. Heat rushed from Rose's soft mouth to burn through every nerve of him. Steven's heart constricted again, and if there *was* a rule against full-blown hard-ons on the hotel's main staircase, he was in trouble.

Rose's breath was warm, her body a soft bit of heaven. Her lips parted as Steven lifted away from her, her eyes half-closed with the stirrings of desire.

No wonder Rose was followed about, no wonder her every move filled the scandal sheets. Every man in London must be falling over his feet to have her, their pursuit giving the scribblers plenty to write about. Now they'd write about Steven as well, and his privilege of kissing this beautiful woman.

Rose blinked a little, no doubt wanting to tell him to go to the devil, but she kept up the pretense and gave him a little smile instead. No one passing would believe anything but that Rose was happily engaged to Steven. He tightened his arm around Rose and led her on up the stairs.

Steven's lips burned from the brief contact, firing him from the inside out. If he got out of this little charade alive, it would be a bloody miracle.

～

"A tricky problem," the solicitor said.

Steven and Rose sat in comfortable chairs in the parlor of

Rose's suite at the hotel that afternoon, the solicitor, Mr. Collins, facing them. Mr. Collins was surprisingly young—Rose surmised he couldn't have been more than his early thirties. But he came highly recommended by both the Duke of Kilmorgan and Steven's barrister brother, Sinclair McBride. Mr. Collins had a shock of bright red hair, a tastefully trimmed moustache, and a neat black suit. Everything correct.

Steven had changed out of his regimentals and had donned a McBride plaid kilt, plain white shirt and waistcoat, and a black frock coat. He wore thick wool socks that emphasized his strong calves, and low leather shoes. Rose could not help surreptitiously running her gaze over him, more than once. More than twice. He made a delectable picture.

The suite he'd procured for her was one of the most elegant in the hotel. The parlor had a cluster of velvet-cushioned sofas and chairs drawn near a marble fireplace, with a heavily carved dining table and matching chairs on the other side of the room. A gas chandelier above them stretched out gilded arms ending in etched globes to soften the harsh light. Tall, draped windows graced the other side of the room, the lace curtains letting in patterns of sunshine.

The bedroom was still more elegant, with a large carved bed heaped generously with pillows, the dressing table more vast than the one she'd had in her dressing room at Sittford House, the Duke of Southdown's estate. Everything Rose needed for a comfortable stay had been provided, including a maid to look after her.

Captain McBride was giving all this to her. When Rose had tried again to ask him why, he'd shrugged and said of course he'd take care of his betrothed. He'd told Miles to go home to his wife—Miles still technically worked for Albert, though Albert rarely came to town. Albert kept Miles and the coach simply so he wouldn't have to take a hansom from the train whenever he did arrive in London.

Steven would arrange for the transportation from now on, he'd said. He'd slipped Miles a handful of banknotes, saying they were compensation for Miles putting Steven up for the night and feeding him in the morning. Miles had been touched, Rose could see.

"The entail is very clear," Mr. Collins was saying. "Albert

Ridgley, the new Duke of Southdown, of course inherits the
title, house, and land, and all moneys and goods tied to the
house. The new duke has no legal obligation to give you anything, Your Grace, except what was specified in the marriage
settlements, or put into trust for you by your own family—but
Mr. McBride has told me that your family was gone before
you married and left you with little."

"That is true," Rose said. "My father had nothing to leave."
She stopped, her grief for her charming but rather feckless
father never far away.

Mr. Collins made noise rustling papers, as though giving
her time to compose herself. Steven was watching Rose,
though, his gray gaze taking in her grief with understanding.

"The new duke is blocking the settlements on you, claiming . . ." Mr. Collins kept leafing through papers Rose had no
idea where he'd obtained. "Here it is. Claiming that your marriage to the duke wasn't quite legal."

Rose nodded. "I know he is. But I don't know how he can
say that. My marriage to Charles was perfectly all right—
Albert attended the ceremony himself. The banns were read
the requisite number of weeks before the wedding day, a
bishop conducted the service, and we signed a register, everything done properly. We didn't elope clandestinely in the middle of the night or anything like that." She waved her hand. "It
was a perfectly aboveboard service, Mr. Collins. I remember
it well." Rose flashed him a smile. "I was there."

Mr. Collins flushed and moved uncomfortably. "Yes, I'm
certain you were, Your Grace. But the new duke's solicitor
showed me the evidence he had when I went to him to challenge him. The new duke is putting forth that the marriage
isn't legal because—my apologies, Your Grace—because you
were already married at the time."

His voice died away, and Rose shot to her feet, eyes wide.
"Rubbish."

Steven was up next to her, a hand on her arm. "What the
devil are you talking about, Collins?"

Collins went as red as his hair, but he rose politely and held
out a piece of paper. "I'm afraid it's here."

Steven snatched the paper from him as Rose clenched her

fists. She liked that Steven came back to stand next to her, shoulder to shoulder, to look at the damning document with her.

It was a copy of a parish register from a church near Dundee in Scotland. On it was a plainly written entry:

Rose Elizabeth Barclay and Keith Erskin, married, June, 1880.

Chapter 4

Rose stared at the two names in shock. One was hers, *Rose Elizabeth Barclay*, in fine copperplate handwriting. The other was Keith Erskin, her first beau, a young man she hadn't seen in years.

Steven was watching her, his shoulder still against hers. His voice was low, calming, but at the same time brooking no lies. "Did you know this Mr. Erskin?"

Rose's breathing came with difficulty, the names swimming before her eyes. "Yes, of course, I knew him. But I never *married* him. Never was even betrothed to him." Rose looked at Mr. Collins, who regarded her with his stoic solicitor's expression. Steven only waited, so close that the heat from his body warmed her side. "It was another scandal, but this never happened. I promise you."

Rose expected Steven to demand an explanation, for her to tell him that she'd lied, and the certificate was true. But he only gazed at her, his eyes light gray among the parlor's garish colors, before he handed the paper to back Collins. "Must be a forgery."

Collins shrugged as he took the page. "I considered that the document was false, and I will look into it. But it is the argument the new duke is using to keep you from any funds, and out of the dower house." He tucked the offending paper away and cleared his throat. "Your Grace."

Rose hadn't moved her gaze from Steven, who looked steadily back at her. "You believe me?"

Steven's eyes were quiet as he gave her a nod. "You'd best know who you married and who you didn't, wouldn't you?"

She couldn't help letting a corner of her mouth turn upward. "And who I'm betrothed to?"

Steven's almost-smile in answer made her face grow warm. "Exactly. It's a forgery, Collins." He guided Rose back to her chair, his hand strong on hers, and they all sat again. "Make the new duke admit it."

"I will do so," Mr. Collins said, sounding determined. "You may at least take comfort, Your Grace, of the duke's bequests to you in his will. You have those, if nothing else."

Rose blinked, her attention dragged from Steven. "Charles left me something in his will? I had not heard this."

Mr. Collins regarded her in surprise that turned quickly to shock. "Are you saying you were not made aware of the will's contents?"

Rose clenched her hands on the chair's carved arms. "Albert and his solicitor told me the will had nothing to do with me. Blast the man." Her temper rose as she realized the extent of Albert's treachery. "He's tried to cut me out at every turn."

Mr. Collins shuffled more papers, apparently his method of diffusing a tense situation. "Your stepson might contest the bequest, of course, but what the late duke left you, I'm happy to say, is to you by name, absolutely, and not dependent on trusts, settlements, and former relationships."

"Get on with it, Collins," Steven said. "Tell her it's something like the sum of twenty thousand guineas, to be settled on her without question."

"Unfortunately not." Mr. Collins looked apologetic and smoothed another paper in front of him. "He names no sum."

"What does he name, then?" Rose asked, as impatient as Steven.

Collins cleared his throat again and read from the page he'd pulled out. "To Rose Elizabeth, née Barclay, whom I regard in the highest esteem, and because of her kindness, patience, and caring nature, I leave two pieces of furniture of her choice from Sittford House, my ducal seat, and all the contents of those two pieces, whatever they may be. To be hers absolutely, for her use, or for her to dispose of as she sees fit."

Collins lowered the paper, and Rose stared at him, puzzled. "Two pieces of furniture? Are you certain?"

Mr. Collins put his finger on the line. "Quite certain."

"What an odd thing for him to do," Rose said softly. Charles had proved he'd had a taste for whimsy, but she wished he'd been more practical on *this* matter. A sum of money, no matter how small, or a pair of diamond earrings, or even Charles's favorite horse, would have been welcome. Furniture was nice, but she had no house in which to put it.

Steven was frowning, but his voice vibrated comfortingly. "Some old furniture can be valuable. Had the duke any good pieces?"

"Charles's collection was famous," Rose said, feeling nothing. "Sittford House has furniture and artwork from many periods of history, handed down through the family. But I thought it was all connected to the estate."

"Much of it is," Collins said, his apologetic tone becoming even more so. "The paintings and the more priceless of the antiques are part of the trust and must remain with the estate." He gave Rose a look of sympathy. "If it's any consolation, your stepson can't sell them either."

Steven frowned and brought his scarred fingertips together. "All the contents of the two pieces. Interesting way of putting it. Maybe he left her something in a bureau somewhere in the house. Jewels or something like that."

Mr. Collins considered. "It is possible. Any jewels, though, that belong to the family stay with the family, unless the duke bought them specially for you."

Rose shook her head. "Anything I wore belonged to Charles's mother." Albert hadn't liked that one bit.

"You're saying Albert gets his paws on everything," Steven said, still frowning. "Except a few sticks of furniture. Not very fair to Rose."

"Not *everything* is attached to the estate," Mr. Collins said. "You'd have to go to the house or look at an inventory, Your

Grace. I suggest you make an inventory yourself. Perhaps there was something your husband knew you liked, but feared to state it specifically in the will, in case his son tried to destroy it or sell it. The new duke can hardly get rid of every piece of furniture in the house to keep you from having any."

"He might," Rose said darkly. "Albert is as tightfisted as they come." She lifted her chin. "But he's kept me from what Charles wanted this long. I believe I'll pay him a visit and take my two pieces of furniture, blast him."

Steven reached over and rested his hand on hers. His fingers were hot, warmth on this cold, rain-streaked day. "Good for you," he said. His eyes too, held heat, and a strength that Rose wanted to draw into herself. When he released her to turn back to Collins, his warmth remained, as though he'd gifted it to her.

"Is that all?" Steven asked Collins. "Nothing else she can do?"

"Not for the moment," Collins said. "I'll work to prove the marriage registered in Scotland never occurred, and fight for your settlements. I am good at what I do, if I say so myself, Your Grace. I wouldn't give up yet."

"Thank you." Rose's anger fell away in a rush of gratitude. "I've not had any hope since the day Charles passed. Bless you, Mr. Collins." She rose and held out her hands to the man, and Mr. Collins, blushing even more heavily, stood up and let her grasp his.

"It's my job," Mr. Collins said, extracting himself, and putting his papers back into a valise. "Thank Mr. McBride for sending for me. He enjoys helping people, does Mr. McBride."

Steven remained expressionless. "Appreciate you coming out in the rain, Collins," he said. "I'll walk you down."

Mr. Collins took his leave of Rose with many expressions of politeness. Steven clasped Rose's shoulder and leaned to gently kiss her cheek. "It will be all right," he said. "I promise you."

The kiss was like a touch of sunlight in gloom, a flicker of hope in a morass of fear. Steven's confidence was so great that it reached through her veil of despair and found the Rose who'd been shivering in the dark since Charles had died.

His touch, his voice, his very presence was daring her to believe in miracles.

"Still helping those in need, are you, Stevie, lad?" Mr. Collins, whose Christian name was Tavis, said as he and Steven left the hotel.

They emerged to fine November rain, which coated the streets and stone buildings, turning the gray scene even more gray. The only contrast was black—carriages and hansoms, dark-colored horses, men in black overcoats and black hats. Collins's bright red head and Steven's kilt were the only colors in the gloom.

"Can't seem to help myself," Steven answered, trying to sound nonchalant.

Collins's look turned serious. "Have you seen her yet?"

He wasn't talking about Rose. Steven shook his head. "She's been out of London. I have an appointment with her in two days' time."

"She already knows, I take it?"

"Yes—a cold, impartial telegram. But I want to see her. She deserves that."

"It might not be easy." Mr. Collins put his hand on Steven's shoulder. "If you'd like me to go with you, I will. I am her solicitor too, you know."

Steven shook his head. "She'll be angry with me, and you need have no part in it." He shrugged, and Collins released him. "I'll cheer myself up helping Rose—the dowager duchess, I mean. Fortify myself for my task."

Collins gave him a knowing look. "The *very beautiful* dowager duchess."

"Beauty isn't everything. I've learned that a time or two." Steven couldn't stop his sudden grin. "This one's beautiful all the way through."

"You've said that a time or two as well, Stevie."

"This is different."

"Heard that one too." Collins returned the grin. "When you get your heart broken, look me up, and I'll pour whiskey down your throat. Again."

"I won't get my heart broken," Steven said. "This is different, because it's not a romance. I'm helping her; she's taking my mind off my troubles."

"Yes, of course." Collins's words were drowned out as a hansom clattered to a stop at the doorman's signal. "Don't you break *her* heart. She doesn't deserve that."

"No fear," Steven answered. "Go do what you're best at, Collins, and stop giving me advice on romance. Be off with you."

Collins stuck out his hand, shook Steven's, and scrambled into the hansom. Steven watched the man drive off, his emotions mixed. Whoever got their heart broken in this business arrangement, Steven was certain, it wouldn't be Rose.

He put aside such maudlin thoughts as he headed out of the rain back into the hotel. His heart beat faster as he ascended the stairs, knowing Rose awaited him at the top. He wondered, between steps, whether his need to make up for his failure had prompted him to help her.

But when he opened the door, and Rose turned from the window with her welcoming look, Steven knew he'd not taken up with her for any feelings of guilt. He'd walk through fire for this woman. Steven had only just met her, but already she'd changed his life.

If nothing else came of this, he'd be a different man when he left her, and for that he'd be forever grateful.

Sittford House, seat of the Dukes of Southdown, lay in Hampshire, far enough from London and other cities to be free of smoke and grime. These days, with trains as swift as they were, the journey was not more than an hour or two.

Steven booked a first-class carriage for himself and Rose. Journalists lay in wait for them outside the hotel, and managed to be in the train station as well. They wanted to know where Rose and Steven were going.

"Business," Steven told them, and let them make of it what they would. "You know how betrothals are."

"When will the banns be read?" someone asked. "Or will this be a Scottish wedding?"

"We'll wed in Scotland," Steven said. "With family." He tipped his hat. "Good day, gentlemen. Ladies."

Rose said nothing at all, only gave them her winsome smile. The smile sent Steven on flights of wicked fancy, but he could see the journalists didn't approve. Perhaps if Rose had been demure and walked about with her head bowed, she might escape more of the scurrilous stories. The journalists might have decided that her late husband had married a nurse to take care of him in his dotage, instead of a lively woman to give him back his youth.

Rose Barclay was anything but demure, Steven thought as the maid fussed around to settle her into the compartment. Though her frock was buttoned to her chin, and she wore only mourning jewelry, her color was high, her eyes sparkling, her head lifted. All the black clothes in the world couldn't repress her vibrancy.

As the train slid out of the city, and the maid left them, Rose looked about her as though this were the most exciting journey she'd taken in some time. Steven enjoyed himself watching her for a while before he forced himself back to business.

"Tell me about Keith Erskin," he said as the farmland, dusted with snow, flowed past, along with low, tree-covered hills. "The man you are purported to have married. Is he likely to cause trouble over this?"

Rose shook her head, looking neither guilty nor embarrassed. "He was a childhood friend, later a beau." Her cheeks went pink. "We were caught kissing at a ball when I was eighteen. He was encouraged to propose to me, but I could see his heart wasn't in it, poor lad. The prospect of marrying at eighteen and settling down dismayed him greatly. So I refused him. This gave me the reputation of being a very fast young lady indeed, and my father took me away to Edinburgh." She looked out the window, her gaze going remote. "In retrospect, perhaps we ought to have married, but we were young and full of stubborn dreams. We each were determined to see the world, I remember, but neither of us has left the British Isles as far as I know." She gave a short laugh. "We might have had an ordinary life, in an ordinary town, and I'd not be followed about whenever I step out of doors."

Steven couldn't stop his smile, which rose up inside him like a light. "You were never made for ordinary, Rosie. There's nothing ordinary about you and never will be."

She flushed, which made her look even more like an exotic siren trapped in the stiff clothing of a less enlightened age. "You aren't so ordinary yourself," she said.

"True." Steven tried to ignore the excitement of having that lovely green gaze on him. He'd left the hotel last night to do quite a bit of drinking before he'd been able to return, precisely to forget that look. Hadn't worked. "I had a strange upbringing—raised by my oldest brother, Patrick, who has twenty years on me. I was the spoiled youngest child, and it led me into a lot of trouble. Made me think there was nothing I couldn't do."

Her interest warmed his blood. "Such as?"

"Tales for another time, dear lady. We're arriving."

The train had slowed, chugging its way into a station. The maid hurried back in to help Rose, who tried to hide her disappointment that their conversation had ended so abruptly.

They descended into cold. Because Steven hadn't written or telegraphed that they were coming—no sense in putting Albert on guard—they had to hire a conveyance to take them to the house. Wasn't difficult to find, because every man, woman, and child in the village of Sittford spied Rose emerging from the train and mobbed her.

"Have you come back to live here?" a young man in a blacksmith's apron asked. "Say you have, Your Grace."

Another was a woman who'd come out of the post office and shop. "Please talk some sense into that stepson of yours, Your Grace. The house has bought my goods for fifty years—now he's sending to a cheap firm in London . . ."

"You're a tart and always will be. You'll never be the real duchess 'round here. *She* were a lady." The last was from an older woman who stood in her front garden opposite the station, her hands wrapped around a cane. A few other women stood near her, nodding agreement.

"Ignore them," Steven said under his breath as he handed Rose up into a dogcart, the only vehicle available.

"She's been saying such things since the first time I arrived." Rose gave the elderly woman a gracious nod, which the woman and her cronies returned with sullen glares. "Her husband treats her poorly—Charles always had trouble with him. I'll speak to His Grace, Mrs. Harrison," she called to the woman who ran the shop. "As soon as he lifts himself from the floor after the shock of seeing me back here. Drive on, Mr. Gains."

A dozen or so children followed after the cart, waving and

yelling, clearly curious about Steven. They gave up as the road bent around a corner from the village and drifted away.

"Thank you for coming with me," Rose said, hanging on to the seat in the rocking cart as they rolled between hedgerows. "I didn't realize how shaky I'd be coming out of the station. I had no idea how they'd receive me."

"I wasn't about to make you face dear Albert alone," Steven said.

He screwed up his eyes against the sunlight on snow, his head pounding. The thought of himself lying randy and uncomfortable in his hotel bed, knowing Rose lay on the other side of the wall, had sent him out last night. He'd met up with friends he hadn't seen in donkey's years, drank too much, dragged himself back at four, and then was up a few hours later to catch a train.

Steven had successfully avoided lying in bed wishing Rose was in it with him, but now his head was punishing him, and all this light *hurt*. It hadn't been as bad in the train, but the dogcart was open to the world, nothing to mute the white glare.

"I know," Rose said, her contralto like a balm on his raw nerves. "But this isn't your fight."

"It is now." Steven put his hand over his eyes. Helped, and also shut out his need to see her smile. "My impetuousness put me in this right up to my neck."

"Still, I am grateful."

Don't make me out to be a hero. Steven's words inside his head were impatient, almost savage. *I'm a frivolous, drunken rake, not a benevolent philanthropist. I'm helping you to make up for the fact that I couldn't help someone else.*

The dogcart jerked, making Steven's headache stab at him. He had to stop seeking out his friends. Perhaps stop even *having* friends.

The cart rumbled over a bridge, a half-frozen stream trickling in the bed below it, and the house came into view. Steven sat up and sucked in a breath.

The place was bloody enormous. Built in the early Georgian style, the house was perched on a wide green hill. It was composed of three huge, boxlike wings, each crowned with a giant triangular pediment. Flat columns marched across the house between tall, many-paned windows and more columns flanked a massive front double door. The structure had been built of golden stone, and when sunshine broke through the clouds, the house took on a bright hue, painfully so.

"Good God," Steven said. He'd spent the past few Christmases at Kilmorgan Castle in Scotland, a pile even larger than this, but it was different somehow. Kilmorgan was always overflowing with families, children, dogs, and horses when Steven visited, and never seemed too large.

This monstrosity had an empty look, as though knowing its master had gone, never to return. Not literally true, because a Duke of Southdown was still master here—he was just a different man. The house seemed to feel its emptiness, however, and mourn.

"I loved this house the moment I saw it," Rose said with a sigh. "My stay in it as a wife was brief, but I consoled myself with the fact that I'd at least continue living on the estate. But that wasn't meant to be."

She looked so sorrowful that Steven wanted to move to her seat and gather her into his arms. He held on to the sides of the cart to keep from doing it.

The drive took them past the dower house, a much smaller version of the main mansion. It too had been built of golden stone, and its three-story, one-winged splendor looked a bit more cheerful than its parent.

As they rolled by, Steven heard barking—a lot of barking. A man came out the front door of the dower house, followed by three hounds, and stopped to stare at the cart.

"That's Mr. Hartley, the steward," Rose said. She lifted her hand in greeting, and Mr. Hartley's mouth popped open. The dogs stared as well, but wagged tails. "Albert has turned the dower house into a kennel for his dogs. Albert loves to hunt, you see."

The steward belatedly bowed, but his gaze remained fixed as the dogcart rattled by.

The driver took them around the last curve of the drive and pulled to a halt in front of the main door. Steven stepped off the back of the cart, slipped the man a few coins, and then helped Rose descend.

Steven shouldn't suddenly feel better with her warm weight against him, shouldn't want to stop in the act of helping her down to press a kiss to her lips. Then again, that was what an engaged couple in love might do. Wouldn't be odd at all.

Steven knew that his kiss wouldn't stop with a light touch. Not by a long way. He had to content himself with a caress to her waist, or else he'd lose control. Regretful, but there it was.

The front door was locked, but Rose had a key. Even as she turned it, the door was wrenched open from the inside, making her lose hold of the key. "Ma'am!" the footman who stood on the threshold exclaimed. "I mean, Your Grace."

The footman was a tall lad, dapper and good-looking in his kit, as the footmen of great houses were meant to be. Many were hired more for their looks than their wit, Steven had learned by experience. His brother Patrick had tended to hire impoverished but well-schooled young men to help in his household—they'd been terrible footmen but had regularly discussed mathematics and classical thought with the brothers, which had been the point.

This footman seemed to be of the decorative but dim variety. He stared at Rose as hard as the steward had done, but with less guilt in his eyes.

"Tell the duke Her Grace has arrived," Steven said to him in his commanding-officer voice.

The young man dragged his gaze from Rose, blinked at Steven, then snapped to attention. "His Grace is not at home. Sir."

"It's all right, John," Rose said. "I've only come for a few things I left behind."

John blinked some more, indecision warring in his eyes. He seemed respectful of Rose, even happy to see her, but he must have been given strict instructions regarding her admittance.

Steven softened his tone. "No one needs to know you let us in," he said. "Her Grace has a key, and you never heard us."

John stared at them a little longer before Steven's words penetrated. "Ah." His face flooded with color. "Yes, sir, that will be what happened." He stepped aside and opened the door wider. "Welcome home, Your Grace. If you don't mind me saying so, ma'am, it's a fine thing to see you back."

Chapter 5

The house opened its arms to welcome Rose. She looked around with fondness as they started up the wide staircase, which rose gracefully in the open hall all the way to the top of the house. Portraits of dukes and duchesses and their sons, daughters, nieces, nephews, great-aunts, reprobate uncles, dogs, horses, and even a few cats covered every inch of the walls. Charles had introduced them all, telling Rose a funny story about each one. What had been intimidating to her at first glance had turned into a gathering of family.

Steven studied the surroundings with less enthusiasm. His eyes were bloodshot, his face a bit puffy, and by the way he'd massaged his temples during the journey, Rose knew he had a bad headache.

"His Grace really is not at home?" Steven asked John as the lad followed them. "Or is that a polite fabrication?"

John had a slight difficulty with the word *fabrication*, but he finally understood. "No, it's not a porky—I mean, a lie, sir. His Grace went up to London on business, so housekeeper said. Not expected back until tomorrow."

"Good," Steven said. "Thank you, lad. Now, remember, you have no idea we're here."

"None at all, sir." John shot him a grin. He gave Steven a hero-worshiping look for another moment, before he realized he'd been dismissed. "Right. It truly is good to see you, ma'am." He bowed to Rose and ran back down the stairs with athletic grace.

"He must make quite an impression on the duke's guests," Steven said once the lad was safely away. "As long as he stands still and says nothing."

"He really is a very good footman," Rose said protectively. "I was never very strict with the servants, which gained me more disapproval from my stepson, unfortunately."

Steven flushed. "Forgive me, Rosie. My head has me growling like a bear this morning." He gazed up the stairs and its seeming miles of railings. "Two pieces of furniture . . . in all *this*?"

Rose understood his dismay. They'd paused on the first landing, which gave them a view of the ground floor below and the first floor above. Both halls were filled with graceful furniture—lowboys and highboys, console and demi-lune tables, straight-backed chairs and Bergère chairs, candle stands and candelabras, cushioned benches and settees. The furniture was valuable, Charles had said, ranging in period from the seventeenth and eighteenth centuries, through the Regency and to the manufactured styles early in Queen Victoria's reign. After that came the cleaner styles of William Morris and his ilk, and the hand-carved, rather sinuous French chairs Charles had purchased in Paris a few years ago.

And these were only the landings. Sittford House had one hundred rooms—exactly—and each was fully furnished.

"Charles was no fool," Rose said. "He knew Albert was exacting and didn't like his father spending any money he might inherit. Charles must have had something specific for me in mind. But what?"

Steven sank to the top stair of the landing, his hand to his head. Rose seated herself next to him, concerned. "You all right?"

Steven rubbed his temples. "My brain is melting, but nothing to worry about. Let us sit here quietly and think about this, my Rose. Instead of tearing all over the house searching every cabinet, we should make a plan. Was there something in particular you admired? That the duke knew you liked?"

"I've been trying to think. But the last year or so is such a jumble, it's difficult."

Steven lounged back on his elbows and looked up at her. "You were fond of your husband."

Rose nodded. "Indeed I was. Charles was a good man."

Steven stretched out his legs, and Rose's heart beat faster in confusion. Steven was a sinfully beautiful sight—a hard-bodied man in a kilt, his reclining position stretching his coat open over his broad chest. Gentlemen didn't lie down in the presence of ladies, unless they had something intimate in mind, but sitting here beside Steven seemed so natural. Rose wasn't afraid, even though they were quite alone, the staff unlikely to come upstairs. Steven was a strong man; he might do anything, and yet, Rose felt comfortable with him, as she'd felt with no one else since Charles.

But here they were, on the floor in the house of a man she'd admired and respected. Though the world had assumed Charles had taken a young second wife to have something pretty on his arm, Rose and Charles had liked each other very much. They'd been able to talk, share jokes and opinions, and laughter. Charles had also not been reluctant where bed had been concerned. The fact that his heart had dangerously weakened had surprised them both.

Steven's touch jolted her back to the present. He closed his hand around hers, his strength coming to her through his grip. "I'm sorry," he said. "I didn't realize how hard this would be for you."

Rose hadn't either. Tears stung her eyes. Steven squeezed her fingers, then he released her and let out a groan. "Och, my bloody head."

"Let me." Rose moved until she sat behind him, and she cradled his head in her lap. She removed her gloves and touched her fingers to Steven's temples.

A mistake, she realized as soon as skin contacted skin. His pulse throbbed beneath her fingertips, his lifeblood. Steven had so much warmth in him, so much *life*.

He closed his eyes as Rose began to massage his forehead, which was a good thing. His gray eyes, even tinged red from his hangover, unnerved her. She didn't tell him she'd lain awake most of the night, worried he'd gone and wouldn't be back. Worried that he'd found another damsel in distress to help, one more interesting than Rose.

When she'd heard Steven stumble in at a small hour in the morning, she'd let out a sigh of relief. She'd wanted to go to him, speak to him, make sure he was all right. It had taken all Rose's strength of will to keep herself in her chamber and away from him.

Now she eased her fingers over his temples, finding his close-cropped hair warm and sleek. She liked the way the shorn ends tickled her fingers.

"Mmm," Steven said. "That's nice."

Steven was nice, and Rose desired him—she knew what the heat flushing her body meant.

"I've always been good at soothing away hurts," Rose said.

Steven's eyes flicked open, his gaze seeking hers. "Have you now?" He finished with an upturn of lips, a wicked one. "Skilled with your hands, are you?"

Her face went hot, but she kept her voice light. "Are you flirting with me, Captain McBride?"

"With my own fiancée? Of course I am." His smile broadened. "I'm not a polite man, Rosie, I warn you."

Rose didn't want to be polite. She wanted to sit here and drown in him, to let him smile at her like that all day long.

She made herself ease away and rise to her feet. "We should get on."

Steven looked up at her from where he lay back on his elbows, his gaze taking in every inch of her. "You're right, Rosie. We should carry on until we're both satisfied."

Rose flushed and turned to the next half of the staircase. "You're being naughty now."

"I'm naughty all the time, sweetest Rose."

He came off the steps and to his feet, moving swiftly for a man with a bad headache. Steven caught up to her and stopped her, Rose one step above him.

The stair took away their difference in height, putting their faces on the same level. Steven's breath touched Rose's lips, reminding her of the all-too-brief kiss he'd given her on the staircase at the hotel.

What was it about staircases? Rose couldn't stop herself reaching out and touching his cheek.

Steven's guarded expression dropped. He looked at her with naked wanting, no disguising it, no holding back. As warmth swept through Rose, answering heat flared in his eyes.

It was nothing to lean a small bit forward and kiss his lips.

Steven's eyes closed as his arm came around her, nothing gentle. He parted her lips with a strong mouth, pulling her close, binding her to him. He swept his tongue into her, no politeness, no reticence. This kiss was insistent and new, and the hot, wild friction of it swept away the rest of Rose's reluctance.

No man had ever kissed her like this before, not with this raw, desperate wanting. These weren't the hesitant kisses of a man who feared to offend a respectable widow. Steven knew what he wanted, and he would take it, to hell with civility.

Rose cupped the back of his neck, again finding the sleek fineness of his hair. Strength and heat came through his body, entering hers at every point of contact. She knew his hunger as his mouth worked. Every part of Rose went shaky—the only thing holding her up was Steven. Her legs had lost all strength.

Steven's mouth was fire. One hand came up between them, cupping her breast in his palm, hand tightening.

She was going to fall. Rose clutched Steven's back, fingers pressing through his coat to the hard strength of him.

Steven pulled away a little, but only to smooth a lock of her hair. "My Scottish Rose." His voice was low, uneven.

Rose couldn't speak, couldn't answer. She wanted to kiss him again. Wanted it more than anything, more than she should, especially standing in this house.

Steven brushed her cheek with the backs of his fingertips. His brows drew together, then he touched the corner of her mouth.

Just as Rose thought he'd pulled away, he made a raw sound in his throat and kissed her again.

Heady sensations, heat chasing shivers, and again Rose had to lock her fingers on to his coat to remain on her feet. Steven closed his teeth over her lower lip, and fire streaked through her, like a lightning storm homing in on one point.

Steven traced her lip with his tongue, then once more slid his mouth over hers. This time, Rose met his strokes with her own, their bodies locked together, touched by the cool draft from the staircase.

Sanity didn't return even when Steven eased back, wiping a tiny bit of moisture from Rose's upper lip.

"Oh, Rosie," he said, his accent thick. "Why the devil did I have to meet ye?"

"We didn't meet." Rose struggled to find her voice. "We stumbled into each other."

"Aye, and I wanted to stay fallen on you forever. You're a beautiful woman, my Scottish Rose. You could be the end of me."

And you, of me, Rose finished silently.

Steven touched her cheeks, his hands caressing as he held her with his gaze. His eyes looked clearer now, the same color as the winter sky through the window behind him.

Love was for warmth, and spring, Rose tried to tell herself. Not for winter, and cold.

But perhaps love knew no seasons—it simply came when it was time.

"We should commence our search," Steven said. "Before young John returns to be shocked."

"Yes." Again, Rose had to search for breath to form the sound. "We should."

Steven smiled at her, which did nothing to help Rose collect herself. He released her from the comfort of his arms, but only to take her hand and lead her on up the stairs.

～～～

Steven hadn't caught his breath even by the time Rose had led him up through the maze of the house to the top floor.

The manor wasn't truly a maze—it had been built at the end of the seventeenth century, when straight lines and symmetrical architecture had been in fashion. But its occupants had, for the past two hundred years, filled it with screens, cabinetry, sofas, tables, chairs, paintings, bric-a-brac, mirrors, chests, highboys, étagères, desks, and credenzas by the score, and every room had mixed and matched styles from over the centuries. A decorator in the past had tried to break up the severity of right angles in rooms by placing the furniture together in the middle, which succeeded only in making everything more of a jumble.

Might have interested Steven more if his whole body hadn't

been burning from Rose's nearness. One taste of her wasn't enough, and never would be.

Steven had sensed a desperate hunger in her, one she might not even realize she possessed. Rose obviously missed her husband, but whether or not he'd satisfied her in bed was anyone's guess. The fact that the man had died on their honeymoon could mean anything from he'd been overexcited making love to his beautiful wife to slipping and falling down the stairs. The journalists would believe the first—that Rose had killed him by being too eager in the bridegroom's bed, but Steven had no idea what the real story was.

Rose walked through the house without worry, looking over everything her husband must have shown her, without guilt. Whoever had been to blame for the duke's demise, it hadn't been Rose.

They went through room after lofty room, Rose knowing her way around perfectly. Steven enjoyed imagining her leading him until he had no idea where he was, and then telling him she'd take him back out for a price of a kiss or two. For more than kisses. She'd smile when she said it, her eyes sparkling.

No, that would never happen. Rose wasn't the sort of woman who went in for naughty games. In spite of the scandal sheets, she was a gentleman's daughter, raised to the straight and narrow. *More's the pity.*

Rose turned around so suddenly that Steven almost ran into her. Reminded him of their first meeting, he falling onto her bosom, then sliding down her welcoming body.

"I've thought of something," she said.

Steven had thought of something too . . . she under him on white sheets, her golden hair trickling through his hands.

He tried to shake off the vision, but it wouldn't leave him. Rose languid against the pillow, her fingers drifting over Steven's skin, both of them sleek with sweat. They'd be joined, the heat between them overwhelming the winter's chill . . .

"Did you hear me?" Rose asked, peering at him. "Are you certain you're all right, Captain McBride?"

No, and he never would be again.

"What?" Steven managed to say. The hangover was making him be in two different places at once—in his chill, square house in reality and the curved, soft bed of his imagination. The true Rose existed in this cold, dull place, instead of in the fantasy in his head. Unfair.

"This way," she was saying. "There was a cabinet I always loved, always raved about. Charles had promised to have it moved into my bedchamber, but he never had the chance."

Her words ended in a sad note, echoed by the quiet swish of her dress as she walked away from him.

Steven caught up to her in the wide hallway. "I'm sorry, love," he said. "What happened to you, I mean."

Rose turned to him, her green eyes softening in the gloom. "You know, you are the only person who hasn't immediately believed his death was my fault." She paused. "Or do you?"

"No." Steven rubbed his hand through his hair to keep himself from reaching for her. "I don't."

"They say I deliberately married a man with a weak heart," Rose said. "And then . . . proved to be too much for him." Her color heightened.

Steven knew exactly why they'd imagined that—beautiful, young Rose would throw any middle-aged man into palpitations. The journalists saw her lush body and red lips and extrapolated that her physical presence had caused the man's death. Steven couldn't blame them for thinking so—wasn't he still fantasizing about having her in his bed?

But they hadn't asked her, or the duke's physician, for the true story. The newspapers had simply declared it, loving the scandal of the young second wife doing in the husband and sweeping up the spoils.

Only Rose had been kept from her spoils.

They entered a room that was little more than a cluster of furniture. At one time, it had been a sitting room of some sort, but now appeared to be a place to store things that didn't fit in the other rooms.

Rose moved unwaveringly to the end of the room, two large windows letting in light there. Her skirts billowed as she knelt before a cabinet and gestured to it. "This."

The cabinet was about three feet long and two and a half high and as wide, inlaid with satinwood and other exotic woods Steven couldn't identify. Rose opened the cabinet's double doors to reveal a stack of shallow drawers.

Steven saw the cleverness of it as Rose pulled out the entire bottom half of the cabinet, drawers and all, on hidden rollers. The top drawers, which were shallower still, stayed in place.

The entire piece, with its burnished wood—deep golds and ambers with a touch of red—seemed to light up the corner it stood in.

It certainly lighted Rose's face, or maybe that was her flush of joy. "I always loved this piece. It's a collection cabinet—for medals or coins, or whatnot." She opened a drawer in the top section, which was empty. "No one's used it for years, but I liked it. I was going to keep ribbons and things in it."

Steven touched the top where a strip of ebony inlay alternated with lighter satinwood to create a chevron pattern.

"It's lovely," he said with sincerity. "Old, I take it?"

"About seventy years old. George Bullock was the maker—very famous in his day, I believe."

Steven liked the feel of the wood under his fingertips. Care had been put into the making of this cabinet, even love.

"This is your choice?" he asked.

"Yes." She pursed her lips in a moue, and Steven's heart hammered again. She really should not do that, shaping her mouth in the perfect form to be kissed. "Now to see if Albert will let it out of his sight."

"Bugger Albert," Steven said. He grimaced. "On second thought, I won't. We have a cart waiting outside, and servants to help move it. I say you take it and to hell with Albert. What about the second piece?"

Rose remained on the floor. "Have you abandoned the idea that Charles might have left me something inside the furniture? That it might hold the key to something else?"

Steven had—it was far-fetched. The duke had been a doting but not very intelligent man, as far as Steven could tell. He'd probably trusted that his son would feel an obligation to take care of Rose and hadn't worried—reasoned he'd live a long while and buy her plenty of things along the way. He'd likely had no idea his son was a turd.

Steven shrugged. "Let us look."

He sank down next to Rose, breathing in the scent of her. He needed her—her body around his, the taste of her in his mouth. Her breast had fit well into his large hand, but he'd felt more cushion of it to explore when she was unfettered. A lush woman, barely contained by her stays. Naked, she must be heaven.

Steven didn't truly believe there was anything in the cabinet, but he couldn't bear to disappoint her. He started pulling out drawers.

They found nothing. After about half an hour of examining the insides and undersides of the many drawers, nothing turned up. Not a cache of diamonds or other costly jewelry or a small painting by an ancient master worth thousands of guineas. The cabinet had been thoroughly cleaned out.

Rose said nothing, but her disappointment was apparent. "The piece itself must be worth something," she said. "To an antique collector if nothing else."

"I can find out for you," Steven offered.

Rose ran her hand along the edge of the inlay of the top, her fingers lovingly brushing it. Steven couldn't stop himself imagining those fingertips running as sensually over himself, and he went hard again.

"I hate to let it go," Rose said, her low-pitched voice completing his ache. "It's rather special to me."

"Then keep it." Steven cleared his throat as he got stiffly to his feet, turning so she wouldn't see any sign of his lust that might be pressing out his kilt. "I'll round up someone to tote this out for you. Hell, I'll carry it on my own back if I have to. It's going home with you today."

"Home." Rose looked wistful. "Only I haven't got one." She met his gaze. "Doesn't that sound sad?"

It did. Steven's hard-on deflated a little, though not much. If he thought about it, Steven didn't have a home either.

Not quite true. Steven was always welcome with his brothers—Patrick, who'd raised him, had a comfortable house in Edinburgh; Elliot had a huge monstrosity of a castle in northern Scotland, overrun with Indian servants and his growing family; and Sinclair had plenty of spare bedrooms in London, even if Sinclair's unruly children did terrorize the house.

But Steven had nothing, no home to return to, no place to put down roots. He enjoyed his visits with his brothers, but in the end they were only visits. His brothers had families. Steven did not. He'd made halfhearted attempts to change this in the past, but put any thoughts of marriage aside when he returned to the army. It was no life for a wife and children—at least, he'd never met a woman robust enough to share it but tender enough to fall in love with.

If he couldn't change things for himself, though, he could change things for Rose. "I swear to you," Steven said, "at the end of this, you'll be able to go home. Wherever you want that to be."

His heart was beating rapidly as he spoke, however, which didn't help his headache. He turned and left the room, unable to take her green eyes gazing at him any longer.

~~~~

Steven couldn't find any servants. The house was dark with the winter afternoon, and no lamps burned anywhere, nor did any fires. The new duke took frugality to an obsessive extreme.

He'd have to go down to the servants' hall and recruit a few sturdy footmen to help. Shouldn't be too much problem—no one was doing any actual work in the house that he could see, and Steven was good at rallying people to obey him.

He did run across a servant standing in near darkness in a parlor on the second floor. The windows faced west, so a trickle of light came in, but only enough to show there was a person in there at all. The man wore a dark suit, like the footman John, but had hunched shoulders and spindly legs. Not much good for moving furniture.

A closer look showed Steven that he was perusing papers on a tall table in front of him. Also that his clothes were wrinkled and looked less costly than even the footman's kit.

This was either a vagrant who'd wandered inside, or the new duke himself, the repugnant Albert.

Whoever he was, he heard Steven's step, and turned with a jerk. The man looked Steven up and down, his hands curling as his gaze lingered on Steven's kilt. "What the devil are you supposed to be made up as?" he snapped.

"A Scotsman," Steven said. "I thought you weren't at home, Your Grace."

Chapter 6

Steven saw a resemblance to the late duke in Albert, but everything that had been strong in Charles was weak in his son. Charles had sported a receding hairline, as did his son, but the older duke had had a robust mane of white hair to go with his, while Albert's graying hair straggled in thin wisps. Charles hadn't been tall, but his back had been straight and strong, while Albert's shoulders were slumped with too many hours of poring over papers.

"A Scotsman," Albert repeated. "What is a haggis-eating, sheep-loving bagpiper doing in my house?"

"I don't eat haggis," Steven said, letting his accent deepen. "And I never mastered the pipes, much to the despair of my poor brother. As for the sheep . . ." He shrugged. "Could never get very far there. Damp wool makes me sneeze."

Albert's scowl deepened. "Get out of my house, sir."

Steven debated explaining his presence, and Rose's, but decided to let the man wonder. "Not until I take what I came for."

"Are you robbing me, then? I'll have the constables on you."

Steven folded his arms. "No, you won't."

However strong-willed his father had been, Albert had inherited only pigheadedness, Steven decided. He was half

Steven's size, yet he swung away from the table, grabbed a poker from the fireplace, and came at him.

Steven easily caught the man's upraised arm as it descended, and twisted the poker out of his hand. He propelled Albert back to the table and slammed him face-first onto it. "Only attack if you have the advantage of surprise or superior strength and position." He pressed Albert's face harder into the wood. "Or prepare to be trounced. I have a raging headache, and see how easily I've bested you?"

"Get off me, you bloody dung-eater."

Steven's temper flared through the hangover. "Your own mouth's plenty full of shit. Thinking about what you're doing to Rose, I've a mind to grind you through this table until you learn some manners."

"Are you her latest lover, then? What happened to the comte?"

Steven pressed Albert down harder until he cried out. Steven growled, "Keep a civil tongue, man, before I—"

"Steven, what on earth are you doing?" Rose's exclamation cut into the room, followed by the rustle of her skirts. "Is that Albert? Good heavens, let him up."

Steven didn't want to. He'd love to beat son Albert into the table until the man's face was bloody. That would be satisfying.

But the note in Rose's voice made Steven release Albert and step away. She was a good woman to feel sorry for Albert in spite of it all, no matter how much Steven didn't share her sympathy.

"You're lucky she's such a sweetheart," Steven said to Albert. "And that she walked into the room just now."

"I'll have the law on you," Albert snarled, wiping his nose with the back of his hand.

"No, you will not," Rose said decidedly. She was an angel in black, her hair and face the only color in the gloom. "Captain McBride is here to help me take the furniture Charles left me, that is all. I've rung for John—he and Thomas and James will carry down the chest from the old parlor."

"What furniture?" Albert snapped. "You can't take any furniture."

"It's in the will," Steven said, stopping himself from slamming the man into the table again. "Two pieces of furniture, her choice. She's chosen one; she'll be back for another."

"My solicitor—" Albert spluttered.

"May contact Her Grace in London." Steven went to Rose and took her elbow. "I think we should be off, love," he said softly to her.

"Don't call her *Her Grace*," Albert snarled behind them. "She's not a duchess—she's the bloody whore who killed my father. She deserves nothing."

Steven let go of Rose and swung back to Albert. Albert, eyes widening, tried to evade him, but Steven caught him by the collar, ignoring Rose's cry.

Slam! Albert's face went once more into the table. "She deserves a commendation for not killing *you*," Steven said, each word tight. "Don't speak to her again except through her solicitor. His card." Steven withdrew a card Collins had given him and slapped it on the table in front of Albert's head. "Good day to you, sir."

He gave Albert another shake before he released the man's collar and left him. Rose was staring, wide-eyed, but Steven turned her away and steered her out of the room.

~

"It's pretty," Sinclair McBride, Steven's brother, said later that evening. "What is it?"

Steven had placed the cabinet in the middle of the parlor of his suite at the Langham. Rain fell outside, droplets lingering on Sinclair's short hair, which was the same shade of blond as Steven's.

Albert had in the end not stopped John and two other foot-men from lugging the cabinet down the stairs and loading it into the waiting cart. The cabinet had filled the small dogcart, leaving no room for Steven and Rose.

Steven had then bade John to fetch the coachman from his tea and have him hitch up Albert's carriage to take him and Rose to the train. Though worried about Albert's reaction, John and the coachman seemed happy to do anything for Rose. Likewise, Miles, the town coachman, had been willing to collect Steven, Rose, and the cabinet from the station in London. Rose had won them over.

Not much wonder. One smile from her red lips, one twin-

kle of her eyes, and men fell over themselves to do her bidding.
Journalists with too much time on their hands had assumed
she'd used that natural charm to make men do her favors,
including in her bed.

Rose was in her bed right now—alone—napping after their
trip. She'd told Steven upon their arrival that, thinking it over,
she was resigned to selling the cabinet.

She'd looked sad, but resolved, and Steven had sent for his
brother to talk to him about the matter. Sinclair had arrived
through the now-falling rain to study the cabinet in curiosity.

"It's a collection cabinet," Steven said in answer to Sinclair's question. "By George Bullock, circa 1815. I'm trying to
find out what it's worth."

Sinclair pinned his younger brother with a hard stare. That
stare, along with Sinclair's ability to obtain any verdict he
wanted in court, had earned him the moniker of the Scots
Machine. His colleagues called him that—the unlucky villains in the dock had named him Basher McBride.

The Scots Machine now assessed Steven. "I'm a barrister,
not an antiques dealer. Why did you send for *me*?"

Steven shrugged. "I thought maybe you'd know someone
who could sell it for Rose. Someone who can be discreet."

"I know many people who can be discreet, but they're not
all on the side of angels."

Steven joined Sinclair in frowning contemplation of the
cabinet. "I hoped it contained some sort of clue or message for
Rose, or had been crammed full of gold coins for her. I've
looked at it every which way, but . . . nothing."

"I met the Duke of Southdown once—the former one,"
Sinclair said. "Maybe he simply knew the cabinet would fetch
a good price, and give his widow a bit of cash. He died, suddenly, didn't he? He didn't know he would go so quickly. How
would he have had time to prepare for her?"

"Well, he didn't do bloody enough while he was alive, that's
certain. Collins is browbeating the duke's solicitors—Rose
will have to put her faith in that." Steven let out his breath. "She
doesn't want to let the cabinet go, but she might have no choice.
Her pig of a stepson wants to see her destitute."

"So you said. He's trying to prove her a bigamist, is he?"

"He won't," Steven said in a hard voice. "She isn't."

His brother's stare became sharper, but finally Sinclair gave him a nod. "If a bigamy case goes to court, I'll advocate for her—I agree with you about her innocence. I warn you, though, juries of middle-aged, middle-class, holier-than-thou men don't like pretty women who marry older men. They know they'd succumb to that temptation too readily themselves, and so they blame the temptress."

Steven balled one hand. His headache was coming back. "Thank you for the optimism."

"This is what happens. Be prepared for it." Sinclair relaxed his stance. "I'll help as much as I can. I'll ram her innocence down the jurors' throats." He studied the cabinet again. "It's an interesting piece. Ask one of the Mackenzie brothers or their wives. They'll either buy it to lose in those huge houses of theirs or know someone interested."

"Yes." Steven had thought of the Mackenzies, especially Eleanor, wife of Hart Mackenzie, who was Duke of Kilmorgan. Eleanor knew everyone in London and everyone in Scotland, plus she had connections via her husband to people throughout the Empire who might like a nice cabinet for displaying their medals.

But he'd hesitated. Rose had asked him, sorrow in her voice, to please help her find a buyer, then had retired to her room. Steven hadn't wanted her to wake to find he'd already sold the bloody thing and had it carted away while she'd slept.

Steven had sent for his brother not only for his opinion, but to help keep himself from picturing Rose, stripped down to her smalls, snuggling in her cozy bed. A single wall stood between her and Steven, a piece of wood, brick, and plaster keeping him from watching her sleep, drinking in the beauty of her.

He needed a cold bath, or maybe a walk in the freezing rain. But Steven couldn't make himself leave the suite.

"Never mind about the cabinet for now," Steven said. "I'll wait until Rose wins back her settlements. She might have a place for it after all." He thought of the warm glow on Rose's face whenever she talked about her husband, and something stabbed at him. He needed to wrap up this business, take himself to Scotland for Christmas, and forget Rose. Hart always invited scores of people to his Christmas parties— maybe Steven could meet a lonely widow there and forget this one.

And perhaps the rain outside would change to showers of gold, and champagne would flow in the streets.

Sinclair was watching him again. "If you change your mind, Eleanor and Hart are in Town for now." He shot a look at the closed door, then one at Steven. "I hope you know what you're doing."

"I don't," Steven said, shaking his head. "I don't at all. Wish me luck."

"Mmph." Sinclair's expression changed. "*I* need luck. Tomorrow, I look for a new governess. Andrew put beetles into the current one's bed."

Steven grinned, his thoughts moving with relief to his energetic eight-year-old nephew. "And the governess fled?"

Sinclair lost his amused look. "No, I sacked her. She decided to lock Andrew into the cellar from whence the beetles came. Because it scared him into silence, she suggested I do this every day. Hence, the sack." The anger fled Sinclair's eyes. "Caitriona managed to get the governess's hair switch off her while the fuss was being made about Andrew. Cat tossed it into the fire. Poor woman was bald as an egg on the back of her head."

"She can wear a bonnet." Steven's sympathy for the governess had died as soon as Sinclair said she'd locked Andrew in the cellar.

"Take care, Steven," Sinclair said, taking up his hat. He looked as though he wanted to say more, settled for his stern barrister glare, and walked out.

～

Rose couldn't sleep. She had undressed for her rest, but only twenty minutes later she rang for the maid to help her into her clothes again.

She needed to speak to Steven. Well, to see him actually. To be in the same room with him. His presence comforted her more than anything else had in a long time, had somehow even when she'd thought him a downtrodden vagrant on the streets.

She stepped out of her parlor and made her way down the hall, then stopped short as a tall man came abruptly out of Steven's rooms.

Rose halted, ready to ask in surprise where Steven was going, when she realized it wasn't Steven. Same light blond hair, same tall physique, same way of piercing her with his gray stare, but a different man.

Steven's intelligence lurked in the man's eyes, but while Steven was restless and moody, even in his hungover state, this man had a quiet intensity about him.

"I beg your pardon," Rose said, though he had been about to step into *her*. "I need to see . . . my cabinet."

His gaze flickered with amusement. "Yes, your *cabinet* is doing very well. It will be pleased for your visit."

"Damn it all," Steven said, coming up behind the other man. "Leave her be. Rose, this is my brother Sinclair, known on the backstreets as Basher McBride. Don't let him intimidate you. Sinclair, allow me to introduce Rose, Dowager Duchess of Southdown."

"Pleased to meet you." Sinclair was immediately polite, holding out a hand and bowing as Rose shook it. He didn't release her hand, but remained holding it in his strong grip. "If my reprobate brother becomes too unruly for you, do not hesitate to send for me. I have a house on Upper Brook Street and chambers in Essex Court."

"That is kind of you," Rose began.

"Don't you have a governess to employ?" Steven said, a scowl creasing his face.

"He wishes me to leave." Sinclair squeezed Rose's hand again, this time in genuine cordiality. "I am pleased to make your acquaintance, Your Grace."

His politeness warmed Rose's heart. So few bothered to be polite to her these days.

Sinclair made a final bow, shot a look at his brother, and departed.

Steven ushered Rose into the parlor. Rose held her breath as she brushed by him in the doorway, his warmth unnerving her. She hadn't been able to sleep this afternoon partly because she craved to be in his presence. She'd had to give in and rush to see him.

Rose made herself walk to the cabinet, which waited for her in the middle of the rug. "Was Mr. McBride interested in buying it?"

Steven closed the door. Rose was very aware she was alone with him, even more so than she had been at Sittford House, when any of the dozen servants could have walked into any room they'd happened to be in. Here, the door was closed, Steven had no regular valet, and any other staff would knock and wait to be admitted.

Rose couldn't look at anything but Steven. The cabinet, a masterwork of craftsmanship, faded to nothing. He still wore his Scottish clothes, his blue and green kilt falling in neat pleats to just below his knees.

"He suggested we ask Eleanor," Steven said without looking at her. "Hart Mackenzie's wife. They have plenty of room and more money than God."

"Really? I wasn't aware God had any money. A stash of gold bars in one of His back rooms, do you think?" Rose tried to smile, tried to joke, but she found it difficult even to breathe. "Probably comes in handy when He needs to repave His streets."

Steven flashed a grin over his shoulder. "I promise you, if God has a stash of gold bars, Hart lent them to Him."

"You're ridiculous."

Steven held out his hand to her. Why did Rose not hesitate to walk to him and take it?

"Keep the cabinet," he said. Rose couldn't hear much over the pounding of her heart, but that's what she thought he said. "You love it, and if Collins is as good as he claims, you won't need to sell it."

"I have to ask you again why you're helping me, Steven." The words were not the ones Rose wanted to come out of her mouth, but they did anyway.

Steven switched his gaze to her, losing his smile. He stood too close to her—she could see the dark ring around his pale gray irises.

"Did you want me to leave you hanging with the pesky newspapermen waiting to pounce?" he asked. "Journalists can shred a person, break them, ruin their lives, and then go home and pour tea. Congratulating themselves on a job well done.

Rumor, gossip, scandal—they dish it out and don't care who they leave in the gutter. I'm not letting that happen to *you*."

Steven's brows were drawn, his anger raw. Rose watched him in surprise. She drew a breath to ask him if he spoke of an experience in particular, when Steven wrapped his arm around Rose and dragged her to him for a savage kiss.

Chapter 7

The breath she'd started to draw didn't reach her lungs. Rose couldn't move. Her world narrowed to Steven, his strength, his lips on hers.

The kiss was fierce, not loving. He scraped her mouth open, invading. The room was hot, the fire stoked high, and Rose went hotter still.

Steven tasted of anger, powerfully so, his hands on her back just as powerful. Rose knew she was surrendering to him, and she didn't care one whit.

Steven lifted her off her feet. As the kiss broke, he deposited her on the smooth top of the chest.

Rose's hands landed on the cool wood, her heart pounding. Steven's knee pushed through her skirts, parting her legs, giving him room to step between them and against her. Rose's throat went dry, her slippered feet sliding to Steven's legs before she told them to.

She felt his arousal through the wool of his kilt, through her volume of skirts. He surrounded her with his warmth, with himself.

He ran a strong hand through her hair, letting curls tumble free. "You should nae be all buttoned and pinned like this," he said. "You were meant to have your hair down, your clothes loose. No reason to hide your beauty."

"But . . . I . . ." Only syllables came out, and those in a stammer.

Steven's fingers undid the first button under her chin. "You're so beautiful, Rosie. Do as you like, and damn them all."

Rose should protest that she was a lady, a respectable widow, that she was buttoned up and prim to keep others from talking about her more than they already did.

She couldn't say anything. *Do as you like, and damn them all.*

He was tempting her. She shouldn't let him. Rose should be adamant, become the prudish, haughty duchess and tell him what she thought of his liberties.

She could only sit still while Steven unfastened another button, and another. His fingers were hot, his fingertips rough. The backs of his hands were crisscrossed with scars, and each of his fingers had been broken at some time and healed—a fighting man's hands.

Steven left off with the buttons and traced her now-exposed throat. "You have the sweetest skin, my Rose. I want to kiss it." He leaned closer. "I want to kiss every inch of it."

Please do, she wanted to answer, but again, her words choked off.

Steven undid more buttons, then pulled her placket apart.

The top of Rose's bodice opened, revealing her breasts swelling over her corset. Rose thought her heart would be leaping out of her chest, but no, everything was whole and smooth, as it should be.

Steven's gaze raked down her, his glance admiring. "I knew you'd be a beauty."

Rose swallowed, and Steven traced the swallow with his fingertips to her breasts. His touch was caressing, smoothing, but left streaks of fire in its wake.

Just as Rose thought she'd never breathe again, Steven took his fingers away, leaned down, and pressed his lips to where his touch had been.

Rose's chest lifted with a sudden intake of air. Steven's mouth was hot, wicked, teasing. She dragged in another breath as he pressed kisses to her exposed skin.

She stretched her legs, her feet flexing of their own accord, while Steven kissed between her breasts, licked, played. He moved his hands down her back to her hips, cupping her there.

Rose was shameless, and she didn't care. The world already thought her a fallen woman—what did she have to lose?

"Rosie," Steven whispered, his Scots accent thick. "Ye taste like heaven. What are ye doing to me?"

His words burned against her skin. Rose felt a sharp pull on her flesh, the bite of Steven's teeth.

He was suckling her, she realized, taking the soft skin of her breast into his mouth. The small pain set her ablaze. Rose hadn't known her body could flush with such need, her nipples tightening until they ached. She was surrounded by Steven's warmth, strength, scent.

She wound her arms around him, holding him while he licked, kissed, suckled. His arousal pressed to the join of her legs, wanting undisguised.

Steven raised his head, his mouth wet, his short hair mussed. He brushed one finger over the mark he'd made on her breast. "You're mine now, Rosie. I've claimed you."

Why did that statement make her all the more excited? "Yes," she managed.

"You are the loveliest lass I've ever had the fortune to meet."

Rose clung to every word. "Yes," she whispered again.

Steven chuckled, his breath warming her. "They don't deserve you. *I* don't deserve you. But I promise you my fidelity, lass. My everything."

Rose had no idea what he was talking about, but hearing him say it in his growling Scots was enough.

Steven hands were on her hips once more, his mouth again opening hers. Rose daringly ran her fingers down his back, finding the tightness of his buttocks through the wool of his kilt. She tentatively caressed his hard, tight hip.

Steven broke the kiss and gave her a swift smile. "Rosie, lass, you're dancing with the devil."

"I am?"

"Doesn't matter though, does it?" Steven brushed another kiss to her mouth. She was pressed so tightly against him that his shirt and waistcoat warmed her bare skin. "I'm going to marry you, after all."

Rose returned his smile. "Yes, I forgot we were betrothed."

"Forgot, did you?" Something hot flickered in his eyes. "Then I'll have to remind ye."

The next kiss showed Rose he'd been holding himself back until now. His mouth burned, his hands were strong, his body hard under her touch. The fact that she was able to hold this virile, amazing, athletic man took her breath away.

Something moved under her buttocks, but it had nothing to do with Steven. She shifted her weight and something well and truly pinched her.

Rose gasped, breaking the kiss, sliding forward into Steven's arms. Steven, surprised, caught her, then he started to laugh.

"Look at that, Rosie," he said, his gaze drawn to the cabinet behind her. "I think we've discovered the first secret compartment opened by ardor."

As Rose turned to look, Steven struggled to catch his breath. He never thought he'd damn a piece of furniture, but he was damning this one. His need shouted at him to forget about the bloody cabinet and drag Rose to the carpet and finish this.

With any other woman, he'd have done it. Steven would have coaxed her to the floor by now and had her clothes off, her cabinet and her settlements be damned.

Rose was delectable with her bodice unbuttoned as she gazed in curiosity at the piece of inlay that had slid aside beneath her hips. A small drawer had popped up, right against her backside, lucky drawer.

"There's something in it." Rose reached an eager hand for it, but Steven caught her wrist.

He'd lived in Africa too long, he decided—a man never thrust his hand into a shadowy opening or lifted a rock without being very careful. All manner of things could be living there. Even in England, ticks, spiders, and other nasties could exist in a drawer closed for so long inside a wooden cabinet.

Steven moved her hand and then gingerly tugged out the papers she'd spied. Rose leaned to look, forgetting to be modest in her curiosity, and Steven clenched the pages to keep from dropping them. Her open bodice bared her to the waist, her plump breasts filling her corset. A dark red love bite marked the pale skin of her breast. She was beautiful, decadent, and innocent, all at the same time.

"They're drawings," Rose said in surprise.

Of furniture. Of course, more bloody furniture. Five sketches in all, done in colored pencils, depicting pieces from the same period as the cabinet.

One was of another cabinet with small drawers, this one shaped like an obelisk whose point had been sawn off. The artist had noted that it was mahogany with silver inlay, in the latest "Egyptian" style. Two pictures showed chairs with gilded arms, the arms of each capped with carved, gilded Egyptian-looking heads like those found on canopic jars. One picture showed a pair of large candelabras, each base in the form of a stele covered with hieroglyphic-like writing. A figure of a woman, carved in ebony, knelt on the top of each stele, holding the gold curlicues of the candelabra on her head.

The last drawing was of a settee. Its green and gold striped cushion rested atop a boxlike structure made of ebony and studded with gold. Scenes from ancient Egypt were carved into the settee's arms and burnished with gold, and a sphinx—half lion, half woman—capped each corner.

The settee was a masterpiece. And hideously ugly.

Rose started to laugh. "I always hated this settee. It was brought over from Paris by one of Charles's ancestors after the war with Napoleon. Ancient Egypt was all the rage then, even though they didn't yet know much about it."

Steven studied the sketch, every gilded, overly ornate inch of it. "I've seen the wonders of the pyramids at Giza and the tombs at Thebes," he said. "And I assure you, Rosie, that no Egyptian pharaoh ever sat on something like this."

"Of course they didn't. It was for French ladies in their salons. It's horrible."

Steven flipped through the sketches again. "This settee is in your husband's house?"

"All those pieces are. His Egyptian collection, he called them. Been in the house for generations. They're somewhere about."

"Then why didn't we see them? I'd have remembered *these*."

"I don't know." Rose managed to look thoughtful and

alluring at the same time. "We didn't have time to do much more than the main floors. Albert might have had them removed to the attics to put them out of my reach. With all the gold on them, they must be worth something."

Steven looked through the drawings again, then flipped the pages over. A few notes had been made on the back of each, in the original hand, describing upholstery or inlay. One had a tiny drawing, made by a pencil invented long after the Napoleonic period, of a single, full-blown rose.

Steven held it up to her, his thumb on the flower. "A message for you, I think."

He saw the swallow move down Rose's throat as she realized that her late husband must have sketched the flower. She turned the drawing over again and forced a smile. "On the ugly settee, no less."

Steven ran his fingertips along the satinwood of the cabinet. "He knew you'd want this cabinet, because you raved about it. Maybe he left these pictures in it for you to find, guiding you to the settee as the second piece you were to take."

"Possibly," Rose said, sounding dubious. "Perhaps he wanted to give me one thing I'd love and one thing I could sell." Her eyes were moist when she looked up at Steven. "If you can find someone to sell the settee for me, you could have a commission on the sale . . . a small one only, I'm afraid." Rose smiled with the lush lips Steven wanted to kiss again.

"Keep your money." He heard the tightness in his voice. "I don't need it."

Rose's smile died. "Oh, I beg your pardon. I didn't mean any insult—"

Steven stopped her words by threading his fingers through her loosened hair and giving her a too-brief kiss. "Not to worry, Rosie, I'll scare up a buyer for you. Right now, in fact."

"Right now?"

The disappointment in her eyes made Steven's heart pound, but he stiffened his resolve. If he didn't leave this room, the hardness of his cock would win over good intentions. "Sooner it's done, the better." And the sooner he went, the better for his sanity.

"I see." Rose relinquished the sketches when he reached for them. "We'll have to return to Sittford and look for the settee before Albert thinks to get rid of it. Tomorrow, if the weather holds."

Steven shook his head. "Not tomorrow. I have another appointment." One he'd give anything to miss, but at the same time, he knew he had to face it.

Rose looked curious and again disappointed, but she was too well-bred to ask for details. "I won't bother you then. I can go to Sittford myself."

"No." The word was sharp. "Not alone. I don't want you at that house without me. I don't trust Albert at all."

Rose grimaced. "Truth to tell, I'd feel better with you there." Her worried look vanished, and she gave Steven an encouraging smile. "You go on then, and we'll plan the trip later. If you're going out, wrap up warm. It's nippy out there."

He stilled, startled, the papers and furniture forgotten. No woman in Steven's history of women—and that history was a full one—had ever told him, concern in her eyes, to wrap up warm. Not one had mentioned the slightest concern for Steven's well-being. They wanted him for what attention he could give them, and that was all.

Steven laid a hand on her shoulder, his heart full. "I will, lass. You rest now, and start making arrangements of your own."

Rose didn't reach to button her bodice, as many women would once they knew the encounter was over. She only sat, open and beautiful for Steven's gaze.

"Arrangements for what? I should wait to see if we can find the settee first, shouldn't I?"

Steven made himself step away from her, but it took every bit of his strength to do it. "Arrangements for our wedding," he said, giving her a wink. "I'm marrying you, remember?"

As Rose gaped, Steven forced himself to turn around, walk across the room, pick up his greatcoat and hat, and wrench open the door. He deliberately did not glance at her one last time—if he did that, he'd never leave.

He heard her say, *Good afternoon*, still polite, though he'd more or less been ravishing her. Steven lifted his hand in acknowledgement but he strode out into the cool hall without looking back and shut the door.

Steven's body thrummed with the heat of her all the way

down the stairs and out of the hotel, and even the freezing winter rain slapping him in the face couldn't cool him.

~~~~~

Steven stayed out the rest of the afternoon and into the darkness of evening. Rose couldn't settle into any task—not mending or writing letters or reading. Steven hadn't let the staff bring in any newspapers this morning, and it was just as well. No telling what the journalists had written about her since last night.

I'm marrying you, remember? The words Steven had shot at her before he'd gone rang in her head.

Had he been joking? Steven loved humor, she'd already come to know. He couldn't *really* mean to marry her—he'd been teasing her, of course. That was what Steven did. He expected Rose to laugh along with him, and she would.

He'd been gone several hours when the maid who'd been waiting on Rose—Alice was her name—tapped on her door. "Begging your pardon, Your Grace," the middle-aged and straight-backed woman said. "There is a lady wishing to speak with Captain McBride. She wanted to come up with me, but the manager has kept her to a back parlor."

"Is she a journalist?" Rose asked in alarm.

"She says not. Doesn't have the look, Your Grace. More like a highborn lady, and a widow at that. She wouldn't give her name, though."

"Hmm." If this lady was one of Steven's friends, why wouldn't she want her name sent up to him? "She was alone?"

"Yes, ma'am. Well, apart from her maid."

A woman conscious of propriety then. Female journalists these days could be seen whisking about alone, which often caused more brow-raising than the stories they wrote, but a respectable lady went nowhere without at least one servant to escort her.

Rose's curiosity wouldn't let it lie. If the woman proved to be a journalist, masquerading as a lady, Rose would be sweet as sugar to her but send her off. If the lady truly was connected with Steven, Rose could at least pass on a message to him.

No, truth be told, she simply wanted to lay eyes on a woman who would come boldly to a hotel and ask for Steven.

"Shall I tell her you are coming down?" Alice asked as Rose straightened her dress and smoothed her hair.

"No," Rose said abruptly. "No . . . I'll just go."

Alice gave her a sage nod. "Yes, ma'am."

Rose's hair was still not right from Steven having pulled it out of its pins, no matter how much she struggled with it. She gave another curl a fierce push into place and left the room.

Chapter 8

Alice accompanied Rose, rather like a guard dog. Rose let her lead the way to a small parlor buried deep inside the hotel's ground floor. Alice opened the door before Rose could ask her to and announced in a rather grand voice, "The Duchess of Southdown. Ma'am."

She curtseyed, and Rose went past her into the room.

The woman who rose from the curved sofa, giving Rose a look of confusion, was certainly no journalist. She wore black, as Rose did, widow's weeds, but her mourning was fresh. Her black hat trailed crepe to her knees, and a thick black veil, which she'd lifted from her face, would cover her completely when down.

"I beg your pardon," the woman said in a cultured voice. "I am waiting for someone."

"For Captain McBride," Rose said. She closed the door behind her, but she was now uncertain she should have come down. "He is out. Is there any message I can deliver to him?"

The woman gave Rose a look as assessing and curious as the one Rose must be giving her. This lady could not have been reading newspapers either, because she showed no recognition of Rose's name, or the fact that it was now coupled with Steven's.

"Only this," the widow said. "Captain McBride has no need to visit while he is in London. Please tell him that." She paused a beat. "Your Grace."

The title was delivered in a skeptical tone, as though she didn't truly believe Rose a duchess of any kind. She thought Rose Steven's paramour, Rose realized, just as Rose suspected this lady of being one herself.

Steven had told Rose the first morning that his vices were too much drink, too much gambling, and too much interest in the ladies. He'd kissed Rose with fire—any woman would be happy to melt beneath him. Had this one? A small pain entered Rose's heart.

Practically speaking, however, though this lady might have been Steven's paramour in the past, at the moment, her face was pale with grief, her eyes red-rimmed. She'd recently lost someone very close to her, and Rose was moved to compassion.

"I will tell him," Rose said, gentling her voice. "My condolences on your loss."

The woman's face started to crumple, but she caught herself and raised a gloved hand to her lips. "Thank you."

Rose went to her and laid a hand on her arm. "If there is anything I can do . . ."

The woman looked up at her, tears fleeing as she gave Rose a startled look. "No. Nothing. Thank you, Your Grace." The honorific was delivered with more conviction this time.

The lady gathered her trailing veil and left the room. A maid came out of the shadows in the hall as she emerged, taking her mistress by the arm to lead her away. The lady leaned on the maid, as though depending on her.

Rose's own maid came forward and stood deferentially, waiting for Rose's orders. "I never learned her name," Rose said, watching the pair disappear through a door to the front of the hotel. "Did you?"

Alice shook her head. "Her lady's maid was properly trained. Never betrayed her with a word, no matter how much I tried."

Rose had to smile. "Curiosity killed the cat," she said,

shaking her head. "Perhaps we should be ashamed of ourselves and feel better by having a large tea."

"I'll have one ordered, Your Grace." Alice returned the smile, and departed to find the kitchens.

Steven walked back into his suite to find Rose there. Two sensations went through him at the same time—a flash of joy that she was there, and a wash of frustration.

She was going to kill him. Steven had been forced to walk around cold, rainy London a long while this afternoon, before his arousal gave him any peace. Once he believed he'd regained a modicum of control, he'd traveled to a street off Chancery Lane to find Tavis Collins and show him the drawings he and Rose had discovered. The errand had taken care of the rest of his impatient desires.

Three cups of tea and a dram of whiskey later, Steven had summoned the courage to return to the hotel.

To find Rose in his parlor, waiting eagerly for him. His desires sprang forth with rampaging enthusiasm, proving they'd been dormant, not tamed.

Steven tried to remain businesslike as he tossed his hat and coat to the rack inside the door. "Mr. Collins suggested what *you* did—that you return to Sittford House and scour it for your furniture. He agrees the hand-drawn rose is a clue directing you. He also telegraphed a minister in Dundee who will come in person to declare that the page in the register with your marriage recorded is a forgery. The man didn't want to travel down—Collins suspects he was heftily paid off."

"That would surprise me," Rose said. "Albert is nothing if not tightfisted."

Steven shrugged. "He might pay a lesser sum in order to hold on to a greater one." He moved to a table where a decanter of whiskey had been left for him, and poured himself a fragrant glass. Rose watched him, a sparkle in her eye. The way she held herself, as though barely containing something, made him stop before he took a drink. "You seem robust this evening. Had a good rest, did you?"

"A lady came to see you," Rose said. "Newly widowed. I don't know who she was."

"Ah." If anything would kill his burning need for Rose it was that. "She came *here*? Why on earth did she, I wonder?"

"She didn't say," Rose said. "She was rather surprised to see me. She told me to tell you that you needn't bother to visit her."

Steven turned the whiskey glass in his hand. "Did she?" He studied the amber contents, debating whether to pour it down his throat and erase the rising pain or opt for staying sober. He chose, and emptied the glass into his mouth.

"I'm sorry, Steven."

Steven swallowed the burning liquid and thumped down the glass. Rose was looking at him in true contrition, her words almost sad. "For what?" he asked.

"It was clearly a private matter between you and the lady, and none of my business. I went to speak to her because of my own silly curiosity. I should not have."

Steven reached for the whiskey decanter, then let his hand fall from it. He shook his head. "No need to flog yourself, lass. If a gentleman had come here asking to see you, I'd have had him against the wall, demanding to know what he wanted."

"But it distressed her, and she wasn't feigning her grief. For that, I am sorry."

"No, she's not feigning." Steven let out a sigh. "She is the appointment I have tomorrow. She told me not to come, did she?" He fingered the empty glass then firmly pushed it from him. "I'll tell you the whole sad story, Rosie, but not tonight. Tonight, I'd like to forget all about it." He gazed at Rose, taking her in, letting the beauty of her soothe him. All the black she wore couldn't shut out the vibrancy of her, couldn't even mute it.

Steven abandoned the whiskey and went to her. "You and I are engaged to be married. We have no need to hide ourselves in this hotel as though ashamed of the fact." He caught her hand and raised it to his lips. "So put on your best dress, my love. I'm taking you out on the town."

Out on the town meant dinner at a restaurant and an evening at the theatre. The restaurant was the Albion in Russell Street near Drury Lane Theatre, where Steven ordered a lavish meal and champagne. He lounged in his chair, looking relaxed and unashamed, caring nothing that so many people stared at them.

Steven focused all his attention on Rose and no one else in the room. Rose's blood heated as she found herself the subject of Steven's gray gaze, especially when he leaned forward slightly to speak to her. She again saw that his irises were ringed with deeper gray, like the dark lining of a sunlit cloud.

He asked her about her life in Scotland with her father. Rose had thought her existence in rural Scotland then Edinburgh dully domestic, but Steven hung on every word, as though her stories fascinated him. He told her a little about his life in the army, making light of what must be hardships—heat, insects, diseases, exhaustion, and living in danger of attack even in quiet times. Steven painted a picture of Africa that was nothing but beauty, of its huge skies, endless rivers, and expansive lands.

"I'd love to see it," Rose said wistfully. The world that she knew, in spite of being a lofty duchess, was small. Charles hadn't enjoyed going out to restaurants like this one, or even coming to London—he'd loved staying home by the fire. Their only outing during Rose's married life had been rambling walks in the countryside. They'd been climbing in the hills near Sittford when Charles's heart had given out. He'd felt unwell during the walk, they'd gone back to the house, Charles had taken to his bed, and he'd not lasted the night.

"No reason you shouldn't," Steven said. "Africa is dangerous for a lady, but some wives do manage it. As a married man, I'd be entitled to larger quarters."

"Indeed?" Rose asked with a sly smile. "Now I understand your quest for a wife. A bigger tent."

Steven's grin widened. "More impetus than that, I assure you." His eyes took on a teasing light. "I can think of many more reasons for a man to marry you, Rosie."

She gave him an innocent look. "Someone to bring you your slippers?"

Steven moved closer, his voice going low. "That could be interesting." He leaned into her, blocking the view of the other diners, and curled his tongue slowly at her.

Rose went hot all the way down. Steven showing his blatant wanting here in a restaurant, in public, made her body tighten, her breasts heavy and warm. She recalled the feeling of him pressed between her legs when he'd sat her on the cabinet, the bite of pleasure-pain when he'd left the mark on her breast. She burned.

"McBride?"

Rose flushed, but Steven sat up without hurry and turned to see who'd spoken. Two men in regimentals were approaching the table, one lifting his hand in greeting.

Steven rose to meet them then held out a hand and assisted Rose to her feet. "Rose, may I introduce Major Clifford and Lieutenant Spencer, from my regiment. Gentlemen, this is my fiancée, the Dowager Duchess of Southdown."

Both men stared, eyes widening, while trying to be polite. "Ah," the major said. "I had no idea. Congratulations, McBride."

"Scots' luck," Spencer, who wasn't much into his twenties, said. "My felicitations, sir."

They shook hands with Rose, bowed, made compliments, and directed more teasing remarks at Steven. Rose answered cordially, and didn't jump when Steven tucked her hand beneath his arm and pulled her close.

Rose kept her surprise hidden. She hadn't thought Steven would extend the pretense of their engagement beyond the ruse for the journalists. These were Steven's colleagues, his friends, and he was blithely standing in front of them declaring himself engaged.

Rose was surprised again when they said good-bye to the lieutenant and major and left the restaurant and rode the short distance to Covent Garden Theatre. The drama had already begun when they arrived, but lack of punctuality didn't seem to be unusual. Others were trickling in, talking and laughing, unworried that they were late.

A pretty woman, her plump body reminding Rose of a dove, waved to Steven. She was on the arm of a tall Scotsman with dark red hair and a handsome face, who kept his gaze fixed on a gilded frieze above them, studying it with grave intensity. He didn't cease his scrutiny even when Steven and Rose stopped in front of the couple.

"Steven, how lovely," the lady said, catching his hands. "I didn't know you were in London. Your brother never tells me *anything.*"

Steven clasped her gloved hands in return, leaned down, and kissed the woman's cheek. "Haven't been here long, I promise."

The kiss drew the attention of the tall Scot very fast. His gaze slammed to Steven's, and though he didn't look directly into Steven's eyes, the ferocity on his face was plain.

Steven released the woman's hands and stepped back without showing concern. "Sinclair keeps to himself. His remembering to mention anything about his personal life is an event. Unless he's whinging on about governesses."

"Still no luck there?"

Steven shook his head. "Afraid not."

The Scotsman did not relax, even with Steven a pace away from the woman. He fixed Steven with a stern eye, seeming to pay no attention to what they discussed. His lady apparently found nothing unusual in this. She continued, "Well, I've exhausted all my recommendations and so have my sisters-in-law. By the time Sinclair finds someone appropriate, Cat and Andrew will be grown."

"The last one objected to Andrew filling her bed with beetles," Steven said. "Can't much blame her. Couldn't have been nice, sliding under the sheets to find them crawling with critters that crunch when squashed."

"Oh, Steven, you are awful." The lady laughed openly, but the Scotsman remained unmoved.

"Beg your pardon," Steven said. "My manners are appalling. Rose, may I introduce you to Beth—Lady Ian Mackenzie. Beth, I present—"

"The Dowager Duchess of Southdown," the Scotsman said, his low and strong voice breaking over Steven's. "Betrothed to Captain Steven McBride, but no official announcement has appeared in any newspaper. Staying at the Langham hotel in adjacent suites. The dowager is a year and three months widowed, her marriage to the Duke of Southdown called into question by the new duke, Albert Francis."

Beth stared at her husband, but again, she didn't look surprised or concerned.

"Oh dear," Rose said when the man closed his mouth and switched his unnerving focus to her. "Has there been a general declaration?"

"I read seven newspapers today," Lord Ian said, still staring at Rose. "All say the same thing. But the engagement can't be real until there is an official announcement, so the newspapers are making it up." He switched his gaze to Steven. "Why are they?"

Steven did not look alarmed. "Let us adjourn to a box upstairs, Ian, my friend." He reached to put a hand on Ian's shoulder then pulled back before touching him, as though thinking better of it. "And I'll explain everything."

Chapter 9

Beth was delighted with the ruse. In an elegant box that belonged to the Duke of Kilmorgan, she clasped her hands and laughed at Steven's tale of meeting Rose and his decision to begin the pretense. Rose listened with some trepidation, but Beth appeared to find nothing wrong with their behavior.

"Marvelous," Beth said. "That stopped a few wagging tongues, I imagine."

"Now they're wagging about this betrothal," Rose said. "Wagging very hard, it seems. Steven wouldn't bring a newspaper upstairs today."

"I didn't want you worrying, Rosie." Steven laced his fingers through Rose's. "You have enough to think on already."

Beth watched him kiss Rose's fingers and raised her brows. "Are you certain it's only a ruse?"

Steven winked at her. "For now." Rose tried to pretend it was all part of the game, but her face went hot.

Ian appeared to have lost interest in the entire conversation. His attention was fixed now on a silk ribbon attached to Beth's sleeve, which he'd untied from its ornamental bow. Now he wrapped one end around his large finger, rubbed his thumb over it, unwound it, and started the process over again. He sat very close to Beth, his thigh overlapping into her chair as he continued to caress her ribbon.

He was an unusual man, certainly. Odd, even. But watching him, Rose saw how gentle he was with Beth, and how he couldn't stay far from her. He liked watching her too, his gaze softening when she smiled at him, while with Steven and Rose he was still a bit stiff. Shy, Rose thought, though this seemed more than simple shyness.

Beth possessed an openness her husband lacked. She engaged Rose in conversation without stiltedness, neither awed by the fact that Rose was a duchess or put off by the rumors about her. Beth spoke to Rose as though they were already friends, and Rose, for the first time in years, had an enjoyable evening.

Rose now understood Steven's insistence that they watch the play with the Mackenzies from this box. Plenty of lorgnettes and opera glasses trained on them from other boxes and the stalls below, and plenty of heads moved together to discuss it. No one paid much attention to the play. But this box belonged to Hart Mackenzie, Duke of Kilmorgan, Lord Ian's brother. None of the staring people would accost them here.

When the drama onstage was over, and they rose to leave, Steven suggested they all go to the Albion for a light meal before they retired. Ian said absolutely nothing, but annoyance flickered in his eyes.

He wanted to be alone with his wife, Rose saw. Sitting with a stranger and even with Steven had been difficult for him, she understood. In any other man, Rose might take this for rudeness, but having watched him all evening, Rose saw that Ian's oddities made him different, and he knew it. He tried to blend in, but he knew.

Rose saw too that Beth loved him. The little glances she'd given her husband to make sure he was all right and the secret looks they exchanged told Rose that theirs was a special bond indeed.

She couldn't help wishing for one exactly like it.

"Perhaps not," Rose said, while Steven waited for Beth's answer. "I am rather tired. It's been a wonderful evening, but we had a long day, and I'm weary."

Steven took her hand and stepped against her, looking down into her eyes. "Of course, love."

For a single moment, as Steven's gray gaze fixed on her and her alone, nothing else existed. The noise of the emptying theatre went away, the draft that came into the box as a footman held open the door, Beth's low voice as she spoke to Ian. Only Steven filled Rose's world, his smile, the warmth in his eyes, his voice wrapping around her as he said, *Of course, love.*

She wanted to save the moment, and never let it go.

Then Steven kissed her hand, released it, and turned to fetch her coat.

As they exited the box, Steven and Beth talking easily again, Ian moved in front of Rose and stopped, facing her. His tall body filled the doorway, blocking her way out. As Rose started to politely ask him to let her pass, Ian leaned to her, pitching his voice low.

"He needs it to be real."

Rose blinked. "I beg your pardon?"

Ian waited for a few seconds of silence, as though thinking through his words. "He needs it to be real," he repeated slowly. "With you."

The words were simple, yet something caught in Rose's heart. She cleared her throat. "Captain McBride is helping me. That is all."

Ian shook his head, his brows lowering. "No. You are helping *him.*"

He turned away, moving to where Beth and Steven waited in the hall. Steven gave Rose an inquiring look, but Ian turned to Beth, the rest of the world forgotten as he absorbed himself in her.

~~~~

Rose pondered what Ian had said on the silent ride back to the hotel. Steven said little, his laughter gone as he looked moodily out the window to the dark night.

He needs it to be real.

Needed what to be real? The betrothal? The affection Rose was developing for him? *More than affection . . .*

Steven McBride did not need her. He was a good-natured, attractive, entertainment-seeking bachelor who liked to play cards and imbibe a little too much—although he'd been quite moderate in his drink tonight. He came from a respectable

Scottish family and had highborn friends and connections like the Mackenzies. His fellow officers apparently thought well of him. Why would Steven need a betrothal to a scandalous woman like Rose?

She had no idea, and no idea why Steven became moodier and more abrupt when they reached the hotel. It was late enough that not many people were about, but couples in evening finery still watched as the two of them ascended the stairs together.

Outside their suites of rooms, Rose started to say good night, but Steven stopped and tugged her hand out of the crook of his arm.

"I can't do it, Rosie."

Rose faced him, raising her brows to hide the rapid beating of her heart. "Can't do what?"

"Stay here and go tamely to bed, knowing you're—"

He broke off, took her key from her and unlocked her door. He opened it and guided her inside, hand on her elbow. The parlor of Rose's suite was still lit, a coal fire dancing on the hearth in anticipation of her return.

"Knowing I'm what?" Rose asked.

Steven closed the door. "Knowing you're in here." The words were almost a snarl. "On the other side of the wall, while I try to be a gentleman and stay away from you." He cupped her cheek with his warm hand. "It's too damned hard."

It was hard for Rose too. She touched his fingers. "The world already thinks it, Steven," she said softly, hearing the tremble in the words. "In spite of our separate rooms. You know they do."

Heat flared in Steven's eyes, then his look turned self-deprecating. "I'm trying to help you win back your good name, not tarnish it more." He laced his fingers through hers and lifted her hand to his lips. "I can't stay in the hotel, lass. I'll never sleep if I do, and I have an appointment to keep tomorrow. I'll be back in time for breakfast."

Rose gripped his hand when he tried to withdraw it. "Don't."

"No choice, love." Steven kissed the tip of her nose but held himself stiffly away from her. "Good night."

"Good night," Rose said faintly, letting him go.

She watched him move across the room, taking up the hat he'd dropped to a table. "Steven," she called.

He turned back at the door, impatient to be away.

"Be careful," Rose said. "You've been . . . ill the last two mornings . . ."

"From overindulging?" His smile was wry. "Don't worry, love. The appointment tomorrow is too important for me to arrive hungover. Sweet dreams." Steven swung away and said nothing more as he disappeared out the door.

An important appointment with a grieving widow. Whoever she might be.

Steven had dropped the silk scarf he'd worn tonight around his neck. Rose lifted it, debated running after him with it, then lifted it to her lips instead. The soft fabric still held his warmth, but it didn't ease the ache in Rose's heart.

Steven was packing up the effects of one Captain Ronald Ellis the next morning when Rose tapped on the door of Steven's parlor and entered to his grunted, "Come in."

Rose stopped in surprise upon seeing the valise and the red uniform being laid inside. "Gracious, are you leaving?"

The note in her voice was one of dismay and alarm, which warmed Steven's heart unexpectedly. She hadn't asked with polite disinterest but with worry that he was going.

Steven smoothed out the uniform. "This isn't mine. I'm taking it to the widowed Mrs. Ellis."

"Oh." He saw Rose readjust her thoughts. "The woman who tried to call on you yesterday?"

"The very one."

Rose came to him and studied the pile inside the valise then reached in and started pulling things out to refold. Steven relinquished the task to her. As a soldier, he'd learned to pack efficiently, but the ability had deserted him this morning.

"Why does she not wish you to come?" Rose asked, shaking out and folding the red uniform coat. "I would think she'd want her husband's things returned."

"She wants the things," Steven said. "Not me." He let out a breath. "But I need to go. To finish this."

Steven had no wish to face Laura Ellis this morning, but he owed it to Ronald. Laura would hate him, and that was fine.

He'd go to her, let her take out her grief on him, and that would be all. He'd promised Ronald.

Rose was watching him out of the corner of her eye as she packed. She had no idea what this was all about, but she wasn't impatient or demanding him to explain. Steven folded his arms and let her warmth drift over him, closing his eyes to it. He wasn't hungover this morning, but somehow he'd prefer a pounding headache and brassy throat to the remorse in his heart.

"Would you like me to go with you?" Rose was asking.

Steven popped his eyes open. "There's no need . . ." He trailed off. Rose's gaze was full of compassion, a softness for Steven. She'd had that even the first night he'd met her and fallen so cravenly into her bosom.

"Yes," he said. "Please. Come with me, Rosie."

Ellis had inherited a house north of Oxford Street, near Cavendish Square. Rose had asked Miles, her former coachman, to drive them, saying that such an errand should not be made in a hired hack. If Albert found out, he'd have to lump it, she said decidedly. Steven was torn between laughter at her resolve and dread of his errand.

Rain had started coming down in earnest. The London streets were soaked, mist rising from the pavements. Miles drove slowly, the roads slippery, but all too soon, he pulled up in front of the house in Mortimer Street.

Steven had dressed in his regimentals for this errand, and rain fell on his bare head as he descended. Rose started to come out after him, but Steven forestalled her.

"No need for that. You stay cozy in here." He took the valise she handed him and gave her hand a caress. "Knowing you're out here waiting for me will be enough to sustain me."

"Please give Mrs. Ellis my condolences," Rose said. "I know how difficult this is for her."

Because Rose herself had lost a beloved husband, she meant. But she didn't understand the half of it, unfortunately. "Thanks, love. Stay warm, now."

Steven squared his shoulders, hefted the valise, stepped to the door, and knocked upon it.

"Steven." Laura rose from where she sat at a writing table as her maid admitted him. The maid had tried to tell him that Mrs. Ellis wasn't receiving, but Steven overrode her. "I asked for you not to come."

"I know." Steven set the valise on a table and opened it. "But I know you'd regret ever after if I didn't. Here it is."

Laura stared at the valise as though it held a snake. She took one step, two, and peered inside.

"He wanted you to have it," Steven said, gentling his voice. "I couldn't not bring it."

Laura ran her hand over the uniform coat inside, fingers catching on the buttons and braid. Her shoulders sagged.

"And this." Steven removed a locket and chain from his pocket and pressed it into her hands.

Laura stared down at it, anguish on her face. "What do we do now? Tell me, Steven. What do I do?"

"We remember him. And honor him."

"Yes. Yes, I . . ." Her voice broke, and as Steven had feared, Laura burst into sobs. "I can't. I loved him. I'll never, ever love anyone like that again."

Her cries were heartbreaking. She rushed at Steven, reaching for him, needing him.

Steven had come here intending to be firm with her, even callous if he needed to be, but he saw now that Laura was truly suffering. He pulled her into his arms, and Laura clung to him, weeping into his shoulder.

The weeping was more than grief, Steven knew. It was guilt for her part in the affair, guilt at cuckolding Steven, fear that she'd driven Ronald to his death. Steven carried his own share of guilt.

The door of the room creaked open, and a breath of air entered the stifling room. "Is everything all right?" Rose asked in her voice like soothing rain. "Can I help?"

Chapter 10

Rose paused on the threshold, torn between pity and jealousy as the woman continued to cry on Steven's shoulder. She reminded herself she had no right to be jealous, but emotions like that had no sense of their own.

Rose had fully intended to remain in the carriage and let Steven attend to his own business. But she'd been able to see, though the parlor windows, Steven speaking to the widowed Mrs. Ellis, and Mrs. Ellis hurtling herself at Steven. Steven had started in surprise, and by the look on his face had no idea what to do with her. Rose had called for the footman who'd accompanied them and bade him help her from the carriage and to the house.

The woman—Mrs. Ellis—raised her head when she heard Rose's voice. Her eyes were red-rimmed with weeping, her face blotchy. She wrenched herself away from Steven as though Steven had been clutching her instead of the other way around, and dragged a handkerchief from her pocket.

"Why did you bring *her* here?" Mrs. Ellis asked piteously. "How could you, Steven?"

Steven's face was flushed, and he balled his gloved hands to fists and cleared his throat. "May I present Her Grace, the Dowager Duchess of Southdown?" he said stiffly. "My fiancée."

"What?" Mrs. Ellis raised her head, her voice ragged. "Fiancée? What are you talking about?"

Steven continued to stand rigidly. "If you'd bothered to look at a newspaper the last few days, you'd have seen it splashed everywhere."

Mrs. Ellis stared at him a moment, then she swung her gaze to the maid who'd followed Rose into the parlor, trying to stop her. "Evans," she snapped. "Fetch me a newspaper."

The maid curtseyed then vanished without a word. She was back quickly, newspapers in her hand. She handed one to Mrs. Ellis, face-up to the place that said, *Captain S— McB— and his tenacious duchess dine together, then head for the theatre with his illustrious McK— in-laws. The play in question was* Medea. *One hopes it is not prophetic.*

Mrs. Ellis read this, her color changing from red to unhealthy pale. "Oh." She looked up, not at Rose, but at Steven, and her expression was one of chagrin but also relief—vast relief. How odd. "Steven, forgive me. I had no idea." She turned to Rose and flushed again. "I'm so sorry, Your Grace." She sank down to the sofa, the spirit gone out of her.

Rose sat next to her in concern. "Are you all right? Evans, please bring your mistress tea."

Evans hurried to obey while Steven stood in the center of the room, a masculine pillar in the midst of feminine hysteria.

"Steven, you should have told me," Mrs. Ellis said, looking up at him, her handkerchief at her eyes again. "I never would have . . ."

"Forget it," Steven said in a firm voice. "It's done."

The tension between them was thick. Rose wished she knew what was going on, but she realized that now was not the time to ask.

"Congratulations." Mrs. Ellis directed the word first at Steven then at Rose. "I hope you will be happy. I truly do."

"I intend to be," Steven answered.

The look he sent Rose seemed to erase all doubt in Mrs. Ellis's mind. She turned a genuine smile on Rose. "My sincerest apologies, Your Grace. Steven was right—I knew nothing, and only assumed. I think this is wonderful. The best thing that could happen. You've brightened my day a bit." She squeezed Rose's hand, and Rose smiled back, more to reassure her than anything else.

The tea came. Rose poured a cup for Mrs. Ellis and pushed it into her hand but declined any herself.

"We have much to do," Rose said, rising. "Everything is very rushed, unfortunately." She took Mrs. Ellis's hand. "Again, I am very sorry to hear about your husband. I know well what it is to lose one so dear. We will never cease missing them, but it does become more bearable. But we wouldn't want to lose the pain entirely, would we? Then it would be as if they hadn't mattered."

Mrs. Ellis nodded, tears filling her eyes again. "You are right. Entirely right." She set aside her tea and got to her feet, becoming again the polite woman Rose had met the day before. "Take care of Steven, Your Grace. He deserves happiness."

She squeezed Rose's hands then let her go. Steven was beside Rose now, his hand on her elbow. "Good-bye, Laura," he said firmly, and steered Rose out.

Not until they were in the carriage, moving through the streets toward the Langham, did Rose venture to speak.

"If you don't wish to talk of it, I understand," she said to Steven, who'd taken the seat opposite her. "But I admit a healthy curiosity."

Steven had been silent since they'd left the house, but he now held out a hand to Rose. "Come and sit with me."

He was asking her to throw propriety to the wind. Ladies and gentlemen who were not related did not occupy the same seat in a carriage, and the ladies always rode facing forward while the gentlemen faced the rear of the coach.

The little rules seemed ridiculous now that they'd broken so many larger ones. Rose didn't hesitate to go to Steven and snuggle in next to him. She laid her cheek on his warm coat, and he slid his arm around her as rain streaked the carriage windows like tears.

"My friend Ronald and I first met Laura five years ago,

when we were on leave for Christmas," Steven began. "And we both fell hard. She was twenty-two and a stunning beauty."

"She is still quite pretty," Rose managed to say. The bite of jealousy rose up in her again, but she would run back to the hotel alone in the rain before she'd admit it.

Steven touched her cheek. "You're a generous soul, Rosie. Ronald and I made great fools of ourselves for her. We were best friends, closer than most brothers, and I think we enjoyed the game for her affections. She certainly enjoyed playing us one off the other. She had us fighting for her favors, each trying to trick the other out of escorting her to whatever outings we'd planned. We both went a little mad, threatening each other with dire fates. Laura sat between us and lapped up every morsel of it. I postured as much as Ronald, even coming to blows with him, but somewhere in the back of my mind, no matter how far things went, I still considered it all a game. After Christmas, we'd rejoin the regiment as best friends." Steven drew a sharp breath. "When Laura chose me as her affianced, I was very proud of myself. What I didn't realize at the time was that Ronald hated me for it."

"Oh." Rose's heart squeezed, and she fought her demon again. No reason for it, she told herself. Clearly the marriage had not come to pass. "But she married Captain Ellis," she said, puzzled.

Steven gave her a nod. "That came later, after I squired Laura about for the rest of that season, very full of myself. She quite played it up as well. What neither she nor I knew was how much Ronald felt it. I had no idea—I was only pleased I'd won the game. I play to win." He let out a breath, sounding bitter. "One night, Ronald cornered me alone in my hotel room. He had a pistol and vowed to shoot me, then himself."

Rose sat up in alarm. "Good heavens. What did you do?"

"He was very drunk, and I was able to wrestle the pistol away from him, thank God. But I saw the misery in his eyes. I realized in that single moment that Ronald loved Laura deeply, and I never had. I'd been infatuated, and wanted to best everybody, as I always do. I'd been gambling as usual, but this time with friendship and our lives."

Rose rubbed her thumb over the inside of his wrist. "Oh, Steven. I'm sorry."

Steven sent her a self-deprecating smile. "No need. I'd been a thorough idiot, and the shock of Ronald truly wanting to kill me woke me up. So I conceded the field. I told Ronald I knew he and Laura belonged together. I'd allow her to break the engagement, then I left for Scotland, taking myself out of the way."

"What did Mrs. Ellis say to that?" Rose tried to imagine the grief-stricken woman she'd met devastated that Steven wanted to break the engagement. No, she'd truly loved her husband. Her sorrow hadn't been feigned, and she hadn't looked at Steven with regret or any sort of longing.

Steven gave a short laugh. "She'd wanted Ronald the whole time, it turned out. Used me to make him declare himself. I doubt she thought he'd go as dramatically far as he did. I walked away, spent my Christmas with my family in Scotland, as per usual, and went back to the regiment. Ronald returned too, by himself, but a married man. He'd obtained a special license and done the deed at New Year's."

"Mrs. Ellis didn't accompany him?"

He shook his head. "She didn't like the idea of living outside England, especially not in such a difficult place as Africa. Which was why I'd never had any fear of taking the game to its logical conclusion. I'd have gotten out of the engagement before it became too entangling. I'd want a wife willing to accompany me."

Rose secretly thought Mrs. Ellis a fool. If Steven had asked *her*, Rose would have eagerly followed him wherever he went, never mind heat and hardship.

"What happened to Captain Ellis?" Rose asked.

Steven looked out the window, but there was nothing to see but drops on the glass and mist beyond. Very little sunshine penetrated the gloom of the day, sealing them in a half light of gray.

Rose rested her head on his shoulder again. "If you don't want to tell me the rest, I understand."

Steven drew a long breath. "No, I want you to know the rest of the story. Ronald and I were on a patrol one night a month or so ago, and got cut off from camp. He'd told me that morning that when he took leave this year, it would be his last. He planned to leave the army and settle down with Laura and raise children. He was happy, and I was happy for him. Things had never been the same between us since he tried to shoot me, no matter how many times he'd apologized for it or tried to make up for it. I was glad we were putting the whole sordid business behind us. But it wasn't meant to be." Steven turned from the window and looked down at her. "We ran into a pocket of rebels, they had guns, and they shot Ronald, right in front of me."

"Steven." Rose slid her arms around him, her heart aching. "How horrible."

"He never had a chance," he said, voice stoic. "I got him away and to a safe place, but he died as I held him."

Rose tightened her embrace. It felt so natural to comfort him, as though she had a right to. "I'm so sorry."

"His last words to me were another apology." Steven gave another short laugh. "Ronald thought I was still in love with Laura, to my surprise. He told me to go back to England and look after her. Gave me his blessing to marry her. I couldn't argue with him, not while he was dying. It was important to him that he made his peace with me this way, so I agreed to take care of her."

Rose said nothing. Steven turned back to the window, the rain increasing outside. Rose thought about how Steven had introduced her to Mrs. Ellis, emphasizing she was his fiancée. And Mrs. Ellis's look of relief.

"She doesn't want to marry you," Rose said. "Is that what she thought you'd come to do? Propose to her?"

"Yes," Steven answered wearily. "Ronald apparently told her that if anything ever happened to him, she and I could be together. But Laura never wanted me. She still doesn't. That's why she tried to put me off. I only insisted delivering Ronald's things so I could fulfill my promise to him, and close the matter."

"I understand." Rose rested her hand on the seat beside her. "Handy that the world thought you betrothed then, wasn't it?"

She spoke lightly, but she at last understood Steven's willingness to have his name coupled with hers, to have the journalists spread the tale that they were engaged. It would send a message to Mrs. Ellis for once and for all that the events of the past were at an end.

"Rose." Steven turned to her, a hard light in his eyes. "I might have seen the opportunity, that first morning. But that's not what it became."

His look made anything jealous in her shrivel in shame. "I'm not angry," she said, her voice quiet. "I am happy to help you in return for the assistance you've rendered me." She tried to smile. "Even to keep you out of an unwanted marriage."

"Not to keep me out—to give Laura her freedom. I know her. She'd convinced herself I was still in love with her, and that it was her duty to marry me for Ronald's sake. Even if I hadn't proposed, she'd have martyred herself, waiting for me to. This way, she can move on with her life, marry someone else if she wishes, instead of either burying herself for me or marrying me and both of us living in horrible guilt. Now she's free."

Rose nodded. "I do see that." She recalled her first encounter with Mrs. Ellis and became torn between amusement and embarrassment. "I suppose she thought I was your paramour."

Steven leaned back against the seat. "At this moment, I don't give a damn what she thought. I've done my part, now we can all rest in peace."

Before Rose could ask him what he meant by that, the coach slowed, nearing the hotel. The street was crowded, despite the rain, and men in black suits waited near the hotel's entrance for their return.

"Oh, God," Steven said, peering out at them. "I can't face that mob right now. Miles!" he called.

Miles opened the hatch below his seat and peered inside. "Yes, sir?"

"Can you take us somewhere a little less conspicuous?"

"Yes, sir." Miles snapped closed the hatch and the carriage turned abruptly. In the mist and rain, perhaps the journalists would not see the crest of the Duke of Southdown on the coach's side.

Miles drove them back to Mayfair, to Grosvenor Street and the mews behind it. He was going to lend them his quarters above the coach house again, Rose saw.

The rain was coming down in earnest as Miles halted the coach. Steven pulled a flap of his greatcoat around Rose as he helped her down, then they dashed together into the warm, horse-scented coach house. A side door took them to a flight of stairs leading to the quarters above, where Mrs. Miles greeted them with tea.

Mrs. Miles helped Steven out of his wet coat, telling him she'd sent hot water up to the spare room he'd used before, if he wanted to wash his face and hands. She chivvied him on up the stairs, then brought a basin and towel to Rose.

Rose rinsed her face and patted it dry, blessing Mrs. Miles for her understanding. It was cozy here, in the small quarters where only Miles and his wife lived. Albert kept no other staff permanently in Town; he employed Miles only because he was paid by a trust settled upon him by Charles. Miles and his wife stayed for Rose's sake, they'd let her know early on, and she was grateful to the pair of them.

Rose finished her ablutions and drank a cup of tea, but Steven did not reappear. After half a second cup and a wonderful scone, Rose filled the cup that waited for Steven and carried it up the stairs to the room at the top of the house.

She'd feared to find Steven on the bed, thinking haunting thoughts of his friend and his death, but he stood at the tiny dormer window, looking out. Rain streaked the window, filming it with an almost constant stream of water. Steven rested his arm on the high sill, his face turned out to the gloom.

"I brought you your tea," Rose said brightly. "Truth to tell, I was getting a bit worried about you."

"Were you?" Steven made no move to take the tea, and Rose set it on the washstand, the only other piece of furniture in the room. "No need. I'll weather my storm. Already have, mostly."

Rose made for the door. "Have a drink of the tea—it's quite good. And come down soon. Mrs. Miles has gone about her errands, and Miles is looking after the horses, so there's no need to make conversation if you don't want to."

Steven turned his head and looked at her, his expression telling her he hadn't taken in a word she'd just said. "Don't go, Rosie."

His voice pulled at her, stirring fires in her heart. "There's more tea downstairs," she said quickly. "And scones. Light as a feather, with plenty of jam—"

"Rose." Steven crossed the cramped room and laid his large hand on her arm. "Stay."

His hand was heavy, strong, but it was the look in his gray eyes that decided the matter. "Yes," Rose whispered, and closed the door.

Chapter 11

Steven went very still as Rose shut the door and turned back to him. No modest protests, no fluttering. Rose understood what Steven wanted, and she wanted it too.

She came to him, resting her hands on his chest, looking up into his eyes.

Their first kiss was unhurried. Steven cupped Rose's face in his hands, parting her lips to kiss her slowly, deeply. He tasted the tea she'd drunk, with its bite of lemon and a little bit of raw brown sugar, a taste he remembered from his childhood.

Rosie, lass, a voice inside him whispered. *I've needed you all my life and never knew it.*

Rose locked her fingers around the lapels of Steven's coat. His heart beat faster as he felt her shaking, knowing she was holding herself back from delving into his clothes.

I'll let you do whatever you wish, my Scottish Rose.

Steven peeled her fingers away and slid off the coat. He tossed it over the foot of the bed and didn't stop moving until he'd relieved himself of collar and cravat and unbuttoned the top of his shirt.

Rose moved her focus to his throat, touching his bronzed

skin as though fascinated by it. Steven smiled at her, his body warming, finding an answering spark in her green eyes.

He pulled off his shirt and rid himself of the short-sleeved undershirt beneath it. Cold air touched his skin, this room again warmed only by the chimney that rose through it.

Rose's lashes swept down as she looked him over, taking in his tanned chest and its brush of golden hair, his flat nipples that were also sun-bronzed. She'd seen him bare when he'd lain in this bed that first morning, but she'd blushed and pretended to look elsewhere.

Not so now. Rose gave him the compliment of a half smile as she ran her gaze over him, as though pleased with what she saw.

The look made his blood burn. More so when she leaned forward and kissed his shoulder. The touch of tongue on his bare skin made him want to groan.

"You're a wicked lass," he said, closing his hands around her elbows. "Do you know what that does to me?"

"What?" Rose slanted him the same eager smile she'd worn when she'd agreed to his deception of their engagement. She'd proved that she loved games, like Steven did, but Rose would win every hand she played.

"It makes me want to be a very bad man," Steven said. He ran his hand up the back of her neck, sinking into her curls. "I'm already a bad man, but I'm holding back for your sake."

"Don't," Rose said, losing her smile. "Don't hold back for me. I need . . ."

Steven read the rest in her eyes. *I need to be held, to be loved, to feel wanted.* Or perhaps those sentiments were Steven's.

"I need it too," he whispered. Maybe he said that—he wasn't certain what was inside his head and what wasn't right now.

He only knew he was stiff with need, and he had a beautiful woman caressing him with both hands.

Steven gathered her close, the press of her body against his hardness, even through his kilt, making him ache. He kissed her as she smoothed her hands over his bare back, and then the kiss turned fierce.

Rose wanted him. That little knowledge made Steven fling away caution and kick self-control out the window. Rose was a beautiful woman, as lonely as he was. They were alone in this aerie, and she was hungry. If she wanted to feed on Steven, so be it. After all, they were betrothed.

Steven finished the kiss by biting down on her lower lip, which made her gasp, then he unbuttoned the front of her bodice and pushed it open.

Her corset cover had little bows on it, white satin ones that beckoned his fingers. Stephen undid one, and Rose laughed at him. Then he saw why—the bows were decorative and didn't open anything.

The hooks in the back did. Steven unfastened them and slid bodice and corset cover off. He kissed Rose again as he unlaced her stays and pulled them away.

Beneath she wore combinations, the top part made of thin lawn and lined with an edge of lace at the neck. In Steven's hurry, he tore buttons, but soon Rose was bare to him.

He stood back to admire her. Now free of the dark cloth that swathed her upper body, Rose was truly the angel he'd thought her the first night. Her skin was replete with color—a pink flush across her throat and chest, the red of her lips, the glorious gold of her hair, and the dark red-brown of her nipples.

Steven cupped her waist, moving his hands up under her breasts. The swell of them filled his palms, just as he'd known they would, and he held them while he brushed his thumbs over her areolas. Her nipples tightened still more as Steven caressed them.

"You are beautiful, Rosie," he said, almost reverently. "Like your name."

"My mother loved roses." The words were so soft they faded against the thrum of rain on the roof.

"I love them too," Steven said, drawing her close.

Her back was warm, smooth, her breasts fine against his bare chest. Rose lifted into the next kiss, her movements fluid. She was good at kissing—her lips fitted smoothly to his, their tongues meeting, no awkwardness.

As though realizing she was enjoying it too much, Rose pulled back. "Steven, what did you mean . . ."

"Shh." Steven quieted her with another kiss. He didn't know what she was asking and he didn't care. Some things could be destroyed with too any words.

He loosened her skirt and the petticoat beneath it, stripping off her mourning. Steven liked to think he was peeling back a cocoon, setting Rose free from the confinement of her grief.

Rose's black skirts dropped away, and Steven unhooked her bustle. Rose said nothing about him knowing how the fastenings worked, but she'd understood him from the beginning. She'd had no illusions about Steven.

With her confining clothes joining his on the bed, Rose was beautiful in nothing but the lower part of her combinations and her stockings. Stimulating as well. Steven's body urged him to take her now, or he'd make a fool of himself.

She looked best against the whitewashed wall. There, all her color came to life, the bloom in her cheeks, the gold of her falling hair. Steven unbuttoned and pushed down her combinations, helping her from them. Setting her free.

Rose naked was a glorious sight, and Steven was on fire. Her soft hands went to his shoulders, she having no doubt about what they were going to do. She wasn't a trembling virgin—she was a woman who knew she liked the touch of a man, and wanted it now.

Steven undid his kilt's clasp and pin and unwound the plaid from his waist. The kilt landed on top of their clothes on the bed, as did the rest of his underwear.

Rose's gaze went to his cock, hard and tight for her, and her flush deepened. But she didn't look away. She wasn't afraid of this part of a man.

Steven couldn't stay from her long. He pushed her to the wall near the window, close enough to the chimney for its warmth. Warmer here than on the bed, well he knew.

His body told him to hurry, but Steven wanted to savor her. He might never have another chance.

Rose drew a sharp breath as Steven leaned and licked between her breasts. Her hands went to his hair, caressing, drawing warmth. He kissed her skin once more then took one of her full breasts in his mouth, curling his tongue around her nipple.

Another quick breath from Rose, this one lifting her further into his mouth. Steven suckled and nibbled her, memorizing her dusky taste, one he'd recall in lonely evenings to come.

There was more of her body to enjoy. Steven licked between her breasts again, then kissed his way down to her abdomen.

He sank to his knees as he went, touching a kiss to her firm belly. The tight lines of it told him Rose had never borne a child, which accounted for some of the sadness in her eyes. Her marriage should have given her that gift.

Steven teased her navel with his tongue, and Rose laughed. She didn't ask what he was doing, didn't try to push him away. She only ran a hand over his head and took another breath as he kissed the swirl of hair between her thighs.

Golden and beautiful. Rose made a faint noise in her throat as Steven leaned forward, nudged her thighs apart a little, and closed his mouth over her opening.

With my body, I thee worship. Steven had always liked the titillating words of the marriage ceremony. *I worship you, Rose. I treasure you.*

He slid his tongue into her, tasting her delights, wondering that he'd waited so long. He'd wanted to fall upon her the very night he'd . . . well, fallen upon her. Or that morning, when he'd lain in this room, unclothed, and she'd leaned over him to gather up his breakfast tray . . .

As Steven rested his fingertips on her thighs and drank her in, he let himself imagine how that would have gone. The tray on the floor, the dishes smashing. Rose on his bed, clothes coming away. The covers pushed aside, she straddling him. Her head back, her breasts moving softly in the rhythm of what they did.

Steven closed hands on her, his tongue doing what he'd wanted to that first morning. Rose made sounds of feminine pleasure, her fingers gripping his hair, but he didn't mind the pain. Steven flicked his tongue over the tight part of her, smiling as she started, her body meeting the wall with a quiet slap.

He couldn't wait any longer. Steven gave her one final lick, then he rose up the length of her, in contact with her all the way, his skin already slick with sweat in spite of the cold.

Rose started to laugh as Steven lifted her, giving him a look of surprise from her languid eyes that he wasn't carrying her to the bed. But Steven was in too much of a hurry for something so tame.

Her laughter changed to a gasp when Steven parted her legs and slid straight up into her.

Rose clutched at Steven as he pressed her open, filling her, finding spaces inside her she didn't know existed. He was hard and hot, and she was wet from what he'd done with his mouth and hands. No man had ever touched her as Steven had today— she hadn't even realized men and women did such things.

But his mouth on her had wiped away all rational thought, erasing propriety and the need for self-control. Rose had fallen against the wall, her legs parting for him, the fires he'd started when he'd drunk her incinerating her from the inside out.

Just when she thought she'd roll away on a wave of incoherence, Steven had risen, the look in his gray eyes intense, and had lifted her into his strong arms.

Her body welcomed him.

"Rosie," he said, a smile spreading over his face. "Ye feel as beautiful as you are."

His accent had deepened, anything civilized stripped away from him. This was raw and basic, nothing to do with civilization.

The world thought Rose a scandalous woman, and now here she was in the heart of scandal. *And what a wonderful place it is, to be sure.*

Rose laid her head back against the wall, amazed that she had this man around her, *in* her.

She'd never made love like this before. She'd thought they'd be on the bed, Steven on her, his weight warming her. Not this primal coupling, with him holding her, thrusting up into her. He was high inside her, making her ache and feel wonderful at the same time.

All Rose could say was his name. It came out of her mouth again and again, as the rain beat on the window and rushed across the sill. If someone could look in from the outside, Rose imagined they'd see a blur of bodies against the white of the wall and the red brick of the chimney. The rain would run the colors together like a beautiful painting that had been tipped while still wet.

The plaster was hard and cool at her back, the warmth from the chimney touching her side. Steven's body in contrast was hot, living flesh, but every bit as hard as the wall behind her.

She could see that his tan ended where his waistband would be, then started up again on his lower legs. That meant he ran about in his kilt and nothing else, or only the lower portion of his military uniform, perhaps with legs rolled up.

The thought of Steven wandering about in the sunshine, half dressed, his golden hair burnished, flooded her with pure desire. Rose felt herself opening even more, embracing him, her body knowing what to do.

Steven responded. His eyes were heavy, a gleam of gray from between his lids. A beautiful man, his face softened, the lines of care smoothed from it. His shoulders worked as he loved her, sweat gleaming on his skin.

Rose touched his face, and Steven kissed her. The kiss was hot, opening her without the sweet touches of lips leading up to it. The flirtation was finished, and this was real.

Steven abruptly pulled away from her mouth. "No," he groaned, his brows drawing down.

His thrusts increased. Steven's fingers bit into her flesh, and at the same time, the wave that had dissipated slightly when he'd ceased drinking her crashed over Rose again.

She heard her voice ringing, crying his name, and his answering words, low and fierce. "Rosie, you're beautiful, lass. Och, *damn it.*"

He held her firmly against the wall, thrusting hard, his face set, while Rose moved with him, body rocking with her pleasure. Sweat beaded on Steven's skin, and trickled from hers, the cold in the room no longer having meaning.

Steven continued to thrust, but gentler now, slowing, his face easing from frustration to warm relaxation.

"I didn't stand a chance," he said breathlessly. "Didn't stand a chance against the completeness of you."

Rose didn't have the speech to ask what he meant. She understood somehow.

Steven kissed her, his mouth warm with what they'd done. He turned around with her as he did so, and lowered her onto the bed, sliding out of her.

Rose lay alone, suddenly cold without him. Instead of joining her at once, Steven paused a moment and gazed down at her. He took her in with a slow glance, the brush of it tingling, as though he touched her.

Steven then trailed his fingers down her body, tracing her nipples, sliding his touch over her soft belly to the join of her legs.

Rose jerked when he touched her there, too sensitive. Steven smiled as though she'd done something pleasing, and slid himself onto the bed next to her. He lay on his side, propped up on his elbow, and moved his hand again to the join of her thighs.

One stroke there made Rose half rise. "What are you doing?"

"Giving you pleasure, love. I was a bit hasty, but you had me too eager."

Hasty? It had been full, wondrous. Steven brushed two fingers over her opening, and Rose jumped again, realizing they weren't yet finished. "I never knew . . ."

Steven chuckled, a warm sound. "There are many avenues of pleasure between men and women. Fortunately, I know most of them."

He knew this one, that was for certain. A few more strokes, and Rose was arching up, her thoughts scattering, as they had when he'd put his mouth to her. She knew she was behaving shamelessly, but she had no intention of stopping herself.

Steven caressed and rubbed her, then thrust a finger inside her. Rose's world narrowed to that feeling—his finger was nowhere near as thick as his hardness, but the small movement made her choke back a cry.

A second finger joined the first, and then a third. All the while, he brushed his thumb over the tightness of her, until Rose bucked against his hand, begging him—for what, she didn't know.

"Hush now, sweet Rose," she heard him say. "I'm only giving you what you gave me."

Rose's cries continued, incoherent, and she couldn't stifle them. Steven laughed again and covered her mouth with a kiss.

When the world went dark, nothing existing but Steven against her, and his hand pressed firmly to her, Rose ceased trying to stop her cries. She let the pleasure wash over her, her joy at being here with Steven become her only thought.

Just when she knew she'd die of this feeling, Steven took

away his hand, rolled her into the mattress among their jumble of clothes, and entered her again.

He thrust into her faster this time, pushing them both down into the bed, his kisses hard. They moved as one, body to body, solidly joined. Their breaths came quickly, gazes holding each other's, both too far gone now even for kisses.

Steven groaned as he lost his seed for the second time. He was holding Rose's hand, his fingers squeezing hers, his face relaxing with his release.

Rose touched his cheek, kissing his lips with her swollen ones, and marveled at what they'd done this day.

Steven lay beside Rose long into the afternoon, not leaving her even as the window darkened with the end of the short day. They'd nestled down under the covers, the blankets heavy with their clothes. Steven had pulled his plaid up over the quilts, adding another layer of warmth.

Rose slept for a while, Steven dozing with her. When she'd awakened, she'd smiled at him, a little shy, but betraying no shame. Steven had touched her, savoring her, before his needy cock had him entering her one more time.

After that they both slept, then awoke and spoke in low voices. About nothing. About everything. Steven heard himself telling her stories about his childhood, how he'd run wild in Scotland with his sister, Ainsley, until their three older brothers dragged them home again. He spoke of the army, his friendships there, his adventures. Rose told him of her life in Edinburgh with her father, her sorrow when he died, her astonishment when a lofty duke asked her to be his wife.

They talked of dreams they had for now and later, and laughed about things they'd seen together. They had only a few memories, two days of them, but it gave them so much to talk about.

Steven could talk to her forever.

The coachman and his wife left them alone. The two downstairs had to know what the two upstairs were doing, and yet, they gave them their privacy. Miles and his wife must have recognized that Steven had come to take care of Rose, and they were letting him get on with it.

"Sittford House tomorrow," Steven said, kissing her shoulder. "I want your legacy in your hands—I don't trust Albert not to sell everything sellable before we can go through it."

"You're still determined to help me win against him?"

Steven noted the surprise and faint worry in her eyes. "Yes. Why wouldn't I?"

"Our bargain will soon be at an end," Rose said wistfully.

"Endings are sad." Steven brushed his fingertips along the softness of her breasts. "I don't like them. Beginnings sometimes can be good. But the middle of the story is always the best part. I like middles."

Rose laughed. "I like the middle of this one."

"That's because all the villains are leaving us in peace." He pressed his palm against hers, their splayed fingers touching. "So are our friends. I'm enjoying it."

The look in Rose's eyes said she was enjoying it too. "We'll have to go back to the real world sooner or later."

"Later," Steven said. "Not right now. Right now is for . . ." He released her hand and slid over her again. "Right now is for loving you. I'm going to do it for as long as I can."

"Good," Rose said with a smile.

That was all Steven needed. He was already aching for her again, a pain that eased only slightly as he slid himself inside her one more time.

~~~~~

The bloody settee was nowhere in the house.

Steven sat on a dusty couch in one of the attics—the be-damned mansion had five—and looked with disgust at the furniture crammed into it. Couches, divans, chairs, tables, bedsteads, most of it rickety and broken. Nowhere had they found an Egyptian-style settee in ebony and gold, decorated with sphinxlike heads.

Rose stood, dejected, near the dusty window. She'd resumed her black clothes, which hid every inch of her. All very proper, but Steven would never look at her the same way again.

He'd seen her beauty. It glowed from her even now until it filled all the spaces in this dingy attic, and all the spaces inside Steven.

"It's not here," Rose said. She made her way carefully

through the mess to Steven and sank down next to him. "Albert must have sold it. How could he have known?"

Steven shrugged. "We'll find him and pound its whereabouts out of him."

Rose did not look hopeful. She leaned into Steven, an intimate move, one she did unselfconsciously.

Steven turned his head and kissed her cheek, which led to a kiss on the lips. That kiss lingered, brightening the gloom around them.

They'd arrived while Albert had been finishing his midmorning tea. The man, it seemed, rarely left the estate—he'd told his housekeeper he'd be in London the day Rose and Steven had first come searching, only so the servants wouldn't bother him.

The man was a fool, Steven thought in contempt. He obviously had no respect from his staff, or else he'd have told them he wasn't to be disturbed, and they'd have obeyed. Steven knew that if servants didn't like an employer, they could find plenty of little ways to irritate him without going so far as all-out rebellion. A man who had no control over his household was a sorry thing indeed.

Steven, brooking no argument from Albert, took Rose on a search of the house. Rose led Steven into every room on every floor, and they looked into every cabinet, cranny, closet, nook, and niche. They'd searched the cellars, rooms down there no one had opened for years. They'd even looked in Albert's private rooms when Albert had gone off with his steward to the home farm.

The home farm would be next. Steven wouldn't put it past Albert to try to hide a priceless antique in the garret of a leaky farmhouse.

The settee, however, was nowhere in sight. They did find the two Egyptian-style chairs depicted in the sketches from the cabinet, but that was all. Steven turned each chair upside down and stuck his hands under the upholstery but found no further clues inside them.

"You can always take one of these," Steven said, motioning to the chairs, which were right side up again. "They'd bring something at a sale."

"I know." Rose eyed them disconsolately. "But I want to

know why Charles pointed me to the settee. Why he wanted me to have *it*, in particular."

Steven slid his arm around her and pulled her close. "No disrespect to your husband, Rose—he was a fine man—but I wish he'd written you a plain note that told you where he'd left you a cache of diamonds."

"Albert would have found that, wouldn't he?" Rose shook her head. "Charles had no illusions about his son."

"Which is why I don't understand why Charles didn't make your settlements and what you received in the will more clear. Why he didn't confound Albert before he began."

Rose sighed. "I don't know. Charles was fond of little jokes, but truth be told, they were jests a child could see through. That's because he had a kind heart, did Charles. Not a mean bone in him."

Steven wondered if he could ever live up to the paragon Charles seemed to be. The man had been kind, yes—Steven had seen that in him, even on brief acquaintance—but Steven had also noted that Charles had not been advanced in intellect. Steven had often been praised for his quick wit and clever mind, but Rose valued softness of heart over cleverness.

Steven cupped her cheek as she looked up at him, and leaned down to kiss her again. He couldn't help himself.

Rose tasted of sunshine and summer days. He'd never be cold with her next to him.

Someone cleared a throat. "Begging your pardon, Your Grace."

Chapter 12

Rose started, but Steven took his time lifting away from her. Let the staff of this house know Steven was looking after her now.

The young footman John stood in the shadows near the door, uncertain whether to advance into the room. Rose struggled to her feet, and Steven, trained to be a gentleman even if he forgot most of the time, stood up beside her.

"It's all right, John," Rose said, giving him an encouraging look. "What is it? Is Albert setting his dogs on us? Not that it matters. I rather like dogs, and they like me."

John listened in perplexity, his handsome face drawn into a frown as he tried to work through this.

"Never mind," Steven said. "Tell us what you came to say."

John stood to attention. "Yes, sir. It's this, sir. Housekeeper said you'd want to know, Your Grace, that His Grace—the duke that's passed, I mean—had us shift a cartload of furniture out to the summerhouse in the months before he married you."

Rose's mouth popped open. "Did he? What on earth for?"

"I don't know, Your Grace." John truly must not know—he wouldn't know how to lie about this or why he should.

"I see." Rose looked thoughtful, and also a little sad, no doubt remembering her sunny wedding on a summer's day. Steven decided not to take it as an omen that since he'd met Rose, the weather had been confounded awful.

"Housekeeper forgot, Your Grace," John said apologetically. "We all did. But she remembered today when you were searching the house and couldn't find what you were looking for. Whatever that is."

They hadn't said specifically, Steven not trusting Albert not to lay his hands on the settee and trundle it away.

"Thank you, John," Rose said, looking a little more cheerful. "We'll have a look in the summerhouse."

John nodded and started patting his pockets. "Housekeeper said you'd want the key. Ah, here it is." He pulled it out in triumph, stepped to them, and handed the key, not to Rose, but to Steven.

"Good on you, lad," Steven said. "Give the housekeeper our thanks."

John beamed like a puppy who'd been praised. He bowed to Rose, mumbled a thanks, and scooted off.

"Curious," Rose said, her excitement returning. "Shall we adjourn to the summerhouse?"

Steven glanced through the high window, which showed nothing but rain and clouds. "The weather is wretched. Why don't you sit in a comfortable room with the housekeeper bringing you tea and cakes, and I'll tramp through the mud and search the summerhouse?"

"No, indeed." Rose leaned to him and closed her fingers around the key. "I'll not sit here, trembling and nervous, waiting for your return. I'm going with you, and that is that."

⁓

Rose regretted her eagerness a bit when they were halfway to the summerhouse, the wind biting them and bringing tears to her eyes. The summerhouse lay on the far end of the huge formal garden, right on the edge of the estate, a lengthy tramp along paths that had become overgrown and rough.

Rose, bundled up warmly, walked with Steven, arm in arm, their heads down into the wind. One of the dogs that had come back to the house with the steward and Albert—a black bird dog with a lolling tongue—followed them, and nothing could dissuade him from it.

Rose had never been to the summerhouse. According to Charles, they'd stopped using it years ago. It was an old thing, apparently, built at the beginning of the century, when every gentleman had to have a summerhouse or folly to simulate Roman or Greek ruins.

This summerhouse was reached by a narrow path beyond a gate at the end of the garden, and up a rather steep hill. The small building was round, imitating a rotunda, with pseudo Roman columns encircling it. It looked as though it had once been painted warm yellow, but years of wind, rain, fallen leaves, and English damp had rendered it a streaked gray, with the original stones showing through. A true ruin, instead of a false one.

Steven inserted the large key into the rusting lock of the summerhouse's door. He had to put all his strength into turning it, grunting with the effort. Just as Rose feared the key itself would break, the lock screeched, the tumblers moving.

"No one's oiled this lately, that's for certain," Steven said.

He pulled at the door—which nearly fell on top of him. The hinges were weak, rust flaking from them as they pulled partway out of the wall.

Steven started to laugh. "I see I needn't have bothered wrestling with the lock. Careful, Rosie."

He propped the door open, took Rose's arm and steered her inside. The dog, who'd sat down patiently while Steven had fought the lock, pushed past Rose, his head up, nose working.

The interior of the summerhouse was dank and dim. The rotunda floor had once been paved with fine marble, but now the blocks were chipped and loose. Light came from windows high above to show them dirt and bird droppings, niches containing now-empty pedestals, and a jumble of furniture, covered with overlapping sheets, in the middle of the floor.

The dog sniffed around this pile curiously, then sat down and wagged his tail as Steven reached for the sheets.

"Hold your breath," Steven advised.

Rose backed away, grabbing the dog by its scruff and dragging him with her.

Steven started pulling the old sheets away. He gathered

them into his arms, trying to mitigate the cloud of dust that
rose from them, but he lost the battle. Rose sneezed, pressing
her finger under her nose. The dog sneezed as well, throwing
droplets of moisture through the air. His entire body rippled
as he drew another breath and sneezed again.

The dust settled over Steven, coating his black coat a light
gray. He ruffled his hair, sending up another cloud of dust, and
tossed the sheets aside.

The furniture beneath didn't look like much. Odds and
ends, much of it broken.

Rose started to express disappointment, then she wiped her
streaming eyes and pointed. "What's that?"

Steven waded among the chairs with no seats, the canted
table with a broken leg, and lifted a shell of a bookcase out of
his way.

Buried beneath the jetsam of mahogany and walnut was a
hint of black and a gleam of gold. Steven started throwing
aside the broken furniture, which shattered to the floor like so
much firewood.

"This is it," he said, then he stopped. "Dear God, what a
mess."

Rose hurried to him. The dog, caught up in the excitement,
dove under the wrecked furniture, emerging with a large stick
that once belonged to a spindle-backed chair. The dog pre-
sented it to Rose, wagging his tail faster.

Rose absently took the stick and tossed it for the dog to
chase. "It's ruined," she said dispiritedly.

Steven pushed more furniture aside, revealing what once
had been a finely crafted, if ugly, settee. "No wonder it was
brought out here with the discards."

Rose had seen the piece before her marriage to Charles,
when he'd brought her to the house to show her where she'd
live. The settee had rested in an unused parlor high in the
house, given pride of place under a wide window and flanked
by tall ebony and gilt candelabras.

After the wedding, Rose had been caught up in preparations for her new life and then Charles's death. She'd never
noticed the settee had gone from the house, hadn't much
thought about it until now.

It had been placed out here for mice to nest in, it seemed,

and for the wood to be split and ruined by damp. Only the inlay had survived, though it was covered in dirt and muck. Steven scraped at the patterns with his gloved fingers to reveal more gold.

"Someone painted over that," Steven said. "What a bizarre thing to do."

"Maybe hiding its worth?" Rose suggested. "Not that sitting out here for a year and a half hasn't destroyed it. Why would Charles do such a thing? Or did the servants lug it away by mistake?"

Steven stepped back to survey the room and the settee's position in it. "No, this was set here on purpose, buried under a pile of useless junk. Charles hid it, love."

"But why would he?" Rose took the stick from the dog, who'd brought it back to her. He sat down and looked at Rose expectantly, so she tossed it for him again. "And why would he draw the rose on the back of the sketch? Not to mention hiding the sketches in the cabinet?"

"He was saving them for you," Steven suggested. "He must have changed his will at the same time, to add you to it and leave you the furniture."

"But he didn't know he was going to die so soon," Rose said. "How could he?"

Steven came to stand next to her, his warmth cutting the chill. "Maybe he did, love. Doctors might not have told him his heart would give out, but maybe he knew, deep down inside. Perhaps he didn't expect it to happen as quickly as it did, but he must have known he'd have to leave you to Albert's mercy."

Tears stung her eyes. "Why didn't he tell me?"

Steven slid his arm around her, pulling her close. "A man doesn't like to confess weakness to a lady, especially not one he loves. Trust me on this."

"Poor Charles," Rose said. Her heart ached for him.

She knew now, after these few days with Steven, that while she'd loved Charles, she'd loved him in a different way than she did Steven. Charles had been kindness, comfort, caring. Steven was passion, excitement, offering her a world behind her narrow confines. Steven was a man who felt deeply, never mind that he covered it up with joking, self-deprecation, and drink.

Steven held Rose close, letting her rest her head on his shoulder. He had such strength, such warmth, a pillar more solid than the columns of this summerhouse for her to lean on. Charles was like this ruined place—Rose's past. Steven was whole and new—Rose's life now. And her future? She couldn't know.

Steven kissed Rose gently on the lips and wiped a tear from her face. "Whatever reason he stashed it out here, Charles wanted you to have this," Steven said. "Let's shift it, and get back to our cozy hotel."

~~~~~~~

Rose helped Steven push the old furniture aside to release the settee. Its once bright seat cushion was a tattered mess, stuffing from nearly a hundred years ago hanging out of it in gray threads. Even the mice had abandoned it.

The dog tried to help, digging at the loose marble tiles around it. Finally Rose and Steven had cleared a path that allowed them to drag the settee to the door and out to the summerhouse's porch.

Rain was falling steadily, coming on gusts of wind that spattered heavy droplets across the steps. Steven shoved the settee to the leeward side of the porch and dusted off his hands.

"I'll go back to the house and tell Albert he is going to lend us transport," he said. He looked out between the trees to the windswept garden beyond. "You can wait here, out of the rain, at least, though it's bloody cold."

"I'm resilient," Rose said. "And I have a dog."

Steven went to Rose and took her hands. It was never cold where he was—when Rose had woken this morning wrapped around him, she'd never been so happy.

"You are the most courageous woman I've ever had the fortune to know," Steven said. "Thank you, Rose."

She stared up at him. "For what?"

"For teaching me what courage means." Steven leaned to her, his breath brushing her lips before he kissed her.

The kiss held all the heat of their loving night, and the light of new day.

Rose pulled Steven close, savoring him. If she had nothing else, she'd remember this, the two of them private in the cold, and the intimacy of waking up next to him in his bed. These were memories she'd hold to her for the rest of her life.

Steven flashed her a grin as he straightened up. "I'll run all the way." He kissed the tip of her nose. "And then we'll feast on hot tea and whiskey."

His smile could change her world. Rose clung to his hands another moment, then she gave a little laugh and let him go.

Rose watched Steven dodge his way through the trees, his head down against the wind. He truly did run, moving so fast his wind-whipped greatcoat and kilt exposed his strong thighs.

Rose kept her gaze on him until the trees obscured him, then she shivered and moved back into the relative shelter of the summerhouse. The dog whined after Steven, but turned and entered the summerhouse with Rose.

Rose stood in the middle of the rotunda, looking over the wreck of the furniture, the dog warm against her legs. "If I had a match, I could build us a nice roaring fire," she said, patting the dog's side. He wagged his tail and gazed up at her, his vitality coming through her gloved hands.

"Then I'd have the constables on you." Albert's voice floated in before his body blocked the open doorway. "When your paramour comes back for you, you go and stay out of my sight. I never want to see you here again, or I will have you arrested for trespass."

Chapter 13

Albert glared at her, the dim light sparkling on his blue eyes. He glared at the dog as well, who shrank into Rose's side.

"I hadn't intended to return after this," Rose said, keeping her voice even. "I will take what Charles wished me to have, and go."

Albert didn't move. "It's criminal you should have anything at all."

Rose frowned at him. "It's what your father wanted. You can dance around with your solicitors trying to tie up my settlements, but this was written out very plainly."

"I intend to prove my father wasn't in a sound mind when he wrote it. Won't be hard to prove. He had to be mad to marry a woman less than half his age."

"There was absolutely nothing wrong with Charles's mind," Rose said indignantly. "He was one of the kindest men I've ever known."

"Kind, was he?" Albert balled his fists as he stepped inside. He hadn't donned a hat, or else it had been torn off in the wind, and his thin, graying hair was a mess. "He wasn't kind to *me*, was he? His own son—his *only* son!"

"You shunned him," Rose said, lifting her chin. "When I

met Charles, he was very lonely. In all the time I was betrothed to him, and then married to him, you never once called on him, or tried to meet with him, or wrote him any letters except having to do with business."

"How do you know? Did you read his correspondence?"

"Of course not. He told me—very sad that you couldn't bother to even have a conversation with him."

"You know nothing!" Albert shouted, the words ringing to the high ceiling. "You stupid tart! My father never had time for me—*ever*. Not when I was a boy, not when I left school, not when I became a man. He never cared that I made my own living without taking a penny from him, and a *good* living. No, he only cared about this sodding house and the bloody title and the family name. He didn't care about *me* at all!"

Rose bit back her next retort, sensing she was wading into murky waters. Charles had always spoken of Albert sadly, as someone estranged from him. *A gap between us, my dear Rose,* he'd said. *More like a chasm. I thought perhaps we didn't see eye to eye because of our ages, but you are younger than he, and you and I rub along very well, don't we?*

"I'm sorry," Rose said to Albert. "It's clear you two had much friction, and I'm very sorry about that. You needn't worry about seeing me anymore. I'll take what he left me and go."

Albert wasn't listening. He took another step toward her. "My father was wrapped up in my mother. The sun and moon rose and set on her. I thought, I hoped, after she was gone, that he'd turn to me. Embrace me. At least *talk* to me. But no. You came along and put paid to that, didn't you? He saw you, and again he forgot I existed. You played him, you little whore. You wrapped him around your finger, and he couldn't see anything but you. Stupid bugger—at his age, what could he really poke? But you stroked his vanity and turned him from me, and I was cut out *again*." Another step, the rage boiling from him. "Then you killed him. He tried to be young again for you, and it killed him. And so, I'm making sure you don't get one penny of Southdown money. Not cash, not a trust, not a house, not a room in a house. You'll get your two pieces of bloody furniture, but only if it's scrap wood."

He took two more strides inside, then started beating the pile of furniture with his walking stick. *Pound, pound, pound!*

Rose skipped well back, the dog hiding behind her, whining. Chairs broke, tables fell, the wood rotted, the cloth and rush seats exploding in dust.

Albert beat it all, his face red, arms straining. Rose saw with alarm that he'd started to smile—a gruesome smile—as though breaking up the furniture his father had put out here released something feral inside him.

Rose started to edge around him. Wind and rain notwithstanding, she wanted to be hurrying up the path after Steven, not shivering while Albert rained destruction inside the summerhouse.

Albert saw her. He snarled at her and rushed her, shaking his walking stick.

Rose yelped and scrambled back. The dog, cringing no more, braced himself in front of Rose and started to bark at Albert.

Albert seemed to come to himself a little. He lowered the stick but swung around and scuttled for the door.

"You can wait in here for you lover," he snapped. "I never want to see you again."

The idea sat well with Rose. Albert could be left alone with his bitterness and rage, and that would be fine with her.

Albert turned around and glared at her again, his face blotchy, eyes protruding. Then he stepped onto the summerhouse's porch, wrestled a moment with the big door, and managed to shove it closed.

The summerhouse shook with the impact, raising dust. Rose started sneezing again, the dog echoing her.

She put her hand over her nose and mouth and headed for the door, stopping in dismay when she heard the key screech in the lock.

No matter, Rose thought in irritation. The hinges were flimsy enough. She'd wait until Albert was gone, then pry the door loose from the wall.

The next moment, she heard a scraping, heavy sound of the ebony settee being dragged along the porch and thumped in front of the door.

"Albert!" Rose yelled. She pounded on the door's flaking panels. "Let me out at once!"

More pounding, as Albert presumably took his stick to

the settee as he'd done to the other furniture. Then came more
dragging—this time it sounded as though Albert piled large
tree limbs, easy to find in this neglected woods, on top of
the settee to block her in. Rose pushed at the door. The hinges
gave a little, enough to let in light, but she couldn't shove the
door far enough to slip out.

"Albert!" she shouted.

She heard another drag, thump, and rattle of a heavy
branch. The light between the slit in the door was muted.

"Damn and blast you, Albert!"

She heard his tread as he stomped away, then silence but for
the wind and rain. Rose balled her fists and beat on the door
again. The dog pawed at it, then looked up at her, worried.

"Oh, it doesn't matter." Rose pressed her hands flat on the
door, then reached down and gave the dog a reassuring pat.
"Steven will be back in a few minutes. Won't he?"

The dog wagged his tail, but looked perplexed, as though
wondering why on earth Rose wasn't letting them out of there.

Rose gazed around at the wreck of the summerhouse and
the ruined furniture in sadness. Charles must have sent the
extra furniture out here to disguise the settee, but still, these
things had been part of the house, part of its history. Albert
apparently hated that history.

It was also sad that Charles and Albert had never had a
chance to settle their differences. Albert blamed Rose, but
Rose could feel no remorse or guilt for that. Either man could
have tried to talk to the other, regardless of Rose's presence.
She'd certainly done nothing to keep Charles from Albert—
she'd barely known Albert. Charles could have made over-
tures to his son, but it was also clear that Albert was a spoiled
brat, even at his age.

These thoughts went through Rose's head distractedly as
she let out an irritated breath. She was cold, rain pounded
down on the roof, and who knew how long it would be before
Steven and Albert's staff could trundle a wagon down here?

The dog left Rose's side to circle the room, his head down.
He might smell rats or birds—the dog would have been trained
to fetch grouse or other game from fields after a shoot.

She watched him abstractedly until he started pawing at

the wall opposite the door. More than pawing. He let out a bark and scrabbled at the paneling with his paws.

Rose went to him, curiosity spilling through her anger. "What have you found, lad?"

The dog looked up at her, tail moving, pleased with himself. He pawed again at the paneling, and it started to come away.

Instead of a stone wall behind it, Rose saw emptiness, and felt a wash of air. "A secret passage?" she asked, bending down to peer inside. "I adore secret passages." Sittford House had several, which Charles had delighted in showing Rose. They'd led between bedrooms—which had set them to laughing at Charles's naughty ancestors.

"Shall we be sensible and wait for Steven?" Rose asked the dog. "Or see what's in there?"

The dog sniffed the opening, looked up at Rose again, then shook himself and plunged inside.

That settled that. Rose moved the panel aside, propping it against the wall, then she ducked into the opening, and hurried after the dog.

～～～

"Rose!"

Steven shouted for her as he jogged up the path to the summerhouse, moving far faster than the wagon creaking along behind him. The wind was biting, icy. The rain would turn to snow before the evening was out, he'd wager. The sooner Steven got Rose back to London, the better.

"Rosie?"

The summerhouse was now in deep shadow from the waning afternoon. The builders had raised it on a fairly high foundation in order to accommodate a set of stone stairs that ran all the way around it.

Woods seemed to have grown up onto the porch since Steven had gone—thick, dead branches blocked the door, reaching halfway up the wall above it.

"Rose!" Steven bellowed.

His shouts turned to swear words as he ran up onto the porch. Someone had dragged huge branches across the door, blocking the way in—or out. Through the limbs he could see the ebony and gold settee, the gilding he'd rubbed clean shining in the dim light.

"Dear God." Steven pulled away the branches, tearing his gloves and bloodying his hands. "Rose!"

No answer. No cries of help from Rose trapped inside, no barks of the dog he'd left with her. Bloody useless animal.

The wagon stopped behind him at the edge of the trees. The driver, one of the farmers, climbed slowly from his perch, his son, whom he'd recruited to help, holding the horses.

Steven yelled to them. "Help me shift this lot!"

The farmer came panting up, stared in amazement at the dead branches covering a piece of broken furniture, then joined Steven in pulling the things away.

Steven's heart hammered, and his stomach roiled. Who the hell had shut Rose in here? He thought he knew the answer, and his rage flared.

"I'll kill him," he snarled. "I don't care if he is a bloody duke. Rosie!"

No answer. Steven shoved the remains of the settee out of the way and reached for the door handle. Locked again, damn it.

Instead of fumbling for the key, Steven simply yanked the door from its hinges. It fell, but he shoved it aside and ran in, calling Rose's name.

The place was empty. Rose wasn't here. Steven's relief was closely followed by another terrifying question—*then where the hell was she?*

He ran out. "Rose!" The woods were growing darker, the rain falling hard. "Rosie! Damn it. Answer me!"

"Guv," the wagon driver who'd follow him inside called out to him. "Come and see this."

Steven charged back into the summerhouse. The driver stood looking at something on the wall, hidden by the broken pile of furniture, which seemed to have become even more broken. A black square about four feet high and three feet wide opened on the back wall, a panel of peeling yellow paint leaning next to it.

The question was not whether Rose had gone into that opening. It was how far had she gone, and what had happened to her once inside?

"I need lanterns," Steven snapped. "Fetch them. Now!"

The driver didn't bother explaining that he didn't work for Steven. He obeyed without question.

Steven was kneeling in front of the opening, peering into the darkness when both driver and his son ran up, each carrying a lantern. Steven snatched the one from the boy's hands. "Stay here in case she turns up," he told the boy then looked at the driver. "You, come with me."

"I should go, sir," the boy said, taking his father's lantern. "I'm smaller."

Steven had no wish to drag a young lad into danger, whatever that might be. The father, though, nodded. "He can wriggle into tight places like a worm," he said proudly. "He's your man."

Steven still didn't like taking a child into that hole, but he had to concede that the driver did not look much capable of crawling about in the dark.

"You stay behind me," Steven said to the boy. "And don't lose sight of me."

"Yes, sir," the lad said.

Without further word, Steven ducked into the darkness.

Chapter 14

Steven had to stoop in the low tunnel, but he kept on. He called Rose's name every few feet, echoed by the boy's "Your Grace?," but silence was their only answer.

At every step, Steven dreaded to come across Rose, lying incoherent, ill, or worse. His entire being filled with panic. He knew the only way he'd relieve it was to find Rose, take her in his arms, and hear her whisper, "Hush, Steven, I'm all right."

He'd plunged into the game of being Rose's betrothed, at first to let Laura Ellis release herself from him, as well as for the fun of it. At least, that's what he'd told himself. Steven knew now that he'd followed his instincts to latch on to Rose and not let her go.

She'd steadied him with gentle hands the night he'd fallen drunkenly into her, and Steven wanted her to steady him the rest of his life. He needed her. No—it went beyond need.

He loved her.

Steven had been telling her the past few days, in a light tone, that he considered them engaged in truth, and that they'd marry soon. Rose had laughed with him as though she thought him joking.

It was no joke. Steven spoke that way because he didn't know how to be serious. Feared it.

When he found Rose, he would put her over his shoulder and run out of here with her. Then he'd shake a special license out of someone and marry her. Tonight.

She was the only woman he'd consider continuing his existence with.

"Rosie!" he yelled, his words echoing hollowly. "Answer me, damn it."

"What's that?" the boy behind him asked.

Steven halted. The boy darted around him, disobeying, as boys did, and pointed ahead of them. Steven flashed his lantern and saw nothing, but then the boy shielded the light and pointed again.

Steven saw it then, a dim outline of something square. A door?

"*Behind* me," Steven said sternly as the boy started forward. The lad sighed and let Steven take the lead again.

The outline grew sharper as they neared it, and the air coming to them turned colder and less dank.

Steven could move swiftly even bent double, having had to run and stay within cover on many occasions in his career. He made it to the dim light to find it was indeed a door, or at least a set of boards nailed together to simulate one.

Steven shoved it open to nearly trip on stone steps on the other side. He hurried up these, finding at the top, in the mud, the precise pointed-toe print of one of Rose's high-heeled boots.

But where had she gone after that? "Rose!" he shouted.

Barking answered him, faint and far away. Logically Steven knew it could be any dog, not necessarily the one from the Southdown estate, but he turned his steps toward the sound without pausing to think.

He shouted again, continuing his path toward the answering bark. Steven pushed through bramble and undergrowth beneath tall trees, the branches tearing at his coat. The boy surged on ahead, unafraid now, but it struck Steven that the lad wasn't worried, because he knew exactly where they were.

"What's over there?" Steven asked him. His heart was in

his throat as he waited for the answer. An old well? A pit? A cliff?

"Come on, sir," the boy said, running nimbly through the trees. Steven hurried to catch up with him.

The woods opened out into a large clearing so suddenly that Steven staggered to a halt. He dropped his lantern, which had already extinguished in the wind, his hand now too numb to hold it.

What was in the clearing had caused him to drop it. First he saw Rose. Second, he saw what Rose stood before—a house.

Not a house. A fairy castle. That was the only explanation. They'd run through the tunnel and emerged in cloud-cuckoo land, where miniature sugar-spun palaces dotted the landscape.

The house was small but done in such exacting detail it was as though someone had built a mansion and then shrunk it. It was two stories, the ground floor filled with many-paned windows, columns, and pediments over the windows and the double front door. The second floor was covered with a mansard roof, with scalloped gray-slate tiles. Dormer windows with curved peaks broke out from the roofline. Half of the cottage was covered with vines, which would bloom a riot of colors in the late spring and summer. Roses.

The columns on either side of the door had been carved with the same kind of vines, except these were covered with carved and painted roses—red, pink, yellow, and white. The roses met in the plaster molding above the door, twining together into a heart.

A garden had been planted around the house, barren now for winter, but the bushes were full and would be fuller in the growing season. It was neat and sculpted, again as though someone had taken the gardens of Versailles and given them a good rinsing until they were small enough to fit here.

Rose stood in the middle of this garden, wind buffeting her coat and hatless hair, staring at the door and its rose motif. She might have been caught in a spell, frozen here to stare at this house for eternity, or until her lover kissed her and woke her.

"Rose!" Steven called.

Rose turned around and saw him. So did the dog. Steven realized that with the wind rushing and roaring in the trees as it was, she'd not been able to hear his cries. She waved to him as the black dog loped to him, then Rose went back to studying the house.

"Isn't this—" she began. Then "Oop!" as Steven barreled into her and dragged her off her feet. He spun around with her once, then set her back down and began kissing her.

Rose was all that was warmth and spice. Her mouth was a point of heat in the cold, her face sweetly smooth, flushed from the wind. Her body fit nicely into Steven's arms. After her first start, she flowed against him, holding him as he held her.

She was alive, and whole, and well. Steven hugged her harder, pressing her to him, kissing her again and again. Rose laughed, and he kissed her smile, taking the whole of her into himself.

He was vaguely aware of the boy, who'd reached the house, patiently waiting with the dog until they finished the uninteresting bit.

Rose tried to push away from Steven, but he held her fast. "Rosie," he breathed. "I thought I'd lost you."

"I was waiting for you," she said. Magical words in this magical place.

But what place was it? "Where are we?" Steven asked the lad.

"We call it the cottage," the boy said, studying it. "Been here forever, my dad says. A lover's nest from two hundred years ago. My dad says."

The architecture put it in the very early Georgian period. Palladian, Steven thought it was called, when classic architecture was revived and Capability Brown had been sought to plan gardens.

The place wasn't a ruin. The garden was neatly trimmed, the house painted, the roof tight.

"No one seems to be home," Rose said. "I knocked, but had no answer. I didn't like to simply go in."

The boy shrugged. "No one lives here. There's always a door open in the back."

He led them around the side, Rose and Steven hand in hand, the dog trotting beside them.

The back was no less a palace than the front, but a short wing stuck out from it like an afterthought. A double Dutch door, with the bottom half opening independently of the upper, as might be found in any of the older cottages around here, opened as the boy raised the latch.

Rose and Steven stepped into a neat kitchen with a flagstone floor, and Rose let out a breath of relief. It was warm here, with a fire in the hearth, and tea things set out on the table. Stranger and stranger.

"I thought you said no one lived here," Rose said to the boy.

The lad shook his head. "They don't. But there's caretakers." He opened the door that led to the main house.

Whoever the caretakers were, they had kept the place very nicely. The architecture might be old, but the furniture was new, chair and sofas strewn with cushions and looking comfortable. The fireplace was stoked, andirons polished, and soft carpets covered the floor. The rose motif continued in the moldings at the top of the walls, in the medallions on the ceiling and above the fireplace, in the patterns on the carpets, and on the embroidered cushions.

The room beyond the sitting room was a dining room, likewise tidy, and a stair at the far end of that presumably went up to bedrooms above.

"Lucky woman," Rose said, returning to the sitting room and looking around in wonder.

"What woman?" Steven, now out of the wind, his panic dissipated, started to grow angry. "Why the devil did you run off like that, lass? And who shut you in the summerhouse? It was Albert, wasn't it? I'm going to kill him—slowly."

"I didn't fancy staying in there," Rose said. "The dog found the secret passage, and when I got to the other end and saw the roof of this house through the trees, I admit to curiosity."

"Bloody hell, Rose."

Steven caught her hand between his, he still needing to reassure himself that she was all right.

"I meant that the woman this house was built for was lucky." Rose glanced around the sitting room again. "Whoever commissioned it for her must have loved her very much."

Steven slid his arm around her. "I wonder if she was called Rose," he said. "This place suits you."

Rose met his gaze, showing no remorse that she'd led him on a merry chase. Perhaps she didn't realize how much the bottom had dropped from Steven's world when he'd found her gone.

"I like it very much," Rose said, giving him the little smile that turned over his heart. "Who does it belong to, I wonder?"

"It belongs to you, Your Grace."

Rose tried to spring apart from Steven at the woman's voice, but Steven wasn't letting her go. Not again.

The woman who'd entered looked like any other in these parts, plump and a bit worn by time, dressed in a plain gown with an apron, her graying hair in a neat bun. She looked like any housekeeper or cook in a country home.

"I beg your pardon?" Rose asked her, flushing.

"We've been waiting for you a long time, dear," she said. "I mean, Your Grace. We've been keeping the place, just like he asked. Thought you'd never arrive."

Maybe Steven *had* stepped into a fairy tale, like the ones he read to Sinclair's children on occasion. Eight-year-old Andrew liked the gory and gruesome ones the best.

Rose stared at the woman, as nonplussed as Steven. "Arrive? From where? Who asked you to keep it?"

"The duke, of course. The one who's passed on, I mean. Young Lord Charles, as my mum knew him when he was a boy, and she his nanny."

"Oh, I see. Then you are Mrs. . . . ."

"Winters, dear. I married Mr. Winters, who was steward before our son took over. Our son tried to tell us matters were bad for you, but we thought that after the will was sorted you'd come. You didn't, not until now, but we kept on being paid to keep the place, and we saw no reason not to. Lord Charles was always a kind man."

"Yes, he was . . . but. . . ."

Steven broke in. "What Rose—Her Grace—means is that there was no mention of this house in the will."

Rose laughed a little. "If there had been, I'm certain the new duke would have heard of it."

"And come to turn the Winterses out and raze the place," Steven finished darkly.

Mrs. Winters opened her hands. "I only know the instructions we received in a letter after Lord Charles had passed. We was to keep the house for you, but when you take possession, you can do with it as you please. Now, I've got tea almost ready. Would you like me to bring it in here for you? Or will you take it in the kitchen, where it's a mite warmer?"

Chapter 15

It had been a day of strange marvels. When Rose and Steven finally found themselves alone in the train heading back to London, the broken settee safely stowed in the baggage car, Steven sank down into the cushioned seat beside her and burst out laughing.

"Good Lord." Steven had stripped off his gloves, ruined beyond redemption, at the cottage, and now he held Rose's soft hand between his bare ones. "We went to look for a settee and came up with a house."

"It's very odd," Rose said, even as she warmed at his touch. "How did Charles suppose I'd find the place? The Winterses had been waiting for me for a year and a half, she said."

"Maybe Charles wrote you a letter and hid it in the Bullock cabinet," Steven said, caressing the backs of her fingers. "Or the deeds to the property—which, if it is entailed with the main house, Albert gets anyway."

"But nothing was in the cabinet, except the drawings of other furniture," Rose said, frowning. "And if anything was inside the cushion of the settee, mice will have eaten it. There was certainly nothing left of that cushion by the time we got it onto the train."

"True." Steven deflated slightly, but then shrugged. "We'll find it, Rosie. I promise you. Now, there's something I decided to do when I thought I'd lost you, and I need to think on it a bit."

So saying, he leaned back on the seat and closed his eyes.

He opened them again when Rose leaned over him and kissed him. She'd been cold all day, until he'd come to her and held her, and now she wanted to imbibe all of Steven's warmth.

Steven's strong hands closed on her wrists, and he pushed her back a little, his gray eyes steady. Before Rose could be surprised that he was rejecting her advances, he gently eased her down to her seat, rose, and pulled down all the shades to their compartment.

Rose's breath caught as Steven returned to her, his eyes dark in the half light and full of promise. Her heart beat even faster as Steven resumed his seat and lifted her onto his lap. Then he proceeded to show her that what he'd had in mind for the journey went beyond more than a few simple kisses.

Rose and Steven entered the parlor of Steven's hotel suite upon their arrival in London, and Rose halted in surprise. She'd supposed Steven had led her there, instead of parting for her to go to her own room, because he'd wanted to continue the seduction he'd begun on the train. Rose still wasn't certain her bodice was buttoned right, in spite of his reassurance, and she was sure her bustle had gone back on crookedly. She reflected that Steven was a proving master at what a man and a woman could do together in tight spaces.

She stopped on the threshold now, flushing, because the parlor was full of people.

One was Mr. Collins, his flame-red hair mussed from the continued inclement weather. Near him stood Lord Ian Mackenzie and his wife, Beth, and Steven's brother Sinclair. A woman with the same blond hair as Steven's greeted them with a wide smile, and another Mackenzie, a bit older than Ian, towered behind her.

"Thank you all for coming," Steven said, in no way surprised, confound the man. He led Rose inside, out of the way of the porters arriving with the broken settee. "Ainsley, Cam, this is Rose. Rose, my sister Ainsley and her husband, Cameron Mackenzie."

Ainsley, the blond woman with eyes the same shade as Steven's and Sinclair's, came forward. "How do you do, Your Grace? I hope you don't mind—Beth has already told me all about you." She winked at Rose and took her hands. "Don't be cryptic, Steven. Why did you summon us?"

And *when* had he? Rose realized now why Steven had been such a long time in the cloakroom at the train station—he must have slipped to the office to wire his friends.

Ian Mackenzie was staring at the settee which now rested in the center of the carpet. As well he might—it was a mess. Albert had finished wrecking what the weather and animals already had done.

"Redecorating, are you?" Sinclair asked in a dry voice.

"Let the man speak," Cameron said in a voice that filled the room. "We'll never have the answer if we keep interrupting."

"I brought you here to make it official," Steven said. He took Rose's hands in his scratched ones, which he'd battered in effort to rescue her. "My sweetest Rose," he said in a quiet voice. "Will you marry me?"

Rose's stared at him. She could have sworn he'd just asked her to marry him, but the world was tilting, and she wasn't quite sure. "Wha—?"

Steven's hands anchored her, and she clung to them, the floor still unsteady. His eyes, clear and gray as the stormy November skies, held no teasing, no joking, only sincerity, and hope.

"Steven," she whispered.

"You'll have to be plain with me, Rosie," Steven said, his grip tightening. "Is that a *yes* or a *no*?"

"Steven," was all Rose could say. If she let go of him, she'd fall. If she held on to him, she was still in danger of falling, because hope and happiness were bearing down on her, threatening to sweep her away.

Beth Mackenzie broke in through the silence. "I believe that is a *yes*, Steven. I can tell by the way she's looking at you."

"Is it?" Steven asked Rose.

Rose's throat closed up, and tears flooded her eyes. She nodded, unable to speak.

Steven let out a long breath of relief. "Thank God." He pulled Rose into his embrace, his own body shaking. "Thank you, God."

He leaned to Rose, wiping away one of her tears with his thumb, then he kissed her lips.

The warmth of his mouth snapped Rose back to her senses again. This was real, not simply a sweet dream she'd wake from all too soon. Steven McBride, the warm, passionate, wonderful man, had asked her to marry him, and Rose had nodded in answer. She'd had to nod because the joy of the moment had closed up her throat and choked off her wild *Yes!*

She broke the kiss and smiled at him. "Yes," she whispered.

Steven laughed. His laughter was always real, deep, and warm. He kissed her again, and the room spun around Rose as she kissed him back, the people in it dissolving into a colorful blur.

"It's wrong." Ian Mackenzie's voice was as harsh as Cameron's but a little more stilted, as though he had to force words out.

Rose turned from Steven to look at him. Ian was staring, not at Steven and Rose, but at the settee.

"Of course, it's wrong," Beth said next to him. "Someone's smashed it."

Rose wiped her eyes and managed a laugh. "I agree, it's a bit of a wreck now. I am hopeful a furniture maker can put it back together, but I imagine its value is lost."

Ian glanced at Rose as though she'd gone utterly mad and hadn't understood a word he'd said. He moved to the settee and went down on one knee in front of it, lifting the broken bits of wood to fit them together again.

The others watched him a moment, then moved their attention back to Steven and Rose, as though finding nothing unusual in Ian's behavior.

Steven put his arm around Rose as his friends and family surged forward to congratulate them. Ainsley and Beth kissed Rose, both excitedly talking about wedding clothes and where and when the deed should be done. Sinclair McBride took Rose's hand once the ladies finally let her go, and kissed her cheek.

"Thank you, Rose," he said. "My unruly little brother

needs *someone* to keep him tame. God knows the rest of us have never been able to."

"I didn't fall in love with her because she keeps me *tame*," Steven said, giving Rose a look that reminded her of the naughty things they'd done in the train. "The opposite. She brings out the wickedness in me."

"Lord, help us all," Sinclair said, but the bleakness in his eyes fled a moment before his warm smile.

"You must let us take you shopping," Ainsley said. "We'll bring Isabella along—she's dressed all of us, and she'll have to dress you too. Your wedding gown will be the stuff of legends."

Steven slid his arm protectively around Rose's waist. "Enough of that. I didn't bring you all here to help plan the wedding. I brought you because I want to marry her right away, and you are the best to help me procure a special license."

Lord Cameron nodded sagely. "Wondered why you wanted the drama. I'll see to it. McBride?" he nodded at Sinclair and Mr. Collins, as though proposing they rush away and hunt up a bishop on the moment.

"Could you exercise a *few* seconds of patience, Cam?" Ainsley said to her husband. "I'd like to at least toast the happy couple. I'll ring for champagne. Or did you telegraph for that as well, Steven?"

Ian Mackenzie continued to piece the settee back together. He'd torn off the tatters of the cushion but pushed the legs and arms back into place, fitting the broken bits as he would a puzzle. The settee looked forlorn without its padding, the wood scratched and splintered, but somehow it wasn't as ugly as it had been. The ebony was strong, and the pure gold glistened in the lamplight.

Beth went to Ian, as though to tell him to leave off, but Rose broke from Steven and joined them.

"I think I see what he means," she said, her interest rising.

Ian didn't stop working. He fitted the last large piece against another, the settee held up by its own tension. Ian ran his large hand along one side, then moved around it and touched the other side. He sighted down the length of the seat and gently touched one of the gilded heads that adorned the corners.

Steven came to examine the thing with Ian, Steven half bent with his hands on his thighs. "What are you looking at?"

Ian glanced at him, then realized that everyone was staring at him. His cheekbones flushed, but he fixed his gaze on the settee again.

"This." Ian pointed at the head he'd touched, then touched a second, walked to the other end and touched a third. He paused—if he'd been anyone else, Rose would have thought he'd hesitated for effect—then he touched the fourth head, and they all saw.

It was different from the others, but only minutely. While the other three had eyes that stared rather unnervingly outward, this sphinx's eyes looked down slightly and to the left. Also, the feminine face was rounder than the others, more human-like, while the remaining three were rigid and fixed.

Ian closed his hand over the carved head and started to turn it. Rose leaned in, holding her breath, while Ian kept turning. All at once, the head came away, and with it a part of the post. It had been seamed so neatly that the crack was invisible when the head was attached. Even the damage the settee had suffered hadn't destroyed its secret.

Ian peered into the opening, then he slid his fingers gently inside and pulled out a rolled sheaf of papers. He handed them to Steven without a word.

Steven unrolled the pages, Rose leaning to look. When she saw Charles's handwriting, her heart skipped a beat. Steven studied the top sheet a moment, then quietly passed it to Rose. "For you," he said softly.

Rose took it, her breath quickening, and read.

My dearest Rose,

If you are holding this paper, I have gone from the world. I have made my peace with it, and my only regret is leaving you alone to face what you must. I have tried to provide the best I could for you, but I unfortunately know that a great lot of money, especially when it is tied to land and a lofty title, brings out the worst in people. My family has had a long history of fighting each other for the smallest scrap, and I fear this will happen again

*with my son. To that end, I have fixed upon a way to
provide for you independently, and hopefully make you
smile in the process. I stumbled across the lovely cottage, which its owner charmingly called "Rose Cottage," but he had no idea what to do with it. It had been
in his family for ages, and he, a city man through and
through, was a bit embarrassed by it. It was free and
clear of any entail, and I offered to purchase it from
him, with the sole purpose of giving it to you. The deed
to the property is enclosed here, and you are to use the
house or do with it whatever you see fit. A copy of this
deed has been filed with a solicitor of my choosing in
case there is any doubt. I know that any will I make that
names you will be contested, for which I apologize, my
Rose. But as you know how much I love my little games,
I made one for you that you'd easily solve. I knew you
admired the Bullock cabinet, which is worth much, and
we made such a joke about the Egyptian settee that I
knew you'd find that too. Rose Cottage is yours, as is
everything in it. As a private purchase it has nothing to
do with my estate, and so I can bestow it on whomever
I wish.*

*I have always loved you, my Rose. I can only hope
that you find as much happiness in your life as you
brought to me at the end of mine.*

*I remain, ever your devoted,
Charles*

The last words blurred. Steven gently tugged the paper
from her fingers and pressed his lips to her wet cheek.

"I'm sorry, love," he whispered. "For losing so much."

Rose swallowed on her tight throat. "Much of it found
again," she said softly.

The property deed, which made up the rest of the papers,
was quite detailed, and long. Mr. Collins reached around Steven and plucked it out of his hands.

"It seems in order," he said after he'd skimmed through.
"But I'll go over it carefully back at my offices. The minister
who can say that the parish record listing Her Grace as

previously married was forged has arrived as well, so that mess will be cleared up at once."

"Good," Steven said. "Then there will be nothing to prevent Rose from marrying me this evening."

"Only the rain slowing us up," Cameron rumbled. "Come on, Collins, McBride. Let's find a license and put Steven out of his misery."

"Oh, for heaven's sake," Ainsley said. She hurried to the door as a footman came through it bearing a tray of glasses, followed by the hotel's croupier with champagne. "Let us at least wish them well. I don't think Rose is about to change her mind."

"No, indeed," Rose said. She held Steven's hand again, borrowing his strength, blessing him for righting her world.

"To the happy couple," Ainsley said after they'd all received full glasses.

"Aye," Steven agreed quietly. He clinked his glass to Rose's. "Thank you, Rosie."

"My pleasure." Rose sipped her champagne, but the enormity of the change in her life swept upon her all at once, and her knees buckled.

Steven caught her in alarm. "You all right?"

"Yes." Rose hastily set down her glass and contented herself with holding on to Steven instead. "I beg your pardon—it's rather overwhelming. I've been a long time alone, you see. Never had much family."

"That's all right, love," Steven said. He gestured expansively to the others in the room. "Welcome to mine."

Suddenly, Rose's shaking evaporated. She saw her life before her, not narrow and barren, lined with people who condemned her, but one full of promise, in the company of those who held together against the world.

Steven's kiss on her lips held more promise still, of a slightly more sinful kind. Rose pulled him close, and surrendered.

Epilogue

Steven lay beside Rose in the comfortable bed of their hotel suite the next afternoon, having made her Mrs. Captain Steven McBride a few hours ago.

He'd agreed to delay at Ainsley's insistence, she backed by his four sisters-in-law, that poor Rose should at least have a decent dress to be married in. Steven gave in to the barrage of ladies, to his brother's and brothers-in-law's amusement.

Somehow the women had managed to come up with a gown for Rose to wear when she and Steven wed at the bishop's house the next morning. They'd chosen a light blue, which brought out the flush in Rose's cheeks, the gold of her hair, and the aquamarine flecks in her green eyes. The fine cloth of the gown hugged her body perfectly, and Steven didn't waste time wondering how they'd cobbled together something so quickly. She was beautiful, and that was all that mattered.

Rose repeated her vows without hesitation, though Steven couldn't remember what the devil had come out of his own mouth. But soon the ring, which he'd borrowed from Ainsley until he could buy another, was on Rose's finger. She was pronounced by the bishop—witnessed by his family and solicitor—to be Steven's wife.

The journalists loved it, of course. This time, when Steven found them all waiting outside the hotel upon their return, he stopped and asked for their congratulations. Steven, with Rose smiling next to him, revealed that he'd fallen so hard for his perfect Scottish Rose that he'd begged her to marry him immediately, and she'd done him the honor of accepting.

They were instantly surrounded by a sea of men and women in black, all bellowing questions, such as *What about the comte? Has he threatened to kill himself? Or Captain McBride?* But most of them looked happy, as though pleased to be able to report good news for a change.

They were equally happy to have the rest of the scandalous Mackenzies walk into the hotel past them—Ian, Cam, Mac, and Hart ignoring the journalists as they always did. Steven had no doubt the men and women of the press were busily making up things about the Mackenzie brothers and their wives, as they so enjoyed doing. All in all, a full day for London's scribblers.

The hotel gave Steven another, larger suite, and the family helped Steven and Rose move into it.

Steven had the devil of a time getting them all to go after that. His leave lasted only until after Christmas, and he wanted every second with Rose.

But food and drink flowed, the Mackenzies and McBrides pleased to welcome the newest addition to their family. At last, after several hours of buoyant celebration, Sinclair and Cameron, perceptive men that they were, ushered the others out.

Now the pretty blue gown was in a puddle on the bedchamber's floor, and Rose dozed next to Steven, her skin warm under his fingertips.

As though she felt his gaze, Rose opened her eyes, their green depths drawing him in.

She gave him a languid smile. "There's something decadent about lying in bed together during the afternoon."

"I like decadence," Steven said, brushing the hair back from her face. "I always have."

"Good," Rose said decidedly. "If the newspapers are going to write about me, I want the fun of having done what they say I've done."

Steven grinned down at her. "That's my Rose." He gave her a thorough kiss, one that had him hard and ready again.

"Speaking of decadence," Rose said. "What shall I do with my cottage?"

Steven shrugged. "It's yours. Collins has proved that. The trust means I can't touch it. So you decide."

"It's very pretty," Rose said. "I wouldn't like to rush to sell it, but I don't see the pair of us settling down in it anytime soon." She caressed the back of his neck. "You promised to show me the world."

"The world is what an army wife sees, every facet of it, the beautiful and the ugly. If you're willing to see it with me."

The sparkle in Rose's eyes was eager. "I am. I don't want to be left behind when you go."

"And you won't be." Steven kissed the tip of her nose. "I won't lie, Rosie. It's a hard life. You now have the little jewel box to settle down in—a peaceful life with people to look after you."

"I don't want that," Rose said quickly. "Not alone. I'd rather have hardship with you than ease without you."

Steven's heart was full. He'd make sure Rose was comfortable wherever she was with him, even if he had to bully his commanding officers to make it happen.

"We could let it," Rose said. "The cottage I mean. To other couples. Have Mr. and Mrs. Winters stay on as caretakers, since they've done so well, if they're willing. It could be a summer hideaway, or a bed and breakfast. Something of that sort."

"Whatever you like," Steven said. "Give you a nice little income. Collins can sort that out."

"He's very useful, is Mr. Collins," Rose said. "I'm grateful to him."

"He likes you." Steven pulled her hand to him and kissed her palm. "I like you," he added softly. Steven released her and rolled partway onto her. "I think you can tell."

Rose flushed as pink as her name as his stiffness pressed her thigh. "My dear Captain McBride," she said, her eyes shining. "I do believe you're about to do something scandalous."

"I hope so, Mrs. McBride." Steven moved himself gently

on top of her, looking down into her beautiful eyes—angel's eyes—as he slid into her. "I hope so."

His teasing dissolved in a rush of desire, and Rose's smile faded. They came together in a thrust of passion, Steven clasping her wrists and pushing them down into the bed on either side of her.

Only one thought stood out in all the madness—in everything that had happened to him in the past few days.

"I love you, Rosie," he said, his words a groan.

His angel smiled up at him, her body meeting his in perfect harmony. "I love you too, Steven. Always."

"Damn right," Steven said, and then words fled, no longer needed.

New York Times bestselling author
Jennifer Ashley returns with an all-new
romance in the Mackenzies series

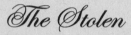

The Stolen
Mackenzie Bride

Available soon from Berkley Sensation
Read on for a special preview . . .

"What morsel is *that*?"

Mal Mackenzie, youngest of five brothers, called at various times in his life *Young Malcolm*, *the Devil Mackenzie*, and *would ye get out of it, ye pain in my arse*—the last mostly by his father and oldest brother—voiced the words as the tedious gathering suddenly grew more interesting.

The morsel was a young woman. What else would it be, with Mal?

"Oh, aye," his brother Alec muttered as he leaned against the wall, in a foul temper. "Of course ye'd notice the prettiest lass in the room. The most untouchable as well."

The lady in question glided through the drawing room on the arm of a man who must be her father. She wore a gown of rich material much like those of the other young women here, but she stood out among them like a fiery bloom among weeds.

They were paraded, these ladies, laced into bodices and tight stomachers that showed a soft enticement of bosom, skirts swaying as they moved. They walked with eyes downcast to indicate what demure creatures they were—suitable wives for the bachelors, young and old, who'd come to view them.

Malcolm's lady, in contrast, had her head up, smiling at all, though the smile was somewhat strained. Her thoughts were elsewhere.

She had red-gold hair that caught the candlelight as she passed beneath the chandeliers, mirrors placed to throw back double the light. Mal couldn't see the color of her eyes from where he stood, but he was certain they'd be clearest blue. Or green. Or gray.

She noted Malcolm staring at her and paused for the briefest moment, the smile fading. Mal, who'd been leaning next to Alec, pushed from the cold stone wall to stand up straight, fires weaving around his nerves.

The young woman took him in—a tall, rawboned Scotsman in a fine coat, dressed like an Englishman except for the plaid that covered his legs to his knees. Malcolm prided himself on not looking entirely like these English whelps—he'd pulled his thick brown-red hair into a queue instead of stuffing it under a powdered cocoon-like wig and had tied his neckcloth in a loose knot.

The young woman's gaze met his, and the answering sparkle in her eyes woke every sense in Mal's body.

Then she turned her head, looking past him as she scanned the crowd for someone else.

The moment—as fleeting as it had been—reached out and wrapped itself around him. The tendrils of something inevitable entangled the being that was Malcolm Mackenzie, changing everything.

Malcolm all but shoved an elbow into Alec, who was pretending to be interested in the interaction of the English and Scottish elite. "Who is she?" Mal demanded.

Alec moodily studied the crowd. "The blond lassie, you mean?"

"Her hair's not blond." Mal tilted his head as though that could help him look under the modest lace cap that rested on her head. "'Tis the color of sunshine, tinged with the fire of sunset."

"If you say so." Alec, two years older and one of a pair of twins, gave Mal a warning look. "She's not for you, runt."

Runt was another name for Malcolm, who'd begun life very small, but now topped three of his four older brothers and his father by at least an inch.

The words *not for you* never deterred Mal. "Why shouldn't she be?"

"Shall I run a list for ye?" Alec asked in irritation. "She is Lady Mary Lennox, daughter of the Earl of Wilfort. Wilfort has an estate as big as this city, more money than God, and power and influence in the cabinet. The family is one of the oldest in England—I think his ancestor fought alongside Henry the Fifth or some such. All of which makes his daughter out of reach of the youngest son of a Scotsman with what the English claim is a trumped-up title. Not only that, she's engaged to another English lordship, so keep your large paws to yourself."

"Huh," Malcolm said, not worried in the least. "Poor little morsel."

Mal followed Lady Mary's progress through the room, noting the polite way she greeted her father's friends and the mothers of the other daughters. Correct, well-trained—like a pedigreed horse brought in to demonstrate what a sweet-tempered creature it could be.

Malcolm saw a little more than that—the restless twitch of her eyes as she searched the room while pretending not to, the trembling of a ribbon on the red-gold curls at the back of her neck.

She was vibrancy contained, a creature of light and vigor straining at the tethers that held her. At any moment, the shell of her respectability would crack, and her incandescence would spill out.

Did no one but Mal see? Those around her smiled and spoke comfortably to her, as though they liked her, but their reactions were subdued, as were hers to them.

This was not her stage, not where she would shine. She needed to be free of this place, these enclosing walls. Out on the open heather, maybe, in the Highlands of Mal's home, Kilmorgan, in the north. Her vibrancy wouldn't be swallowed there, but allowed to glow.

And she'd be with him, the layers of her clothing coming off in his hands, the warmth of her body rising to him, their mouths together. This woman belonged in Mal Mackenzie's bed, and he intended to take her there.

It would be a grand challenge. Lady Mary was surrounded, protected. Her father and the matrons circled her like guard dogs, to keep wolves like Mal at bay.

Mal made a noise in his throat like a growl. If they considered him a wolf, so be it.

"What are you grumbling over?" Alec answered, not happy. He did not want to be here; he hated Englishmen, and only duty to their father kept him calm in the corner instead of racing around picking fights.

"At last, something interesting in this place, and you have no use for it," Malcolm said. Alec was his favorite brother—well, the one who drove him the least mad—but Alec had his own tribulations.

"Let her be, Malcolm," Alec said sternly. "I'm supposed to be watching after you. You go near her, and you'll stir up a world of trouble. I'll not be facing Da's fists because I could nae keep you out of it."

"I could put you in the way of Da's fists, and maybe have your neck broken, with a few words, and you know it," Malcolm reminded him. "But I don't, do I? Why? Because you're me best mate, and I don't want you dead. The least ye could do is help me meet yon beautiful lass."

"And I'm calling to mind the last time I did you such a favor. I remember pulling your naked arse out of a burning house, and taking shot in my upper arm, which still hurts of a rainy morning. All because ye had to go after what wasn't yours."

Malcolm flushed at the memory, but only a little. "Aye, any husband should be angry to find a strapping lad like me in his place next to his bonny wife, but he had no cause to set the bed on fire. Nearly killed the poor woman. Not surprised she left him behind and went to the colonies with her mum."

"He's still looking for you, Mal, so stay clear of him."

"Nah, Da' put the fear of God in him, and it was three years ago. And *that* lass isn't married." He waved a hand in the direction of the delectable Lady Mary.

"No," Alec said. "It'll be her father's pistol you'll have to dodge instead."

"So, you'll not help me?"

"Not a bit of it."

Malcolm fell silent. He would never betray Alec's secret to their father—to anyone in the family—and Alec knew it. No leverage there.

"Ah, well." Malcolm's slow smile spread across his face. "I'll have to solve this conundrum on me own."

"That's what I'm afraid of," Alec said darkly.

The innocence of it, Mary was to reflect later, should be astonishing. That moment in time—she at Lady Bancroft's soiree in Edinburgh, her only worry her role of go-between in the forbidden liaison of her sister, Audrey, with the man she loved.

The simplicity of it; the nothingness . . . If Mary had left that night for home, if they'd reached Lincolnshire without her ever having seen the broad-shouldered Scotsman who gazed at her with such intensity, Mary would have lived the rest of her life in peace, moved out of the way like a chess piece sheltered from the rest of the board.

That night, she stepped into the wrong square at the wrong time. A storm had kept them in Edinburgh, and her father and aunt had decided they might as well accept the invitation to Lady Bancroft's fashionable gathering.

Malcolm would not have been there either, if his father hadn't sent his brother Alec to spy for him. Alec had brought Malcolm along for camouflage, and also because Alec didn't trust Mal alone on the streets of Edinburgh—for very good reason.

Mary's life would have been so very different . . .

For the moment, Lady Mary Lennox existed in a bubble of safety, sure in her betrothal to Lord Halsey, and more worried about her shy little sister than herself.

Tonight's gathering was a decidedly political one. Lady Bancroft had invited prominent Scotsmen to her soiree to reassure those in Edinburgh that rumblings of the Jacobite rising were just that—rumblings. Never mind that Charles Stuart had landed somewhere in the west, never mind that he was trying to raise an army. He'd never succeed, and they all knew it.

Highlanders were harmless, Lady Bancroft was implying,

thoroughly adapted to civilized living—enlightened men of science. They blended effortlessly with the English aristocracy, did they not?

In that case, Lady Bancroft ought not to have invited the two young Scotsmen warming themselves near the great fireplace at the end of the hall. Mary saw them as she scanned the room for the Honorable Jeremy Drake, the note to him from Audrey burning inside her stomacher.

The Scotsmen looked much alike, brothers obviously. But civilized they were not.

They'd dressed in waist-length frock coats with many buttons, linen shirts, neat stockings, and leather shoes. Instead of breeches, they wore kilts, loose plaid garments wrapped about their waists.

Other Scotsmen here, in knee breeches and wigs, were indistinguishable from their English counterparts, and moved quietly among the company. These two, on the other hand, looked as though they'd risen from the heather, rubbed the blue paint from their faces, put on coats, and stormed down to Edinburgh.

They wore their dark red hair pulled back into loose queues—no wigs—and lounged with a restlessness that spoke of hunting in long, cold winters, bonfires on the hills, and the wild ruthlessness of their Pictish and Norse ancestors.

Though the two stood calmly, their stances relaxed, they watched. Eyes that missed nothing picked out every person in the room. Wolves, invited to stand amongst the sheep.

When Mary's scanning gaze passed that of the younger one, his eyes caught hers, and she paused.

The sparks in his gaze seared her in place. In that moment, Mary smelled the sweetness of heather under wild wind, felt the heat of the sun in a broad sky. She'd been to the northern Highlands once, and she'd never forgotten the raw beauty of it, the terrifying emptiness and incredible wonder.

This Scotsman embodied all of that, sweeping her to the place and time, under the never-setting sun, when she'd felt afraid and free in the same breath.

The moment passed, and Mary turned away . . .

To find her life completely changed. One *tick* of the clock ago, she'd been serene about the path she'd agreed to, ready to fulfill her duty to her father. At the next *tick*, she felt herself plunging into a long, dark pit, and she'd consented to step off the edge.

Mary turned away, shaking off the sensation with effort. She had a mission to fulfill, no time for idle thoughts.

She drew a deep breath and said, vehemently, "Frogs and toadstools!"

A few ladies jumped, but her aunt Danae, used to Mary's epithets, turned to her calmly. "What is it, my dear?"

"My fan," Mary said in feigned exasperation, making a show of patting the folds of her skirts, her bodice. "I've left the aggravating thing in the withdrawing room."

Aunt Danae, a plump partridge in a too-tight gown, put a soothing hand on Mary's wrist. "Never mind, dear. Call for Whitman, and have her fetch it for you."

Their hostess, Lady Bancroft, who stood near, began to signal for one of her many footman. Mary, who'd hidden the fan for the express purpose of going after it, said, "No need. Won't be a moment," and ran off before anyone could object.

Mary's fan was safely in a pocket under her skirt, so she quickly passed the withdrawing room and made for the stairs that led to the upper reaches of the house.

The Bancrofts' home had been purchased, not inherited, when Lord Bancroft had returned from the colonies with a vast fortune and been elevated from plain Mr. Drake to Viscount Bancroft. The house lay a few miles outside Edinburgh, a tall structure built in the modern style but with enough stonework and crenellations to bring to mind an ancient castle in the wilds of Scotland.

A bit ridiculous, in Mary's opinion, but at least the fires drew well, and there were comfortable carpets on the floors.

Lady Bancroft was not spendthrift enough to waste candles lighting staircases that would not be used by guests, so Mary groped her way upward in the dark, only the moonlight through a few undraped windows to light her way.

Jeremy hadn't been in the vast drawing room below, nor had he been in any of the anterooms, so he must be waiting in his chambers above. Likely languishing there, distraught that Lord Wilfort had forbidden the match between him and Audrey. No matter, Mary would soon cheer him with Audrey's letter.

She made it to the upper landing, out of breath, and turned the corner for the wing that would take her to Jeremy.

A tall man stepped out of the shadows and blocked her way. Moonlight fell on a light-colored frock coat stretched over wide shoulders and a kilt of blue plaid wrapped around his waist.

He was one of the Highlanders from below, the younger one who'd caught and held her with the heat in his eyes.

Primal fear brushed her. To be confronted by this man, a Highlander, in the dark, in this deserted part of the house was . . . exhilarating.

Mary also was touched with curiosity, wonder that such a being existed and was standing less than a foot from her. A warmth began in Mary's breastbone, spreading downward to her fingertips and up into her face.

The man did not move. He was a hunter, motionless in the dark, sizing up his prey. At the moment, that prey was Mary.

Fanciful nonsense, Mary tried to tell herself. Likely he was staying in the house, perhaps on his way to his bedchamber.

Where he'd pull off his coat, unlace his shirt, lie back before the fire in casual undress . . .

Mary's throat went dry. She'd been listening too hard to Aunt Danae's tales of her conquests when she'd been a young woman. Aunt Danae had lived on passion and desire, but Mary was far too practical to want such things for herself.

Wasn't she?

"I beg your pardon, sir," she said. "My destination lies beyond you."

She spoke with the right note of haughtiness—after all, the Scots were a lesser people, drawn into civilization by the English. Or so her father claimed. Not that Mary truly believed in the natural superiority of Englishmen. She'd met too many Englishmen who were decidedly *in*ferior.

The man said nothing, only stood in place, eyes caught by moonlight.

A touch of fear began to rise. Mary was alone and unprotected, and he was a creature of the uncivilized wilds. The clansmen raided each other's lands, it was said, stealing cattle . . . and women.

Those women were as barbaric as the men, she'd heard,

wielding swords in battle alongside them. Not what a proper young English lady had been raised to do.

"No matter," Mary said when he did not speak, her voice scratchy. "I will simply go 'round the other way." The house was built around a courtyard, four square wings surrounding cobbled pavement below. "Good evening, sir."

She swung away but had taken only a step before the Scotsman pushed past her and stood in front of her once more.

Her heart beating rapidly now, Mary swung around again, ready to make a dash for Jeremy's chamber. Jeremy was not a small man—he would clout this Highlander about the head for frightening the woman he hoped would become his sister-in-law.

Mary stumbled and nearly fell as the Scotsman put himself in front of her *again*. A large hand on her shoulder pushed her back onto her feet.

"Steady, lass." His voice was a deep rumble, starting from somewhere in his belly and emerging as a warm vibration.

The hand on Mary's shoulder remained. No gentleman should touch a lady thus. He could grip her hand, but only when meeting her, dancing with her, or assisting her. The Highlander had stopped her from falling, yes, but he should withdraw now that she was upright again.

Instead, he kept his hand on her, the appendage so large she was surprised his gloves fit him.

He stood close enough that Mary got a good look into his eyes. They were unusual, to say the least. Not blue or green as a red-haired man's might be—they were tawny, like a lion's. The sensible side of her told her they must be hazel, but the gleam of gold held her in place as securely as the hand on her shoulder.

"Please let me pass, sir," Mary said, trying to sound severe, but she sounded about as severe as a kitten. In his opinion as well, because he smiled.

The smile transformed him. From a forbidding, terrifying giant, the Highlander became nearly human. The warmth in the smile reached all the way to his eyes, crinkling them at the corners.

"I will," he said in a voice that wrapped her in heat. "As soon as ye tell me where you're going, and who ye intend to meet."